MIDAS
TYLER JONES

Midas
First published 2023
in a deluxe limited edition by Earthling Publications

ISBN 978-1-59021-687-3

This Lethe Press edition © 2025 by Tyler Jones

For more information about Lethe Press publications, visit us at: lethepressbooks.com

Cover art by Ben Baldwin

Interior art by Dave Dick Illustration

Cover and interior design by Scott Cole | 13visions.com

For more information about the author, visit tylerjones.net

For Rae Lyn

We work in the dark, we do what we can, we give what we have

BY TYLER JONES

Longsight M40

Night of the Long Knives

Turn Up the Sun

Heavy Oceans

Midas

Burn the Plans

Enter Softly

Almost Ruth

The Dark Side of the Room

Criterium

"How wicked it would be, if we could, to call the dead back!"

—C.S. Lewis

INTRODUCTION

WHEN A GOOD MAN HANDS you a book and asks you to write the introduction, it's thrilling to imagine yourself constructing an erudite analysis of the text you were given. Fantasies spring: here, you can play teacher, presenter, reader, and informant all at once. You are given a headstart! The chance to read the book before almost anybody else! And with this opportunity comes the scholarly responsibility (coveted, indeed) of being the first to deliver an eloquent, articulate take. What writer wouldn't froth at the chance to wax first, solo, alone? What intellectual wouldn't bask? Glory be, we say, glory be.

And so, with all academic potential in mind, this literary authority bestowed allows me to give my esteemed, cultured, learned response:

The book fuckin' rules.

Oh, I apologize. This may be the only swear word amongst the thousands you now hold, but oh my goodness, God if that wasn't my full and sophisticated response.

Midas is one of the best books I've read in years. It's the sort of story I will be recommending for a long time at the end of podcasts when the hosts inquire as to what you've recently loved. It's the book I will be slurring about at the end of the bar with my writer friends here in Michigan as I try to describe the brilliant placement of the Midas myth in the Old West where gold, of course, is God.

You can taste that appetite for *Au* on the first page when our man, Jeremiah, is approached by the riderless horse. You know then the emptiness upon that saddle is an emptiness unlikely to be filled, more likely to spread. And you know it for certain when Jeremiah discovers the first of the golden objects, a morning glory flower, which is too detailed and *real* to be a carving. Life recognizes life, after all.

But ambition and greed tend to find one another as well.

Birds of a feather, one might say, even if said birds are rendered gold by the touch of one who wields such power.

Tyler Jones wields such power.

I met Tyler in a legendary way. I'd come to the McMenamin's Edgefield outside Portland with John Skipp, Allison Laakko, April Peterson, Rose O'Keefe, and more. Tyler and I had written about meeting up in the pool hall area, and he was easy to spot. Bright-faced, wearing a stylish and studious blazer, he had a brick of a book on the booth table before him. We hit it off so quick it felt akin to having met up with an old friend, but the two of us hadn't ever met in person before. There's a photo from this night I now cherish. *Midas* leans more toward "The Monkey's Paw" than it does the golden touch, and even that isn't giving its due.

Here's its due:

Midas is smart. *Midas* is rich. *Midas* is full of golden hope despite its centerpiece of grief. My favorite writers are the ones who can take a subject as horrible as the loss of a child and, rather than sinking the reader in soul-darkening grief, deliver a thrilling, transcendent arc of a man. Here, that man is Jeremiah, brother to Elijah, husband to Emma. And boss, it seems, to possibly be my favorite character in the novel, Abigail. He's also the target of Solomon, a man after the power Jeremiah was led to by that riderless horse. Jeremiah doesn't do a thing in this book that any one of us wouldn't have done. He's not driven by mania or madness, power or pride. He's driven by pain. And what man doesn't gravitate toward that which eases his pain?

Oh, I am excited for you to get to the piano lesson scenes in this book. These images will never leave my mind and have made space for themselves in my private library of treasured horrors. But there are many: Tyler Jones may wanna write the play Jeremiah and Emma attend and present it in actual theaters. And the castle of Charwood! A construction Tyler describes as an ongoing, ever-increasing place to hold Emma's ever-growing grief.

There is propulsion here without pandering, plot without pushing. I underlined many passages as I read, and I'd like to share one here.

"To transform a living thing into gold," (Emma) said. "Isn't that something worth pursuing, even if it leads to death?"

"I don't know," Elijah said. "I've always thought the pursuit of life is better."

There's that rising above the grief, a play on words, too, and a philosophy I can't help ascribing to Tyler himself, as this book is teeming with energy, purpose, and prose.

I'm a horror fan. So are you. And we read the books and we watch the movies and we even listen to the frightening tones of the dark, moody music, always on the lookout for that gem, that classic, that piece of gold. Yes, we dig through the genre and find ourselves admiring even the worst of it because, good or bad, it's still found in the corner of the artistic world we call home. And when we do find those nuggets of gold, our souls brighten, our body stiffens, and it feels something like we've been touched by two fingers, crossed in a way to become one, and with that touch, we are rendered something new, something changed, something shiny.

Something gold.

Here's a book you've been looking for.

Tyler Jones should be proud, beyond proud, for having mined himself for such a story, and pulled forth the gold to prove it.

Midas will remain with me forever.

–JOSH MALERMAN

BLACK HAWK, COLORADO

THE RIDER IN THE BLACK robe tore through the night, the hooves of his horse pounding a steady rhythm over the hard ground. One hand clutched the satchel strapped around his chest while the other hand gripped the reins. What he carries close to his heart may be what he has been seeking for so long.

Days, weeks, months, years. Following maps drawn from visions. Images telegraphed to him from places just behind what could be seen. A world inside the world. He sometimes saw shadows moving within this place and heard their voices inside his head. They showed him things, these shadows, whispered instructions, bestowed upon him this monumental task.

When he started having visions, he was still a young man, and his hair was still dark. After he emerged from that first trance, dazed and overwhelmed, his hair had turned completely white. Though he was much older now, his hair was still as white as the moon, casting its pale light down on the road.

The shadows taught him about the threads that connected every-thing and determined every outcome. They hummed with every choice a man made. They created motion and momentum and propelled everyone to invisible destinations, each thread vibrating, touching other threads and making them hum. Each thread carried a different tone, a different frequency, and if one could tap into the network, the celestial spiderweb, he might be able to see future events before they occurred.

The road angled upward as though it led straight into the sky, and the rider brought his horse to a stop at the summit. He looked down into the valley, the lights of Black Hawk hanging like a halo above the town.

Not much longer now.

He kicked his heels, and the horse began to move again. The rider went around town and ventured into rocky hills to the north. He kept watch for the small pyramid of stones he'd stacked at the entrance of a narrow pathway that led through the trees.

A pyramid because it was something he'd seen in one of his visions. Something from the shadow world. What it meant, the rider didn't know at the time. But he found out eventually. A representation of when the shadows crossed over into this world and interacted with man, changing the course and direction that history's river would flow.

Deeper into the woods, the rider saw the lantern light of the abandoned mining settlement he and his family had lived in for the last month while he searched the nearby mountains for the cave.

As he neared the settlement, a man wearing a white robe ran out to meet him. He bowed. "Were you successful?"

The rider smiled and touched the satchel on his chest. "Gather the family," he said.

The man in the white robe bowed again and ran toward the buildings that made up the encampment. It was late and the rider knew many would need to be awakened for the ritual. But he couldn't wait, and they would all want to know if this cave was the one they'd been searching for.

The rider took the horse to a large, round canvas tent set in a clearing just outside the settlement. He tied up the animal, gave it hay, and entered the tent. A small fire burned in a pit at the center of the room, the smoke rising through a hole above it.

Against the far wall sat a desk covered in books, journals, and papers, one of which was a hand-drawn map of trails, towns, mines, and rivers. Scattered across this map were six dark circles, each one representing a cave. Written next to them were two dates: the day, month, and year the family first camped at that location and the day, month, and year they moved on after discovering the cave did not contain what they were looking for.

The rider removed his shoes, took off the satchel, and laid down on the furs that covered the tent's wooden floor. He kept his legs together and spread out his arms, palms up, as though his body were an arrow. He closed his eyes and focused only on his breathing until every other sound vanished.

He waited.

Breath.

Heartbeat.

Breath.

With his eyes closed a hazy image came into view. He began to see figures moving around him. He heard their voices whispering to him, words that seemed to float in and out of an invisible wind. He only ever caught pieces of what they said. Fragments he'd then write down in a journal once the physical world came back into focus.

Their voices—speaking in a language he could not recognize but one he somehow understood—hummed inside his head.

And slowly, his body lifted from the furs until he no longer touched the floor.

An hour later, the rider staggered out of the tent, blinking furiously in the light of a thousand stars that suddenly seemed brighter than they'd ever been, holding the satchel in both hands. And the moon, full and scarred, shone down on the settlement, illuminating every bunk and shed. The creek along the edge of camp sounded like tiny bells, and even his footsteps seemed more real than real. He could hear and feel the crack and crumble of every piece of dirt his feet crushed.

He came to the largest building, the Gathering Room, and stopped. Two women stood near the door, one of them with both hands folded together, held tight against her chest, above her heart. She shifted uncomfortably, and the moonlight made the tears on her face glisten. The other woman gently rubbed her back as the rider approached.

"Solomon," the first woman said, "please. There has to be another way."

The rider walked past them and put his hand on the door. The woman reached out and grabbed his black robe.

"Look at me," she pleaded. "Solomon, please. Anything…" her voice broke, and she started to cry, "…anything but this."

Solomon jerked his arm from her grip and opened the door of the Gathering Room.

"Solomon, please!"

He closed the door behind him but could still hear her crying.

A bright fire burned at one end of the room, bathing the space in warm light. The entire family was gathered—except for the children—all dressed in white robes. Forty-seven men and women sitting on the floor in concentric circles around a table upon which sat a large black bowl carved out of porous stone. The white robes covered their legs, so it appeared as though they were half-bodies growing up out of the wood. None of them turned when Solomon entered. They all remained motionless, eyes closed, hands resting on their knees.

Solomon made his way through the circles of white robes until he reached the table. He took off the satchel and set it down on the table. He waited as the family opened their eyes and looked at him. He turned slowly so all could see him.

Solomon held out his arms and spoke in a strong voice. "Brothers and sisters, sons and daughters, here we are again. The day has come once again when we find out together if we have found what we have been seeking for so long."

Smiles broke out on the faces of those gathered. They looked at one another, nodding and murmuring.

Solomon reached into the satchel and took out an object wrapped in cloth, holding it gently as though it were made of glass. He unwrapped the cloth to reveal a stone the size of his fist. Bright veins of gold coursed through the grey chunk of rock, glowing brilliantly.

He lifted a small mortar and pestle out of the bowl, then took a knife from the satchel and dragged it over the rock until chunks of gold came off.

"It has never been about what we gain, but rather who we are becoming," Solomon said as he took the pestle and ground the gold into a fine powder.

"I know what comes next is difficult and painful for some of you, and it is for me as well. It tears my heart in two, but I promise you there is no other way."

He made eye contact with two men in the back and said, "It's time."

The two men nodded and rose, their faces stern, and left the room.

Solomon then took a canteen from the satchel, filled it with water from a lake near the cave, and poured some into the mortar. Solomon set the rock down and stirred the strange liquid with a finger. When he pulled it out, bits of gold clung to his skin. He held this finger up to the light, turned it over, and stared at it.

Then Solomon closed his eyes, held the mortar to his mouth, and drank the liquid.

Without opening his eyes, Solomon said, "We are here as one, let us breathe now as one."

He started breathing louder, slowly and methodically. Each seated man and woman fell into rhythm with their master, matching their breathing pattern to his. Soon, the sound of rushing air filled the room.

They all continued breathing together when the door opened, and the woman Solomon had passed outside, came in, the two men on either side of her. She now carried something in her arms, something wrapped in a blanket. It moved slightly as she walked past the bodies on the floor. Something under the cloth jerked once as the woman placed the bundle in Solomon's outstretched hands. Solomon took the blanket over to the pedestal, and the woman remained standing, arms still outstretched, hands shaking. Her whole face went pale, and her mouth twisted into a thin, crooked line. The skin around her eyes folded into a network of wrinkles as her chin shook.

"Please," she said.

Solomon ignored her and nodded at the two men. Each of them took the woman's arm, led her to the back circle, and helped her to the ground. Tears slid down her cheeks.

Gold dust glistened on Solomon's lips as he held the bundle in one hand and unwrapped the layers of blankets with the other until the entire family could see the infant—no more than a few weeks old, eyes clenched tight, hands bunched into fists—lying in Solomon's hands. A baby boy.

Solomon cradled the infant and stared at it for a long time. Sadness flickered across his face for a moment, then disappeared. He ran his gold-stained finger across the child's forehead, leaving a glittering mark on the skin.

He gently placed the infant into the bowl, and when the cold stone hit the child's skin, it began to cry, making a small and trembling sound. The mother buried her face in her hands, whimpering. Solomon looked around the room. Everyone's eyes were fixed on him, but a few members of the family sat up straighter, their jaw muscles tightening. They all knew what happened next. But no one knew better than the child's mother. She was weeping freely now, trying so hard to keep her mouth shut, to keep any sound from coming out. But she couldn't hide the tiny, wet moans of pain that slipped through her fingers. Tears dripped from her chin, making dark marks on her white robe. Her eyes weren't just closed, they were clenched together as tightly as they could be. Her chest shook.

The stone bowl caused the baby's cries to echo horribly.

Solomon reached into his robe and removed a wicked-looking jade dagger. Something twisted and old. The blade was dark green, chipped, and dented as though it had been struck against a thousand bones. The handle was wrapped with dark and hardened leather.

The baby's cries grew louder, more frantic. Solomon leaned over the bowl and put his hands on the rim. The dagger scraped against the stone, and when the child's mother heard that sound, the blood drained from her face. Her eyes rolled back so far that they turned pure white. She slumped over, head falling into the lap of the man next to her. He put a hand on her shoulder and focused his eyes straight ahead.

Solomon took one last look at the infant, and his expression was something between pain and euphoria. Lifting the blade in both hands, Solomon whispered, "To remake the future."

"To remake the future," the family repeated in unison.

The infant's cries reached a fever pitch, its voice becoming hoarse. Wailing echoed from the bowl.

Then the blade fell, and the cries were silenced.

He withdrew his hand—eyes wide open, chest heaving—and extended his trigger and middle fingers, crossed them, and touched the blood-covered blade. He closed his eyes and waited. Nothing happened. He crossed and uncrossed the fingers and touched the dagger again. He waited. Nothing.

The corners of his mouth twitched. The knuckles gripping the dagger went white. His nostrils flared.

"The search continues," Solomon said quietly.

"The search continues," the family replied as one.

PART I

CHARWOOD

1

CHARWOOD, 1859

The preacher who was no longer a preacher, awakened while it was still dark, but troubled thoughts kept him from falling back to sleep. He lay with his eyes open, listening to Emma's breathing stop and start as her body twitched in the grip of another nightmare.

He got out of bed, made some coffee, and went outside. He stood on the front porch and watched as a silver fog crept in from the forest. Smoky fingers moved over the field, stirring the dead grass with tiny shivers. Across the field, the town of Charwood was a black silhouette against a gray sky. All was silent. He could just make out the shape of the church in the distance. It made him cold inside to think of the years he had spent in that building, teaching from a book he no longer believed in. Back when he was known as Jeremiah Pevensie, the preacher, the reverend. Even now, whenever he heard the bell ring, it sounded more like a warning or an alarm than a call to worship.

Beyond the field to the west lay the forest, obscured by fog. The tops of the pines seemed to rise suddenly out of this fog with no base to support them. A ghost forest that hovered halfway between earth and sky.

Jeremiah saw a dark shape moving toward him from within this silver curtain, growing clearer as it came closer. Soon, a horse's head broke through the fog, followed by its saddled back with full bags strapped on either side. But there was no rider. Steam trailed from the animal's nose as it walked across the field with slow, tired steps.

Jeremiah did not move from the porch, expecting to hear the voice of the horse's owner echoing from the trees at any moment or to see a human shape running through the fog after the animal.

The horse was so close now Jeremiah could hear the air rushing from its flaring nostrils. Froth dripped from its mouth, and its ribs were visible, pushing against the skin with each heaving breath.

Jeremiah opened the door of his house a crack to see if his wife had awakened, but the house was still and quiet.

The horse came right up to the porch, and its glassy eyes looked at Jeremiah without blinking. Its hair was a dusty brown, brittle to the touch when Jeremiah stroked its neck, a dirty white diamond between the eyes. Jeremiah took the reins and led the animal around the house to the barn, where his two horses stood in their stalls chewing hay. Neither made a sound as the new horse entered the barn, they simply watched and chewed.

Jeremiah poured some water into a metal bucket, and the horse drank as Jeremiah removed the heavy bags from the animal's back. After the horse had drunk its fill, Jeremiah led him to one of the empty stalls and put fresh hay in the feeder. He made soothing sounds while stroking the horse's mane and told him to slow down, but the animal continued eating as if it had not had a meal in many days.

Jeremiah wondered how long the animal had been wandering and if there was a rider lost somewhere, stumbling through the woods, trying to find his way out. Maybe something had spooked the animal in the middle of the night, causing him to abandon his owner. Jeremiah had overheard some of the men in town talking about a wolf stalking the forest. That beast had even ventured into town recently. Isaac Cutter, who kept a number of sheep on his farm at the south end of town, bolted awake one night to the sound of frantic bleating, and when he ran outside with a lantern, he discovered blood-matted wool, paw prints near the fence, and a missing ewe.

Jeremiah almost said a silent prayer for the poor horse's owner, wherever he may be. The words formed on his lips, but then he stopped and hit himself in the thigh as hard as he could. The pain was so bright that it scorched the prayer from his mind. Jeremiah shook his head to clear any thoughts of God and man's ability to change his mind about what he had already decided.

The morning wore on, and the fog lifted slightly until Jeremiah could see the entrance to the forest. Dark clouds had rolled in and covered the sun, making the morning feel like dusk, and he knew the day would not get much brighter.

Jeremiah returned to the porch, where he finished his coffee and continued to watch the forest. After an hour, he decided to venture into the woods, but not too far, to see if the horse's owner had set up camp nearby. He entered his house and quietly filled a satchel with some venison jerky and bread in case the journey took longer than expected and in case the horse's owner, if found, needed nourishment. He strapped on his gun and knife, put on a warm coat, and went back outside, carefully latching the door as softly as he could.

Though the sky was dark, the air was warm and charged with electricity, which made the hair on his neck stiffen.

Jeremiah made his way across the field, stopping only to remove some dry weeds from a small mound of dirt. A grave he had dug with his own hands only three months earlier. He tried not to imagine the state of decay of the body buried beneath the earth, tried not to picture worms eating holes in the pine box that held his son, but these images developed in his mind, and Jeremiah struck himself once in the face to erase them.

His eyes stung as he looked up at the stone-colored sky. "You are a thief," he said. "A cruel and heartless thief."

Then Jeremiah spat in the dirt and trekked toward the floating forest, mist swirling around his legs like the smoke of a world on fire.

He paused where the field met the trees and turned back to look at his home. The cluster of buildings that made up his small farm were distant and alone. The high whinny of the lost horse traveled the distance and reached his ears.

He hoped Emma's sleep was peaceful because it rarely is these days. Sometimes, he watched her eyes moving back and forth behind closed lids, her lips forming soundless words, the skin between her eyes folding in pain. He knew what she dreamed about, even though she never told him. He sometimes dreamed the same days, the same moments. Hours filled with so much pain it was a wonder his heart didn't just stop beating. How could something hurt so much and not kill you?

2

AS HE CROSSED INTO THE woods, Jeremiah was struck by how quiet it was—no animals scurrying in the trees, no flapping of wings—only the sound of his boots as they broke twigs and dry leaves.

The sun arced across the sky, a dim light rolling behind gray clouds, casting twisted shadows on the ground. Minutes stretched into hours, and the walk became hypnotic—the crunch of his steps, the rush of his breath. A thousand trees surrounded him, and he could almost believe he'd been walking in place and the world was spinning beneath him.

After several hours, Jeremiah came to a large, moss-covered rock. He leaned against it and took out his canteen. His throat was so dry he could have easily drunk all the water, but he stopped himself to have some for the return journey. A gentle breeze stirred the leaves, carrying a faint but familiar smell.

Smoke.

He stood and kept going along a path between two trees, the trunks of which were so wide three men standing fingertip to fingertip could not have wrapped their arms all the way around.

The smell grew stronger, and he slowed down, wincing at the crack of dead leaves under his boots. Someone was out here, but that did not mean it was the horse's owner. The forest was known to be a place where men on the run went to hide. It was the reason the children of Charwood were not allowed to play in there alone. Sheriff Brennan had arrested or shot more than one outlaw within these woods. It was also not uncommon for a gold prospector to come back into town with black eyes, a bleeding gash on his head, and empty bags.

Jeremiah stopped and listened but heard nothing. He moved forward carefully, stepping only on the bare ground until he came upon a circular clearing where someone had set up camp. A breeze blew through the trees and knocked branches together, moving the flap of a canvas tent with a sound that made him think of ship sails. A campfire lay smoldering nearby.

Jeremiah called out, "Hello?" and waited. No answer. He called again, hiding himself behind a tree in case gunshots were given in response. Still nothing. Jeremiah called one last time, then approached the camp, crouched down, fingers touching the gun on his belt. Even as he circled around the back of the tent, Jeremiah knew the campsite was abandoned. He could sense it in the stillness of the air.

Jeremiah gave up caution, stepped into the clearing, and saw a man lying on the ground in front of the fire pit. Jeremiah took out his gun and came up slowly from behind. He leaned down and gently pushed on the man's shoulder. It felt stiff and cold to the touch, and he knew, without even seeing the man's face, that he was dead. One arm was stretched out, the fingers twisted into a claw. The other hand clutched his chest. Jeremiah came around the body and knelt in front of it. He sighed, took off his hat, and wiped the sweat from his brow.

The face was sliced open in four diagonal lines from the hairline to the chin. One eye had been punctured and was just a bloody mass. The other eye bulged from the socket. The nose was ripped away, and there was a hole in the cheek, open so wide Jeremiah could see the man's teeth. One ear dangled by a thin piece of skin. The neck and throat were mostly gone, with torn skin and shredded muscle covered in dried blood. A dark pool of congealed blood covered the ground in front of the man and spilled from the open throat.

Jeremiah had seen enough injuries to know a bear attack when he saw one, and a quick glance at the nearby ground showed deep, paw-shaped impressions twice the size of his own hand.

Flies buzzed in the air, landing on the bloody dirt. A few crawled through clumps of flesh stuck in the man's beard, their spindly legs moving over his split lips.

Jeremiah sat back, staring at the body. Memories of his son, Samuel, flared up inside his mind. He shook his head to clear them, but it was too late. Specific moments, images, and voices came alive, and pain so fresh it did not feel like it was three months old…it felt like all of it had just happened.

Jeremiah gripped one hand with the other and squeezed until the bones scraped together, and the memories faded. He wiped his eyes and took another look at the body.

The man's age was impossible to determine because his face was so destroyed, but Jeremiah guessed him to be somewhere around fifty years old by the wrinkles on his forehead, around his eyes, and the streaks of grey in his beard.

Jeremiah stood and shivered, then started collecting wood to rebuild the fire. Once the flames were going, he went over to the tent and stuck his head inside. A bedroll was laid out but not slept on, and other than a satchel, the tent was empty. Jeremiah grabbed the bag and carried it to the fire.

As he neared the body, he saw tiny flashes of light coming from the dark puddle of dried blood. He crouched down and looked closer. Thousands of small glittering pieces dotted the stained dirt. Even the open wounds on the man's face flickered in the firelight. Nothing else on the man's body—not his skin, hair, or clothes—sparkled with this strange substance. Only the blood.

Jeremiah took out his knife and used the blade to scrape some of the dried blood out of the laceration on the man's cheek. He carried it to the fire, turning the blade first one way, then the other. Something in the blood shimmered with a metallic glow.

An illness? Jeremiah wondered, walking back to the body. He had never heard of any ailment that caused the blood to shine like this. He patted the dead man's clothing, but the pockets of the shirt and pants were empty except for a broken pencil. Jeremiah was about to go and search the tent again when he saw another flash of light, this time coming from the hand clutched to the man's chest.

The fingers were stiff and claw-like, grasping at something. Jeremiah managed to move one finger, and the object in the man's hand caught the firelight and reflected it brilliantly. He moved another finger and another. His breath caught in his throat when he saw what it was. He pulled back the last finger with a brittle snap, and a large piece of gold tumbled from the man's hand.

Jeremiah picked it up, his heart beating so fast his legs went weak. It was more gold than he'd ever seen, and the color and texture were flawless. No impurities. It weighed as much in his hand as a small stone. And, somehow, this gold had been fashioned into the exact size and shape of a morning glory flower.

Jeremiah slipped the flower into his pocket and immediately searched the camp for more gold. He tore through the tent, ran his hands along the stitching of the canvas, overturned the bedroll, and dumped out the contents of the satchel, but there was nothing to be found. He wondered if the man had been a prospector or perhaps a jeweler and was murdered by a partner in his operation. Jeremiah knew of many men who had left their families and traveled into the mountains in search of riches. But he'd never heard of anyone coming back with this much gold.

He looked back down at the stiff and lifeless body. His eyes moved over the man's legs, bent and pulled up toward his chest, the one hand curled against his stomach with its broken finger, and the outstretched hand...those twisted fingers, curved and misshapen, the cords beneath the skin pulling it into something deformed. It reminded him of Samuel's hands near the end. At night, when the boy could not sleep because of the pain that ripped through him, his hands would sometimes contort into such shapes.

But every memory of Samuel was connected to another memory, a whole string of them that went backward to when there was no pain. A long black tunnel Jeremiah could not always stop himself from falling into. His chest burned as he fought to breathe, to not lose control over what his mind saw. The memories came anyway, and with them all the sights and sounds of the moments in which they belonged. Each of them sharp.

Jeremiah closed his eyes and hammered a fist into his thigh until the pain overtook his thoughts.

3

JEREMIAH STARED INTO THE FIRE in a trance as the day wore on. He knew he should go back home, that his absence would be like a team of black horses dragging Emma's thoughts into dark places. But he stayed, turning the golden flower over and over in his hands, watching the firelight make the gold seem alive and moving.

He opened the man's satchel and dumped out the contents: a smooth stone, two coins, and a creased piece of paper covered in wild, almost illegible handwriting.

A valley, a town, a wide-open field. To the west through trees, travel until you see water. Up the mountain that can only be seen when standing upon the flat stone, to the rock that stands as a doorway. Pass through the rock and into a place where time has no meaning, where the sun sets on days and hours outside the world. Still water, green grass. A place of darkness with writing on the walls. Find it there and beware the cost.

Beneath this, written in different handwriting, were the words,

Solomon's second vision. The words came to him through a whispered voice, and he wrote them down, eyes closed, as he listened. Directions, landmarks? He says each piece will become clear with faith, and when they do, I am to draw a map that will lead us all to the place he describes.

Jeremiah folded the paper back up and put it in his pocket. He wondered if the note was referencing Solomon, Israel's wisest king. There were no stories of Solomon having visions in the Bible, though, unless the man had been looking at an apocryphal text.

When the night came, Jeremiah went into the tent and lay down on the dead man's bedroll, covering himself in a blanket that still smelled of someone else's skin. He faced toward the opening of the tent so he could see outside, and he lay there for some time as the fire slowly died.

A twig snapped, a sound like a gunshot in the quiet.

Something moved in the darkness, stalking at the edge of camp where the circle of light ended. Just a faint shape, like a lean dog with pointed ears and eyes that glowed red. The animal stopped and looked at Jeremiah. Their eyes met, and Jeremiah wondered if this was the wolf that had made off with Isaac Cutter's sheep. He went to reach for his gun, to either kill the animal or scare it away, but his hand never made it. His head spun like he had drunk too much whiskey.

"It was you, wasn't it?" Jeremiah said out loud. "You killed him."

Then Jeremiah heard a voice inside his head, a voice that was not his own. It was low and dark and liquid.

NO. I MOVE THROUGH THE WORLD, AND EVENTS UNFOLD. THIS MAN'S THREAD STRETCHED THROUGH MANY OTHERS AND BECAME A KNOT THAT HAD TO BE UNTIED SO THE FUTURE COULD HAPPEN AS IT IS SUPPOSED TO. YOU WILL UNDERSTAND IN TIME.

"I am not afraid of you," Jeremiah said out loud. "I am a man. I'm more ruthless than you'll ever be."

YOU SHOULD BE AFRAID. BECAUSE YOU ARE MORE RUTHLESS THAN I.

"Stay away," Jeremiah said, and his words came out slurred. "Stay...."

He slipped into a black sleep and dreamed his own memories, scenes from the past that he spent every waking moment burying within himself. While he slept, they all came clawing back up to the surface, like a rotting corpse coming out of the grave.

When he awoke, the sun slowly moved up the sky, shooting light through the trees and casting long shadows on the ground. Jeremiah reheated what little coffee there was, then he took the small spade he found inside the tent and scraped away at the hard ground until he made a hole just big enough for the dead man's body. By the time the grave was finished, Jeremiah was soaked in sweat and weak with hunger. There was a half-full canteen inside the tent but no food, so he ate sparingly from the venison jerky and bread he'd brought.

He dragged the body into the grave, but one of the dead man's arms was so rigid that it rose up above the edge of the hole. Jeremiah pushed on the arm until he heard a muted crack beneath the flesh, and the arm folded. He then shoveled dirt over the man's body until it was covered.

The sight of the mound made Jeremiah's heart heavy, and he sat for a while staring at it, thinking about how strange it was that all the thoughts, dreams, and ambitions of a man could disappear so completely beneath the dirt—so completely that one could almost believe no dead person had ever existed at all. Jeremiah removed his hat and bowed his head, but he did not pray.

4

WHEN JEREMIAH EMERGED FROM THE forest, the sky was dark. He walked halfway across the field before he saw the lights of his house. He put his hand into his pocket and rubbed the smooth gold of the morning glory. There would be a fight waiting for him when he came through the door, he knew that much. He hadn't planned to leave and stay gone for as long as he had, and surely Emma was mad with worry by now.

His fingers touched the golden flower and he tried to think of what he would tell his wife. He had never lied to her before, but as his skin ran over the rough stem and around the jagged petals, he knew he could not tell her the truth. Not yet. He needed to be certain of what he had found.

Jeremiah knelt and tried to calm his breathing. He had done nothing wrong, except perhaps take the golden flower. He set out with nothing but good intentions to find the owner of the lost horse, and Jeremiah promised himself that he would tell Sheriff Brennan where the man was buried as soon as he could. Still, he could not stop his hands from shaking.

Jeremiah walked the remaining distance to his house. He almost didn't stomp the mud from his boots for fear of waking the child, but then he remembered there was no child to wake.

The door flung open, and he found himself looking into his wife's face. Her expression was hurt and fear and anger, all at the same time. Her black hair hung in strands around her green eyes. Emma flung her arms around his neck and squeezed so hard he almost couldn't breathe. She touched his face, his neck, as if feeling to make sure he was real and not a ghost. Jeremiah pulled her close and held her. It had been so long since their bodies had touched that he found her shape felt foreign.

"I lost track of time," Jeremiah said.

Emma's chin shook. Her eyes were red and full of tears.

"I'm so glad you came back," she said, then put her face to his chest and wept.

Jeremiah filled the tub with hot water while Emma warmed some stew. He sat in the bath until the water turned tepid and the tips of his fingers were wrinkled, then he got out and put on clean clothes.

He found Emma sitting by the fire, sewing a hole in one knee of the pants he had worn into the woods. Jeremiah could not remember what caused the tear.

"Oskar Wellford had an accident while you were gone," she said without looking up. "His horse threw a shoe, and when he went to pick it up, the horse kicked him in the head."

Jeremiah watched his wife and was struck by how much older she looked, aged not with time but with grief. The crying and screaming lasted for several weeks after Samuel's death but were then replaced by a tired indifference. Something in her died with the boy. This new Emma moved through the house and did many of the same tasks as the old Emma, but she was not the same. Motion without meaning.

Her fingers deftly moved the needle and thread, pulling the two torn edges of fabric together. "He's been asleep since yesterday. The doctor doesn't know what state he'll be in when he awakens."

Jeremiah took a bite of stew and remembered a passage from the Bible. He tried to push it aside, but the words were already in his mind. When Jesus heard Lazarus had died, he told his disciples their friend was only sleeping.

Sleep, Death's brother.

The fire crackled, and Emma's chair creaked as she rocked back and forth. Jeremiah put down the spoon and pressed his hands to either side of his head. He wanted nothing more than to sleep for weeks, maybe months, as long as it took for the pain to go away.

Quiet. Everything so quiet without Samuel.

Later that night, as Jeremiah lay awake in the dark, Emma lying next to him, he kept seeing the cold, stiff body of the man he'd found in the woods, buried now in a shallow grave. Jeremiah had always believed that the Angel of Death had two faces—one he showed to the righteous and one he showed to the wicked. He wondered which the man in the woods had seen at the moment of his passing. A beautiful angel glowing with light, or a dark hooded creature with dripping fangs and sharpened claws?

Emma shifted and rolled toward him. "I know why you went out there," she said.

"Why?"

"I've thought about it too," she said. Jeremiah couldn't see her face in the dark, but her voice came from only inches away. "I want to be with him, wherever he is. You're the only reason I haven't done it. Maybe God has a plan in all of this."

Jeremiah reached under his pillow and touched the cold metal of the morning glory. "There is no plan," he said. "There never was."

Emma let out a soft sigh, and Jeremiah felt the weight of her hand on his chest. He lay there until Emma's breathing changed, then got up, put on a coat, and walked outside into the cold night.

5

WHEN JEREMIAH ENTERED THE BARN, the horses were quiet and still. He found the dead man's horse lying down in its stall, eyes open, breathing heavily. The food and water Jeremiah had put out before he left looked untouched. The other two horses seemed to be watching over the new one, with ears turned back and eyes wide.

Jeremiah took his pipe from the shelf and filled it with tobacco. After lighting it, he paced the length of the barn, a cloud of smoke trailing behind him.

The sound of labored breathing coming from the dead man's horse echoed in the space like the voice of a ghost. It reminded Jeremiah of the way Samuel sounded near the end. He hit his face once to stop the memory from becoming any clearer, and it was then that Jeremiah remembered the saddle bags he'd removed from the creature earlier.

He opened the bags and pulled out a pouch of tobacco, a tin of coffee grounds, a broken compass, three smooth stones, the feather of an eagle, a journal, a piece of rolled-up parchment paper, and a clump of gray and white fur tied together at one end with a piece of leather string. The fur looked to be from a coyote or a wolf. Jeremiah rubbed it between his fingers, imagining what it would be like to be covered in such hair. He wondered if this fur was from the wolf he'd seen at the campsite. He swallowed hard, and his chest burned when he did.

When Jeremiah opened the journal, he expected to find entries detailing the dead man's journey and perhaps even his final days. Instead, the writing was indecipherable, scrawled in a language Jeremiah could neither read nor understand.

There were no words, only strange square-shaped symbols, each a self-contained image. They depicted acts of violence and sacrifice: A man stabbing his own eye with a knife, a man eating a human heart, a man impaled on the branches of a tree. There was something ancient and unsettling about the symbols, as though each one told its own blood-soaked story.

As his eyes moved over the lines, each pictogram seemed to whisper with a voice that came from inside him. An echo that hissed the pronunciation of the images without explaining their meaning, and the pictograms appeared to rise off the page, gaining shadow and dimension as they floated before his eyes. He wished he had a key to decode the symbols, to understand why the dead man had taken such great pains to write them all down.

He unrolled the parchment paper, hoping the answer would be there. What he found instead was a map—a crude charcoal drawing of shaky lines, as though made in haste—of a trail that led through a forest to the top of a mountain. The trail ended at a black circle, and next to this was a sketch of a man on his knees, both arms raised, his mouth open and screaming in pain. Above the kneeling man's head, a disembodied hand hovered, radiating light in every direction. The hand was poised curiously—pinkie and ring finger were bent down toward the palm, with the thumb touching them. The remaining two fingers, index and middle, were pointed straight up and crossed. It was a familiar gesture, similar to old paintings of the saints, even of Christ himself, in books he had read long ago. Except in those images, the two fingers remained uncrossed.

As Jeremiah looked at this image, a sound began to grow in his head. The wolf's voice, rising in pitch and volume until it became a scream that seemed to match the sound that would have been coming out of the drawn figure's mouth. Jeremiah quickly turned the map face down and slammed his hand on it.

Jeremiah started to replace the dead man's belongings when he felt something shift inside one of the bags. He reached in and pulled out a small but heavy object wrapped in cloth. It was only about the size of an apple, but it weighed as much as a rock twice that size. Jeremiah slowly unwrapped the cloth to reveal a bright and metallic object that glowed in the light.

A golden bird, a thrush, lay on the cloth. With wings folded against its body and eyes still open, the bird looked so real it might stir and fly away at any moment. Jeremiah took the gold morning glory from his coat pocket and compared it to the thrush. The color and brilliance were the same. As Jeremiah looked closer at the bird, he couldn't understand how such a thing was made. The lines of the feathers, the bumps on the legs, the sharp point of the beak, and the way the eyes seemed frozen in time—if it was a piece of art, it was unlike anything Jeremiah had ever seen.

The bird was heavy, but it felt hollow, and as he moved the object from one hand to the other, he felt and heard the sound of dust shifting around inside it.

Jeremiah started sweating the longer he stared at the two golden objects. They seemed to pulse with life, like an ember in a fire. Even the horses became troubled, stamping their hooves and snorting. The dead man's horse merely moaned and moved its legs uselessly against the hay.

Jeremiah weighed the bird and flower in his hands, feeling their warmth on his skin. It was then he realized he was not just holding two strange objects, he was holding money, more money than he had seen in his entire life. He could pay off all his debts, buy a new house, buy Emma anything she wanted. They would have everything.

6

THE NEXT DAY, WHILE EMMA went to the Wellford's house to help Leanna with chores, Jeremiah visited the blacksmith in town and asked to use the forge to make a gift for Emma. The blacksmith was a member of the church where Jeremiah had once taught, and he agreed to let him have use of the shop for a few hours while he went out to the farms to shoe horses and sharpen plows.

When he was alone, Jeremiah put the bird into a crucible, which he then placed in the furnace. He wasn't sure the heat would be enough to melt the gold, but within minutes, the metal began to soften and collapse. As the bird lost shape, a hole opened on its side, spilling out gold dust. It melted into the bright liquid and disappeared. The outside of the bird—its eyes, beak, and feathers—had all been perfectly preserved, but the inside of the animal had somehow crumbled away, leaving just a hollow shell.

Jeremiah poured the molten metal into a small brick mold and let it cool while he smoked his pipe and watched people going about their business in town. Those who saw and recognized him turned away or acted like he wasn't there. Many had been sitting in the pews when Jeremiah delivered his final sermon.

The day he cursed God.

He waited until the brick had cooled enough to remove it from the mold, then put it in his satchel and walked down Main Street to the bank. Not a single person said hello or looked him in the eye, and he had a strange feeling that he had ceased to exist.

The bank manager could not hide his surprise when Jeremiah showed him the gold. The small, balding man had to remove his glasses and wipe the moisture away more than once as he held the still-warm brick, the distorted reflection of his round face floating over its surface.

Jeremiah kept his story simple: he had gone panning for gold in the river and stumbled upon an outcropping of rock eroded by the water. He saw what appeared to be gold in the stone, and when he finally managed to dig it out, he found it to be a much bigger piece than he had expected.

The bank only had enough money to give Jeremiah half of the sum of the gold bar, and the rest would have to be brought in from San Francisco. When the bank manager gave Jeremiah what money he had, Jeremiah held the coins and ran his fingers along their cold edges. He kept thinking the moment was false, a dream that would turn to vapor as soon as he tried to leave the bank. But the money was real, and it was his.

After signing a receipt and leaving the gold with the still stunned bank manager, Jeremiah took only a small bag of coins with him and kept the rest locked up in the vault. He went back outside and walked down the street as dusk fell.

Men trudged in from the fields covered in dirt, bits of straw clinging to their hair, their beards. Some waved goodbyes to each other and went home, but most made their way straight to the tavern.

Jeremiah went along the boardwalk until he came to the tavern doors. He could hear the piano playing a jaunty tune just beneath the clamor of too many voices all talking at once, the percussive sound of the dancing women's boots as they slammed on the stage.

He thought about going inside and buying everyone a drink, but they all knew who he was, what he used to be. They would stare at him and wonder what he wanted. They would want to know where he had gotten the money to buy so many glasses of whiskey.

Besides, they would never trust him. How many times had he stood at the pulpit and preached against the sins of drunkenness and lust? How many times had a worried wife awakened him from sleep and begged him to come down here and drag a glassy-eyed Sandy Dearborn or Colin James back home to their children before losing an entire day's wages at the poker table?

At the time, Jeremiah believed he was doing right. Now, he wondered if he'd been living in an upside-down world and insisting everyone else do the same.

Now, standing there at the doors, seeing all those men stagger in from a long day of physical labor, Jeremiah thought he understood why they needed this. A sanctuary at the end of the day. What did Jeremiah have but a son who was no longer alive and a wife hovering dangerously close to becoming a ghost herself? Maybe a few drinks while watching a pretty woman kick up her skirt wasn't the worst thing in the world.

Jeremiah turned away and walked the dusty main street. The weight of the coins in his pocket was unfamiliar and made him feel guilty in some vague way. He stopped when he came to the clothes shop. The mannequin in the window wore a long, bright blue dress, and he thought of how beautiful it would look on Emma, how it would complement her black hair and pale skin. He went inside and told the woman working there he wanted the dress. Her eyes widened a bit, but she took down the dress and boxed it up. He then picked out a pair of shoes and a hat to match. While the woman boxed these up as well, Jeremiah added a pair of white gloves to the counter. Something stirred in him as he pictured his wife in these beautiful things, and he wondered if this gold was the path to somewhere better for them. Somewhere joy and purpose could be found again.

7

JEREMIAH CAME HOME TO FIND Emma sitting by the fire, a torn dress on her lap, a needle and thread in her hand. She stared into the flames as though in a trance, the skin around her eyes swollen and red from a night of restless sleep. Jeremiah had felt her body spasm and jerk as she dreamed.

She looked up when he closed the door, and a thin trickle of blood ran down her finger, soaked red into the fabric of the dress. Emma muttered something and put the finger in her mouth.

Jeremiah set the boxes on the table as Emma carried the dress over to the wash basin, dipped the corner in, and scrubbed it, turning the water pink.

Jeremiah watched as she hung the dress to dry, her other fingers dotted with small pinpricks of blood. Stray hairs stuck to her cheek. He saw strands of grey at the back of her neck, strands that had not been there three months earlier.

Emma wiped her hands on her apron and eyed the packages. "What are those?"

Jeremiah pushed them to her. "An apology."

She sighed and gently touched the bow, afraid to undo something so beautiful. Jeremiah knew she recognized the boxes and the store they came from. A store she'd purchased clothing from only twice during their marriage. He tried to smile at her, to make the moment something more than it was.

The ribbon came undone and fell to the table. Emma's lips tightened as she lifted the lid and pulled out the dress. It hung in front of her body, the fabric crisp and bright. She held her bleeding finger out, careful not to stain the dress.

When she looked up at Jeremiah, her eyes were redder than before. "You know I can't accept this. We don't have the money."

Jeremiah came closer and opened the other boxes for her. Emma's body seemed to shrink with each new item he pulled out.

He held the shoes, the hat. "I thought you would look beautiful in these."

"Jeremiah," her eyes moved around the house, left in a permanent state of disorder since Samuel. "I can't."

A gust of wind rattled the window and creaked through the door. The flames flickered in the fireplace. But she still held the dress, the fingers of the hand that wasn't bleeding slowly caressing the fabric. A deep navy blue. Jeremiah always loved the way dark blue made her black hair shine.

Jeremiah reached into his pocket, took out the small bag full of coins, and set it on the table. Emma looked at him with confusion. He pushed the bag a little closer. "Open it," he said. She did as he asked and took a sharp breath when she saw what was inside. The hand with the bloody finger covered her open mouth.

She lifted the bag and let the coins fall onto the table. "How?" she asked, then her eyes narrowed. "What did you do to get this?"

Jeremiah took her hand in his. He tried to remain calm, but it was difficult because he was about to lie, and Emma had always been able to sense a lie.

"When I was in the woods," he said, "I found a piece of gold. Bigger than anyone around here has found before, or likely ever will."

Her green eyes settled on his and remained there, searching for the untruth. "Why didn't you tell me?"

"I had to be sure it was real. I took it to the shop and melted it down. That's when I knew."

Emma looked at the money, then at the open boxes with the clothes. She picked up one of the coins and turned it over in her fingers.

"This belongs to us?"

The words were right there, but he wasn't sure he wanted to say them. Emma raised her eyebrows, watching him. "I think it's a gift," he said. "Or an apology. God has given this to us because—"

Emma clutched the dress to her chest and took a step back. The swollen flesh around her eyes tightened, and she pointed a trembling finger at her husband.

"This is not payment for Samuel," Emma said, in a voice so low Jeremiah had to strain to hear it.

She shook her head, making no effort to wipe away the tears. Wood cracked in the fireplace, collapsed into the bed of glowing embers.

"It is not," she said, folding the dress over her arm and putting it back into the box.

She turned and left the room, and the sound of their bedroom door slamming shut echoed in the quiet house. Jeremiah ran his fingers over the dress. A dark spot shone on the fabric. He touched it and his finger came away wet with blood.

Emma came out later when it was dark, her eyes puffy from crying. She sat on Jeremiah's lap, rested her head against his shoulder. He had let the fire die and the embers pulsed red like the beating heart of something alive. He put his arms around his wife, held her close.

She had lost weight since Samuel died and her shape was foreign to him, fragile. How unfair, he thought, that almost everything broken could be fixed, except other people.

"The quiet bothers me," she whispered. "Without him, all I hear is the house."

Jeremiah's eyes moved to the window, to the darkness outside. The shadow shape of a small headstone rose up from the field. He had not wanted to bury the boy where they could see his grave from the house. He had wanted to bury him out back, but Emma insisted and he did what she asked. How many times a day did he catch her staring out the window at that mound of dirt, one hand held over her heart, crying silently as she pictured their son's small body dressed in his Sunday clothes?

"The walls make sounds," she said. Jeremiah felt tears fall onto his neck. "The floors creak like someone is walking over them. All these things I never noticed before."

Sometimes Jeremiah dreamed that he dug a second grave next to Samuel, a grave he crawled into and scooped handfuls of dirt over himself until he could not see the stars.

"I miss his voice," she said. "I miss the sound of his feet running from one room to the other." She sat up and looked at Jeremiah, her eyes quivering in the dim light. "Why are these the things I miss?"

Because, first you miss him, Jeremiah thought, *and then you become aware of how different everything is without him. You see the empty shape he's left behind.*

He held Emma tighter, feeling her bones where he had not been able to before. Before...

"I try," Emma said, "but I can't see the day when this will hurt any less." She put a hand on Jeremiah's cheek, turned his face to hers. "I want you to tell me that you would have found the gold even if Samuel were alive."

Jeremiah looked away from his wife but she moved his face again. "I need to hear you say it. Tell me we are blessed and it has nothing to do with Samuel."

Jeremiah swallowed painfully and forced himself to meet Emma's eyes. He saw pleading etched into her face, a need to believe what she was asking him to say. Wrinkles that had not been there three months prior were now dark shadow lines in her skin.

He swallowed again, and looking at the headstone in the field, said, "Even if Samuel were still here, I would have seen that horse and gone into the woods looking for its owner."

Emma put her head back on his shoulder. Jeremiah felt air leave her body as she exhaled.

"Who was he?" she asked. "The man you found. Who is missing him?"

Jeremiah held his wife and watched as the embers glowed in the dark like small red eyes.

8

LATE IN THE AFTERNOON, JEREMIAH came in from feeding the horses and found Emma standing in front of the mirror, holding the new dress up to her neck. Her face turned red when she saw him.

"It would look better if you put it on," he said, smiling.

She looked down at her feet in the new shoes. "If I put it on, will you take me somewhere?"

Jeremiah leaned against the doorway, still struck by her beauty after all these years. From the day they met she did something to him, filled his heart with love and lust in equal measure.

"Where do you want to go?" he asked.

"I want to be where there are people," Emma said, holding up the dress again and looking at herself in the mirror as though the person in the glass was someone else. Someone she could be.

She scooped up her black hair in one hand, twisted it, and held it on top of her head. "I don't have friends any longer, besides Leanna, not since…" she stopped and her face turned red again.

She didn't mean "not since Samuel," she meant not since Jeremiah had cursed God in front of the whole congregation and gave up his position as minister. He could still hear the gasps and crying as he hammered his fist into the pulpit and screamed out his pain in front of all of them.

"I want to be surrounded by people," Emma said, as she walked closer. "I can't remember the last time I left the house."

She took Jeremiah's hand in hers. "I want to remember that there was an us before Samuel, and there can be again in these… these after days."

Jeremiah pulled her hand to his mouth and kissed it, felt her cold skin on his lips.

He nodded and said, "Then you better get dressed."

9

THEY WALKED SIDE BY SIDE down the main street. The sun had slipped behind the trees, and the sky was still burned at the edges. Light shone from the tavern and inn windows, from the jail and the restaurant. Children ran in circles around the blackened skeleton of the lightning-struck oak tree, which gave Charwood its name, and their laughter carried on the still air.

Jeremiah wore the only suit he owned besides his clerical garments—a black wool coat and pants, a vest, white shirt and tie—clothes he had not worn since he stood at the edge of Samuel's grave with a small crowd, mostly members of the church who came to pay their respects.

Jeremiah didn't want anyone to perform a service as the small pine box was lowered into the earth. He did not want to hear about God's love or heaven. Instead, he wanted to hear wailing and screaming. He wanted fire to fall from the sky and burn everything around the dark hole in the ground. He wanted to throw himself on top of the casket and let himself be buried with his son. But Emma insisted that Carlson Reid, the young man from San Francisco brought in to replace Jeremiah, say something.

Jeremiah disliked Reid from the moment they shook hands. His skin was smooth and free of calluses. His blond hair was too bright and perfectly combed, and he smelled of cologne, a scent that made Jeremiah's head ache.

Emma walked stiffly in her new dress and shoes, a much older coat worn over the top. When they reached the theater, Jeremiah held the door open, and they stepped into a lobby full of men and women dressed in their finest clothes, with a hundred voices all talking and laughing at the same time.

Men stood on one side of the room smoking cigars and drinking whiskey, and the women on the other fanned themselves and talked about trips to the city. Emma smiled nervously as they headed for the ticket booth, and Jeremiah noticed several women stopped talking and stared at his wife.

Heat moved up his back and into his face. He stood behind Emma, as if to protect her from their eyes, their loud voices now whispering behind gloved hands. Jeremiah took Emma's coat and gave it to the man at the counter, thinking he needed to buy her a new one—a whole new wardrobe—something to make the wall of whispering women jealous.

Jeremiah put an arm around Emma and guided her to the lobby's center. He smiled and told her he paid for seats in the very front row. He tried to move her gently to the doors that led into the theater and steer her away from all those staring eyes, those red lips that moved almost silently, but Emma glanced over and saw them. Saw how the women looked away from her, pressing closer together. Women Emma knew or used to know. Women from the church who would meet weekly for Bible study and friendship.

Emma turned and walked faster toward the doors. Jeremiah's jaw tightened as he looked into the faces of those women. The blond in the white dress with the fluttering eyelids was Laura, Carlson Reid's wife, and Jeremiah didn't know if he had the strength to see that man.

He moved to keep up with Emma when he felt a hand on his shoulder. Jeremiah spun around, expecting another hostile face, but found Sheriff Charles Brennan instead. Alone, dressed in the same suit he always wore to church on Sundays. He wore no hat, and Jeremiah had forgotten how gray his hair was. As gray as the fur Jeremiah had found in the dead man's bag.

"Jeremiah," Brennan said, holding out his hand. "I'm so glad to see you two out together." He smiled, a genuine expression in a room full of false ones.

Emma heard the sheriff's voice and turned around.

"You look lovely this evening," Brennan said as he kissed her hand. Emma smiled in return, and Jeremiah was relieved to see it was also genuine.

"I didn't know you enjoyed the theater," Emma said.

"Oh, I was never much for watching people make believe on a stage. But Helen always loved it. She'd drag me here for every new show." Brennan nodded to the front doors. "I think you can still see my claw marks on the street. After she passed, I've just kept coming."

After, Jeremiah thought. *So many afters. A person dies and leaves a dividing line. Everything before, and everything after.*

Brennan looked directly into Emma's eyes. "It's a shame I finally appreciate it now that she's gone." He smiled sadly, and all the lines in his face deepened. "But that's the way it goes. The only thing I don't like is the crowd. Too stuffy." He puffed out his chest and laughed.

Emma laughed with him, and Jeremiah caught Brennan's eye, gave him a small nod of gratitude. An usher came into the lobby and announced the performance was about to begin.

Brennan followed them into the darkened theater, told them to enjoy the show, and left to find his seat. Jeremiah and Emma walked down the aisle to the very front row, center stage. The rest of the crowd filed in, and soon the room was full.

When the first actors took the stage, Emma reached over and laced her fingers through Jeremiah's. The play was called *Empty Monuments.*

It took place in an unknown time, in an unknown country. The king of this place sent a man, whose young son had recently died, on a mission. The king heard rumors that a mysterious hole had opened in the ground just outside a far-off village. Anything broken thrown into the void would reappear the next day, whole again.

Leaving his wife behind, the man traveled to the village to see if the story was true. When he arrived, a town leader demonstrated the power of the strange hollow. A mug was shattered, and the pieces were thrown in. The following morning, the restored mug appeared inside a small stone circle near the hole.

The man, stunned by what he had seen, rode home as fast as he could and, under the cover of darkness, went to the graveyard and dug up the rotted corpse of his son.

Emma's hand clenched Jeremiah's tighter during this scene. He glanced over to see if she was crying, if the story was too much for her to bear. But her eyes followed the actor, her mouth open slightly as the man wrapped the boy's body in burlap and laid it on the back of his horse.

One hand rose to cover her heart as Emma watched the man carry his son to the hole's edge. Her body tensed, and she leaned forward.

When the bundle of bones and decomposed flesh fell into the abyss, Emma took a deep breath and held it. Even with her gloves on, Emma's nails dug into Jeremiah's skin.

The man waited all night by the hollow, occasionally slipping into fitful sleep. When the sun rose, he crawled to the stone circle, crying out for his son, but the boy did not appear. The day wore on, and eventually, the man understood he had found the one thing the mysterious hole could not do: It could repair what was broken, but death was not something to be fixed.

The man mounted his horse and started the journey back home, and as he did, he sensed something following him. Blueish smoke floated over the ground from the side of the stage and followed him all the way back to his house. He told his wife nothing of what had happened.

In the middle of the night, the man awoke to his wife shaking him violently.

"It's our son," she said, but she was smiling. "He's come back. I feel him in the walls, the floor, the air around us."

All the man heard was a ghostly moaning. A child's voice pleading to be sent back to where it came from.

"We only wanted our boy returned to us," the man said to the audience. "Now, we are haunted." Then he hung his head, and the curtains closed.

Emma stood immediately, her gloves making a muted sound as she clapped her hands. Jeremiah stood next to her and glanced behind him. They were the only two standing. The rest of the theater only offered subdued applause.

The curtain opened to reveal the entire cast standing on the stage. They all joined hands, took a bow, and the curtain closed once more. Emma continued to applaud even after the rest of the crowd had stopped and begun exiting the room.

Jeremiah touched her arm again, and Emma looked over, startled, then sat beside him.

"Shall we go?" Jeremiah asked.

Emma took his hand in hers. "I want to sit for a moment."

The two of them sat, staring at an empty stage.

10

WHEN THEY REACHED THE LOBBY, the cast was already mingling with the audience. Champagne was poured and passed around. Glasses clinked together. Voices and laughter filled the room. A man carrying a tray came by and handed them each a glass. Emma took a sip, pursed her lips together, and smiled.

"What is it?" Jeremiah asked her.

Emma's eyes moved around from person to person. Her lips were still curved in a slight smile, but her eyes were wide, nervous.

"I'm still your wife," she said, holding the glass with both hands, "but I'm no longer a preacher's wife." She took another drink and laughed. "I'm not sure how to behave."

She looked down into the mostly empty glass and swirled the liquid inside. Her smile disappeared. "This is different than what I expected," she said. "Like that man from the play, we just carry something with us, I think. Something that fills a room."

She glanced around again. Husbands and wives conversed with other couples, their laughter loose and easy. No one looked their way. No one even acknowledged their presence.

Emma finished her champagne and said, "Let's go."

Jeremiah put a hand on her shoulder. "Are you sure?"

"I don't want to be here anymore."

Jeremiah nodded and pulled away to get her coat. He walked sideways through a group of people, some of whom he had met with and prayed for during their own tribulations. People who confessed their secret sins to him and received forgiveness. Now, he wandered right through their midst as though he were as insubstantial as the blue smoke that had drifted over the stage.

The man at the counter handed Jeremiah the old coat, its elbows thin and tattered. He put it over one arm and started back to his wife. As he drew closer, he saw a man speaking to her—a man dressed in fine clothes. He stood straight and tall, his head tilted toward Emma's ear.

The heat came back, ignited in his stomach, and spread up his chest and neck. He could not see Emma's face or see if this man's presence was welcome.

Jeremiah slipped between two men discussing a bridge that was being built in north Arrow County. He looked directly into the eyes of Lloyd Fletcher, a man who not infrequently played poker and watched the girls dance while his wife thought he was taking part in an important town committee overseen by the mayor himself. He was even known to offer his own daughter, Abigail, to travelers when the women at the tavern were occupied.

Fletcher made eye contact, ignored Jeremiah, and continued talking without missing a word. As he got closer, Jeremiah smelled the well-dressed man's cologne and saw the man's hand briefly touch Emma's bare arm.

The heat burned brighter inside Jeremiah, scorched up his face and scalp. His shirt stuck to his back with sweat.

The man with the tray of champagne came up to them, took Emma's empty glass, and gave them two full ones. Jeremiah shouldered his way through more people, some of whom moved out of the way, while others, he felt, deliberately stayed where they were.

He could hear the man's voice now, even though he still couldn't see his face, a measured and arrogant voice. But he could not make out the words. Emma laughed, an effortless sound, bright and real, and the heat in Jeremiah's gut flashed down the back of his legs.

He went up to Emma and handed her the coat. He tried to relax his jaw and lips when he saw Charles Fairfax the Third. The man's hair shone in the light, his cheeks flushed red from drink. He was a strange combination of masculine and feminine, what his mother would have called "a beautiful boy" with his full lips and long eyelashes.

Fairfax gave a small bow. "Good evening, Jeremiah. I'm so glad you both could make it. I was just telling Emma—"

Jeremiah ignored the man. "We should go," he said to Emma.

Now, her cheeks turned red with embarrassment. She looked around for a place to set down her fresh glass of champagne.

"There's no need to rush off," Fairfax said, touching Jeremiah's arm. "This is your first time out in how long? Enjoy it."

A beautiful woman broke through the crowd and grabbed onto Fairfax's arm. She held no glass, and her movements were as quick and precise as a small bird's. She smiled widely when she saw Emma.

"What a lovely new dress," the woman said as she embraced Emma. "I've seen it in the shop window. Oh, it looks wonderful on you!"

Was it Jeremiah's imagination, or did Fairfax look disappointed that his wife had found them? The heat scalded Jeremiah's hands, and his palms itched to make fists.

"I ran into Emma, and we were discussing the play," Fairfax said, giving Emma a smile. "We both found it be insightful and heart-wrenching."

The woman held out her hand to Jeremiah. "I'm so glad you two came."

He tried to remember the woman's name, but he couldn't. The elder Fairfax came to church every Sunday and tithed more than ten percent, but his son and daughter-in-law rarely attended. Fairfax the Third met her somewhere out east while in university. Some claimed she studied to become a nurse, a woman of science, which is why she didn't need the church.

But Jeremiah recognized her, and he said, "It's very nice to see you again."

Emma shrank a little in this woman's presence, her shoulders rising. Fairfax's wife spoke with such ease, moved with such confidence, and laughed so easily, it made Jeremiah think she had not endured a single hardship or loss during her life.

"I was just talking to the Harringtons," the woman said. "Their oldest son got engaged to the Searcy girl."

Fairfax nodded at what she said, but his eyes stayed on Emma, watching her as she looked at the floor.

"Dear," he said, and touched his wife's arm. "We should probably leave these two to enjoy their evening. They don't need us talking their ears off."

He smiled brightly, and the woman joined in. "Of course," she said. "I'm so sorry. It was truly wonderful to see you both. We should have you over for dinner soon."

Jeremiah thanked her for the invitation, which he knew would never come, and said goodnight. Emma watched the woman's dress disappear into the crowd, sadness filling her eyes. She looked at her drink again, lifted it in a silent toast, and downed it in two swallows. She tried to smile at Jeremiah but looked like she was trying not to cry. The smile had a twisted quality that made his gut ache.

"I think I'd like one more," Emma said, looking around for the man with the tray.

"We should go," Jeremiah whispered, taking her coat and helping her into it.

"No, we're out, and I want to enjoy myself," she said, and the words came out forcefully, almost angry. She noticed Jeremiah still held his full glass, and she took it from him, drank it all in two swallows. She blinked long and hard and tried to smile again, and Jeremiah hated the way it hardened her features and made her look like she was in pain.

"Emma," he said. "Let's go home."

The noise in the room was so deafening that it pressed against Jeremiah's skull. He wanted to be outside in the cool, quiet air. Emma turned a full circle, searching for someone or something to give them a reason to stay. Finally, she hung her head. "Okay, let's go."

Jeremiah took her hand and pushed into the crowd, bodies packed so closely together he couldn't even see the front doors. Emma's hand suddenly jerked out of his, and a moment later, he heard her voice, full of pain, screaming above all the other voices.

"What have you ever lost?" she yelled, and when Jeremiah shouldered through the people in his way, he saw her, legs bent, pointing a finger directly into Margaret Thorson's face. She stood with several other well-dressed and wealthy women, all backing away from Emma.

Emma looked different to him, as if the drink had pulled up all of the hurt, bitterness, and anger in her heart and plastered it right on her face. It contorted in ways unfamiliar to him.

"Has the world ever opened up beneath your feet and swallowed you whole?" Emma said, still pointing her finger. "Have you ever cried so hard you thought your heart would cave in?"

Her words came out slurred and shaking. Tears ran down her face. Jeremiah came up behind and wrapped his arms around her. She leaned into him even while she still shouted.

"All of this," she said, waving her arm at the room, "all of this doesn't protect you from it. Someday, death will sneak up and rob you of something you didn't think you could live without. Who will you be then? What do you have that will take the pain away?"

"Emma, we need to go," Jeremiah said gently.

At the sound of his voice, Emma spun around in his arms and pointed at the woman. "She said her son was a burden, and sometimes she wished she'd never had him at all."

Jeremiah pulled his wife closer. "We don't belong here," he whispered. Emma looked up at him with wet and quivering eyes. She nodded once as tears slid down her cheeks and dripped off her chin.

She turned once more to the women, her eyes moving over each one, and said, "God damn you all."

Jeremiah kept his arm around her shoulder and led her out of the room. The crowd parted to let them through. Everyone was silent. Jeremiah turned around once and saw Charles Fairfax watching them with concern.

As they reached the door, Sheriff Brennan came over, pushed it open, and followed them out into the street.

"Wait here," he said. "I'll get the wagon from the jail, give you a ride home."

"We don't want to trouble you," Jeremiah said.

Brennan waved his hand. "It's no trouble. She ain't in no condition to walk, just hold on."

He took off at a brisk pace, heading into the dark and quiet town.

Jeremiah kept his arms around Emma as she shivered against him. She had fallen apart in front of them, just like he had. He had told them God was nothing more than a cruel tyrant and a heartless thief. And now Emma had cursed them all.

Jeremiah knew the party would continue, and they would be the subject of conversation for the rest of the evening. But he didn't care, and Emma was right. Everything she had said was true.

What did any of them have that could take away the pain?

11

WHEN THEY GOT HOME, JEREMIAH helped Emma out of her dress and into bed. He waited until she fell asleep, then went to the barn to retrieve the map and journal. He unrolled the parchment paper on the kitchen table and used books to hold down the edges.

He stared at the map until his eyes went blurry, until he had memorized nearly every detail. He sat with both elbows digging into the table, hands gripping the sides of his head. The childishness of the drawing forced him to think about things he did not want to think about, of all the pictures Samuel would never draw.

Even though he never said it to Emma, the quiet bothered him too. Especially in the evening, when the sky was dark blue and a breeze shivered through the tall grass. When he heard the distant shouts of parents calling their children for dinner.

He and Emma never had any trouble talking, and after they were married, evenings were often spent in each other's arms, discovering the other's thoughts and dreams. Uncovering their fears. Then Samuel was born, and something new came into the house, something bright and alive. Evenings were filled with cooing, crying, and laughing.

They had a togetherness before the boy, but the child transformed them into different people, and wherever they were now, it didn't feel like before Samuel. He was still there between them, somehow—a thought, a memory, a ghostly fog that made the other person harder to see.

Jeremiah rubbed his eyes, blinked a few times, and looked at the map again. Some of the lines were smudged, and the paper was stained dark in places, probably with sweat. He traced the crude lines with his finger, imagined the hand that held the charcoal shaking as it drew, trying to create from memory a map to get back to someplace he had just run from.

A hand on his shoulder startled Jeremiah from his thoughts. He turned to see Emma standing behind him, looking at the open map. Her brow furrowed as she looked at the images, the mad scribbles of trees and water, and that dark swirling hole.

"I've been trying to figure out where he started from," Jeremiah said. "It's only half a map. These woods could be anywhere."

Emma leaned over and tapped a finger on the floating hand above the kneeling figure. "What does that mean?" she asked quietly, as though asking herself.

Before Jeremiah could answer, she moved her finger to the kneeling man, his mouth wide open, screaming. Only this figure and the floating hand above him seemed drawn with any real sense of diligence. The map was drawn in a hurry, probably propped up on the dead man's knees and sketched in firelight. But those two images were done carefully, and with not a small amount of artistic ability.

The screaming man's face was wrinkled around the eyes. The mouth was misshapen, locked open, the eyes squinted shut. The hands, held up in front of his chest, had gnarled fingers curled into claws. Somewhere, down a long dark hallway that led to the back of his mind, in a place where Jeremiah stored all the things he couldn't face, he almost heard that scream echoing.

Emma's finger slid down the paper to the edge of the woods, followed the jagged tree line, and came to rest on an object in the lower left-hand corner.

"Does that look familiar to you?" she asked.

After staring at the map for hours, Jeremiah wasn't sure which pencil lines were intentional and which were the mistake of a shaking hand.

The shape was familiar, but he couldn't think of why.

Emma dragged her finger farther down until it came off the paper and stopped at the table's edge.

"Here," she said. "This is where Charwood would be."

Of course. Why hadn't he seen it before?

"Fang," he said quietly.

To the south of town was a large open field, similar to the north field he and Emma lived in, and at the center of this was a giant stone that stood as tall as two men. The children called it "Fang Rock" because it curved to a sharp point. The rock could not be seen from town, but everyone knew where it was. Out there alone in the field, looking like a giant fang that had come ripping up from under the earth, as if the world itself had grown teeth.

"Charwood was his starting point," Jeremiah said.

Emma's hand left his shoulder. She pulled out a chair, sat down, and looked at her husband.

"Why do you need to know where he started?" Her eyes, circled with red, stared at him, unblinking.

Jeremiah's breath went shallow as he tried to think of what to say and how to say it. He put his hands under the table so she couldn't see him twisting his fingers together.

He took a deep breath and said, "I need to tell you about the gold."

Emma listened as he told her about the bird he had found, the flower. He believed those objects were not sculptures, but once living things that had been transformed. The bird was hollow and inside was a fine gold powder. Her eyes never left his face as he spoke, and her expression remained so blank that he wondered if she had taken some of the druggist's powder earlier.

Emma waited until he had finished telling his story, then said, "You know how this all sounds?"

Jeremiah expected this. How could she possibly believe him? The story was unbelievable. He wasn't even sure he believed it, but his hands still went numb at the memory of holding the bird and somehow knowing it had once been alive. A knowing that had passed through the grooves of the hardened feathers, the beak, the claws, and into Jeremiah's skin.

"Why would you think those things you found were real?" Emma asked.

Words tumbled through Jeremiah's thoughts, words and phrases that explained it all to himself, internally. But spoken aloud, they wouldn't really explain the feeling he got from the bird.

"It's impossible, Jeremiah," she said. "You know that."

He shook his head silently. Emma sighed, rubbing her forehead. "I don't want to hear anymore. This talk makes you sound crazy."

Silence passed between them, grew into something uncomfortable, and lingered. Emma closed her eyes and pressed two fingers into each temple.

How could he explain the distinct shock of holding something in his hands, something that his mind was unable to dismiss? He imagined it was what people who witnessed Christ's miracles must have felt.

Then he remembered.

"Wait here," he said and got up. He went to their bedroom and reached under the mattress, searching until his fingers touched cold metal. Jeremiah came back to the table and held out his closed hand. He placed the object in front of Emma, then sat down.

Her eyes went wide when she saw the golden morning glory, she couldn't hide that. She felt it, too, he knew she did. Her eyes narrowed as she picked it up, turned it over, and ran her fingers along the petals and stem.

"Tell me how an artist made that," Jeremiah said.

She lifted her eyes to meet his, tilted her head. "Just because I don't know how an artist sculpted this doesn't mean he didn't."

"How did he create the grooves on the stem, the shape of those petals?"

Her face changed suddenly. A look of disgust. She put the flower back on the table and crossed her arms. The skin under her eyes was dark and swollen. "I don't see it, Jeremiah. I don't see it like you do."

"The bird was the same way," he said. "So flawless that I hated to look at it, because I knew, just like you know, it used to be alive."

Emma stood up so fast the chair scraped the floor. She shook her head back and forth but kept looking at the flower. Firelight cast dark shadows against the right side of her face. That one gray-green eye stared out from the center like a pale moon shining on a lake at midnight.

"I could feel the lines of every feather, the roundness of its eyes," Jeremiah said. "One claw was chipped just a little."

"Stop it," Emma said, backing away from the table. "Stop. I don't want to hear anymore."

"If Aaron could turn a staff into a serpent, and Christ could turn water into wine, why couldn't there be the power to turn living things into gold?"

Emma kept walking backward until she bumped into a shelf and rattled the bowls. "I don't want to hear anymore."

Jeremiah stood and picked up the flower, feeling again that strangeness he first experienced in the woods, a quiet hum that told him of impossible things. He held the morning glory delicately between two fingers.

"You know it as well as I do, Emma. This was not sculpted. This flower was picked from the dirt and then changed."

He grabbed the parchment map with his other hand and held it up. He pointed at the drawing of the hand, two fingers extended, rays of light shooting out all around it.

"You asked what this means. If I follow this map, I think it leads to the place where the power is."

12

IT WAS LATE AFTERNOON THE next day when a rider came out of the east woods. Jeremiah heard the rolling thunder of hoofbeats before he saw the horse crossing the field. There was something familiar about the rider, about his silhouette.

Jeremiah sat on the porch smoking a pipe. As the rider came closer, Jeremiah stood up and squinted into the distance. There was no mistaking the figure now. He set down the pipe and ran out into the field.

The rider brought the horse to a stop, jumped off, and threw his arms around Jeremiah.

"Elijah," Jeremiah said, "I've missed you." He held onto his brother, his only living flesh and blood, like something might steal him away at any moment.

"I'm sorry it took me so long to get here," Elijah said. He put his hands on Jeremiah's shoulders and stepped back, looking into his brother's eyes. They hadn't seen each other in over a year, and Jeremiah searched for time's marks in Elijah's face. He was tan, with a full day's growth of stubble on his face, and except for some of the lines around his eyes, he looked the same. He still had their mother's dark, almost black hair. He was like her in so many ways. In fact, there was very little of their father in him at all. That had been passed to Jeremiah.

"Thank you for coming," Jeremiah said, taking the horse's reins and leading it to the barn. Elijah walked beside them, looking at the house.

"Every time I come back, the place looks smaller," he said. "It doesn't fit with what I remember."

Jeremiah followed his brother's gaze and tried to remember it as it had been when they grew up there. A family of four gathered around the dinner table, their father's cracked hands and rough voice, like pebbles scratching together, as he prayed over their meal. The brothers shared a room and a bed, which meant that one often took the blows for the other when their father came home drunk and angry.

Elijah stood just outside the barn, shielding his eyes with a hand as he looked at the house. Jeremiah wondered what his memories felt like and if they were different from his own.

He took his brother's horse to an empty stall at the back, and as he passed the dead man's horse, Elijah's shook its head and whinnied. Its ears flicked back and forth, eyes wide.

Jeremiah managed to get the animal in the stall and closed the door. He took off the saddle bags and put hay into the feeder. The horse turned in circles, always keeping one eye on the boards its stall shared with the other horse.

Jeremiah got some more hay for the dead man's horse, and when he leaned over the door, he saw the animal lying on the ground, foam coming out of its mouth. Its ribs rose and fell with ragged breathing. It moaned in a voice like a man's, low and full of pain.

Elijah's horse suddenly kicked the wall with a sound like a cannon, and Jeremiah's whole body jerked, his heartbeat feeling like an echo that bounced around in his chest. The boards shook and swayed. The animal snorted in quick bursts and stamped its hooves.

As he walked back through the barn, he checked on his two animals only to find them standing at the far ends of their own stalls, as far away as they could get from the dead man's horse. They, too, were alert, standing very still, ears twitching with each echoing moan.

When Jeremiah came out, he found Elijah staring across the field to the church and the white crosses and headstones of the graveyard where their parents were buried.

"How long has it been since you went to their graves?" Jeremiah asked. He set the saddlebags on the ground between them.

"Too long," Elijah said.

And why go to the graves at all? Jeremiah thought. *There was no comfort there, no peace. Just bones buried in dirt.*

"Was it as bad as you said in your letter?" Elijah asked.

Jeremiah looked at the church as well. The cross atop the steeple cut into the grey sky.

"Worse."

"He is a God of forgiveness," Elijah said, still shielding his eyes. Eyes that were the exact same light blue as their mother's, the color of a spring sky on a cloudless day.

Jeremiah lowered his gaze. "I've done nothing to forgive."

Elijah nodded slowly and turned in a circle, looking at the field he had grown up playing in. So many wars and adventures in the tall grass. So many nights spent catching fireflies and racing back and forth between their house and the church.

Elijah stopped turning when he saw the grave, the small hill of bare dirt rising from the ground. He put his hands down and walked toward it. Jeremiah stayed behind. He remembered the fear as he stood at the pulpit as if it was a fresh cut from a knife. A wound still screaming in the open air, dripping blood all over everything he touched.

A lifetime of believing what he said and did had some effect on outcomes, only to find that lying prostrate on the floor, praying so hard sweat puddled under his forehead, did nothing to change what had already been decided.

A lifetime of being afraid that God would punish him for wrong thoughts, words, and actions. Yes, he was afraid as his fingers gripped the sides of the pulpit—as if a dark hole might open in the sky and pull him up into it—and the words were like coals in his throat, burning there, and the only way to relieve the pain was to speak them.

His voice shook when he started. Sweat crawled down his back in a slow itch. Part of him expected lightning to come tearing through the roof, slam into his body, and burn him alive. But there were no storm clouds, no wind or rain. Just a clear sky and birds chirping from the trees outside the church.

Even though he was afraid, he spoke, and even as his mouth formed the words, they ignited the air. They floated over the pews and burned everyone who heard them. But once he started, he could not stop. Some in the congregation began to weep and moan, and Jeremiah didn't stop even when many of them got up and walked out. Those who remained sat in shock, mouths open, eyes wide. The reservoir was already empty, so none of them saw tears, and none of them saw how afraid he was.

The fear was gone now, but the anger remained.

Jeremiah walked over to the grave where Elijah knelt, one hand grasping the cross that hung around his neck, the other resting on the dirt.

Jeremiah heard him say, "May angels lead you in," then Elijah stood with a heavy sigh and embraced his brother again.

"I'm so sorry, Jeremiah." He put his hand to either side of Jeremiah's face and pulled him closer until their foreheads touched, and Elijah made no effort to wipe away the tears that ran down his cheeks.

Seeing his brother's fresh pain made Jeremiah want to cry as well, but he had been poured out so many times he had nothing left.

Three months, he thought. *Is that all the time it takes to be emptied?*

"It happened so fast," Jeremiah said. He folded his hands together and squeezed until the fingers went white. He spoke between gritted teeth. "I prayed and I prayed and I prayed. I lay on the floor of his room for three nights, begging God to take his fever away and give it to me."

Jeremiah hit his chest with a fist, his face turned to the sky. "He didn't listen. He never listens."

Elijah stepped back and used his shirt sleeve to wipe his face. "The Hopi I was with performed a ceremony in the boy's honor. I wish you could have seen it."

Jeremiah didn't know what to say, but it meant something to him that people hundreds of miles away, people he had never met, had acknowledged Samuel's life and death.

"How is she?" Elijah asked, nodding to the house.

Jeremiah closed his eyes and saw the pain in Emma's face when she had screamed at Margaret Thorson after the play, saw the droplets of blood that dotted her fingers, the bruise-colored flesh under her eyes after Leanna Wellford came and took away the clothes, said the women of Charwood did not want a blasphemer to mend their dresses.

"She's still grieving," Jeremiah said.

"And you?"

Jeremiah looked back down at the mound of dirt and felt a heavy, dark wave wash over him. It covered up the joy he had at seeing his brother and the excitement and curiosity of finding the gold. Just as suddenly as it appeared, the wave pulled away and vanished, leaving a cold emptiness in his mind. All strength left his body, and he had to will himself to remain standing.

"The whole world feels empty," he said.

Elijah wrapped his arms around Jeremiah again and pulled him close. "I'd like to stay with you for a while and help however I can."

The two men made their way to the house as the sun fell into the west and the sky grew dark.

13

WHEN EMMA OPENED THE DOOR and saw Elijah, her eyes widened as she tried to fight the tears. Looking into his face and seeing his pain was like seeing her own pain reflected. She threw her arms around his neck and embraced him, weeping.

Jeremiah closed the door and watched them. The wound was not new, but it was seen anew through his brother. His brother, who had not yet mourned with them, had not yet poured out his grief.

Elijah smiled through his tears and put an arm around each of them. They stood in a tight circle, arms laced together, heads bowed.

"I am so thankful to be with you both," Elijah said quietly. "I've been praying for you since I got Jeremiah's letter, and I want you to know I'll be here for as long as you want me to stay."

Emma smiled back, gathered up her apron, and wiped her face with it. "It's wonderful to see you," she said. She took a deep breath and let it out, smiling again. I'm sure you must be hungry. I've made some stew."

The men sat down as Emma poured helpings of stew into bowls and placed them on the table. After she sat next to Jeremiah, Elijah closed his eyes and bowed his head. Jeremiah watched his brother's lips moving silently and wondered how he could still pray, knowing that God was deaf to their voices.

Jeremiah took hold of his spoon and was surprised at the heat that burned up his neck. It spread like fire up his face and into his scalp. His knuckles turned the color of bone as he gripped the spoon tighter. His arm actually ached to stab the table and scar the wood. He was faintly aware of his breathing, harsh exhalations coming from his nostrils that sounded like an animal. He glanced up and saw Emma watching him with an expression he could not name. He thought it might be a concern, but it looked like embarrassment. She shook her head slightly.

When Elijah opened his eyes, he gave them each a smile and took a bite of stew.

It was the same feeling Jeremiah had when he stood at the pulpit on that day three months ago. The Sunday after Samuel's burial. He felt drunk even though he hadn't been drinking. The world was thin and hazy, a distant mirage of pews and people that wavered in his vision like air above hot stones.

"You know damn well prayer changes nothing," Jeremiah said.

Emma shut her eyes tightly and shook her head again.

"It changes me," Elijah said, and resumed eating.

Jeremiah's hand gripped the spoon so tight the metal dug into his palm. He would not allow himself to say things he could not take back. He clenched his eyes shut until white sparks burst inside the black.

After dinner, Emma laid out some blankets for Elijah, said goodnight, and went to the bedroom. Jeremiah poured two glasses of whiskey and filled his pipe with tobacco as Elijah's eyes moved over the bookshelves, which were now nearly empty. They had once held a number of biblical commentaries, books that Jeremiah read and re-read. Passages were underlined, notes were made in the margins. Elijah also noted that he had not seen a single Bible in the house. Not the large leather-bound volume that had been given to him by their father, nor the smaller one Jeremiah used for personal study.

Elijah noticed Jeremiah staring at him and smiled, holding up his glass. "It's good to be with you, brother," he said, and took a drink. "Although it's strange to be in a house again. A house of wood, anyway. The Hopi live in dwellings made of clay bricks."

Jeremiah lit his pipe and blew a stream of smoke toward the ceiling. "How much longer do you think you'll be with them?"

Elijah's shoulders rose and fell. "I have more than enough for my book, but each question only leads to more questions. You know, they're not warriors. In fact, the word Hopi means 'peace'."

He swirled the last of the whiskey in his glass, watched the firelight pass through it and paint golden lines on his chest. "They believe that everything has a spirit. Animals, plants, rivers, mountains, everything. Their history teaches that the world has been destroyed three times, and the world we live in now is the fourth. Every time the people forget the Creator's plan, he destroys all they've built and only the faithful survive to start again."

Elijah swallowed the last of his drink. "I can't think of a reason to not go back. Someday."

Jeremiah glanced out the window, grateful he couldn't see the grave in the darkness. He looked to the black trees of the forest, their jagged tips cutting into the sky, and for a moment, he saw something slip between the trees. Something with red eyes. He leaned forward, face almost touching the glass, and watched for movement. *Probably just a reflection*, he thought. *Nothing more.*

He took another drink and closed his eyes.

"I need to show you something," Jeremiah said. He set down his pipe and glass and then took the flower from his pocket. He kept it hidden between his hands as he held them out to his brother. When he opened them, the morning glory glowed brilliantly in the firelight. Elijah took it and gently ran his fingers along the petals and stem.

"This is remarkable," he said. "Truly. Is this a gift for Emma?"

Then Elijah jerked one hand away, as though a spark from the fire had landed on his skin. His expression changed. He held the flower up, squinting at it. One finger kept caressing its surface. He looked to Jeremiah, then back to the flower. He turned it over, then upside down, feeling it, inspecting it. He blinked several times in a row. He opened his mouth to say something but could not find the words.

"It's real," Jeremiah said, leaning forward. "I'm convinced of it."

Elijah shook his head. "How is that possible?"

Jeremiah finished his whiskey, walked to the hallway, and listened for a few seconds before crossing the room to an old trunk hidden in shadow. He pulled out several blankets, set them on the floor, and lifted a small journal and a folded piece of parchment.

"I found it in the forest on the body of a dead man," Jeremiah said.

He then proceeded to tell his brother the entire story.

14

ELIJAH STILL HELD THE MORNING glory, touching it the whole time. He did not say a single word as Jeremiah told him of finding the body, the blood that sparkled with gold, the bird, and the money he got from melting it down. Elijah only shook his head and looked at the flower, proof of his brother's story.

When he finished, Jeremiah knelt in front of the fire and spread out the parchment paper. He opened the journal to one of the pages with all the strange symbols.

"These were in his bags, along with the bird."

Elijah knelt next to him and gently touched the paper. His eyes were wide open, flickering with firelight as he traced a finger over the map. It came to rest on the drawing of the screaming man.

"The dead man drew this?" he asked.

"I don't know for certain, but I think so," Jeremiah said.

Elijah sat back and put both hands to his face. He rubbed them up and down.

"Do you remember my ninth birthday?" he said through his fingers. "We didn't have any money for presents because father spent it all at the tavern. So you took your folding knife, the one I'd always wanted, and you wrapped it in cloth and buried it in the woods. Then you drew a map leading to it and gave it to me."

"I remember."

"Tell me this isn't like that."

Jeremiah put a hand on his brother's arm. "I swear to you. Every word I speak is the truth."

Elijah exhaled, and the air shook as it came out of him. "I don't know what to say, or even what to think."

Jeremiah tapped the journal. "What do you make of these?"

Elijah picked up the book and pored over the symbols. His lips moved silently. His finger moved over an image of a bird pecking at an eyeball, then on to a figure holding a knife over the body of an infant. One man seemed to be wearing the skin of another. A hand gripped a cut-out heart. A stone city with dark liquid running down its walls. A kneeling woman clutching at her belly, the same dark liquid oozing from beneath her hand.

Finally, he shook his head. "I haven't seen anything like these before."

Jeremiah tried to hide his frustration. "Not with the Hopi? Not in any of the cities built into the rock?"

Elijah shook his head again. "These look much older. They're not Egyptian, but they remind me of Egyptian writing. The way a picture is used instead of words. But look," he said, turning the journal to his brother, "they all tell stories of death and suffering. Sacrifice. They can't be used to tell any other story. Except, maybe this one," he pointed to an image of a man holding up an orb. Rays of light shot out of it.

Jeremiah pushed his fist into the floorboard until his knuckles burned. A log shifted in the fire and sent out a shower of sparks.

"I've seen some of the cave drawings done by the Hopi and other tribes, and they look nothing like this," Elijah said. "I think these came from much farther away."

Jeremiah spread a hand over his face and rubbed both temples. "Then why write them down? Why go through all that trouble?"

Elijah turned pages in the journal, which were filled with more symbols. Only rarely did they repeat. "Maybe the map and the journal are separate," he said. "Maybe one has nothing to do with the other."

Jeremiah sat up and grabbed the map, putting his finger on the black circle. "What about this?"

"A hole perhaps, a well? Maybe a cave."

"Whatever it is, I think that's where we find it," Jeremiah said.

Elijah sighed, set the journal down, and pushed it away from him, like it was something he no longer wished to touch. "Find what?"

Jeremiah pointed at the floating hand with the crossed fingers.

"Jeremiah…" Elijah began.

"Ever since I found this map, I can't think of anything else," Jeremiah said, looking into the orange glow of the fire. Shadows flickered on his face. "If there is something up there that can give a man the power to change living things into gold, I need to find it."

"The last man to find it died alone in the woods, bleeding gold. Is that where you want to end up?" Elijah stood quickly, clenching his fists. He walked to the window and looked out into the dark.

"I think God wanted me to find that man," Jeremiah said quietly.

Elijah turned. "You don't know this is from God."

Jeremiah started to speak, but Elijah held up a hand. "We are guessing at all of this," he said. "We have a map, a journal, a dead body, and a flower made of gold. We know nothing."

Elijah picked up his glass, tried to take a drink, saw it empty, and set it back down. He scratched at his neck. "Even Pharaoh's magicians turned their staffs into serpents, turned water into blood. You don't know it's from God."

Jeremiah held up the morning glory. It gleamed in the dimming firelight, so bright and pure. "If there is a power that can do this, what else can it do?"

Elijah's shoulders fell as he looked at the flower.

"I want to find it," Jeremiah said. "And I want you to come with me."

15

ELIJAH WOKE UP WHEN HE heard the bedroom door creak open, and Emma came down the hall into the room, still in her nightgown. Her dark hair, almost as black as their mother's had been, was bed-messed and tangled. Elijah could not help but imagine her thrashing around and sweating in the grip of a nightmare. She stepped further into the light, and he saw the dark skin beneath her eyes, eyes that held the sleepless look of someone not yet ready to face the day.

She smiled when she saw him and raised her hand in a little wave. He waved back. She slipped on a long sweater and folded her arms across her chest, walked to the window, and looked out at the grave.

"Jeremiah went into town," Elijah said.

Emma nodded slowly, her eyes still on that bare patch of dirt.

"He showed you the flower?" she asked. "The map?"

"He did."

"What do you make of it?"

Elijah crawled over to the fireplace and added more wood to the flames.

"It's remarkable, but I think it's a dangerous pursuit," he said. "Chasing after something like that. Everything has a purpose, whether we see it or not, and it bothers me that I can't understand what the purpose is of this gift. The reason for its existence."

Emma's face was blank as she stared out the window. Elijah knew there were probably a hundred thoughts tumbling through her head as she gazed at the ground where her son was buried.

"To transform a living thing into solid gold," she said. "Isn't that something worth pursuing, even if it leads to death?"

Elijah watched her stillness. She looked like a painting. A portrait of a grieving woman, not moving in the gray morning light that poured through the glass. He couldn't even hear her breathe.

"I don't know," Elijah said. "I've always believed the pursuit of life is better."

Emma turned to face him, and even though her expression did not change, it seemed different—sadder somehow but also colder.

Her gray-green eyes looked directly into his. "Everything leads to death eventually," she said.

She came and sat down next to him on the blankets, grabbed the edge of one, and wrapped it around her bare legs. Elijah felt heat radiating off her body, almost as warm as the fire. She gazed into the flames, arms around her knees.

"Ashes to ashes," she said.

"Just because death is at the end of everything, that doesn't mean we shouldn't chase what makes us feel more alive," he said.

"Do you really believe that?"

"What's the other choice? Misery? Bitterness? All things have to end, but that doesn't make the end something to be afraid of."

Elijah noticed Emma's fingers, dotted with small, red needle pricks, picking at the frayed edge of the blanket. Twisting loose threads into a knot.

"Does he seem different to you?" she asked without looking at him.

"He's lost a son," Elijah said. "I didn't expect him to be the same."

Emma's body jerked at the mention of her son as though startled. She sat up straighter, more alert. Her fingers moved faster. Up to that point, Elijah had seen her as just a hazy outline. A grieving mother whose loss hung about her like a fog. But when she thought of Samuel, she became solid, glowing. More real than real. There was pain in her eyes and anger as well, like Jeremiah. But Emma's was different somehow, hotter. It burned the edges of her profile, a shimmering heat that distorted the air.

She looked at him curiously, watching her, and said, "His faith is gone, but mine isn't. How can the same loss affect people so differently?"

She noticed what her fingers were doing and stopped, letting the blanket fall. With a sigh, she lay down on the blanket, one arm under her head. The nightgown slid up her leg, and Elijah saw smooth, pale skin covered in gooseflesh. He pulled the blanket up over her, and she smiled gently.

"You haven't aged," Emma said, and Elijah realized for the first time how close she was. Her smell came to him—her skin, her hair. Soft and feminine. He was overcome with the desire to wrap his arms around her and bury his head in her hair. He wanted to feel her body pressed against his, and the desire came on so strongly and so suddenly that his hand gripped the coffee mug tighter.

"I would love to hear about your travels someday," Emma said. "You've seen so many things that I dream of seeing." She leaned in a little closer. "I once dreamed of living in Europe, did you know that? I wanted to study art and literature, learn how to create beauty."

Her black hair was spread out like a pool at night as she looked up at the ceiling.

"Do you think it's too late for me?" she asked. "Do we only ever have one chance to do certain things?"

Elijah fought the temptation to lie down beside her. He remained sitting, looking into the fire. Emma shifted a little, and the swish of her nightgown was loud in his ears. Such an intimate sound, fabric on a body—the rustle and whisper of things moving across skin.

"I don't think we can look back at the past and see it clearly," Elijah said. "It's too blurry, too distant. But I believe each moment has a way of determining its own outcome, and sometimes we are incapable of choosing anything other than what we chose."

"The future is such a headache," she said.

"Or it's something beautiful you haven't seen yet."

Emma rolled over on her side and looked up at him. Her eyes were large and wet and glistening. "If Jeremiah finds what he's looking for, what will it change? He's pulling away from me. I've felt it every day since Samuel died. I've tried to reach him, but I can't. All the gold in the world won't change that."

Her whole body convulsed as she wept. Elijah reached a hand out to her shoulder. She took it and pulled him down, gently, until he was lying next to her. His hands moved without his permission, and her body came closer to his until they were touching, embracing. Her face pressed against his chest, and his hand on her back felt every lungful of breath. She lifted her face, and Elijah's head went dizzy and heavy all at once as her lips brushed his chin. Needles pricked the back of his legs, and he wanted so badly to taste her breath. He reminded himself that this was his brother's wife, his brother's wife, his brother's wife...

He held her head against his chest. Her fingernails dug into his back as she sobbed.

After a while, her cries subsided and then stopped altogether. She spoke with her face still to his chest, her hand still clutching his back.

"He's not the same," she said. "He disappeared into the forest for two days and came back carrying something with him."

"He's still grieving," Elijah said. "You both are."

"It's more than that. I know you feel it too."

The sound of carriage wheels and horse hooves pulled Emma from his embrace. She sat up and wiped her eyes. "He's back."

Guilt swelled in Elijah's chest, a feeling so powerful he almost couldn't breathe. Emma stood and smoothed out her gown. She ran fingers through her hair and composed herself, then went to the bedroom without saying a word.

16

THE BEDROOM DOOR CLOSED JUST as the front door flew open and Jeremiah came into the house, breathing heavily.

"We need to leave immediately."

His boots stomped across the room to the kitchen where he poured water from the pitcher into a cup, drank it, and poured another.

"Two men came into town last night looking for me." His mouth clenched, tensing all the muscles along his jawline. He turned to the shelves and took down bread, coffee, oats, and jerky and set it all on the table.

"Maybe they have nothing to do with the gold or the dead man," Elijah said, but his own heart was beating faster now.

Jeremiah shook his head and kept gathering food.

"You think they knew him?" Elijah asked. "The dead man?"

"I don't know if they knew him, but they're here because of him," Jeremiah said without looking up. "I'm sure of it."

"How is that possible?"

Jeremiah's hand slammed down on the table so hard a fork clattered off the edge.

"I took the melted gold to the banker!" he shouted. "I got money for it. He probably told someone, or maybe he'd already been paid off, instructed to let someone know if a man brought in a large amount of gold."

He slammed the table again. The palm of his hand stung, throbbed in time with his heartbeat.

"I didn't think," Jeremiah said. "I didn't think ahead. He had to request more money from another bank in San Francisco."

Elijah stood in stunned silence. His brother placed both hands on the table and lowered his head. He let out a deep groan as if he was going to vomit.

"We need to leave," Jeremiah said. "Right away. They can't follow us."

Elijah came closer and touched Jeremiah's shoulder.

"You're only guessing," Elijah said. "It could be nothing."

"They didn't even know my name," Jeremiah said, still looking down at the table. "They were asking for the preacher whose son had died." He looked up at Elijah with bloodshot eyes. "We need to go."

Elijah pulled his hand away. "What about—"

The bedroom door opened. Emma came into the room, dressed in riding clothes and boots, and carrying a bag. Her black hair was done in a long braid that hung down her back. Jeremiah stood up straighter when she approached the table and dropped the bag.

"I'm not staying here," she said. "I'm coming with you."

Jeremiah looked from his wife to Elijah. He laughed without humor.

"Emma—" he began.

"You're going out there to find something. Something impossible." She stabbed a finger at her chest. "I need to find something too."

"No, absolutely not. It's too dangerous and I—"

"I'm not asking you for permission."

Jeremiah took a step closer. "I won't allow you to come on this journey. I could never forgive myself if something happened to you."

He reached out to touch her arm and Emma pulled away.

"You don't own me, Jeremiah Pevensie. I don't care how dangerous it might be. You are not the only one in pain. Do you understand that?"

Her chin shook as she blinked furiously to keep the tears that flooded her eyes from falling. "He was our son, and I lost him, same as you." Her finger stabbed again. "I will not stay here and waste away."

She stood a little straighter. "Besides, I'm a better shot than both of you."

Jeremiah's body sagged, as if all the air had gone out of him. "Gather your belongings," he said. His eyes met hers but there was no warmth. "We leave in one hour."

Emma went out to the barn to saddle up her horse, and the two men were left alone.

Jeremiah turned to his brother. The skin on his neck was splotchy and red. "You should have said something."

"She'll be safer with us than she would be here alone," Elijah said.

Jeremiah shoved the food into a burlap sack, flung it over his shoulder. "Now we have to worry about her."

The supplies he had purchased at the general store were in a heap by the door. He went over and pulled a leather coat from the pile. The inside was lined with cloud-white wool.

"I didn't see a warm coat in your belongings," he said, and threw it at Elijah. The coat sailed across the room, unfolding as it did, empty arms waving.

Elijah caught the garment in one hand. "It's not my place to interfere," he said.

Jeremiah made it halfway to the bedroom, stopped and pointed a finger at Elijah. "She'll slow us down. You should have said something."

The bedroom door slammed and Elijah was alone. His eyes moved down to the coat, and he caught sight of his shirt and the small dark stains that marked it. He touched one and it was still wet. Emma's tears. He wondered if Jeremiah had noticed.

17

THEY RODE UNTIL THEY CAME to the dead man's camp. The tent still stood but it was now in tatters. Claw marks were raked across the sides. Pieces of bedding lay strewn about.

Jeremiah jumped down off his horse and went over to the fire pit. He knelt and poked at the ashes with a stick. Elijah dismounted as well and his instinct was to help Emma, but he stopped himself. Jeremiah was already upset, and treating Emma like anything but another member of their expedition would only anger him more. Instead, Elijah smiled at her, to let her know he was not bothered by her company.

"This is where I found him," Jeremiah said, scraping a dark spot on the ground. "Look, it's still here."

Elijah joined his brother and saw all the tiny, shimmering dots in the dirt, like sparkling grains of sand. From the stained ground, he could almost see how the body had been lying, where the face and mouth had been pointing. Emma passed by them and walked toward a mound of dirt on the other side of the tent.

"I buried him," Jeremiah said. "It didn't seem right to leave him where he was."

Emma approached the grave, took off her brimmed hat and bowed her head. Her lips moved silently and Elijah wondered if she was praying. Jeremiah didn't seem to notice. He went into the tent and dug through it again, looking for anything he might have missed.

Elijah looked back down at the dirt, at the shining dust embedded within the dried blood. He noticed something else on the ground, next to where the body would have been lying. Paw prints, like a dog's. They weren't deep impressions, but the dirt within each print was darker than the dirt around them.

Elijah was about to kneel down and take a closer look when Jeremiah came out of the tent, brushing aside a torn flap with one arm.

"We need to keep riding," he said. "Put as much distance between us and town as we can before nightfall."

Emma finished her prayer, if that's what it was, and put her hat back on. Again, Elijah wanted to help her as she climbed up on her horse, even though she had no trouble getting in the saddle, and they were off again. They had not gone far when Elijah looked back toward the camp, but it had already been swallowed up in all the branches and brush, the twisted path of the trees.

They rode in a line, Jeremiah in front, then Emma, and Elijah behind her. He followed the black braid that fell down her back, swinging back and forth with the horse's movement, and he found himself thinking back on the morning, the warmth of her body as she pressed against him.

The going was slow and before long the temperature fell. The light that streamed through the trees turned dark gray, and the air became hazy and dreamlike.

When they came to a small clearing, Jeremiah brought his horse to a stop and held up a hand, head tilted as if listening.

"Do you hear that?" he said.

Emma leaned forward, closed her eyes. Elijah did the same and heard the music of water flowing over rocks.

They all dismounted and tied the reins of their horses around tree trunks. Elijah grabbed the rifle out of the saddle bag, and they set out on foot. They had not gone far when the trees thinned out and opened on a clear shallow creek that ran as far as they could see in either direction.

Jeremiah went to the creek's edge, cupped his hands and scooped water into his mouth. "This is it," he said. "The water on the map."

Emma knelt on the bank. Her skirt floated around her knees as she brought handfuls of water to her face and washed off the dust. She looked up at the small ribbon of sky above her. Dark blue with white pinpoints of light. The forest on the other side of the creek was just as dense and tall as what lay behind them.

"Somewhere beyond those trees is the mountain," she said, still looking straight ahead.

Elijah followed her gaze, and for a moment it looked like the woods were moving closer together. Contracting around a narrow space, as if to hide whatever lay ahead.

Nothing but a trick of the light, he told himself.

"We need to set up camp," Jeremiah said.

When they made it back to the clearing, Jeremiah took all three horses by the reins and led them to the creek while Elijah set up the tent. Emma made a fire and cooked some beans in a pot she'd carried from home.

The tent was large enough for only two people to sleep side by side. Elijah watched as Emma cut up pieces of jerky and threw them into the pot, stirring it. Without Jeremiah present, Elijah could almost imagine that he and Emma were out here alone, off to seek a new life, a new future, somewhere neither of them had ever been.

He untied the bed rolls and laid them out in the tent. Another image from that morning flashed in his head like a bolt of lightning—her nightgown as it slid up her leg. The smoothness of her skin. He saw them lying together in the tent, the same way they had on the floor. His face buried in her hair as she breathed into his neck.

Elijah fought the urge to hit himself the way his brother did, to punish himself for thoughts he didn't want. In his head, he repeated *She is my brother's wife* until guilt came and covered up the waking dream.

Elijah realized he had not spoken to her since they had left the house. He felt ashamed and hoped this did not hurt her heart. He was about to say something, anything, when he heard the sound of horses approaching.

Jeremiah emerged from the now dark woods, the horses behind him, and for a moment Elijah was overwhelmed by a feeling so close to hatred his back started to sweat. In that moment, it didn't matter that Jeremiah was his brother. If he had not come back from the creek, if he had slipped and smashed open his head on a rock, that dream of Elijah's could have been real.

The thoughts came fast, uninvited, and Elijah shook his head to erase them. Jeremiah led the horses into the clearing. His brow creased when he saw his brother.

"Are you feeling ill?" he asked.

Elijah tried to smile. "Tired and hungry."

Jeremiah tied the animals to a nearby tree and then inspected the tent. "It's smaller than I remember."

Elijah nodded. "I'll sleep outside."

"I'll take tomorrow night," Jeremiah said.

18

AS THEY ATE, ELIJAH COULD not see any difference in how Emma treated him. She dished up his food with a tender smile, then gave the same smile to her husband. She took her bowl and sat atop an empty saddle bag, while Jeremiah and Elijah sat on the dirt. The fire crackled, sending occasional pieces of ash, still burning at the edges, up into air so black the tops of the trees were invisible.

"There's sky somewhere up there," Elijah said, looking up.

Jeremiah looked up as well and nodded. Emma stared at her plate, moving the beans around with a fork. Jeremiah hadn't said a word to his wife, he didn't even look at her, and if Elijah didn't know they were married, he never would have guessed it. She knew her husband didn't want her here, and Elijah had said nothing in her defense. He wished he had. Even something minor, just enough to let her know he was on her side.

Elijah offered to clean the dishes, but Emma shook her head and collected everything.

"Take a gun with you," Jeremiah said. He had the map open on his lap and did not notice Emma's hands were full.

Elijah stood, picked up Jeremiah's gun belt, and, standing so close he could smell the sticky sweetness of her sweat, wrapped his arms around her waist and buckled the belt. She kept her eyes focused straight ahead and gave only a slight smile when he finished. It was a strange thing to him, to see that gun hanging at her waist, plates piled in one hand, pot and silverware in the other. Strands of black hair had come loose and hung curled around her cheek. One side of her face was in the light, and the greenness of her eye caught him off guard, all those speckles in the color, like treasure at the bottom of a pond.

She said, "Thank you," and set off into the dark, toward the creek. Elijah sat back down, wishing he had some whiskey to turn the day and all his guilt into something duller.

"I've been thinking about the map," Jeremiah said, taking a folded piece of paper from his shirt pocket and handing it to his brother. "But it's not how the dead man found the mountain. He was carrying this with him."

Elijah unfolded the paper and read what was written.

"Whoever Solomon is, he had a vision or knew something that led this man here. He was following those instructions. The map he drew just filled in the details of a path he'd already followed."

"It's not very clear," Elijah said. "There must be a hundred towns with burned trees. How would he know to come here instead of some other town?"

Jeremiah reached into his pack and pulled out the dead man's journal. "Maybe there was more Solomon saw, and this man didn't write it down. In case someone robbed or killed him, they wouldn't know exactly where to go."

"On the map he drew, there was another person."

"I don't think he traveled by himself, but he came back from the mountain alone."

Elijah snapped a twig in half and tossed it into the flames. "Is Emma as good a shot as she says she is?"

Jeremiah smiled. "Better."

"The Hopi are master archers," Elijah said. "Even the young ones can hit small targets while riding a horse. The chief said motion is the key. They never stop moving when they shoot."

Jeremiah took the paper from Elijah and put it inside the journal. "How long has it been since you fired a gun?"

"Years."

"Not since father?"

Elijah shook his head.

Neither of them needed to retell the story, they had both lived it. When they were just boys, their father had taken them into the woods to teach them how to shoot. After hours of waiting, he sighted a deer, handed Elijah the rifle, and gave him instructions. But when it came time to pull the trigger, Elijah could not do it. He didn't want to kill something. Their father got so angry he jerked the gun away, shot the deer, then dragged his youngest son by the collar and shoved his face in the animal's blood. When Elijah got up, his father beat him until the boy was unconscious. Jeremiah tried to help but ended up taking a beating himself. Elijah had not held or fired a weapon since.

The men did not speak until footsteps coming through the brush made them sit upright. Emma emerged with a pile of still-wet dishes. She silently packed everything back up, said goodnight, and went into the tent.

"We should get some sleep," Jeremiah said. "We'll leave at first light."

He stood and looked into the forest. "Keep an eye out. If you see or hear anything, wake me."

Elijah stretched out in front of the fire. He wanted to add more wood for warmth, but he was suddenly alert and nervous and didn't want to draw attention to their camp. So he lay awake as the fire died, listening to every branch as it bent in the breeze until his eyes grew heavy.

He heard a voice speak inside his head that was not his. DREAM A DREAM OF A THING THAT WILL NEVER HAPPEN, it said.

19

ELIJAH JERKED AWAKE. IN A dream, something with fur had brushed up against his face. He sat up, breathing heavily, and saw a shape moving around in the darkness outside the clearing, stalking between the trees. He thought immediately of the paw prints he had seen at the dead man's camp. The burned earth inside each mark.

Elijah stood and squinted into the trees. The animal moved back and forth, and its eyes shimmered red. It turned around, looked at Elijah, then walked into the dark.

Elijah suddenly felt a need to follow the animal. It made no sense, but the feeling stung the back of his neck like the slow crawl of sweat. He reached his hand back there, and it came away dry. It didn't make sense, but he remembered the Hopi chief telling him that sometimes ancestral spirits took the form of an animal and helped guide them.

Elijah took a quick look at the tent, then made his way into the dark woods, following the wolf-shaped shadow that moved through the trees.

Occasionally, he lost sight of the animal as it went through a thick patch of brush, but when he made it to the other side, the wolf was always there waiting. Elijah did not know how long he had walked when the wolf stopped and sat at the edge of an embankment. Even in the dark, Elijah could tell the ground sloped downward. The wolf stared at something Elijah could not see, so he approached cautiously.

An orange light glowed down below. Two men sat around the fire, eating. Their horses stood nearby, ears flicking, faces turned toward the wolf. Elijah crouched down and watched the men. It was impossible to see their faces clearly, but the smaller of the two had a beard and wore a black hat with a round crown. The other man looked taller, and his head was bare. They ate in silence.

Elijah tried to breathe calmly, still, the air he exhaled sounded far too loud. The muscles in his thighs started to burn and cramp, but he was afraid to shift his weight and make a sound.

He thought these had to be the men looking for Jeremiah. He knew the world was full of coincidence, but the fact that these two men were traveling in the same direction in an otherwise empty forest was beyond coincidence.

Elijah's hands began to sweat. His pulse throbbed in his throat, making him want to swallow his heartbeat back down to where it belonged.

When the two men got up and went into the tent, Elijah finally allowed himself to stand up straight. He looked at the wolf. Its dark fur blended so much into the shadows that it seemed partly made of shadow itself. The wolf turned its head toward him, and the eyes flickered with red light, as if reflecting a fire.

The voice spoke in Elijah's head again, but it was so low that he could not understand what it said. Some intelligence radiated from those eyes, and Elijah felt that the wolf knew and understood things. *It may look like a wolf, but it's not a wolf. A wolf is just what I see.*

The thought made no sense, but neither did following it out here, and it had brought him to this place to warn him.

The animal lowered its head and walked back into the woods the way they came. Elijah followed. He wanted to run back to camp as fast as he could, but he had to be cautious. Any loud sound, like a dead branch snapping in half, would carry like a gunshot.

By the time Elijah saw the smolder of his own fire in the clearing, the wolf had disappeared. He went over to the tent and moved aside the flap.

"Jeremiah," he whispered. "Jeremiah, wake up."

One of the bodies stirred, the other sat straight up. Jeremiah crawled out of the tent and slipped on his boots. "What is it?"

"We have to leave now. The two men who were looking for you are here."

"How close?" Jeremiah reached back into the tent for his gun belt and strapped it on.

Elijah pointed south. "They're camped about half a mile away."

Jeremiah's eyes searched his brother's face. He looked to the woods, then back to Elijah.

"You heard something out there?"

Elijah nodded, breathing too loudly, too fast. The embers of the fire pulsed orange. Thunder cracked above them, and the horses moved about nervously.

Jeremiah stared at him for a moment, then knelt and touched Emma's leg. "Get up. We have to go."

She came out of the tent, still fully clothed, eyes wide. "What's wrong?" she asked.

Jeremiah was already gathering up their supplies. "Pack up," he said. "We're being followed."

20

THEY RODE UNTIL GREY LIGHT fell through the trees, and with it came rain—softly at first, then pouring by the time the trees began to thin out. They emerged from the forest into a large open field, surrounded by a vast expanse of trees. Dark clouds filled the sky.

"Where's the mountain?" Jeremiah said, turning his horse in circles. "It's supposed to be here."

Lightning flashed and briefly illuminated the field and the forest beyond. There were no mountains, not even a hill, rising up. Jeremiah rode further out into the field, past boulders and rocks, deposited there like they'd fallen from the sky. To him, the whole field looked like an empty impression. A place where something should have been, but no longer was.

"God damn it," he hissed.

Thunder cracked, echoing across the open space.

Elijah kept an eye on the woods they'd just come out of, watching for the other two men. Rain fell harder, turning the ground to mud underneath his horse's hooves. The animal's eyes were wide, alert.

They were missing something, but what? In his memory, he pulled up the map, the journal, and the paper Jeremiah had shown him back at the campsite. He went through each piece, searching the images. Then he remembered.

He turned to Emma. "Start looking for a flat stone on the ground, big enough to stand on."

She nodded once, her face tight and grim, then yanked the reins and galloped north. Elijah kicked his heels into the horse's side and rode to Jeremiah.

He pulled alongside his brother and yelled over the roar of the rain. "The vision on the paper the man carried. 'Up the mountain that can only be seen when standing upon the flat stone.' Emma's looking for it."

Jeremiah turned and saw his wife's silhouette riding along the treeline. She stopped, jumped down from the horse, and stood still, her face turned up to the sky. Then she lifted one arm and began waving. The two men took off, riding across the field toward her.

As they approached, they saw Emma standing on a bright patch of solid ground, large enough to fit at least six horses standing side by side.

Flat stone, Elijah thought.

She didn't look at the men as they dismounted and led the horses to her. Her eyes were fixed on something in the sky, something neither of them could see. Elijah had never seen a rock so large and flat, like a giant table nearly level with the dirt.

He stepped onto the stone and pulled the horse behind him. Jeremiah stood beside him, watching his wife. She grabbed Jeremiah's arm, pulled him closer, and pointed up. Elijah came alongside them and followed her finger until he saw it.

Within the rain-sliced darkness and misty air, a massive mountain trembled into view, towering above them, shifting and flickering like a shadow through warped glass. A narrow path, carved in dirt, twisted up the side of the mountain.

Elijah went to the edge of the stone and, still looking up at the mountain, stepped off the stone onto the muddy ground. The mountain shifted as he did, blending into the dark sky until it was invisible. He stepped back up on the stone, and the mountain came into focus again.

Jeremiah climbed up into the saddle and turned to look back at the forest. "Let's keep moving."

He spurred his horse off the stone and toward the mountain. Emma and Elijah mounted their horses and followed Jeremiah as he crossed the field and started up the trail, riding single file behind him. Elijah craned his neck, and he couldn't even see the top of the mountain. It was somewhere above the storm.

The mountain rose up on one side of them, and the other side dropped steeply into the valley below. The skeleton of some animal, possibly a horse, lay just off the path, half buried in debris. Scavengers had mostly picked it clean, but there was still some blood and hair, and small strips of rotted flesh hanging from the bones.

Elijah kept glancing over his shoulder, half expecting to see two horses charging around the corner. Emma's long braid was soaking wet and coming undone. He turned his face toward the sky and let the water fall on his skin.

The rain looked like a torn curtain fluttering over the valley, disintegrating into pieces. Hours passed as the horses moved slowly on the steep, muddy ground. Torrents of water ran down the mountainside, cutting through the trail and spilling out over the edge of the cliff. Rocks broke loose and tumbled off the path. Elijah could feel the mountain shuddering, as if it were coming apart.

Thunder boomed in the clouds with a sound like dynamite, and Elijah counted the seconds until a streak of lightning tore across the sky and slammed into the forest below in a shower of sparks. He watched the small orange flames until he rounded the next corner. The sound of the storm made the horses nervous, and Elijah's animal kept looking toward the cliff with one wide eye, her ears twitching.

Halfway up the mountain, they came to a level clearing off the trail. It was a small space between trees with a stone circle of a fire pit at the center.

"I say we camp here," Jeremiah said. "We have a better chance at defending ourselves if we're not constantly looking behind us."

Elijah and Emma agreed, so they tied the horses to nearby trees and set up the tent with the opening facing the trail. The three of them crowded into the tent and lay there listening to the water falling from the sky and running down the mountain. Rain beat at its sides, a sound like war drums.

"I'll take first watch," Elijah said.

"Don't hesitate to shoot," Jeremiah said, handing him the rifle. "Because they sure as hell won't." He put a hand on his brother's shoulder. "Aim true and fire quickly."

Elijah lay on his stomach with his face at the tent flaps. He folded one back just enough to see out and pointed the rifle's barrel through it. He felt Emma's boots resting gently against his ribs. Soon their breathing patterns changed, and Elijah felt the day's travels ache in his body. The world beyond the tent was all silhouettes and shadows, shades of grey and black. The rippling underbelly of the clouds hung over the valley, blocking any stars. Sometimes the ground trembled beneath him, and he couldn't tell if it was horses coming up the path or rocks worked loose and tumbling down the mountainside.

The rain eventually slowed, and the tones of water droplets hitting puddles and trees became gentle and soothing, like the earth was playing itself as an instrument. Elijah closed his burning eyes for just a few seconds.

The first thing Elijah saw when he startled awake was the wolf's red eyes staring at him from the edge of camp. Elijah gripped the gun and sat up. He pulled the tent flap back and peered into the darkness. There was no thunder, and the rain was just a drizzle now, but something had stirred him. He felt it in his sleep.

The wolf stalked back and forth, never taking its eyes off Elijah. Then a voice spoke inside him. It felt exactly like one of his own thoughts, but it came from somewhere farther back in his mind.

The wolf asked, ARE YOU READY?

"Ready for what?" Elijah whispered.

Elijah felt the vibrations before he heard the source—horses pounding up the trail. Two of them sprinting. Elijah hit Jeremiah's leg and said, "They're here."

21

JEREMIAH JERKED UPRIGHT, PISTOL IN hand. He knelt next to Elijah and looked outside as the pounding grew louder. The wolf stalked back into the shadows, and Elijah wondered if his brother saw the animal. Emma threw off the blankets and crawled to her husband, rifle in hand.

"We have to leave the tent," Jeremiah said to Elijah. "Move into the trees. You go right, we'll go left. Wait for a clear shot."

Elijah tried to answer, but his mouth had gone dry. Jeremiah patted his brother's shoulder, and the three of them ran out of the tent. Jeremiah and Emma sprinted for the trees, keeping their heads low until they reached the covering. Elijah was behind them until his foot slipped and he fell to his knees. He picked the gun up from the thick mud and kept going, his clothes heavy with soil and rain.

Within minutes, the sound of hooves reached their camp. The two men sat upon their horses, silhouetted against the sky, the cliff and valley behind them. They both raised rifles and took aim at the tent. Gunshots rang out, one after the other. Bullets punched through the canvas, sparking against rocks on the other side. The gunfire briefly illuminated the men's faces: a blast, white light, a stern face, jaw set, black, another blast.

After the echoes rang out, a deep voice spoke. "If any of you are still alive, come out now."

His horse stamped and turned in a circle. "What you're after doesn't belong to you. You know it's wrong to steal, preacher. If we have to come get you out, you will be killed. If you come out on your own, you will be spared."

The man waited a few moments, then nodded to his partner, who dismounted and walked slowly toward the tent, rifle to his shoulder. The man with the deep voice said, "Make your peace with God."

As soon as the man reached the tent, the wolf burst from the trees and ran straight for the man still on his horse. The wolf snapped at the animal's legs and neck, sending it into a panic. The horse reared up, kicking wildly, and released a terrified bray. It started to run back down the path, but the wolf moved in front. The animal screamed and tried to turn around, and the wolf darted to the other side, snarling and snapping. Desperate to escape, the horse spun away from the sharp teeth and ran in the only direction it could. It took four steps and tumbled off the edge of the mountain, its rider still in the saddle. An echoing scream followed them down, then stopped abruptly.

The second man turned when he heard the commotion, and he stood still for a moment, a perfect shape. Elijah raised the rifle—willing his hands not to shake—and pulled the trigger. The hammer fell with a quiet clink.

Elijah tried to clear the mud and pulled the trigger again. It still didn't fire. There was a muzzle flash and a crack from the trees to his right, and the second man howled in pain as he fell to the ground, clutching his stomach. His horse reared up and bolted away down the path.

Emma emerged from the trees, her rifle still trained on the writhing man, smoke curling from the barrel. Even in the pale light,

Elijah saw how tight her lips and jaw were. She stared at the man on the ground, watching him struggle to breathe, but her face showed no emotion. Jeremiah came out of the trees to the left of her, his gun also pointed at the man.

"Elijah, go check on the horses," Jeremiah said in a low voice. Elijah did as he was told, feeling heat rise in his face, fearing that his brother, and even worse, Emma, believed he had chosen not to fire his weapon. That he had risked their lives because of some inner wound he wouldn't let heal. His stomach ached at the thought of what might have happened had the wolf not chased the first man off the edge.

Emma lowered the gun and stood with her face toward the sky, letting the cool water fall on her skin.

Jeremiah knelt next to the wounded man, one hand grasping fistfuls of mud, the other hand pressed to his gut, thick blood leaking between the fingers. His heels scratched at the dirt, and foam pushed through his clenched teeth with each breath. He looked at Jeremiah and tried to speak, but the words fell into a moan of pain.

He opened his mouth, and the teeth were stained with blood. "It...doesn't belong...to you."

Jeremiah kept his finger on the trigger of his gun. "It does if I find it first," he asked.

The man coughed, and more blood poured out of his mouth. "Solomon...knows you."

"Who is Solomon?"

The man's red teeth clenched together in a pained smile. "He'll... find you."

The wolf appeared at Jeremiah's side, close enough to touch, to smell its wet fur and hot breath. Jeremiah looked into the wolf's eyes and saw the reflection of some unclear future, vague red shapes, lonely and aimless.

The wolf turned its gaze to the man on the ground. ᴅᴏ ʏᴏᴜ ʙᴇᴄᴏᴍᴇ ᴀ ᴋɪʟʟᴇʀ?

"I don't want to take a life," Jeremiah said.

AND YET, IT MUST BE DONE.

Jeremiah placed the gun barrel directly against the man's temple. His eyes went wide, and his breathing quickened. He opened his mouth to say something, and Jeremiah closed his eyes and pulled the trigger.

22

ELIJAH TRIED NOT TO LOOK at the gaping hole in the side of the man's head, but the torn and bloody flesh, the splintered skull, kept drawing his attention. The dead man's eyes were still open, looking straight up at the sky.

"Where did they come from?" Elijah asked.

Jeremiah knelt in the mud next to the body, holding a piece of paper he had pulled from one of the man's pockets. A page from a notebook, soaked through with red. Jeremiah put one hand to his head as he read it, the fingers digging into his scalp. Then he curled his fingers into a fist and hit himself in the thigh. He crushed the paper and hit himself again.

He dropped the crumpled note on the ground. "The man I found, he was sent. When he didn't come back, these two were sent to find him." Jeremiah looked up, his eyes as red as the dead man's throat, enclosed in dark circles. "Someone else will come."

Emma came behind and knelt beside him, wrapping her arms around his neck. Elijah hated the way he felt seeing her touch him.

"Remember what you told me," she said. "If this is real, if things can be changed into gold, what else is possible? We're closer than they are. We can find it first."

She put one hand over her husband's clenched fist and held it there. She turned to Elijah. "Even if we turn back now, that doesn't mean they won't send someone else to kill us."

Jeremiah stood, brushing mud from his knees. "We need to move the body away from the path."

"Into the trees?" Elijah asked. Jeremiah shook his head and looked over at the cliff. It made Elijah a little sick to think of it, but he understood. If the bodies were found, they would be found together, broken, covered in mud and debris. It would look like an accident that resulted from the storm.

Jeremiah grabbed the man's legs, and Elijah took hold of the arms, and they staggered over to the cliff. The jagged hole in the man's head leaked cold blood on Elijah's arm. They each planted their feet and hurled the body out over the edge. Neither of them stayed to watch or listen for the impact.

The horses stamped their hooves and moved about anxiously. Jeremiah reached out, and his horse jerked away, looking at him with one black eye. Jeremiah felt the animal sense something about him, something not right. Perhaps it was the smell of the wolf.

As Jeremiah and Emma finished folding up the tent, Elijah quickly snatched the paper Jeremiah had dropped. He went into the trees like he had to relieve himself and spread the paper on a rock. Handwriting was so scribbled that it was hard to read, and the page was covered in bleeding ink. Only a small section, not covered in blood, was legible:

A town in the place where the tree is burned.
A son buried in the field.
A preacher who abandoned God when God abandoned him.
A body found amongst the dead leaves.
He seeks what we seek. He seeks what is ours.

To the mountaintop where time does not move. To the place in the dark where the writing is on the walls. To the glassy lake and the motionless grass, to a sun that crawls across the sky and sets upon a day in which it did not rise.

Take back what belongs to us. Steal back our birthright like Jacob stole from Esau.

No wonder Jeremiah is afraid, Elijah thought. *Someone out there has been searching for this. Waiting for it. And Jeremiah was right, more would come. It was only a matter of time.*

Elijah looked over his shoulder. Both Jeremiah and Emma had their backs to him as they loaded their supplies on the horses. He crushed the piece of paper again and hid it in his fist. As he walked out of the trees, Elijah dropped it near where the body had been and stepped on it, driving it into the puddle of muddy water and blood.

Once the horses were calm, they saddled up and started on the trail. As they rode, it occurred to Elijah that none of them had said a single word about the wolf. Then he noticed dark red spots on his hand that held the reins, bright and accusing against his skin—splotches of dried blood that were not his.

The trail eventually leveled out, and riding became easier. A few rays of sunlight cut through the cloud covering and shone down on the valley. The going was slow because of the mud and rocks, but after several hours, they came to a flattened space where the trail ended—a point that looked out over the valley, all the way to the mountains on the other side. They drank water, fed the horses, and walked around the point looking for a sign.

"We're not at the top yet," Jeremiah said.

They mounted the horses again and rode into the trees without a path to guide them. They rode for another two hours, stopping only once to inspect a small pile of stones stacked in a pyramid. This sat atop a larger rock, safe from the rainwater that had carried so much debris down the mountainside.

Jeremiah reached out to touch the stone pyramid, then stopped himself. "A marker," he said.

The air grew thinner the higher they went, until they breathed in shallow gasps. Jeremiah assured Emma they would get used to the altitude in time, but Elijah felt as though he were suffocating.

He watched the gun at Emma's hip, watched it move with each step of the horse. She turned and caught him looking, strands of hair stuck to her cheek with sweat. She gave him a slight smile and turned back around.

They moved through the trees, some so close together their legs scraped against the bark. The horses trudged slowly, unsure where they were going. Eventually, they came across another pyramid of stacked rocks, reminding them they were moving in the right direction. They rode without speaking until the trees parted, revealing a large, oval-shaped boulder blocking their path. It rose half as high as the trees around it, and was cracked completely open in the center, from the bottom almost all the way to the top, like an upside-down V. They could see all the way to the other side. A hole big enough to walk through.

Jeremiah got down off his horse and touched the stone. "The doorway." He put his hand into the cool, dark space and smiled. "The rock that stands as a doorway."

Jeremiah went over and touched Emma's leg. He smiled up at her. "This is where we're supposed to be," he said.

To the right of the boulder were more rocks, pressed together so tightly they resembled a manmade wall. Behind these, the trees and brush were thick and impenetrable. They had no choice but to go through the rock or turn around and try to find another way in. But Elijah knew that even if they looked, nothing would be found. *You enter a house through the door.*

A faint metallic ringing buzzed in Elijah's ears, like the sound of a shovel striking stone, and when he peered into the woods, he caught a glimpse of the wolf walking between the trees. With its sleek body low to the ground, the wolf stole behind Emma and Jeremiah and entered the doorway, disappearing into the dark.

Jeremiah helped Emma down and laughed as he hugged her.

He said things that Elijah could not hear because the metallic ringing had grown louder. The opening in the rock, the doorway, tugged at his insides, pulling the breath right out of his lungs. His legs went numb the longer he looked into that dark opening, and he wanted to turn away and run as fast as he could down the mountain. *It's just a rock. A broken rock, nothing more.*

Still, the fear remained. It was senseless and unfounded, but it hummed away inside him like a string plucked on a guitar, vibrating through his arms and legs, making them weak.

He saw Emma looking over her husband's shoulder, arms down at her sides. She stared at the opening, her eyes narrow and intense, their green faded. Did she hear that metal ringing, too? An endless buzz like a hive full of angry bees?

Jeremiah kept one arm around Emma and pulled Elijah closer with the other arm. "This is it," he said, still smiling. Elijah studied his brother's face and did not like what he saw. Both he and Emma felt something was wrong with the rock, but Jeremiah didn't seem to feel any fear. And the wolf. There was a moment last night, right before Jeremiah shot that man, that looked like he talked to it. Like they had a conversation.

There was a bit of madness in the excitement Elijah saw in his brother's eyes.

"Guns out," Jeremiah said. "I'll lead. Elijah, you bring up the back."

Elijah saw Emma's hand shake slightly as she took out her gun. Her knuckles turned the color of milk as she gripped it in one hand and took her horse's reins with the other. Jeremiah paused at the opening in the rock, looked back, and smiled again before walking into it. Emma led her horse to the entrance and passed over into the cool shadow inside the rock. The moment the horse's face touched the shadow, it stopped and took two steps backward. Emma pulled the reins hard, but it refused to move. It shook its head and stamped.

Elijah took a blanket from his bag and draped it over the animal's head.

"They're not that different from us," he said, rubbing the horse's neck. "If they can't see it, they think it can't hurt them."

Sweat ran down the side of Emma's face, along the curve of her jaw, and down her neck. She walked into the opening without looking back. Elijah hurried to follow, holding the rifle on his shoulder and pulling on the reins. His horse moved forward without any prodding and allowed itself to be led. As soon as Elijah's foot crossed over into the rock, the sound of ringing metal grew so loud he clenched his teeth until they scraped together. It hurt worse than the time his father had hit him in the side of the head when he was just a boy. The man's hand had struck Elijah's ear and left a stinging heat that stayed for days.

He slid the gun back into the bag, wrapped the reins around his arms, and plugged both ears with his fingers. It did nothing to drown out the sound. If anything, it felt louder, like it was coming from inside him and moving out through his body. He imagined it was like having your head inside a church bell while it was being rung.

The rock was bigger than Elijah could see from the outside. He and the horse were completely inside the cool darkness of a tunnel made of stone. He walked as fast as he could, closing his eyes and pushing forward to the air he felt blowing from the other side.

The dark he saw behind his closed eyes grew brighter. The damp coolness gave way to the smell of pine and clean air. He opened his eyes and squinted into a grey sky.

Jeremiah and Emma stood looking out over a large, flat clearing of long grass, enclosed on all sides by forest. To the south was a small lake, and although there did not appear to be any tributaries entering or leaving, the water was clear. To the west, on the other side of the grassy field, a bare piece of the mountain rose as if it were the only piece left of a peak cut away.

There was an unnatural stillness in the clearing—the trees did not rattle with wind, the grass was stiff and unmoving, and there were no birdsongs or insect hums. Even the surface of the lake was unbroken, shimmering like glass. Jeremiah left his horse and started walking toward the mountainside, moving through grass so green it looked painted, unreal. Elijah called out to Jeremiah, but he kept moving.

Emma shivered a little and squinted in the direction of the lake. She crossed her arms over her chest, lips tight, and jaw set. Elijah grabbed the rifle again, let go of the reins, and ran to catch up to his brother. As he got closer, he saw a bright glimmer in the distance, sunlight bouncing off two objects on the other side of the lake. Nearby lay the remnants of a camp.

Jeremiah stopped when Elijah came near and stared straight ahead at a large black hole carved into the center of the mountainside.

"It's the circle from the map," Elijah said. He turned to Jeremiah, but his brother was now focused on the glimmering objects. He went toward them, cautiously, as though the shining things might suddenly wake up and attack. Elijah stayed close behind him, holding a hand over his eyes to shield them from the sun.

When Elijah saw the objects clearly, he stopped moving. The only sounds he heard were his brother's footsteps crunching the grass and his heartbeat pulsing in the back of his skull. He swallowed hard and forced his legs to keep walking, closer to something he could not understand. The bodies of two men—one kneeling, the other standing with his hands lifted, as if in worship—their faces frozen into masks of terror and pain. Elijah's stomach clenched violently, and his throat burned. Jeremiah stared at the two bodies as a faint smile grew on his face, because the men were made of solid gold.

23

TOOLS WERE SCATTERED ABOUT THE campsite, blankets and clothing lay on the ground, soaked and muddy from the rain. A lantern lay smashed near the tent, surrounded by pieces of broken glass. A heavy pot hung over the fire pit, charred black on the bottom. Two tents had been blown away from the camp, one of which hung impaled on the branches of a tree, the other half-buried in the mud. Only one tent still stood, with black mold growing in ominous patterns on the canvas.

Jeremiah and Elijah walked past the two frozen bodies, so lifelike that Elijah expected them to blink at any moment. He felt as if their eyes watched him as he went by. The brothers held their guns and approached the tent cautiously. Elijah trained his rifle on the opening while Jeremiah moved one of the flaps aside with the barrel of his revolver. He looked inside and waved Elijah over.

Loose sheets of blank paper, the same parchment paper the map had drawn on, covered the floor and bed. A journal and several small nuggets of gold sat atop a small folding table, also strewn with paper. The air was stale, thick with the smell of mold. Jeremiah picked up the journal and opened it.

"Cornelius Griffin," he read aloud from the cover. "The man I found was named Cornelius Griffin."

He turned the book around and showed it to Elijah. Nearly all the pages had been torn out. Jeremiah threw it on the ground.

They went back outside and saw Emma moving toward the lake, arms still crossed over her chest. The tall grass hid her legs, so it looked like she was floating through the field.

From a short distance, Elijah could almost believe the golden men were sculptures made by an artist and abandoned here on this peak to serve as a warning. But up close, he saw every pore, wrinkle, whisker, and scar. Even the dirt under the fingernails had been turned to gold, and from the open, screaming mouths, the process by which they were transformed was excruciating.

Jeremiah ran his fingers over the kneeling man's face, feeling his golden whiskers and eyebrows. Elijah did not want to touch the men, but he had to, because he couldn't believe otherwise. Part of him expected his hand to pass through the statue, for it to evaporate like mist.

He put his fingers on the arm of the kneeling man, and as soon as his skin touched the cold metal, he jerked his hand away. Like the flower Jeremiah showed him, but so much worse. He touched the statue once more, and a sick, nauseous feeling moved up his chest. The golden skin and hair were of a texture that no artist could have created, no matter how skilled. Elijah's breathing grew heavier and deeper. Each heartbeat felt like it took up too much space in his chest.

Elijah backed away, his head going light, his skin still sparking from the feel of all that metal, all that gold, and the reality that these men had once been alive, had moved through the world, spoken words, gripped tools, just ripped Elijah's thoughts apart.

The kneeling man had a look on his face Elijah had seen only one other time in his life—when a member of the Hopi tribe had been trampled by a spooked horse. A look of pain so severe it was difficult to witness.

The gold looked almost liquid in the sunlight, like it should come off on his fingers. Elijah leaned in close to the face of the frozen man, forcing himself to look, to imagine what sorts of horrible sensations consumed this man in his final moments, what memories and regrets darkened his thoughts before they came to an end. The longer he stared into the man's face, the more Elijah felt his own face contorting to match the man's expression, until Elijah himself was a living mirror of the lifeless statue.

Emma's voice came from the lake. "Elijah, Jeremiah!"

Jeremiah stood up fast and ran toward his wife. Elijah stayed where he was, staring into the statue's golden eyes. Something about them unnerved him, but he couldn't tell what it was. Then he realized there were no pupils. The entire eye was a golden orb, all one color. It made Elijah feel as though he were looking at something not human, something that shouldn't exist.

He straightened up and crossed the field to where his brother knelt at the edge of the lake. Emma stood off to the side, holding one hand over her mouth.

A decayed body lay face down in the grass, one arm hanging in the water. Unlike the others, this body had not been turned to gold. What was left of the pants and boots told them the body was that of a man, his flesh now picked apart by scavengers, exposed to the elements. All that remained was a rotted corpse, a still red skeleton with thin strips of meat hardened on the bones. Wispy bits of dark hair still clung to the skull. The teeth were dandelion yellow.

Near the body was a tree stump carried to the lake to be used as a makeshift table. A mortar, a pestle, and a metal coffee cup were on the stump. Elijah picked up the mortar and saw traces of powdered gold coating the sides. He ran his finger through the dust and held it up so Jeremiah could see. The lines of his fingertips sparkled in the sun.

Jeremiah looked out over the lake. "Why isn't he like the others?"

"The man you found in the woods," Emma said, looking at the corpse, "he must have killed them all. Maybe he murdered this one before he had the power."

Jeremiah nodded slowly, one hand absently tearing out blades of grass and dropping them into the water. "If he killed them all, then why was he running?"

Like the statue's golden eyes, the quiet stillness made Elijah uneasy, fearful. He felt they had all stepped out of the world into another place where time moved at a different speed. He watched the clear water for any signs of fish. He had not seen a single animal, insect, or bird since they stepped onto the mountaintop.

Nothing was living.

Since their tent was in tatters, they had no choice but to sleep in the only tent standing. Jeremiah started a fire while Elijah and Emma carried the belongings inside.

"You should sleep on the cot," Elijah said.

Emma shook her head and grabbed one end of the frame. "I'd rather sleep on the floor," she said, dragging it outside. She returned, and they laid out the three bedrolls side by side. Elijah peered through the flap and saw his brother unpacking food for dinner, his back to them.

Elijah reached out and touched Emma's arm. "Are we going to ignore what happened yesterday?"

Emma sighed. "This isn't the time."

"If not now, when?"

Her green eyes met and held his gaze until he had to look away. "I need something," she said, "I just don't know what it is yet."

"Is it me, or just someone other than him?" Elijah felt guilt as soon as he said it, but it was a thought on his mind since she came and lay in his arms.

She sighed again. "You didn't need to ask that."

She crossed her arms, and her fingers searched the skin on her elbow until they found something to dig into and pick away at.

Jeremiah sat by the fire-pit, stacking kindling.

Elijah knew he should just be quiet and give her space, but he could not stop himself. "What do I do with what's in my heart?" He had to fight to keep his voice quiet.

"Bury it, for now." She watched her husband pull something out of the ashes, hold it up, and blow the dust off it. "I don't know what the future holds."

Though they were close in age, Elijah felt he was looking at a much older woman. Someone who knew more of the world than he did, who knew of the pain it could cause and the things it could steal. And that made him conscious of his own understanding and beliefs about the world. It was like speaking to someone who had visited a country he had never even heard of. What could he possibly offer?

Emma stopped picking at her elbow, reached out, and touched his arm. There was sadness in her smile. "This isn't the time," she said, and turned and left the tent.

Elijah looked down, and there was a smear of blood on his shirt where she had touched him.

24

ELIJAH WALKED OUT INTO THE field, away from the firelight, and looked up into the night sky. A few clouds, as thin and faint as smoke, hung there unmoving. The dust of the galaxy stretched above him like a shotgun had blasted a thousand holes through the black canvas of sky.

Emma was asleep in the tent, her bedroll on one side, Elijah's on the other. Jeremiah would sleep between them. Since leaving the valley, Elijah had found himself wrestling with something he had not felt since he was a child. It was a feeling that started as a whisper, a nagging voice in the back of his mind, and over the last several hours had grown louder.

A soft snap came from the campsite where Jeremiah was breaking twigs into pieces and tossing them into the flames.

The voice in Elijah's head repeated the same thing over and over—*I am better than my brother. I am better.*

He hated the voice and what it said, but it kept echoing endlessly.

Elijah closed his eyes and prayed, asking God for strength and wisdom. He didn't want to hate his brother, and what he felt, if it was hate, was senseless and corrupt. Elijah came here to help his brother, so why did he resent every word he spoke, every expression?

He looked back at the fire, at the lonely figure of his brother, his shadow a giant cast against the tent behind him.

It was the quietest night Elijah had ever heard. The mechanics of his own body suddenly seemed very loud to him. His heart beating, his lungs filling with air, and even his thoughts seemed to be an internal voice shouting.

When Elijah returned to the campsite, his brother was smoking a pipe and staring into the dying fire, his eyes glassy.

Elijah sat. "I haven't stopped thinking about what happened here," he said, nodding toward the lake and the corpse. Jeremiah nodded and snapped a twig in half. The fire made his eyes look orange.

Elijah looked away from his brother's face. "The Hopi believe there are places on earth that are more than what we can see. Tunnels and caves a man can enter in one place, and come out at a different place hundreds of miles away. Some of these are good, some are bad."

Smoke from the fire drifted into Elijah's face. He coughed once and looked at the stones around the fire-pit. Probably stacked together by one of the men now dead on this mountaintop.

"They believe certain things can stain a place," Elijah said. "Violence, sacrifice, acts of vengeance and love can turn the ground sour, or cause it to become fertile."

Elijah looked at his brother again. He tried to silence that voice inside him. "Jeremiah," he said, "this place is bad. I felt it from the moment we came through that rock."

Jeremiah nodded again and made a small humming sound in his throat.

"Do you feel it?" Elijah asked.

"I feel something," Jeremiah said. "But I don't know what it is."

"I think we need to leave," Elijah said. He tried to strengthen his voice, but it sounded weak and afraid.

Jeremiah reached into the pocket of his coat. "You said the Hopi believed caves could lead to other places."

Elijah frowned, nodded silently. Jeremiah held out his arm and handed Elijah a small piece of paper, the edges were torn and burned black. The paper itself had turned brown but there was still some handwriting visible on it.

> "...to step into the cave is to step out of...
> ...I almost forgot who I was...
> ...feel so very alone...
> ...the night is still...
> ...I thirst..."

Elijah stopped reading. His brother was looking directly at him. "We can't leave," Jeremiah said. "Not yet."

Elijah turned and looked over his shoulder at the jagged mountain that cut into the sky. The cave, a hole blacker than black, like a dark eye, stared back.

25

ELIJAH AWOKE WHILE IT WAS still dark. He heard Jeremiah and Emma breathing out of time with each other. He got up, pulled on his boots, and went outside. The fire had burned down to coals. The statues were just black shapes in the night, but the sight of them still made his head feel dizzy.

He picked up a canteen and made his way across the field to the lake. The moon, bright and almost full, reflected on the glassy surface, as if there were a second moon floating just beneath the water.

Elijah walked past the corpse, its one arm drifting in the unbroken water. He went a little further down and dipped the canteen into the lake. The water tasted fresh but slightly metallic. He drank the whole canteen and filled it again, but his throat was still parched. He filled it a third time and drank so fast that water ran down his chin, soaked his shirt. Still, his throat scratched like he had drunk no water at all.

Elijah was about to refill the canteen once more when he heard grass moving behind him.

He stood up and peered into the darkness. "Jeremiah?" he said. The sound kept moving, coming closer.

He gripped the canteen, ready to swing it at whatever came at him. A shape, low to the ground, emerged from the grass. The moonlight pulsed in its red eyes.

YOU SHOULD NOT HAVE COME HERE, the wolf's voice spoke inside Elijah's head.

"You led us," Elijah said.

I FOLLOWED.

Elijah shut his eyes, and when he opened them, the wolf was still there. It walked over to the corpse and licked at the red bones.

THE MAN YOUR BROTHER FOUND, THIS WAS HIS SACRIFICE. The wolf looked at the tree stump with the mortar and pestle. HE DRANK THE GOLD AND COMMITTED THE SIN. HIS SOUL WAS CORRUPTED, BUT HE RECEIVED WHAT HE CAME FOR.

"Did you lead him here, too?"

I LEAD NO ONE. THOSE WHO ARE MEANT TO FIND THEIR WAY.

"I don't understand this place," Elijah said.

IT IS A WORLD WITHIN THE WORLD. NOT EVERYONE WHO PASSES THROUGH THE DOORWAY MAY RETURN.

"Are you…are you Death?"

The wolf shook its head. I AM MUCH OLDER THAN DEATH.

The wolf turned and went back into the grass. Elijah followed the thin path the animal made. Soon they were in front of the cave. A lit lantern sat just inside, casting orange light on the walls. The wolf lowered its head and made a motion toward the entrance. Elijah walked forward, feeling a chill pass over his skin as he stepped inside.

The lantern illuminated one wall covered in symbols, pictograms like those in the journal Jeremiah had found. They filled the wall from top to bottom and continued deeper into the cave where the light did not reach.

Elijah ran his fingers over one of the rust-colored stains and heard a whisper inside him. He pulled his hand away and the voice went silent. He put his fingers on the next symbol and the whisper returned. As he ran his hand along the wall, the voice hissed the meaning of the symbols, each one of them a piece of the story about an ancient culture whose belief in a dark figure drove them to perform increasingly terrible and bloody rituals in order to achieve oneness with this being. Amputations, beheadings, cannibalism, and eventually infanticide were undertaken in efforts to absolve sin and become something more than human.

Elijah walked further into the cave, carrying the lantern in one hand, the other hand touching the symbols on the wall.

The story shifted, became instructions for how to perform a ritual, given to this ancient culture by the god they worshipped. He taught the people how to transform anything they desired into solid gold. This gift, however, came at a terrible cost—a human had to be sacrificed, and only one person could hold the gift at a time. Gold from a certain mine was ground down to powder and mixed with the water of a specific lake, and then consumed while the sacrifice took place.

Over time, fathers murdered sons, brothers killed brothers, wives killed husbands—all to obtain the power. The gift passed from one person to another, from one family to another, until objects made of gold were commonplace. Homes were solidified into the substance, which came crashing down upon the families who lived there. Cups, plates, tables, chairs, floors, and even streets were all transformed.

The capital city of this civilization was made entirely of gold, and the brightness of it led some to blindness. For a time, these ancient people were exceedingly wealthy as they traded and bartered with other nations until they wanted for nothing. But their cruelty and selfishness were also known, and eventually other nations and cultures would have nothing to do with them, and they were shut off from the rest of the world. Their gold became worthless because it could not be used to purchase anything within their own cities, it was in such abundance. They cried out to the being they worshipped and begged him for something more. So he gave them more rituals to perform in order to...

Elijah stopped. This was a symbol he could not understand. He rubbed his hand over the stone and closed his eyes, listened for that whisper that told him the meaning, but the symbol was silent.

He moved on and the whispers continued.

There was death and bloodshed, torture and brutality on a horrific scale, and the golden city was no longer gold, it was red. Painted in blood.

Elijah backed away from the wall. He tasted the salt-sweat that ran over his lips. His breathing was heavier, frightened. The last symbol he touched suggested that this outcome, this ocean of blood, is what the dark god wanted all along.

The symbols ended at a place where the light of the lantern did not reach. It stopped as though hitting a wall, and beyond was a blackness so thick it seemed to be made of oil. Elijah reached his arm into the dark and felt a sudden cold so intense it was like being burned. When he pulled his arm out, the darkness still clung to it, dripped off his skin in thick drops.

A voice came out of the dark. A woman's voice, sweet and familiar. "Elijah, darling. Listen to me. Jeremiah will not leave here without the gift. Someone has to be sacrificed, and you know he won't kill me."

Elijah put his hand back up to the dark, felt the cold of it on his palm. "Emma, how did you get back there? Are you okay?"

"You read the wall," she said. "It's only a matter of time before he knows what needs to be done. You have to do it first."

"Emma, I can't...."

"There can be an us," she said. It sounded like she was crying. "He won't let you leave this mountain, do you understand that? He is beyond reason. He believes this gift, this power, will make everything right again."

"I've tried to tell him, all the gold in the world will never fix what's been broken, and it won't bring back what we've lost. But he won't listen to me."

Was she trapped in there? She didn't sound hurt, but Elijah wanted to run into the dark and pull her back out into the light.

"Please come out," he said. "We can talk about this."

"You need to do it first."

"I can't kill my own brother," he said.

Her voice grew deeper, stronger. "If you don't kill him, he will kill you. You will be just another corpse left to rot on this mountaintop."

He imagined the act, he had to. He saw himself plunging a knife into his brother's gut and watching the light go out of his eyes. He saw himself with his hands wrapped around Jeremiah's throat. He growled and smacked the side of his head. Some of the dark on his fingers smeared on his cheek. He saw a rock in his hand, saw himself kneeling over his brother and slamming the stone into his face until it was unrecognizable.

He said, "It's not right to ask this of me."

"Then your choice is made," the voice said. "We could have had everything, but now you'll get nothing."

The voice seemed impossibly closer, whispering right next to his ear. "You won't leave this place alive."

Elijah waited for her to say something else, but there was only silence.

"Emma?" he called out. "Emma, please!"

Something caught Elijah's eye, something glinting in the dirt wall. It glowed like amber held up to sunlight, pulsing with color, and when Elijah touched it the piece fell away easily in his hand and warmed his skin.

Elijah put the gold in his pocket and left the cave, some of the darkness still trickling down his fingers. The wolf was not waiting, but Elijah knew where to go next.

26

JEREMIAH JERKED AWAKE IN THE quiet tent. He sat up and felt for Emma, but his hand only touched empty blankets. The tent flaps swayed a little, gave him a view of the fire-pit outside, the eerie orange glow on the ground reflecting off the statues.

Jeremiah went outside and looked at the field, the lake. He knew the mountaintop was quiet during the day, but this silence was deathly. It made him feel like he was still locked inside a dream.

He cupped his hands around his mouth and called for Emma, Elijah. Silence. A dark shape came out of the tall grass and lowered itself next to the statue of the kneeling man.

HE ONLY WANTED RICHES, the wolf said, staring into the statue's frozen eyes. HE TRIED TO KILL THE MAN YOU FOUND.

Jeremiah looked at the statue's face, so distorted by pain it made his chest tighten.

"What about him?" he asked, nodding toward the lake.

The wolf turned its head in the direction of the water. HE IS ANOTHER STORY.

"Where is my wife?" Jeremiah asked. "My brother?"

The wolf looked back at him, its eyes bright. SHE IS IN THE CAVE.

"Together?"

The wolf blinked.

Jeremiah clenched his fists. He wanted to hit himself, to stop the thoughts that sparked in his mind, but strangely, he didn't want the wolf to see him do it. The wolf tilted its head and watched him.

THE CAVE IS WHERE YOU FIND IT.

Jeremiah clenched until his knuckles burned. Emma and Elijah, alone in the cave? Why had they gone without waking him? He couldn't find an answer in all his scattered thoughts. He walked past the wolf and went toward the cave. The muscles in his forearm quivered and when he finally released his grip, his fingers had gone numb. The torn rock of the mountain rose into the sky like the tip of a knife.

He didn't want to believe they had turned against him. Could not believe it. Why would they? Maybe Elijah had awakened and made his way toward the cave. Maybe Emma awoke, saw him walking, and followed, thinking he was her husband. But how could she? He was sleeping right next to her.

Jeremiah's hand struck the side of his face. The sting of it focused his mind. He was looking for an explanation that did not exist. If they were in the cave together, without him, it was only because they didn't want him there.

The skin on his throat went sticky. His heart pushed up in his chest, like it was fighting to climb out of his mouth. It beat heavier, stronger. The dark entrance of the cave stood before him, a deeper darkness than the night. He clenched his fists one last time and went inside.

A lantern sat at the center of the floor, casting light on either wall. There was no one else he could see. Jeremiah went over to the wall with all the symbols, the same symbols Cornelius Griffin had carefully transcribed into his journal, even if he did not understand them.

The wolf entered the cave and watched as Jeremiah put his hand to the wall. Jeremiah heard a voice whispering in his ear, and keeping his hand on the stone, listened while he walked further into the dark, dragging his fingertips along the markings.

Images flooded his mind as a voice hissed the story of the dark god and the city of blood and gold. The wolf followed closely behind until Jeremiah reached the wall of darkness. He shivered as he stood beside the black veil. The air was as cold as winter. The hair on his arms stood up.

"Is it all true?" Jeremiah asked the wolf.

The wolf blinked. IT IS A VERSION OF THE TRUTH.

"There was a marking I couldn't understand," Jeremiah said. "The ritual, the sacrifice."

YOU ASKED ABOUT THE BODY AT THE LAKE. THE MAN YOU FOUND, THAT WAS HIS SON.

At the word "son" Jeremiah's teeth ground together. "He killed his own son?"

THAT IS THE COST. YOU MUST SACRIFICE YOUR OWN BLOOD.

Jeremiah shook his head. "Nothing is worth that."

YOU SAW WHAT HE COULD DO.

Jeremiah pressed the palms of his hands into his eyes and groaned.

NOT EVERYONE CAN GIVE WHAT IS REQUIRED.

Jeremiah's legs suddenly went weak and he lowered himself to the ground. He heard footsteps echoing from behind the dark wall, a dark so thick he couldn't see anything beyond it. He touched it and it burned his skin like the water under the ice of a frozen pond. He pulled his finger away and the dark came with it. A thin line ran to the floor.

More footsteps.

"Who's there?" Jeremiah called out.

A voice echoed back there.

"Jeremiah?"

The voice came closer. Jeremiah leaned his head in close to the dark. It sounded like crying, like a woman sobbing behind the veil.

"Emma?"

Jeremiah ran to one side of the cave and felt the stone, looking for a way around the black veil, but it went all the way to the wall. He ran to the other side. He called her name again, louder, but she kept crying like she could not hear him.

Jeremiah took a deep breath and pushed his whole arm into the dark and held it there. His skin started burning immediately. He reached further in, trying to feel for a place where the dark ended, but the burning cold moved up into his shoulder, as though it were freezing his bones into solid ice.

He screamed and pulled his arm out, wiped off the liquid darkness and rubbed his skin to get the heat back.

How did she get back there? She must have found a way around, Jeremiah thought. But the voice he now heard came from only a few feet away. Close enough to touch.

He leaned his mouth close to the wall of darkness. "Emma," he said. "Tell me if you can hear me."

The voice came from inches away. "I can hear you."

"What happened?"

"It was Elijah," she said.

"Are you hurt?"

The voice shook. "He read the wall, Jeremiah. He knows what to do."

The faint light from the lantern caught something embedded within the walls that glittered.

"He won't do it," Jeremiah said. "Neither of us will. We'll all leave and go back home. We shouldn't have come here."

She was crying again, speaking through the tears. Jeremiah's heart ached to hear that sound. The dark wall shimmered a little, and beyond, back where Emma was trapped, he could see thick swirling currents of blackness.

"He's changed," Emma said. She took a breath and sniffed. "He grabbed me, Jeremiah, grabbed me so tight it hurt and he wouldn't let go. He kissed me and told me he wanted us to be together."

Jeremiah felt air push out of him, as if he had been struck in the stomach. A sick feeling churned in his guts, burned up his chest. He clenched his fists and lowered his head, so close to the dark wall that his hair touched it. Cold skittered across his scalp.

"I tried to get him to leave the cave, to find you and talk this over, but he wouldn't listen. He kissed me again and said he had to kill you. He told me it would hurt at first, but eventually I'd understand."

Each breath was shallow and Jeremiah's lungs ached for more air.

Emma's voice fought to keep from crying. "He said…he said God took Samuel from us because he knew how evil you would become."

Jeremiah's knees buckled and he had to lean against the wall to keep from slumping to the ground. His heart sped up until he feared it might disconnect from the machinery of his body.

"This place has poisoned him," he said. "We have to leave this mountain."

He still couldn't see her, but Emma's voice was so close the hair on Jeremiah's ear shivered with her breath. "Your brother is determined to take the gold. You have to kill him before he kills you."

The darkness shimmered and Jeremiah thought he saw a shape moving inside it.

"I'll see you on the other side," Emma's voice said.

27

A CLEAR MOON RIPPLED ON the surface of the lake, beneath its perfect mirror in the sky. Elijah hurried to the tree stump table. He took the piece of gold from his pocket, placed it in the mortar and starting grinding. Sweat dripped down his face and fell into the powder as he ground fast and hard, until the muscles of his arm burned.

He knelt by the corpse, the white bones of its fingers distorted in the water, and dipped the bowl into the lake, filling it with water. He picked up a small twig and used the end to stir the powder until it dissolved, and the water turned into a swirling gold-colored liquid sparkling in the moonlight.

The stillness of the mountaintop made him feel as though he were in a dream, that his actions were predetermined and he was merely going through motions without understanding why. Elijah lifted the bowl to his mouth, took one last look at the world around him, wondered if he would remain the same person after drinking, or if something inside would detach, become a separate self.

He put the bowl to his lips. The liquid tasted bitter and grainy, as if filled with sand. He swallowed, felt the grit of powder between his teeth.

His throat was immediately filled with heat. It moved down his chest and scorched his stomach. He doubled over and fell to his knees, one arm wrapped around his belly. Elijah heaved and heaved, trying to make the liquid come back out. The pain was so severe Elijah feared the liquid was going to melt through his guts, come spilling out over his legs and eat at them until nothing remained.

Elijah sank to the ground, his fingers clutching handfuls of grass, and just as he was on the verge of losing consciousness, the pain subsided. Not all at once, but gradually, until it was just a heat in his belly, a heat that moved and spread into his arms, his legs, his fingers and toes. Up to his chest until it entered his neck and covered his head.

He lay in the grass, breathing heavily. A chill passed over his skin as the sweat cooled. He lifted his hand, looked at it in the moonlight. It looked the same. He still had skin, still had the scar he had accidentally carved in his knuckle while whittling a fishing pole.

But the process was not complete. Drinking the gold was only part of the ritual. There was still one thing left for him to do.

Elijah stood and looked across the field to the two golden statues. Frozen there in the dirt was more money than even the wealthiest men in the world ever saw. And Elijah would have that power soon. But even more than that he would have...

A shadow moved and came around the tent, went and stood next to the dying embers of the fire. A figure that seemed to face him, to be looking across the blue grass.

"Emma," Elijah whispered.

Somehow, she had found a way out of the cave. She was looking for him.

Elijah walked toward her. The future was so clear to him now. He was not afraid anymore.

She stood, arms crossed over her chest, watching as he came closer. Her face was creased with worry. "Where's Jeremiah?"

The question caught Elijah off guard. He looked over her shoulder at the tent.

"He's not in there," she said.

Elijah reached out, caressed her arm.

Emma took a step back, eyes wide. "Don't touch me."

Elijah let his hand fall, and a golden smear remained on her coat.

"I want us to be together," he said. "I want you to know that I can protect you, take care of you."

The look on her face cracked whatever certainty he had. "Elijah," she said. "What are you talking about?"

He felt as if the ground was no longer solid, and he was sinking into it. He glanced at the black mouth of the cave.

"Back there, you said I had to prove myself. You said—"

Emma crossed her arms even tighter. She shook her head. "You're confused. I woke up to an empty tent and I just came out here."

Elijah held out his hands, heart beating wildly in his chest. "That's not true. Why would you say that?"

Her voice, the same voice he had heard coming from the darkness of the cave, spoke to him like he was a child. "Elijah, I haven't seen you since the evening. I haven't been out of the tent. Now tell me, where is my husband?"

The heat he felt after swallowing the golden liquid burned his insides again. Thoughts rushed through his mind. Violent, angry thoughts that weren't his, *couldn't* be his. It was like watching a train rush by, each car full of haunted passengers, each car on fire.

He took a step closer, still holding out his hands. "You're lying. Did Jeremiah make you do this? Make you pretend to love me?"

She looked over her shoulder, slowly backing away toward the tent. "I don't know what you're talking about."

Elijah moved fast and grabbed both her arms. His hands squeezed so hard she let out a frightened cry.

"Was it all just to get to this mountain?" he screamed. Drops of spittle sprayed on her face.

Emma closed her eyes, head jerking as he shook her. The gun was just inside the tent next to her pillow. If she moved quickly, she just might be able to reach it before…

She opened her eyes and saw someone moving across the field. The figure hurried to the lake and knelt down. Elijah saw her looking and glanced over his shoulder.

When he turned back around the anger in his eyes was gone. Instead, what Emma saw was a hurt so deep it was painful to look at.

"Elijah," she said. "I'm sorry, I don't understand what's happening."

His eyes moved over her face, from her lips to her cheeks.

"You used me," he said.

His fingers tightened around her arms, squeezing even harder. She knew she couldn't overpower him, so she took a deep breath and looked directly into his eyes.

"Elijah," she said, trying to keep her voice steady. "Let go of me."

His hands released her and some emotion passed over his face, an awareness, shame maybe, and then it was gone. He took a step backward, looking at her and shaking his head, then another step.

"You're a liar," he said. He started to turn around but stopped, pointed his finger at Emma. His mouth opened, but his face twisted up like the words were right there inside his mouth and they tasted bitter. He put a hand to his head, fingers gripping his skull, and hunched over like he was about to vomit. His eyes met hers and she saw that hurt again. "You are a mother without a son," he said, "and soon, you will be a widow."

Elijah stood up straight, then turned and left, became just a shape moving through the tall grass. The moon slid over the surface of the lake. The silhouette of a man knelt by the water.

Emma's legs gave out and she sank to the ground. Rocks cut into her shins but she didn't feel it. She watched Elijah move closer to the lake, but she could no longer see her husband's shape by the water.

Feeling came back to her legs. First pain, then the warmth of blood as it crawled on her skin. She stood up and stumbled to the tent, felt around in the dark until her fingers touched the rifle. Then she ran outside and screamed with all her strength.

"Jeremiah, he's coming!"

28

THE MOON SHONE DOWN LIKE a blind eye. The light reflected off the lake and made the world a hazy dark blue. Warring thoughts clashed in Elijah's head as he approached the water. Two voices, one he knew and one he did not, struggled against each other.

One voice said: He is your brother, reason with him and leave this mountain.

The other voice said: He has always had everything you wanted. You deserve this one thing and all that follows.

The figure he had seen from the campsite was gone. The corpse by the water looked like nothing more than a pile of sticks and rags in the pale light. Griffin's son. Left here to rot while the father ran away with a terrible gift, but he ended up with nothing at all.

Elijah didn't want to do it, but he wanted the gift more than he had ever wanted anything and he did not understand why. The desire was a red-hot coal inside his chest and it ignited every other thought in him, turned it to ashes. Even then, he could not imagine life without his brother. He couldn't see any future without Jeremiah in it.

He walked closer to the tree stump, stopped and tried to think of what was missing. Grass moved in the stillness, a small sound made loud by the quiet.

Where was the metal bowl?

The corpse by the lakeside shivered and moved. Elijah stood paralyzed as the bones of the arms lifted. The legs pulled in and the rotted skeleton began to rise. It stood slowly, trembling, and staggered toward him. The gaping holes of its eyes lunged closer, tangles of hair swinging. The stench of rotten flesh filled Elijah's nostrils. He jumped back and opened his mouth to scream but the sound caught in his throat.

The skull fell forward, jawbone hanging open. The whole corpse collapsed to the ground and Elijah found himself looking into the hardened face of his brother, the skeleton a disintegrated pile at his feet. Their eyes locked for one moment, then Jeremiah swung his arm and smashed the metal bowl into Elijah's face.

A bright light exploded in Elijah's vision, something popped behind his eye and his mouth filled with blood. He went sideways, falling, and crashed into the grass. He blinked rapidly to clear away the light. A metallic ringing, the sound of a blacksmith's hammer striking a blow, echoed endlessly.

Weight pressed into Elijah's chest and pushed the breath out of him. Jeremiah's knees fell on either side of his head, pinning him down. Elijah put up his hands to protect his face as Jeremiah threw punches that slammed into Elijah's fingers and numbed them.

Elijah scrambled backward and lashed out with a kick that cracked Jeremiah's cheekbone. He fell back and knelt on all fours, groaning.

"Don't do this, brother," Elijah said, panting.

Jeremiah raised his eyes, blood ran down his chin. "And let you take everything?"

"I don't want this. I don't want anything."

Jeremiah stood on shaking legs. "You've always wanted everything I earned. You wanted Emma from the first day you met her."

Elijah spit out a mouthful of blood. "We have to leave. This place is twisting our thoughts."

"I will not allow you to take what's mine," Jeremiah said. "I've already lost too much."

Elijah waved an arm at the campsite, the cave. "There's nothing but death here. It's not worth it. I don't want the gold—"

"You only want what it can get you," Jeremiah hissed.

He crouched low and ran straight at Elijah, ramming his head into Elijah's gut. They both fell to the ground and Jeremiah landed one hard blow on his brother's ear. Elijah moaned as the sound of rushing water filled his head. Hands grabbed his shirt and pulled his head off the ground.

"Stop," Elijah said. "Listen to me." He thrashed as hard as he could, throwing his body in every direction, but Jeremiah stayed locked above him, keeping Elijah's fists from hitting him.

They had moved closer to the lake and the ground was now damp.

"Jeremiah, I'm your brother," Elijah yelled. "Don't do this."

Jeremiah pulled Elijah's arms to the side and smashed the top of his head into the man's face. Jeremiah felt Elijah's nose collapse and blood came pouring out of his nostrils. Elijah screamed in pain but he kept fighting, inching them closer to the water.

He kicked again and again, trying to knee his brother in the back, trying to throw him off balance. But Jeremiah was too strong and Elijah was too wounded. In one swift motion, Jeremiah moved Elijah's arms so they were pinned under his knees, which gave him enough time to let go and grab Elijah's throat with both hands and squeeze.

Emma walked across the field, gun at her side. She heard the men shouting, heard the smack of skin against bone. She moved as if in a dream, getting closer until she could see her husband kneeling over Elijah.

The moon hung above them, a pale spotlight that shone down on the two brothers as they fought. Emma stopped and raised the gun, closed one eye and trained her sight on Jeremiah. She could pull the trigger and end the battle, save Elijah's life.

She moved the barrel of the gun until it came to rest on Elijah. He was on the bottom now, but there was a chance he could find the strength to fight back harder and overpower his brother.

The gun moved back and forth between the two men.

Or she could kill them both, be rid of them and their jealousy, their violence.

But she knew, deep down, she could never kill Jeremiah. Sometimes when his features softened and the skin around his eyes was not creased with pain, Emma saw glimpses of Samuel in him and she could not erase that last connection to her son.

She lowered the gun.

The back of Elijah's head slipped into the lake, and Jeremiah pushed him further down until he knelt in the water. Elijah hit the side of Jeremiah's face, beating at his back and chest with frail blows. Jeremiah squeezed even harder and forced his brother's head back down. Elijah still thrashed, but his movements grew weaker. Jeremiah loosened his grip for just a moment, long enough for Elijah to lift his head and take a gasp of air.

"Don't do this," he said, coughing weakly. "Don't do this."

"You would have done the same to me," Jeremiah said, and pressed his thumbs into his brother's throat, shoving him back under the dark water and holding him there until Elijah stopped hitting, stopped thrashing.

His eyes were wide open, staring up through the water. His body spasmed once, twice, then went still. Jeremiah lifted his hands and Elijah's body stayed where it was. His arms floated uselessly, his hair waved in the water, his face swollen and strange.

Jeremiah put his hand on his brother's chest and willed the flesh to become something else, but it didn't change. Jeremiah looked at his hand with confusion. He had followed the ritual, so why wasn't it working? He tried again, touching Elijah's body in different places, but it still stayed the same. He clenched his hand into a fist and hit Elijah's arm, his leg. Water splashed as he struck the lifeless body again and again.

Jeremiah stopped to catch his breath. He sensed a presence behind him and turned to see the wolf standing on the shore.

A low voice spoke inside his head. THE MAP. THE PICTURE.

Jeremiah closed his eyes and tried to visualize the scribbled map that led them to this place. His closed eyes moved over the paper, remembering each detail. Then he saw it. The glowing hand that hung above the drawing of the kneeling body. The trigger and middle fingers pointing straight up, crossed. The other two fingers bent to the palm, and the thumb folded over the palm to touch the two bent fingers.

Jeremiah made this motion with his own hand, then reached down and touched Elijah on the leg with his two straight fingers.

Elijah's leg began to glow with a deep orange light. It spread slowly down the leg and up Elijah's chest, leaving a solid, shimmering surface. Jeremiah kept his fingers pressed down, eyes burning at the brightness. The change kept moving up Elijah's neck, over his face, freezing his features—eyes still open, mouth agape—and into his hair, which became rigid.

When the glow covered Elijah's body completely, there was a sound like something heavy being dropped onto the dirt, and a cloud of dust exploded from the motionless body. It hung in the air for a moment—a ghost shape of Elijah made of dust. The particles drifted down, fell over Jeremiah, and floated on the surface of the water.

The metal statue sank beneath the water and settled into the mud. Elijah's face, frozen in fear and pain, stared up through the rippling water.

Jeremiah scrambled backward to the shore. His chest ached and his eyes burned. A sharp pain stabbed at his gut. He couldn't breathe right. Jeremiah put his hands to his face and a whimper came out of him.

Elijah, his brother.

Even when Elijah was traveling, Jeremiah knew he was out there somewhere in the world and it was only a matter of time before he saw him again. Now he was nowhere and there was a dark empty space in Jeremiah's mind where his brother had been, and the guilt was a red hot stone that tore through his insides.

He lifted his hand and looked at it in the moonlight. The two fingers he had crossed and used to transform his brother were the same gold color as the statue under water. It looked as though he had dipped the two fingers into melted gold, and it hardened on his skin. He grabbed hold of his shirt and tried to wipe it off, still his fingers remained marked.

He stared at the lake and saw his brother's shape, shimmering golden in the moonlight.

I've created another hole in the world, he thought. *Another empty space. A monument that will still be here long after I'm dead and gone.*

PART II
THE CASTLE

29

THE SOUND OF HAMMERS AND saws had echoed from the field outside town for the last seven months. A small army worked from sunup to sundown—a crew brought in from the nearby town of Ashville—and slept in rows of tents on the property.

The house in the field was gone, and in its place a castle had risen, built of dark stone. At first, it was just a large home, but the construction never stopped. The home continued to grow until it spread east and west toward the edge of the forest that encircled the valley. Then two additional wings were added that stretched to the north.

Scaffolding rose into the sky at the center of the courtyard, a giant tower built of stone so dark it always looked wet. Once construction on the tower was complete, a third north wing would be added to close off the entire structure, making it a giant square with a tower rising out of the middle, like a finger inside a ring.

At first, the town was unsure what to make of the endless construction, but Jeremiah hired local men to build a new schoolhouse and jail. He also funded repairs to all of the buildings along the main street and the boardwalk. Roofs were patched and repaired. Doors and signs were repainted. Even the windows that shattered during an especially bad storm were replaced. A flower garden was planted in the town square, and a new fence was built around the blackened skeleton of the oak tree.

Over the seven months the castle was constructed, the town of Charwood looked as though it were aging backward until even those who had lived there their entire lives believed it had never looked better.

The church was the only building in town that remained untouched by Jeremiah's funds. The white paint continued to peel off the siding, and the bell that hung in the steeple darkened.

Inside the castle, a woman wandered up and down long, dark hallways, her footsteps echoing all around her. The fabric of her dress, imported from Italy and ordered from New York, swished about her legs. A hundred other dresses, all expensive and made of the finest materials, were stored in a large wardrobe in the bedroom she shared with her husband, who she was looking for now.

Five floors up, she walked along the north hall of the west wing, past countless empty rooms. She paused at one open doorway, looked in, and watched rain patter against the windows. The masons would not work on the tower today, not with the rain.

She moved on, and a thought formed in her mind as she did. It was not the first time this thought had materialized, and every time it happened, she did her best to snuff it out like a candle before it could become bright. But this time it caught her off guard, and that was all it took for the thought to flicker into existence.

The echo of a child's footsteps running up and down the halls, the stairs. Such a massive house, so many rooms, so many places for a little boy to have adventures.

It did not hurt like it used to, but it did not hurt less. Just differently.

Emma swallowed hard and resumed walking.

She knew the castle was far too big and extravagant, but that was the point. She wanted it to be something the town could not ignore. Whenever travelers pass through, they ask, "Who lives there?" And the townspeople would have to tell them.

The richest couple in the biggest home.

The ones who made this town beautiful again. The ones who gave so much.

Whenever Emma went into town, she kept her head up and smiled at everyone she saw. She could sometimes feel the stares of the other women, and Emma knew they were envious of her dresses, shoes, jewelry, and even her hair. Those women who had scorned her and talked behind her back now watched with looks of jealousy they could not hide.

It made Emma feel better, but not as much as she had hoped. When she went back to her home, her "fortress," as Jeremiah called it, she was alone. Jeremiah was often busy overseeing the construction or locked away reading a new shipment of books, and she had no friends except Abigail Fletcher, who worked as both cook and maid. But the girl was young, more like a daughter than a friend. Emma hired her because they needed someone to handle the business of the house, but also to get the young woman away from her drunken parents, and her father who was known to whore her out.

So Emma wandered the halls in her fine clothes, trying to tell herself that once the house was finished, things would change.

She came to a large room halfway down and went inside. She crossed to the far wall, where a framed painting of an elk hung. The picture was nearly as tall as Emma, the frame thick and gilded with flowers and vines. It was a gift from Mayor Haskins for the many contributions the Pevensies had made to the town.

She gripped the edge of the frame and pulled until a portion of the wall swung away to reveal a door. She had only been inside twice, when Jeremiah invited her. She did not quite understand why he needed such a room, all it held were books, scrolls, and artifacts from long-dead civilizations. Objects and manuscripts he had ordered from various sellers in New York and San Francisco. A secret library no one else was allowed to see.

Emma pulled on the door handle, but it was locked. A bright glow came from the gap under the door. She knocked once, waited, then put her ear to the wood and listened. A faint hum came from the other side. She knocked again and said Jeremiah's name. No response.

In their old house, each knew where the other was at all times, but now, she rarely saw her husband. There were so many rooms, so many places to be alone.

She missed Jeremiah. Three months earlier, he had taken a trip to San Francisco for "research," and she'd hardly seen him since he returned. He spent most of his time in this secret room. She pulled on the door and felt the deadbolt catch.

She hated locked rooms.

If Jeremiah were in there, he would have answered, so he must have gone into town.

Emma went over to the window and put her fingers on the glass, watching as clear beads of water slid across the surface. She looked out at the field, the rows of tents shuddering in the wind and rain.

Her eyes moved over the muddy field and dead grass until they came to rest on something that made her stop breathing. Her fingers pressed harder into the glass. When she finally gasped for breath, her heart thudded against her ribs.

30

IT WAS DARK BY THE time the rain stopped, and Jeremiah began his trek back from town to his home. A single light shone from the study window at the front of the castle. The other windows were dark. Torn grey clouds drifted across the sky, and a pale sliver of moon hung like the blade of an axe.

His boots sloshed through the mud as he approached the tent city, where many construction crews gathered around the fire after work to talk and play cards. Their conversations and laughter carried on the air.

The talk died down as the men became aware of Jeremiah making his way between the tents, carrying a jug of whiskey in each gloved hand. When he came into the light of the fire, it was silent. Two poker games were in progress, but the players sat motionless, holding their cards. Cigar smoke drifted in small clouds.

Garrett, the foreman, sat on a log near the fire, his mutt curled in the mud at his feet. Garrett took the pipe from his mouth and stood when he saw Jeremiah, touched the brim of his hat with one hand, and nodded.

Jeremiah handed one whiskey jug to Garrett and the other to a man whittling a piece of wood into an animal shape. "I thought you all could use a little something to help warm you up," he said.

The men raised a quiet cheer. A few got up and collected whatever mugs and cups they could find.

"Thank you, sir," Garrett said. "Much obliged."

Jeremiah nodded but looked distracted. His eyes were set on the castle, on the dark silhouette of the fortress he had built. Even though he knew it was monstrous, it was what Emma wanted. She had studied books with pictures of European castles, and they interviewed a dozen architects before they found one who could draw what Emma saw when she closed her eyes. A structure telegraphed from a nightmare. She said it comforted her, the size of it, the foreboding nature of it, even the darkness of it.

"It's something, isn't it?" Jeremiah said.

Garrett followed his gaze. "It is indeed."

He had never seen anything like it. Not even close. If he wasn't building it, he could easily believe that a monster, or a madman, lived there. Even though Garrett didn't know Emma very well, in fact, he had only spoken with her a few times, he recognized her grief as surely as if it were painted on her face. A heaviness, a weight that she dragged around with her. This house, if it could be called that, was an external structure built to mirror the house that grief had built inside her heart.

"Everything is on schedule," Garrett said. "Even the rainy days haven't set us back too much."

Jeremiah kept looking at the castle. "I don't know that it will ever end."

"What do you mean?" Garrett asked. He handed the whiskey jug to a man who poured generous helpings into cups.

"She talks about making it higher," Jeremiah said. "Adding more towers. In her mind, it just keeps growing."

Garrett tried to imagine the castle any larger than it already was. As it stood, it already took up most of the field. The only directions it could grow were north and south, but by then it would stop being a house, or even a castle, and become a town unto itself.

Jeremiah's gaze moved along the jagged spires. "She says it helps, this constantly growing thing."

Garrett grabbed one of the cups and gave it to Jeremiah, then picked one up for himself. They clinked the cups together and drank.

Garrett swallowed and sucked at his teeth. "That's strong enough to melt steel."

Jeremiah laughed.

Garrett took out his tobacco pouch and shoved some of the leaf into the bowl of his pipe.

He said, "I once knew a man and his wife who lost a child. A boy. Seven, I think he was. Seven or eight. Anyway, the woman never could be okay with what happened. You see, it was just a stupid accident. Boy went down to the creek, slipped on a moss-covered rock, and hit his head. He fell asleep that night and never woke up."

Jeremiah took another drink while Garrett lit his pipe. The dog stood, stretched, and rubbed against Garrett's leg.

"Wasn't nobody's fault," Garrett said, "just bad luck is all. But the woman thought it was God, her husband, the world. She started burning things a few months after. Little things at first. The boy's clothes. His toys. Then she started dragging their furniture outside and setting it on fire. She'd watch the whole time the thing burned, whatever it was. Had this look in her eyes like she was punishing someone or something."

Garrett glanced over at the house. "The husband didn't know what to do, thought his wife had gone crazy, but what could he do? The man had to work. He couldn't just sit around all day and make sure she didn't burn things. Well, one day she broke a lantern on the floor of the house, and all that oil running between the boards gave her an idea. She threw a match and watched the whole house go up in the flames. Must have given her a thrill because next thing you know, she's going from house to house all over town, setting fires."

Garrett's hand rubbed the dog between the ears. Its tail thumped contentedly. "Most of the town had caught fire before anyone realized why it was happening."

Garrett looked into Jeremiah's eyes and then nodded toward the castle. "What I'm saying is, when you lost something you thought couldn't be lost, building something seems like a better choice."

Jeremiah's brow creased as he stared at the massive stone structure before him. What Emma had created was certainly not beautiful. The castle, which Jeremiah thought of as a "fortress," was austere and frightening, like something out of a child's fantasy book—a place where a dark and evil queen dwelled.

And sometimes, when Jeremiah lay awake at night, he heard the voice of the wolf whisper in his thoughts. A WORLD WITHIN THE WORLD.

And he knew that Emma was not building a way out of her pain, she was building a space for it to exist, to keep it alive. A place where she was both prisoner and jailer, a fortress where nothing could get in—not death, not the dark…and not even the light.

31

JEREMIAH KNEW ABIGAIL WOULD HAVE already gone home, so if he wanted something to eat, he'd have to make it himself. He didn't have much of an appetite these days, anyway. Emma was probably asleep by now. That was one good thing about the construction. She spent so much time poring over drawings and meeting with Garrett that her mind was exhausted by the time night fell.

A part of him wanted to go to her, get into bed, and wrap his arms around her, but even more than that, he wanted to be in his secret room.

He walked down the corridor to the west wing. Even the lanterns on the walls could barely fight the darkness that filled the space. The shadows and contours on the stone made him think the walls were made of liquid.

A small fire was dying in the great room of the west wing, but Jeremiah didn't stay there long. He made his way to the staircase and climbed, his hand trailing along the smooth wooden banister.

If he was honest with himself, Jeremiah was not even sure why he had the secret room built. It was as if his mind knew he would need it before the rest of him did. Now, it was where he spent most of his time. He knew it bothered Emma, but what he was preparing would make her forget her anger.

He paused on the third-floor landing and looked down the hall. There was no light except what little moonlight fell through the windows and cast pale rectangles on the narrow carpet.

So many empty rooms.

He continued climbing.

When Jeremiah reached the fifth floor, his heart thumped heavily, and his breathing was loud. He paused for a moment, swallowed hard, and walked to the large room where his other room was hidden.

He made it halfway to the wall when a figure stepped out of the shadows in the corner. Jeremiah jumped back, his heart galloping like he had just climbed twice as many stairs.

The figure came forward into the moonlight that poured through the window, making its skin seem to glow. A stained dress hung limply around its thin frame. Hair curled around the face, and the eyes were set deep in shadow.

It took Jeremiah several breaths to recognize his wife.

Jeremiah took a step toward her. "Emma?"

She stared at him and lifted a finger. Dirt was underneath the nail. She pointed at the wall with the hidden room.

"What's in there?" Her voice was hoarse, deeper. Her dress was soaked through and muddy.

Jeremiah stopped moving. "I don't understand."

Her voice grew louder. "I want to know what's in that room." Emma stepped out of the moonlight and into the shadow. She seemed to age right before his eyes. The lines on her face filled with dark, and her eyes shone like an animal's. "What are you hiding from me?"

Jeremiah's heart sank. He was not ready, but he had no choice. If he didn't, she would break the door down and see for herself. "Darling," he said. "Give me more time, please."

"Show me," she said again, and this time, her voice sounded broken, close to tears.

Jeremiah's hands lifted. He wanted to pull her close and tell her that he had a plan, a way out of the dark. But he knew she wouldn't listen until she got into that room. She wanted what she wanted, and nothing else would do.

He sighed, let his hands drop, and walked over to the far wall, her footsteps behind him the whole way. He grabbed the framed painting and pulled the wall open. From under his shirt, he pulled out a key that hung from a leather necklace. He put the key into the lock.

He wanted to say something before he took her inside, but he couldn't think of anything worth saying. He turned the key and pushed open the door to his hidden room.

The room behind the wall was about half the size of the room they had just left. It was completely dark and windowless. He took down a lantern from a nearby shelf and lit it. Emma stood beside him, her hair and makeup ruined, her dress mud-splattered and wrinkled. Her eyes were so wide that it unnerved him to look at her.

The lantern illuminated walls full of shelves containing leather-bound books and scrolls. The air was musty, but there was also a sharp, metallic odor. Strange stone artifacts filled some shelves. Weapons that appeared to be made of bone, others of jade.

Jeremiah led her toward the center of the room, carrying the lantern before him. The light bounced off several objects on the floor in front of the shelves—a bright yellowish light that reminded her of the men on the mountaintop, the statues, and Elijah on the lake bottom.

There was some sort of energy in the room, Emma could feel it crackle in the air, the way she felt lightning before it struck. She looked past her husband to a table in front of the fireplace. Something lay on top of it, covered with a sheet. Emma walked closer.

Her shadow fell on top of the sheet, a dark shape against the white. Jeremiah came up behind her and set the lantern down. The sound of Emma's breathing filled the room. Each inhale like wind over a cave, each exhale a trembling sigh.

Jeremiah grabbed the sheet, looked at his wife, and said, "This is for you." Then he gently folded the cloth back. The lantern light hit the object on the table and broke apart. It rippled along the ceiling.

Emma's hands went to her face, covered her mouth as she sucked in a shallow breath. Her fingers crawled up her cheeks, around her eyes, across the wrinkles in her forehead, and threaded into her hair.

"What have you done?"

32

SAN FRANCISCO (THREE MONTHS EARLIER)

Jeremiah arrived in the city by coach and had the driver take him straight to a hotel in the heart of the city. He had come to the city only one other time, years ago, to speak with Reverend Kerry not long after he'd taken over as the church pastor in Charwood. That seemed like another lifetime, lived by another person, and the city looked far more populated and chaotic than when he'd last visited.

The windows of the fourth-floor room looked out over the bay. Jeremiah drank a glass of whiskey and watched a dozen or more ships moving through the harbor. From this distance, the ships looked small enough to fit in the palm of his hand. Fog rolled in over the water, wrapped itself around the masts and sails like fingers, making them look like ghost ships that slipped in and out of existence.

He opened the window and smelled the salt-tinted breeze, fluttering through the curtains. Voices carried from below as people moved in tight crowds. There were more people on the street than in all of Charwood. He heard the distinct patter of other languages, a foreign and musical sound, voices like instruments, and he wished he knew what the sounds meant.

He finished the whiskey, put on his hat and gloves, and went downstairs. At the front desk, Jeremiah asked a young man in a suit, hair greased with a harsh part in the center, how to get to the library. He memorized the directions, then went out into the street, to the bustle of bodies and voices. Coaches and carriages rattled past, leaving long grooves in the mud.

He shouldered his way through a crowd of Chinese and smelled the strange odor of their pipe smoke. Long braids hung down their backs. One of them held out a hand and showed him a piece of silver, asked a question Jeremiah could not understand. Jeremiah shook his head and kept walking. The man's voice followed him until he turned a corner.

He walked past taverns and restaurants. The smell of cooking made his stomach ache, but he wouldn't stop. Not yet. He saw trash piles overrun with rats in the narrow alleys between brick buildings. In one, a man lay on the ground, groaning, blood leaking from his mouth. Jeremiah clenched his right hand. The leather glove creaked with the motion.

He was not afraid. He knew he could easily kill anyone who tried to attack him and take his money. But the strangeness of the city, its hostility, made the muscles in his shoulders tense. Too much was happening all at once, and he could not keep track of everything around him.

Finally, the library came into view. A large building with stone pillars. Jeremiah walked up the steps, marveling at the giant columns supporting the entryway. Inside, he found a man behind a desk writing in a ledger.

The man looked up when Jeremiah approached. "May I help you, sir?"

Jeremiah took off his hat. "I'm looking for books about the ancient civilizations of Latin America."

The man raised his eyebrows. "Anywhere in particular?"

Jeremiah shook his head. The man sighed and closed the ledger. "Well, that doesn't help us narrow it down. There were many cultures, now vanished, scattered throughout the region."

"I'm looking for the oldest."

The man rose and stood very straight. Everything about him seemed stiff and proper. His face had few wrinkles, but his hairline had receded and gone grey.

"That would be the Maya," he said. He came around the desk and beckoned with one finger. "Follow me."

Jeremiah followed the man down aisles of tall bookshelves. Their boots clacked on the tiled floors and echoed. The librarian led Jeremiah to a winding staircase, and they ascended to the second floor. They turned down one aisle, and the man held out a finger, ran it along the spines, and spoke under his breath. He stopped and tapped a thick brown book, took it down, and handed it to Jeremiah.

"This may have what you want. It was written by an explorer, one of the first to document the ruins of Mayan civilization," the man said. "There is a table over there. You may leave the book when you're finished. I will be downstairs if you need me."

Jeremiah carried the large volume over to the table and opened it. He read until his eyes burned and his vision grew blurry, then he skipped forward several chapters and skimmed the words.

The book was mostly self-serving and unbelievable. This explorer, whoever he had been, was more concerned with the tales of his adventures, most of which painted him as a hero surrounded by weak-minded and faithless underlings, than he was about the actual history of the Mayan people. By the time he reached the ancient cities, Jeremiah did not believe most of the explorer's conclusions about the culture, its people, or their rituals.

Jeremiah slammed the book shut and rubbed his eyes. He heard a light cough and looked up to find the librarian standing in front of him.

"Not what you were looking for?" the man asked.

"I don't know what I'm looking for."

The man reached for the book, picked it up gently, glanced at Jeremiah, and cradled it as though it were an infant.

"Much of it is guesswork," the librarian said. "How they lived, what they believed. Unfortunately, there is much we don't understand about them."

"Is there anything else?" Jeremiah asked, looking at the rows of books on either side of him.

"Not here," the librarian said. His eyes held Jeremiah's for a moment. "You may find something more at Abernathy's Books. You're obviously not from here. I can draw you a map if you'd like."

The man re-shelved the book, and Jeremiah followed him down the staircase to the front desk. The librarian took a piece of paper and drew a picture of the streets with an arrow pointing to a place several blocks west.

"If he's there, tell Abernathy I sent you. He's a prickly old fool, but he makes a living selling the kinds of books of which only one copy is made."

"Why would there only be one copy?"

The librarian raised his eyebrows. "Because they are books which contain information only certain types of people need to know. Books that aren't created to be read, but rather to contain secrets. Treasure chests, if you will. Often locked with language that must be decoded, and the material within them is…questionable to most, fascinating to others. But if you seek information that cannot be found here, Abernathy either has it, or has read it."

Jeremiah took the map from the librarian, thanked him, and went back outside to join the surging crowd.

33

A BELL JINGLED WHEN JEREMIAH opened the door to Abernathy's. The shop was small and made smaller by the towers of books that lined the walls. A narrow staircase, lined with stacks of books, went up into darkness. Books were piled along the railing of the balcony above him. The smell of dust and old paper drifted through the air.

The dark shop was lit by only two lanterns—one on a table between two high-backed chairs, and the other on a desk near the back of the store. An old man sat at the desk, his bald head covered in dark spots, the shapes of spilled liquid. Three books lay open in front of him. The man's gnarled fingers gripped the nub of a pencil and scratched out illegible words in a notebook. He did not look up.

"The shop is closed," the old man said in a raspy voice. His other hand held open one of the books, blue veins roped beneath the skin.

Jeremiah unbuttoned his coat and took out the journal he kept in the pocket. He opened it and set it down in front of the old man.

"I couldn't find what I was looking for at the library," Jeremiah said. "The librarian sent me here, said you might be able to help me."

The bony fingers that held open the book moved slowly to the journal. A yellow fingernail traced the symbols written there. The old head lifted. Cloudy eyes looked at Jeremiah from above, a pair of spectacles perched on a crooked nose. White hairs sprouted from the ears.

"Where did you get this?" The man's voice creaked.

"It's mine. I didn't get it from anywhere."

The old man's Adam's apple bobbed up and down a few times. His glasses were smudged and dirty. He let go of the pencil and closed the notebook.

"I can't help you," the man said. "Like I said, the shop is closed."

"The door was unlocked," Jeremiah said.

The old man's eyes were large and blue behind his glasses.

"I forgot to lock it," he said, moving one hand slowly to his lap. His eyes stayed locked on Jeremiah's. "Try Cartwright's," the man said, a little out of breath.

"The librarian sent me to you."

The old man moved fast. His hand shot under the desk and came back up holding a pistol, the barrel shaking as he tried to aim. Jeremiah threw himself across the desk, scattering books and papers to the floor, and grabbed the old man's arm with one hand. Jeremiah felt the bones of the man's wrist grind together under the pressure. With his other hand, Jeremiah pulled out his own gun and had it against the man's temple before he could even rise from his chair.

Jeremiah squeezed tighter and twisted the old man's wrist until the gun dropped to the desk, then Jeremiah let go and snatched it up, took a step back while keeping both barrels trained on the man's head.

Anger filled the old man's eyes. "You said I could have more time," he said. "I'm not finished yet. You have to let me finish."

He buried his face in his hands. A hacking sound came from the old man's throat. When he spoke again, his voice was even more hoarse. "I'm so close. Please, just let me finish."

The man took a handkerchief from his vest pocket and wiped his mouth. The cloth came away stained with a bright red smear.

Jeremiah backed away, still holding the guns on the man, until he reached the door. He turned the key in the door to lock it and pulled the shade down over the window. He put his own gun back in his waistband and kept the other gun pointed at the old man.

"I'm not whoever you think I am," Jeremiah said. "I'm just looking for information."

The old man eyed him as Jeremiah walked back across the room. One curled finger tapped the journal. "Where did you get this book?" he asked.

"I told you already, it's mine."

"Do you know what these symbols mean?" he asked.

"I want to know where they come from," Jeremiah said.

The old man coughed again into his fist, a sound like a distant ax against the bark of a wet tree. His hand came away wet with blood. "That's not what I asked," the man said.

"I know what some of them mean."

"Then you know they are terrible instructions. A whole language created to describe death."

"Who did you think was coming?"

The old man ignored him and continued tracing the symbols in the journal. "Did you copy these from a book, or did you find them written in stone?"

"I found them on the wall of a cave," Jeremiah said.

The old man looked up again, his milky eyes wide. Silver whiskers covered his chin.

"Was this cave at the top of a mountain?"

"I was told you'd be able to help me."

The old man waved his twisted fingers. "Was it at the top of a mountain?" he almost yelled.

Jeremiah reached for the journal, but the old man snatched it up before he could. "Some of these I've never seen before," he said. "I knew they were out there, I just didn't think I'd live to see them."

He coughed again but made no motion to cover his mouth. "Tell me, please. Were they at the top of a mountain?" The man's voice grew softer, and his breath wheezed out of him.

"They were," Jeremiah said.

The old man lowered the journal and looked again at the symbols. Then he set the book down and took off his glasses. He closed his eyes for a long time, and when he opened them again, red veins were glowing in the cloudy white.

"You aren't the first," the old man said. "Someone else has been asking about these."

34

THE OLD MAN CLOSED THE journal, replaced his glasses, and stood with a groan. "I think I'd like a drink." He came around from behind the desk and shuffled to the front of the shop. Jeremiah followed him with the gun. The man was hunched over, his spine a crooked line of bumps under his coat. He winced with each step.

He shuffled to one of the high-backed chairs and collapsed into it with a wheeze, clutching his injured wrist to his chest. A small cloud of dust puffed up from the cushion. He motioned to the other chair, and Jeremiah sat down.

"I'd offer you tea, but I'm out of water," the old man said, reaching under the chair and pulling out a bottle. "And I think you broke my goddamn hand."

"Are you Abernathy?"

The old man nodded, uncorked the bottle, and took a long drink. "Though not for much longer, I'm afraid." He looked around the room, at the enormous piles of books leaning precariously. "One day, that front door will not be unlocked. People will walk by unaware that just inside is a dead old man. By the time I'm found, my body will be stiff and my skin will be dust on the floor."

Abernathy shifted his weight in the chair and stifled a cough in his fist. "All these books will be auctioned off, and my life, such as it is, will be forgotten." He handed the bottle to Jeremiah and said, "I've been thinking about death a lot these days. Far more than is healthy."

A thin line of bright blood ran down from the mouth of the bottle. Jeremiah handed it back without taking a drink.

Abernathy squinted over his glasses at Jeremiah. "What is it you're looking for?"

"I want to know where these symbols came from. Who created them."

The old man's eyes narrowed, his lips puckered as if tasting something sour.

"Why?"

"I'm curious," Jeremiah said.

One side of Abernathy's mouth curled in a grim smile. "I'm no fool, boy. This is more than curiosity." Looking now through the glasses, the cloudy eyes fell to Jeremiah's gloved right hand.

Jeremiah suddenly wanted to hide his hand, slip it inside his coat. The old man's eyes moved to the desk, to a series of wooden crates along the back wall. "It's all in there. Everything I know came from those books."

Jeremiah was no longer worried about Abernathy leaving, so he went to the crates. Each was filled with old volumes, stacked up and surrounded by sawdust. The covers were made of worn leather, reddish-brown, and creased.

Abernathy took another pull from the bottle while Jeremiah put the gun on the desk, picked up a book, and opened it. Certain words seemed to glow as his eyes scanned the pages. The book told of a massive city deep within the jungle and of a mysterious man who appeared one day and demanded to be worshipped. The man performed miracles and resurrections, things that were thought to be impossible.

Much of what Jeremiah saw fit with the story the symbols from the cave told, but what made the skin tingle like spider legs walking down his neck was the fact that the book was written in first person, seemingly by someone who had been alive at the time, or someone who was pretending to be. It didn't make sense, though. Several lines spoke of golden people walking around the city.

"Your journal, those symbols, aren't a complete history, you understand?" Abernathy said.

Jeremiah took another book out of the crate. The pages, stiff and yellow, crackled as he turned them. A dictionary of some kind. Drawn symbols along with their meaning. He recognized some of them but not others.

"Where did you get these?" Jeremiah asked.

Abernathy held the bottle to the light to see how much whiskey was left. "There's a house east of here, in a valley near a lake. Do you know it? A great stone house, one side covered in moss. It once belonged to the Burkes, a cursed family if there ever was one. The last remaining Burkes, Nathaniel and his young son Christopher, disappeared several years ago, and their estate was sold to pay off various debts. Nathaniel had been a collector of things rare and unusual, and after he vanished, I was asked to come and assess his collection, which I then bought. These books were among those I purchased."

Jeremiah dug out more books, some older than others. "Have you read them all?"

"Every word," Abernathy said, and wiped the blood off the bottle with his sleeve.

Jeremiah opened one book to a page that showed a large map of the states and territories. He counted six points marked with bold Xs, places where symbols from this culture had been found. "When I came into the shop, who were you expecting?"

Abernathy sighed. Breath rattled in his throat. "There's a man, goes by the name Solomon Anders. He wrote me a letter, said he knew I had bought the book collection, and he wanted several of the volumes. Sent a piece of gold as proof that he could pay whatever I asked. I wrote back and told him the books weren't for sale. Sent the gold back, too, though it pained me to do so."

Jeremiah froze when he heard the name "Solomon." His memory flashed back to what the dying man had said on the mountain, shot through the gut and lying in mud.

Solomon knows you. He'll find you. His final words before Jeremiah ended his life. Solomon. Not just a name, but a man somewhere in the world, searching for what Jeremiah had already found.

Abernathy took a long drink from the bottle, closed his eyes, and held the liquor in his mouth. He swallowed hard and shook his head back and forth.

"A few weeks later, Solomon writes back and tells me the books are his property and he will have them. I could either accept his gold and send him the books, or he would personally travel here and slit my throat, take the books, and then burn down my shop."

"And you believed he would?"

Abernathy looked down at the floor. Small droplets of his blood glistened on the wood.

"Not at first. But not long after, someone started following me. A figure in the background, always waiting in the shadows. I thought it was just coincidence at first, but I started seeing his shape everywhere I went, even here in the shop. Of course, when I opened up the shades or lit another lantern, no one was there."

His fingers tightened around the bottle. "I used to have a cat. A harmless old thing, no good at anything except keeping me company. One day I come to work and it's hanging above the desk. Its throat had been cut open, and its guts were pulled up through the hole, wrapped around its neck, and nailed to the ceiling. There's a puddle of blood all over the desk, my books."

"You're lying."

Abernathy held out the hand with the bottle and tilted it toward the desk. "Stain is still there. Look for yourself."

Jeremiah turned to the desk, brushed some paper aside, and saw it. A dark, wine-colored shape soaked into the wood. He traced the outline with a finger. A shiver gathered at his shoulder blades and inched up his back.

"If he came all the way here, why wouldn't he take the books?" Jeremiah asked.

Abernathy smiled. His teeth were rust colored from the blood. "Oh, I don't think he was here, not really."

Jeremiah looked back down at the crates. "You're sending him the books."

Abernathy nodded. "But I've been copying them down as best I can. Word for word, drawing for drawing. I've asked around, sent letters, but no one else has ever seen them. It is my belief those are the only copies."

Jeremiah put the books back into the crate and started digging through another. Slim volumes, some handwritten in ink so old it had faded to ghost words.

"Why copy them?" Jeremiah said. "You said you don't have much time left, so why bother?"

Abernathy smiled again. A fuzzy halo from the lantern hung above his white hair. "If half of what those books say is true, any man alive would search for what those people had."

"What did they have?"

The wrinkles around Abernathy's face deepened. He lifted the bottle and took a drink, then ran his tongue over his rusty teeth.

Jeremiah picked up his gun and came closer to the old man. "What did they have?"

Abernathy chuckled, an ugly, phlegmy sound. "Your journal here is just instructions. But there's more, so much more."

He sneezed, and a red mist hung in the air before gently settling onto the withered hand that held the open journal. Red dots blossomed on the pages.

Jeremiah put a hand on each arm of the chair and leaned his face close to the old man's. "I'm taking those books with me."

Abernathy's eyes grew sad and tired. "I can't stop you. But if I were you, I would hurry. You won't be unknown for long."

"When will they come?"

Abernathy swallowed the last of the whiskey and let the empty bottle roll off his lap. "Soon," he said.

"Will you tell them I was here?"

"Son, I don't know what I'll say when the time comes. It depends on how much they hurt me. Does that change your plans?"

"It might."

"If you do it, will you do it quick?"

Jeremiah nodded.

The old man's eyes closed and fluttered behind the wrinkled eyelids. "I think I've had about enough of this world. I don't know why I keep on going, keep on fighting through each day. I'm ready for whatever comes next, whether it's nothing or everything my heart has ever wanted. Take the books, the scrolls, take all of it. Just know they'll come for you. This man, this Solomon, has been searching for a long time. He'll find you."

"He may have already."

"My Celia's in the ground already, barren womb and all. I've got nothing to live for."

Jeremiah tried to remain calm, but he suddenly felt time slipping away from him, like fuel in a lantern being burned up.

"I'm going to ask one more time," he said. "What else did they have?"

Abernathy's eyes opened. He reached up and covered Jeremiah's right hand with his own. "Whatever you've lost, let it remain lost. Don't try and fix what can't be fixed. There are some things in this life that are permanent, and it's best if we accept that. Those books are a path. It looks bright at first, but they lead somewhere dark." His hand tightened on Jeremiah's. His eyes went wide, and his voice dropped to a raspy whisper. "I see the pain in you, son. It's all over your face as clear as a fresh scar. But listen to me, they want to stay where they are. They don't want to come back."

Jeremiah jerked his hand away and stood up straight. He paced in front of the chair, his heart pounding like a fist at a heavy door. His legs went weak like he had just run up a mountain. His mouth was dry, and he smelled his own sweat.

"Are you saying…" Jeremiah swallowed, then knelt so that he and Abernathy were eye to eye. "Are you saying this power can bring the dead back to life?"

35

ABERNATHY TOOK OFF HIS GLASSES, breathed on them, used his shirt to wipe the lenses, and then put them back on. His dark pupils seemed to float in milky liquid.

"I have one request," Abernathy said, "which I think you owe me, seeing as how you're stealing my property, and quite possibly my life."

Abernathy's eyes fell to Jeremiah's gloved right hand. "Will you let me see, just once?"

"I don't know what you're talking about."

Abernathy coughed and made no effort to wipe away the blood that dribbled down his chin. "I may be an old fool, but I'm not blind." He leaned forward in the chair and clasped his hands as if praying. "I'm begging you. Change me. Make the sign and transform me into something more than this flesh and blood. Let the last thing these eyes see be the world as it looks through gold."

The muscles in Jeremiah's arm twitched. The gun in his left hand suddenly felt heavier. Some part of him wanted to remove the glove and turn the old man into gold. Jeremiah wanted to see it and feel the power flowing through him. But he couldn't leave a golden statue. Not here.

"I can't," Jeremiah said. "I'm sorry."

Abernathy let his fingers unfold, and he held out his empty hands. "So you will take all I have and leave me nothing in return?"

Jeremiah's finger tightened on the trigger. "That's the way the world works," he said. "It has teeth, and it rips everything you love away from you."

Abernathy laughed. "No, that's not the world, son. Everything is temporary, but your choices determine what you keep and what is ripped away."

The old man's cloudy eyes looked into Jeremiah's, and he could not bear to see them any longer. He took a step forward, shoved the barrel of the gun against Abernathy's temple, closed his eyes, and pulled the trigger. The blast was deafening. When he opened his eyes, a cloud of grey smoke hung in the air. Blood and white matter were sprayed across the room, splattered all over stacks of books, and the floor.

Abernathy's mouth hung open, and his eyes were locked onto the ceiling. His head fell sideways against the wing of the chair. A dark stain grew in the upholstery and spread down the cushion.

Jeremiah stepped around a puddle of blood and put the gun into the old man's hand. He went upstairs, found a moth-eaten blanket, came back down, and covered Abernathy. He propped open the front door with some books, then carried each crate outside and set them in front of the window.

A man passed by, pulling an empty vegetable cart down the mostly empty street. The sky was dark. Two men, obviously drunk, stumbled their way home, oblivious to the world around them. Jeremiah talked to the cart driver and gave him a few coins to help load up the crates and take him to the hotel.

A few hours later, the books were spread out on the floor, arranged into categories as best Jeremiah could make them out. His body was tired, and he wanted to sleep, but his mind was racing like a horse at full sprint. He knew there was no way he could sleep tonight, not with all these books that held the key to some door he had not even known was there.

Jeremiah filled a glass with whiskey, picked up the first book, and started to read. He continued reading until the sky grew lighter and the sounds of the city waking up came pouring through the open window.

He read until the whiskey made his head feel light, and the room shifted whenever he turned to look out the window. When the words on the pages bled together into shapeless pools of ink, Jeremiah lay on the bed and slept.

When he woke up, the sun was going back down. He left the hotel and walked into the cool dusk until he came to a dark and quiet tavern. After sitting near the back, Jeremiah ordered beef and vegetables and ate silently while watching the people walking outside.

He tried to think about what he had read, but his thoughts were washed out, dissolved. He caught glimpses of their faint shapes hovering in his mind, but they weren't solid enough to make sense of. It reminded him of when he was young and playing warrior with Elijah. His brother had accidentally struck him in the side of the head with the tree branch he was using as a sword. The blow set off an explosion of white light that momentarily blinded Jeremiah and left him senseless. His name, age, memories, all of it dissolved into the white, and he had never felt so afraid.

Elijah.

Jeremiah put a fist to his temple and rapped the knuckles against the bone, hard.

His stomach turned at the thought of his brother.

Jeremiah felt as though the books were erasing and remaking his interior. All he could think was what they said, and he didn't know if he was more afraid of their words being true or being false.

36

JEREMIAH REMAINED IN THE HOTEL, each day a repeat of the last. He lost track of morning and night, and slept only when he was too tired to stay awake, or too drunk to make sense of the books.

By the third day, he had read through every book. Then he went back to the first and started reading them again, this time taking notes in a journal he bought one evening when he went out for dinner.

He thought of going by Abernathy's to see if the old man's body had been discovered, if the old man's prediction about his life being forgotten and all his books being auctioned off had come true. But Jeremiah didn't want to see that place again. Whenever he stopped reading, guilt snuck out of the fog of his thoughts and made his whole body ache. He told himself Abernathy was dying anyway, but it didn't help, because he knew that was true of every person.

Death is the end of all things, he thought, and the voice in his head didn't sound like him at all. It sounded like the wolf.

Every day, Jeremiah ate one meal at the same restaurant, and on the fourth day, when he ordered food, his voice sounded strange, and he realized he hadn't spoken more than a few words to another person since leaving the book shop.

By the morning of the tenth day, Jeremiah had two journals filled with notes written in feverish handwriting, often falling off the edge of the page. He'd read through all the books at least three times. There were several he went back over even more, to make sure he was not missing some important detail.

He slept most of the eleventh day, and when he awoke late afternoon to sunlight streaming through the window, Jeremiah felt some of the fog inside his head begin to lift. He packed all the books back into the crates and hammered the nails with the heel of his boot. Then he went downstairs to make arrangements for his trip back home.

37

THE COACH RUMBLED INTO THE south end of Charwood, near the courthouse and burned tree—as Jeremiah had instructed the driver—so Emma would not see him arrive. Most of what happened at the north end of town was visible from the front windows of the castle.

The crates of books filled the seat opposite him, and the floor was covered with cases of lead toy soldiers, similar to what Samuel used to play with, that Jeremiah would melt down into ingots and transform into gold. The toys rattled together with a metallic sound as the coach bounced along the outer edge of town. Orange windows glowed in the houses they passed. The town was mostly quiet, although Jeremiah heard a few voices shouting from the tavern.

The coach driver took him along the eastern line of the forest towards the castle, a dark shape with burning windows that rose up into the black sky. It had spread so far in either direction that it nearly touched the trees on either side of the valley. The white tents of Garrett's crew looked like an invading army camped outside an enemy fortress.

The coach came to a stop at the barn, and the driver jumped down and opened the door for Jeremiah. He had to crawl over the cases of lead toys to get out, and then asked the driver to carry them into one of the empty stalls in the barn.

When the job was done, Jeremiah took a small bag from his jacket pocket and shook out five coins.

"This is what we agreed on," he said, handing them to the driver. "And this," he shook out three more, "is for a room at the inn above the tavern. Get your horses fed and watered and have a drink and a meal yourself."

The driver took the coins. His mouth hung open. "Thank you, sir."

Jeremiah pointed at the town. "Go back the way you came, and quietly."

"Of course, sir."

The driver tipped back his hat and wiped sweat from his brow. He held up the hand with the coins, smiled a warped smile, and climbed into his seat. The man gently whipped the reins and drove off silently.

A fire glowed at the center of Garrett's camp, but no one was outside. The men were probably all asleep. The whole way home, it was all Jeremiah could do to stay awake, but now that he was here, he felt weak with all the energy humming inside him.

He paced the length of the barn, from one end to the other, in the dark. He tried to picture himself following through with his plan, but whenever he imagined it, his stomach twisted and he felt sick.

Jeremiah took off the gloves and wiped his sweaty hands on his pants. He felt as though his heart had turned into a rock, and it beat against his ribs so hard it was painful. As he neared the front of the barn, he saw a shovel leaning against the wall. Moonlight gleamed off the blade.

He closed his eyes and tried to remember exactly what the books said, what he could do now.

Jeremiah heard the crunch of grass, of something walking through the field, coming closer. He grabbed the shovel and held it up, ready to swing at whatever came toward him. The footsteps kept coming, gently, and then stopped. Red eyes hovered in the tall grass.

YOU KNOW NOW.

Jeremiah lowered the shovel. "What I read, is it really possible?"

FOR CENTURIES, MAN HAS ALWAYS STOPPED AT THE SURFACE OF THIS GIFT. BUT WHAT GOOD IS GOLD IF YOU ARE NO LONGER ALIVE TO USE IT?

"I don't know if I can do it," Jeremiah said.

The wolf stalked back and forth, always keeping one eye on Jeremiah.

EVERYTHING IS CIRCULAR. THERE HAD TO BE DEATH AT THE BEGINNING SO THERE CAN NOW BE LIFE. THERE IS NO BIRTH WITHOUT BLOOD. It stopped moving and stared at him. IF YOU WERE CAPABLE OF ONE, I BELIEVE YOU ARE CAPABLE OF THE OTHER.

Jeremiah's eyes burned. "I don't want to see what he's become. I want to remember how he was when he was alive."

He closed his eyes and tried to pull up a memory of Samuel vibrant and alive, but all he saw was his son's gray face, covered in beads of sweat, each breath the sound of a dog scratching at a door. His small, hoarse voice wheezed out the last words Jeremiah had ever heard him speak. "Make it stop hurting."

MAKE EVERYTHING NEW. NOTHING NEEDS TO STAY AS IT WAS. THIS IS HOW THE FUTURE IS MADE.

When Jeremiah opened his eyes, the wolf was gone, and the shovel was in his hand.

38

TO HIS RIGHT, THE HOUSE loomed above him, the dark stone cutting into the sky. To his left, the faint outlines of tents in the light of a dying fire. Jeremiah walked softly, careful not to let the shovel he carried hit the ground.

He made it to the edge of the castle and kept going out into the field. He could not see the grave in the dark, but he had walked to it so many times that he knew exactly where to go. The air was cold, and by morning, the field would be covered in frost. But for now, the ground was still damp and soft.

The sharp ends of the grass pricked Jeremiah's shins as he walked, but he didn't feel it. His breathing grew faster, heavier, as he approached the mound. He could see it now. A lump of earth covered in dead grass. He looked up at the castle, at the light burning in the bedroom window he and Emma shared. He wondered if she was asleep.

When he was in San Francisco, in the hotel, he knew what needed to be done. On the ride from the city, that knowledge became certainty. Now, standing at his son's grave, one thought kept running through his mind.

What if I'm wrong?

Could he live with himself if he didn't try?

The mound had settled with the rain and looked even smaller than he remembered.

He's there, Jeremiah thought, *just under the dirt. And I put him there. I dug this hole with my own hands and laid my son inside it. I can dig it back up.*

Abernathy's words echoed in his head: *They want to stay where they are.*

"But where are you?" Jeremiah said aloud, looking up at the clear black sky.

He took off his hat and coat, rolled up his sleeves, and stabbed the shovel into the mound.

Over time, the weakness in his arms and legs faded, and the rhythm of digging took over. The moon slid across the sky. Push the blade into the earth, heave a shovelful of dirt onto the growing pile. The temperature fell and each breath burned his lungs, but Jeremiah was hardly aware of it.

He stopped for a moment to wipe away the sweat that had cooled on his brow. He looked up at the castle, at the light in the bedroom window. Emma had not been the same since Samuel died, as if some part of her was also buried in this grave. He didn't just want to bring his son back he wanted his wife back just as much. He wanted what they used to have, in what seemed like another lifetime. Simple moments, taken for granted. Reading in front of the fire, walking through the field as it bloomed with multicolored flowers. Birdsong echoing from the forest, the world bright and alive.

Samuel.

Everything was new and pure. Laughter, smiles, voices, memories—all of it swirled together in Jeremiah's mind. He saw the world as it was and wondered if time was frozen in the places they left it, waiting for them to return to those days when life felt like a dream and pain was something distant.

There was a clear hole now, the size and shape of the one he had dug seven months ago. He stepped into it, and the dirt walls reached to his knees. He kept digging.

The light had left Emma's eyes after Samuel, and he'd hoped the house, the fortress, would bring some of it back, but she had only slipped further away from him since construction began. Jeremiah knew for certain they were not a family anymore. They were, once. Now they were just husband and wife, wandering the halls of a castle too big for them as people, but not big enough to hold all their grief. He wanted to get them back to that place, that moment in time when everything felt right. When everything *was* right.

This isn't right, Jeremiah thought.

IT ISN'T RIGHT THAT YOUR SON IS DEAD, a voice said from the field. It sounded like the wolf, but Jeremiah could not be sure he wasn't only hearing his own thoughts in response.

The pile of dirt grew larger. Jeremiah's muscles burned, but he ignored the pain and kept digging, the dirt walls now up to his chest. Sweat crawled down his back and face. The sweet smell of the damp earth filled his nose. The shovel struck something solid and vibrated with the impact. A burst of rancid air bloomed upward and hit him. Jeremiah gagged, then swallowed hard.

He told himself it wasn't the odor of his son's rotted body. It was something else, something in the earth. But the smell grew stronger as he shoveled away more dirt, and in the ghostly glow of the moon he saw a rectangle shape inside the hole.

Turning the shovel sideways, he scraped away more dirt until the outline of the coffin lid was exposed, a dark crack in the wood where the shovel had hit. The smell was stronger now, overwhelming. Jeremiah held an arm over his nose and brushed the lid clean of debris.

That stone in Jeremiah's chest beat wildly, slamming into the bones of his ribs. He knelt closer to the lid. It creaked with his weight. There was a wet snap as one of the boards cracked.

The stone grew inside him, took up too much space, and he felt like he was suffocating as he put his hands on the wood.

It wasn't too late to cover it all back up and bury Samuel again. He closed his eyes and tried to see the boy's face, find that smile, those eyes, and he knew that what he was about to do would destroy that memory. He knew that if he opened the lid, he would never again see Samuel as he was, he would only see whatever lay buried here.

But if the books were true....

If what they said could actually be done, the whole future would glow the color of gold.

Everything new, everything pure.

Jeremiah curled his fingers around the edge of the lid and pulled. The nails that held it in place groaned, but the wet dirt had weakened the wood, and they began to pull out. The odor came in a putrid wave. Jeremiah covered his mouth with a hand, stood up, and vomited onto the ground.

"Hold on," Jeremiah whispered. "Just a little longer. I'll fix this. I'll fix you, I promise."

Once the nausea passed, Jeremiah bent over again and got a better grip on the lid. He pulled until the wood broke in half, and he was looking down at his son's face. Jeremiah grabbed his stomach when he saw the boy. His throat spasmed, and he stood again to vomit, but there was nothing left in him.

He put an arm to his face and bit his shirt sleeve to stay quiet. He wept until his throat was raw and his head throbbed with blood rush.

Jeremiah didn't know how long he had been digging, but he knew he needed to fill the hole before daylight. He wiped his eyes with the back of his gloved hands. The books, he told himself, remember what the books said.

He straddled the coffin, closed his eyes so he didn't see Samuel, and tore away the rest of the lid. He threw the pieces up onto the ground and lowered himself closer. Jeremiah turned his head away as he slipped his hands under the rotted body of his son and gently lifted.

The boy was so much lighter than he had been in life. Jeremiah's eyes started burning again when he thought of everything inside his son that was now gone, decomposed into liquid at the bottom of a pine box, running in thick lines down his arms. A fresh wave of odor hit, and Jeremiah kept his head turned, breathing through his mouth.

He told himself the strange shape in his arms was not Samuel—not anymore. It was just a husk, a thing of skin, muscle, and bone—an abandoned house made of flesh that his son could return to. But this thing—it was not his son—not yet.

He set the body down on the ground and covered it with his coat. Then he shoveled dirt back into the empty grave.

An hour went by. The hole was filled in. A new mound, bigger than the old one. If Emma saw it and asked what had happened, Jeremiah knew he would lie. He would tell her he added more dirt to make it stand out again. To make it clear where their son was buried. She wouldn't want to think that coyotes had been digging in search of food, so she would believe him because she wanted to.

The sky turned a deep shade of blue. He needed to get the boy inside before it got any lighter, so he laid the shovel against the castle wall, out of sight. Then he went over and picked up Samuel's body. He focused on the books, on the words he had read. He refused to look down at the thing he carried in his arms. He was grateful his coat covered most of the body, but the legs dangled, swinging back and forth as Jeremiah walked toward the front door.

This is just a shell. Nothing more.

39

"What have you done?" Emma said.

She knew the thing on the table was her son. But it wasn't. Not really. The golden body had wasted away. The nose was mostly gone. One eye socket was just an empty hole, the other was closed. Part of his right cheek had collapsed, and his beautiful black hair was nothing but thin, hardened strands now. Large patches of his golden skull shone. The lips had rotted away, leaving a grim smile that exposed his metal teeth. Most of his arms and legs were bone, but some places glistened like fresh frost.

She felt that electricity again. She looked at his hand, and that golden frost was slowly growing, making a soft sound like melting ice. It moved up the exposed bone, and what was left behind looked like new skin, only golden and shining.

The missing parts are growing back, she thought, then she gagged.

Emma tried not to think of what he had looked like before Jeremiah changed him.

She knew the statue of her son's corpse was not her son, but Emma could not stop herself from moving in closer. One hand reached out and touched the boy's shoulder. When her fingers felt the coldness of the gold, she started crying.

"What have you done?" she said again. She looked at her husband as he stared at the small body lying motionless on the table.

"What have I done?" Jeremiah said. "This is our son, Emma. This is Samuel, your boy."

Her voice cracked. "I don't want to see him like this."

Jeremiah put his hands on her shoulders and tried to look into her eyes, but she turned away, and he felt like something had just stabbed him in the stomach.

"Look at me," he said, "please. Our family was torn apart, but I'm putting it back together again."

Whatever Samuel was, whoever he had been, it was nowhere inside this statue of a decomposed body. Emma had a memory she held onto and often visited when she had trouble sleeping. A few nights before Samuel died, she told him a story about how she had fallen into a pond while trying to pet a duck. Samuel's eyes grew bright, and he smiled at the picture of his mother splashing around in a pond wearing her best Sunday dress. That was the last time she heard him laugh. The last time she saw him smile. Every memory after that was of him in pain. Coughing up blood into a bucket they kept by his bed. His sweet face twisted in pain, covered in sweat.

Emma looked at the statue and felt this memory being pushed aside, replaced by the thing she saw in front of her. She shut her eyes tight and tried to hang onto the memory, but it was fading. All she could see was the golden body, the grotesque statue of her son, and she was repulsed.

Emma saw Jeremiah's face through the mist of her tears, and she lashed out, striking him in the face. Her nails left bloody marks on his chin. Jeremiah let her hit him again. She felt his skin rip beneath her nails, felt the slickness of blood as it dripped down his cheek. She hit him again. And again.

"Why couldn't you just leave him alone?" she said, breathless. "Why did you have to take him out?"

Her arms fell to her sides. Red lines were scored all over Jeremiah's face. A trail of blood ran around one eye.

"I can make everything new again," Jeremiah said, holding up the two golden fingers of his right hand. "Just be patient, and I can bring him back."

Emma pointed at the statue. "This isn't my son. I want it out of this house immediately."

Jeremiah looked into her eyes and stared for a long time. "This is Samuel. This is our son."

"I want it out."

A sound, like fingernails tapping against metal, came from the table. Jeremiah went around his wife and got closer. He gently stroked the boy's forehead and whispered to him. The eyelid on the golden corpse fluttered. Emma's breathing sped up and got louder. The eyelid opened halfway, then closed. Fluttered some more.

Emma's hand gripped Jeremiah's shoulder to steady herself. Her knees were giving out.

The eyelid opened all the way. A golden orb stared out, a slightly darker shade of golden in the center. The eyelid fluttered once more, then opened again, and the orb rolled in its socket until it came to rest on Emma.

It saw her, and she felt it cut through her. An icy feeling pierced her chest and left her completely breathless. Her knees buckled, and she fell to the floor. The golden eye kept staring at where she had been.

Emma sank down to all fours and tried to fill her lungs with air, but each breath was shallow and painful. Cold fire burned along her scalp. Pain. Everything hurt, and she wanted it to stop. She wanted to die.

Finally, she pulled in enough breath to scream. A broken and horrified sound that filled the small room.

40

EMMA LAY IN BED, BUT she couldn't sleep. The metallic clang of hammers chiseling stone echoed across the valley, and each blow sent a vibration through the floors and walls of the house. The rain had stopped, and the builders were putting up the final wall of the north wing that sealed off the courtyard.

The curtains were closed, but gray light still came in around the edges. She wished it was night. She wanted to sleep for days. She wanted to wake up and find Samuel back under the ground, not a golden statue inside their house.

As she lay there, Emma listened for the sound of Jeremiah's footsteps. She heard nothing except the house as it grew around her.

Each minute felt like a finger pressing down into her chest, until the weight of the hours kept her pinned to the bed, body aching and tired. She kept seeing that golden eye open and looking at her. Her chest had gone cold, like each breath was frigid air, and she knew Samuel was somewhere inside that shining corpse. Pieces of him anyway. What she saw in that eye was something partially alive. She recognized her son, but did he recognize her?

Emma started crying. She reached for a pillow, put it over her face, and screamed with all the strength she had. She screamed and cried until her throat was raw.

She told Jeremiah to get rid of it, and she meant it. Pieces of her son may be trapped inside that statue, but they were incomplete, and no matter how bad she wanted Samuel back, she wanted all of him.

There was a soft knock at the door. Emma ignored it and kept the pillow over her face. She thought of pressing it down harder until she breathed in her own hot breath and the pillowcase filled her mouth. She thought of a narrow black tunnel eating up all the light, of losing feeling in each finger, each toe. She imagined something inside her pulling away, detaching itself from her body and slipping down through the mattress to settle on the floor beneath the bed. She would break apart and slide through the walls, roaming a shadow world in search of her son. Then, together, they would find their way back to the light, if such a light even existed.

Another knock. Emma waited for whoever it was to give up and leave her alone.

Abigail's voice. "Ma'am, is everything alright? Can I get you anything?"

Emma pulled the pillow from her face and breathed in the cool air. The thought of dying did not frighten her like she thought it should. When the things that give life meaning are taken away, what use is there in continuing to hurt, to fight through each day in hopes it will get better when it never does?

"I'm fine, Abigail," Emma said.

"I could bring you some food," Abigail's voice said.

Emma thought, *Your life had meaning before Samuel. It could have meaning again. You still have your husband, and you could have another child.*

"I'm not hungry," Emma said. Even she could hear the tears and rawness in her voice.

"Are you sure, ma'am?"

Emma sat up so quickly that the room tilted sideways, and she felt dizzy. "Goddamn it, Abigail, I'm not hungry."

Silence from behind the door. A shuffle of feet.

Finally, Abigail's voice again, quieter than before. "Yes, ma'am. I'll leave you be."

Soft footsteps echoed down the hall, and Emma put her hands to her face. She felt the tears as they ran between her fingers.

Death.

She kept repeating the word in her head over and over. At first, it sounded like a curse, but as time passed, it started to sound like the name of a place, a destination she wanted to reach.

41

SHE AWOKE IN THE MIDDLE of the night to a black room and her heart pounding in her throat. It had started in a dream, the pounding, and when she opened her eyes, it kept going, thudding in time to something in the house, a faint sound and vibration.

Emma sat upright and swallowed painfully. She put a hand to her chest and held it there, pressing against a burning pain that spread up her neck.

Footsteps coming from above her, around her. A staggered rhythm that sounded like a child just learning to walk. Heavy, and with a faint metallic ring.

She put two fingers to the skin of her arm, gripped flesh between the nails, and squeezed until a tear came out of one eye. She was not dreaming.

The footsteps stopped, started again, moving as if with a limp. She pulled back the covers, stood on the cold floor and felt the wood shudder through the bottoms of her feet.

That metallic sound rang in her ears again. Someone hammering, she told herself. Someone from Garrett's crew, still out there, still working. But it was a lie, and she knew it.

Like a small, distant bell made of thick steel, the ringing echoed in her head. A throbbing sound that felt as though it were coming from inside her own heart. A bell encased in muscle that vibrated with each ring and sent quivering blood shooting through her veins.

Her palms grew wet. Her hands shook. Weakness spread behind her knees and up her thighs.

A sound like a horse being shod, clanking in an off-kilter rhythm.

She breathed faster, and her head felt lighter, as if it were lifting off her shoulders. She closed her burning eyes and tried not to cry.

42

EMMA WAITED UNTIL THE FOOTSTEPS stopped and the echoes faded, then she crept to the door. She put her ear to the crack and listened. Nothing but the hush of air as it moved down the hall, like the house itself was breathing.

She opened the door slowly and stepped out into a hallway so dark she could hardly see anything except moonlight coming in through the windows of the first floor. She followed the light to the stairs and went down to the entryway.

The house creaked and groaned. She looked through a window at the tents of the construction camp outside, the red embers glowing in the fire pit, the outline of the town beyond the field.

She knew she was awake, but this nighttime world didn't feel real.

Emma turned and went down the corridor that led to the west wing. Her fingers dragged along the stone as she walked through narrow bands of moonlight that came through small windows and lay across the floor.

She walked through the great room, making her way around the dark shapes of furniture that were hardly ever used. The room was stale and cold. She stopped halfway across and listened again. Blood rushed through her head like distant ocean waves.

At the foot of the stairs, Emma dug fingernails into her arm again. Pushed as hard as she could until she felt the slickness of blood as it leaked up from the crescent-shaped wounds.

Her hands would not stop shaking.

The shuddering metallic sound continued, coming from somewhere above her, in one of the empty rooms. A house full of empty rooms.

Emma's hand grabbed the railing to support her weak legs, and she started climbing.

If it was really her son, why was she so afraid?

By the time she reached the fifth floor, Emma's dress clung to her back, and sweat stung her eyes. She paused to catch her breath, then went down the hall to the large, empty room that hid Jeremiah's secret room.

Seeing her son's decomposed body shimmering and solid made her feel like everything inside her, every organ, bone, and muscle, had disintegrated. Decomposed, like Samuel, from the inside out. And the pain, she didn't have words for the pain that sliced right through her thoughts, turned them to dust.

She swung open the painting that revealed the hidden door. It was unlocked. A fire still burned in the room. Her pulse sped up, tapped at her temples. She tried to breathe deeply, but the air only went so far and her lungs seized.

She could still feel that electricity in the air, but it wasn't as strong now. As she walked past the shelves with all the artifacts, the books and scrolls, she felt small pops on the hairs of her arms. Little sparks.

Something caught her eye on the floor in front of the shelves, hidden in shadow. She found a lantern nearby and some matches. She lit it and held up the light. The thing she'd seen glowed.

Emma knelt, reached for the object, and picked up a golden mouse. It took her a moment to realize that what she held was not another artifact, it had once been alive. It was light, hollow, and she could hear and feel the dust shifting around inside it.

She stood up quickly and dropped it to the floor. It thudded on the wood, clanged into another object. The circle of lantern light wobbled over the bookshelves and walls and illuminated a row of animals, all transformed. Several birds (one of which had its wings unfolded as if trying to escape), squirrels, more mice.

The disgust Emma felt slowly melted into fascination. She walked along the row of animals, inspecting each one.

Scattered in between the animals were smaller objects—ants, spiders, and moths. She picked up a beetle and held it to the light. Perfectly preserved, "changed," as Jeremiah had said.

As she came near the end of the row, the light fell on another object, this one bigger than the others. She got down on her knees and stared at it. Tears burned her eyes, though she wasn't sure why. She slipped her hands underneath and gently lifted the object.

Its skin was smooth. The long head was still being formed when it died. Small bumps on either side where the eyes would have developed. Four legs curled in toward the stomach, sharp at the ends where hooves would have been.

She remembered Jeremiah telling her that one of Garrett's horses had given birth last month, but the foal was stillborn. This must be that creature.

She cradled the fetus in her hands as though it were something still alive, sleeping, and might awake at any moment. She gently put the foal back on the floor and stood. Her shadow fell across the table at the center of the room.

She slowly approached the table where she'd seen Samuel lying before. The fire crackled and the light made the shadows shift and slide, flutter and breathe. Emma kept her head turned, not wanting to see him again, needing to see him again, to touch him, to be sure he was real.

She reached the table and looked. A white sheet lay crumpled on the surface. The golden boy was gone.

Her body jerked at a distant, rhythmic pounding. A stumbling, clanking sound.

It's walking, she thought.

He's walking.

He walks.

43

EMMA RAN BACK DOWN THE stairs, across the west wing, and down the corridor to the main house. As she climbed the stairs back toward the master bedroom, she tried to picture Samuel's face, but all she could see were the collapsed features of the golden boy on that table. She saw its one eye staring at her. More than anything, she hated the guilt that lived inside her because she could no longer find the living Samuel in her memory.

She paused when the sound came again. A thin sliver of orange light glowed from under a closed door just down the hall. The room where they had put all of Samuel's things—his small bed, his toys and clothes and books. She never called it "Samuel's room" out loud, and neither did Jeremiah, but she always thought of it as his. The room that would have been his.

She walked to it, turned the handle, and opened the door slowly. A fire burned in the fireplace, lighting the room in a warm orange glow. At the far end she saw her husband, lying on the floor beside Samuel's bed. Within arm's reach of his body were a line of toys—a tin lion someone had given Samuel, Emma could not remember who, a worn leather ball, a stack of wooden building logs, a tin soldier on top of a horse with wheels.

Each and every toy had been changed into objects of gold.

And Samuel was beside Jeremiah, lying on his back, staring up at the ceiling with his one open eye.

Golden, damaged. One half of his face caved in. The fact that he was changed should have made him easier to look at, but it didn't. It made it worse, somehow.

Jeremiah had dressed the boy in a pair of pajamas he used to wear when he was alive, so all Emma could see were his golden hands and feet, neck, and head. He lay there stiff and unmoving, much as he had on the table in Jeremiah's secret room. But Emma sensed him somehow. Sensed his consciousness in the room with her.

She breathed in sharply, put a hand to her chest to settle the burning she felt there.

The single eye rolled downward, and that discolored circle in the middle of the orb saw her. The golden mouth opened, but no sound came out.

Emma backed away, fresh sweat running between her shoulder blades, and closed the door.

44

EMMA AWOKE TO THE GRAY light of early morning and the sound of flowing water. She looked to the windows, expecting to see the glass splattered with rain, but they were dry.

She sat up and listened harder. It was definitely water, not flowing exactly…but being poured, running down into deeper water.

Emma got out of bed and went into the hall. The sound was louder and clearer there. It came from the bathroom, the next room down. She walked to it and put her ear to the door. She heard Jeremiah speaking in low tones but couldn't make out the words.

The sound of water cascading into a full tub. A jug dipping into the bath and being poured again.

She cracked open the door just a little so she could hear what he said. Warm, moist air came out.

"Give her time," Emma heard her husband say. "She'll come around. We've missed you so much. Your mother has been in a lot of pain since you've been gone. Pain like that doesn't just go away. It takes time."

Silence. Then a low moan, like the sound that lingers after a bell has been rung and the tone is no longer audible. A metallic vibration in the air.

The jug dipped back into the water and poured.

"The house is different," Jeremiah said. "It's much bigger, but the town is the same. And your mother and I are the same. All your friends are still around, but you won't need to go to school anymore. We can teach you everything you need to know."

The jug dipped and poured again. The music of water flowing into water.

"I don't have to work anymore," Jeremiah said. "And I don't want you to worry about anything. Wherever you were, you'll never have to go back there again. I promise you that."

Emma felt like she was going to throw up. Fear pricked her scalp like hot needles. Her right leg buckled, and her knee hit the door, pushing it open further.

A single lantern on the floor cast a circle of light around the brass bathtub. Jeremiah sat in a chair next to the tub. He turned and looked to the doorway, a frantic look on his face. Emma doubled over when she saw the figure sitting in the water. She could not see his face, just the smooth golden skin of his back, full of holes where the flesh had deteriorated.

Jeremiah set down the jug and stood. Emma wanted to run, but her legs wouldn't move. Her husband came over and held out his hand, and she didn't know what to do, so she put her hand in his, and he helped her stand.

He led her to the tub. "Samuel, your mother is here. She wants to see you," he said.

The boy's golden face turned slowly, and she saw the gap where his right eye used to be. She saw the golden bone of his skull inside it. The head continued to turn until the good eye looked at her. The boy's expression didn't change, but Emma felt something different radiating from him—recognition, maybe.

Emma's legs gave out, and Jeremiah caught her, guided her to the chair, and helped her sit. He knelt and took both her hands in his.

"I know this is not what you expected," he said, "but the books I found told me what needed to be done."

Emma lowered her eyes and looked at their hands intertwined. Jeremiah pulled his right hand away and held it up. His two fingers glowed the same golden color as Samuel's body.

"This is what the gift is for," he said. "But it can't happen all at once. It's a process."

Emma's eyes drifted to Samuel. The boy now stared straight ahead, unmoving. There was just enough of him there to confuse her heart, and a different kind of pain was in that confusion. The pain of being unable to accept that this thing was her son. She closed her eyes and felt hot tears running down her cheeks. Her skin burned.

Jeremiah reached for the jug and put it in her hands.

"This is your son, Emma. The same soul, the same body. It just looks different. He needs you just as much now as he ever did. Maybe even more."

He took her hand with the jug and put it into the water, then he helped her lift and pour it over Samuel's back. The golden skin shimmered as water rolled over it.

"Just like you used to," Jeremiah said. "No different." Jeremiah guided her hand once more. "Now you do it."

The boy sat as still as a statue. The damaged face created a profile different from what Emma remembered, and it made her stomach churn. Jeremiah's eyes studied her face, and his expression was pleading. He smiled, but it looked like he was trying not to cry.

"He needs you," Jeremiah said. "We can be a family again."

Emma shook her head. "This isn't Samuel."

Jeremiah put one hand on her wrist and the other under the jug. "Bathe your son, Emma. This is Samuel, sitting here in the bath, and he needs his mother to bathe him."

Emma's hands shook. Her stomach burned like she had swallowed a hot coal. "I can't. It's not him."

Jeremiah pulled his hands away. His expression grew cold. His blue eyes seemed to lose color as he stared at her. "Don't talk about him like he's not here. Now, bathe him."

Emma tried to lift the jug full of water, but it felt as heavy as a stone. It fell from her grip and shattered on the floor. Emma stood up so quickly that the chair fell backward.

"I can't," she said. "This isn't our son."

Her husband's face twisted up, and his lips curled back to show his clenched teeth. The skin between his eyes folded into deep grooves. He opened his mouth, but a sound came out of the golden statue in the bath that made him stop.

Emma heard the sound before—the low echo of a metallic ringing, a moan bouncing around in a hollow space.

Emma saw the boy's face in profile. His mouth was closed, his lips were together, and he made the moaning sound again.

"Mmmmmm...."

Jeremiah cast one hard stare at Emma, then sat on the edge of the tub, and put a hand on Samuel's back. "Are you trying to speak?"

He gave the boy a chance to respond and then asked again, "Samuel, are you trying to say something?"

The golden boy's head turned stiffly, and that strange, dead eye fell on Emma.

"Mmmmmmm...."

"Try again. One more time."

Emma's heart fell through her chest and landed somewhere in her gut. "Mother," she said. "He's trying to say, 'Mother.'"

45

EMMA WALKED AROUND THE TUB to look directly at the golden boy. His head moved, following her until she stood in front of him. She knelt down so they were eye to eye.

His face was a frozen, expressionless mask. She wished his eyebrows could move, wished his mouth and lips could twist and curl into a smile. Something other than this blank stare. Emma looked into the boy's eye, trying to ignore the gaping hole where the other should have been. She forced herself not to look at the indentations in his face.

Emma put a hand to her chest. "Do you know who I am?"

The golden lips pressed together, and the sound came out. "Mmmmm...."

"Say it again," Emma said.

Jeremiah stood a few feet away, watching with an intense gaze.

The boy's golden eye closed as he made the sound. Nothing like human speech, just the dissonant noise of vibrating metal, but Emma heard something else within it. A voice spoke inside her head whenever Samuel moaned. It was faint but unmistakable. She looked at Jeremiah to see if he heard it too, but his expression stayed the same.

"One more time," Emma said, gently.

"Mmmmm…."

The voice she heard was not real. It was a memory of Samuel's real voice telling her about his day at school, learning, and playing with his friends. Her mind had deceived her, pulled from some old memory of her son speaking, and played it inside her head. Emma stood and backed away.

The boy's frozen face did not change, but Emma thought she felt hurt spilling off him. The hurt of being rejected by his mother. He moaned again, but this time there were no words in the sound, and it made the inside of Emma's head go tight.

She clamped her hands over her ears and ran out of the bathroom. Jeremiah didn't even move to stop her.

Emma went to her room and closed the door. She stood with her back against it, barricading it until her breathing finally calmed. Then, she got into bed and pulled the blankets up to her chin.

After a few minutes, she heard the gentle flow of water again and the hum of Jeremiah speaking to Samuel—a hum that continued until her eyes grew heavy and she fell asleep.

46

HE SLEEP. WARM. SHAKE. LONG, DARK. HOUSE SLEEP. FEET HEAVY ON FLOOR. NO QUIET, TRY QUIET. SEE NO GOOD. WALK SLOW. TOUCH WALL. THINK THIS LONG DREAM. NO REAL. AM I HERE?

COME TO DOOR. OPEN SLOW. SMELL HER. SMELL SWEAT. SAD.

SKY CIRCLE SHINE LIGHT. WHITE, SOFT. FALLS ON BED, ON MMMM.

CLOSE TO BED. GLASS OPEN, COLD. SEE HER. FACE TIRED. OLD NOW. NO YOUNG. LINES.

NO TOUCH. LOOK. ALL IS CLOUDS. SMOKE. HURTS DEEP. NO SLEEP. NO DREAM. CAN'T STAY.

ME IN PIECES. OVER THERE. NOT ALL OF ME, HERE. HURTS SO DEEP. SHE FEELS TOO. SHE FEELS HURT IN DEEP PLACE.

NO SAD OVER THERE. HOLD HAND OVER FACE. HEAT THERE. FACE IN PAIN. MY HAND, NOT MINE. CHANGE. SHE RIGHT. NOT ME. PIECES ME. NOT ALL. AND HURT.

SHE SEE THE NOT ME. SHE HEAR BURIED ME. SHE HELP. PLEASE HELP. PLEASE HEAR AND HELP. GO BACK. WANT GO BACK. NO BELONG. NOT HERE. OVER THERE. NO HURT, NO MORE. YOU, ME. NO HURT. OVER THERE.

47

GRAY MORNING, FRIGID AIR. THE teeth of a saw cutting through wood. Men's voices drifting through from outside. Emma opened her eyes and smelled the breakfast Abigail was cooking in the kitchen.

Emma got out of bed, went to the large window overlooking the field, and opened the curtains. Men in Garrett's camp lined up at a large table while someone scooped food into metal bowls. Garrett stood off to the side, directing those who'd finished eating to various tasks. His mangy dog stood at his feet, panting, breathing clouds.

The grass in the field was covered with frost. It wouldn't be long before the snow came. Emma had been looking forward to spending the winter in this house, decorating it in bright colors for Christmas, but now...

Now she didn't care. This world and everything in it felt like a thin shadow of something real. Every person, object, wall, and ceiling was like the breath from that dog's mouth. Insubstantial vapor. A thing that looked solid until a breeze blew it apart.

Emma wanted to get to the world that cast the shadow over this one—the real, the solid—a place where time had no meaning and hurt was just a word that had forgotten its purpose.

Samuel.

Emma put on a warm robe, slipped on a pair of shoes, and walked down the hall to the room that would have been Samuel's. Knocking on a door in her house felt strange, but she knocked anyway.

Footsteps, Jeremiah's, came closer. The door opened a crack, and half of Jeremiah's face peered out. His eyes grew wide when he saw Emma, then narrowed.

"I want to try again," Emma said. "I was wrong. You knew what you were doing and the outcome, but I didn't, so this is all new for me."

Jeremiah lowered his eyes and nodded. "Is anyone else here?"

"Abigail is in the kitchen."

He nodded once more and opened the door slowly, glancing into the hall as he did. Emma went into the room, and Jeremiah shut the door behind her. All the curtains were closed, and the room was dark. An unlit lantern sat on the bedside table. Samuel sat on the floor before the fireplace, watching the flames. He was dressed in pajamas again, and Emma's heart seemed to twist upside down when she saw them.

Her boy's clothes on another boy's body.

No, the body was his, but not his.

"The light bothers him," Jeremiah said, nodding at the windows. He looked tired, worn down. The stubble on his face was more gray than Emma remembered.

The toys Jeremiah had changed sat next to Samuel, but the boy didn't touch them. He didn't move at all. He sat with his back straight, legs stretched out before him.

Jeremiah watched his wife watch their son. He smiled. "This is all I've wanted," he said, " the three of us, together."

Emma went over to her husband and gently touched his face. "You've given up so much to make this happen."

Jeremiah blinked hard. His eyes filled with tears. "I wish there had been another way. But having him here now makes it all worth it."

"I know," Emma said. "Thank you."

Jeremiah wrapped his arms around her and pulled her close. Emma smelled the sickly-sweet scent of illness coming off him. The faint odor of whiskey on his breath.

"I want to spend some time with him," Emma said. "Just he and I alone together."

Jeremiah squeezed her tighter. "Be careful with him, he's fragile. He's not finished yet, and he's confused and afraid."

Jeremiah pulled himself away, took another look at his son, and then left the room. As soon as the door clicked shut, Emma walked over to it and turned the key as quietly as she could. It made a small metallic noise, and Samuel turned his head at the sound.

Emma crossed the room and knelt in front of the fire so that she faced him. Both of his golden hands rested on his thighs. Small hands, long fingers. She had wanted him to learn to play piano someday. A memory she'd not thought of in a long time. His fingers sparkled like jewelry in the firelight. She put her hand on his and held it.

She looked into the boy's face, into his eye. The gold at the orb's center seemed to swirl in constant motion.

"Samuel, can you hear me?"

The boy's mouth opened, and Emma put a finger to his lips.

"Just nod if you can hear me."

The golden head moved up and down slowly. He stared at her with his blank expression. The golden hand squeezed Emma's hand just a little.

"Do you want to go back to where you were?" she asked.

The golden eyelid blinked, and he nodded again. Emma put her hands on either side of the boy's face and looked directly into that yellow swirl at the center of his eye.

"Is that really you in there?" she asked. She held her son's face and put her forehead to his, feeling the smoothness of it, the warmth. "I've missed you so much. I'm sorry he brought you back."

She pulled away and looked into his eye again.

"I'm going to get you back to where you belong, but you won't be going alone. I'm coming with you. You and me, together. Do you understand?"

Another blink, another nod.

48

JEREMIAH WENT DOWNSTAIRS TO THE study, took a bottle of whiskey out of the cabinet, and poured some into a glass. He knew how it would feel when he took the first sip—the burn at the back of the throat, the warmth in his stomach, a head that got lighter by the second—but maybe he didn't want to feel that way.

Jeremiah put the glass down and sat in one of the high-backed chairs. There was no fire going, and the room was cold. Condensation ran down the windows, and he shivered a little.

He always felt a cloud of thoughts and memories chasing him, and if he slowed down, they would all gather around his head like a swarm of black flies. Slip in his mouth and eyes and drive him mad.

It was the first time Jeremiah had rested without a drink in his hand or studying some ancient text, and he did so now because his heart felt so full he could hardly breathe. Emma was upstairs with their son. Just the two of them, alone in a room. He'd been so afraid she would reject the boy because he was changed. He hoped she would come around but didn't know for certain. Sadness hung over her like a dark fog, and he wasn't sure she would ever find her way out.

Even he found Samuel difficult to look at sometimes, but he thought it was better to have the golden corpse of their son living with them than to have no son at all.

The smell of eggs, sausage, and coffee drifted in from the kitchen. Somehow, they would have to keep Samuel hidden from Abigail, perhaps by keeping the boy in the west wing and making it off-limits. Abigail was a good worker and wouldn't ask questions if she wasn't allowed in certain sections of the house.

As he sat in the chair, the guilt Jeremiah had been outrunning found him, and a memory of Elijah flashed in his mind so quickly and clearly that his stomach clenched. He pushed the image aside and thought of his wife and son together upstairs. He imagined her touching the boy's golden skin, looking into his golden eye, and slowly accepting that this impossible figure in their house was not a statue, but the vessel that held their son's soul.

Jeremiah closed his eyes and let himself feel everything he had been trying to drown since Samuel died. He let himself believe that everything could be new again.

49

EMMA STOOD IN THE BATHROOM looking at herself in the mirror. She wiped steam from the glass with the sleeve of her dark blue dress and saw a face looking back that did not seem to belong to her. Red-rimmed eyes stared out from swollen flesh. Fine lines around the eyes deepened when she squinted. Her wet hair, which had not been cut in months, now had streaks of silver.

She felt as though she had lived an entire lifetime since Samuel died, as though each hour had lasted days while the rest of the world moved at a normal speed.

Emma put her hair up and rubbed a small circle of rouge on her cheeks, then lightly darkened her eyelashes. The steam from the bath cleared away and Emma could see herself better. She stood up straighter, shoulders back, and forced herself to look at the woman in the glass. Even without making any expression, Emma thought she looked sad. It was etched in her face.

The pain, the crying, it carved lines in the skin.

She couldn't remember the last time she'd gone into town, the last time she'd seen people. But she would today, and she didn't want them to see a woman cloaked in sadness.

Emma breathed out, imagined herself seeing Laura Reid at the store, and smiled into the mirror. She pretended to laugh silently and watched her face transform. She didn't like the way it looked. It looked like pretending, even more sad than just being sad.

She heard Samuel's staggered steps clanking in the next room, the heavy thud of his golden toys as they hit the floor. The sound of those steps made Emma tense up, like a hand squeezing the back of her neck. Emma felt each step shudder up her sternum. Her breath shook a little. The way he looked unnerved her, the way he walked. She felt a stab of anger whenever she saw him in old pajamas and didn't know why. Maybe it was because they belonged to the old Samuel, the child who lived in her memory, and she hated seeing those clothes hanging on something that did not fit those visions.

The incessant hammering, sawing, and stone-chipping never went away, but at least those sounds were outside the house. Samuel's footsteps echoed from the room down the hall and straight into her skull.

Emma sat on the chair and slipped on her brown boots, lacing them tight around her ankles. She left the bathroom and went down the hall to the master bedroom. She opened one of the wardrobes and picked out a long black coat. It hung alongside two dozen other coats of various colors. Coats she had purchased but never worn.

She selected a gilded brooch from the jewelry table with a red stone in the center. The brooch was thin and cheaply made, but Jeremiah had changed it to gold when they first came down from the mountain, and the piece now sparkled.

Samuel's footsteps pounded the floor. Emma's hands shook, and the sharp end of the pin stabbed into her finger. She lost her grip on the brooch, and it clattered to the ground. The red stone came loose from its setting and skittered under the bed.

She held up her hand and saw a red pearl of blood growing on the tip of her finger. She put the finger to her lips and sucked away the blood. The copper taste filled her mouth, and a quick but vivid image flashed in her mind.

She saw her son's coffin being lowered into the ground, and she knew that over time, everything in him would decay and come leaking out. She had this thought as she stood by the grave the day they buried him, but she pushed it aside, down as deep as she could. It came back now, vicious and angry, and she couldn't help but think the taste in her mouth was something other than her own blood.

Another red pearl grew from the wound on her finger. She carefully dabbed the blood into the setting where the cheap stone had been, and it glistened again.

50

EMMA STOOD INSIDE MENDELSON'S CLOTHING store, looking at a boy's suit while trying to avoid eye contact with Wallace Lancaster as the elderly Mendelson knelt beside him and measured the seam of a new pair of pants. The store's sign that hung outside above the door had been weatherworn and faded before Jeremiah paid to have it restored.

Emma took off one glove and ran her hand over the rough gray wool of the jacket. It came with short trousers and a matching vest. She held up the jacket and tried to picture Samuel wearing it. It seemed like the right size, and most of all, it was something the old Samuel had never worn.

Emma put the suit over her arm and went to the shoes. She was not sure how they would work on Samuel's stiff feet, but it couldn't hurt to try. If anything, they would muffle the awful sound of his staggered, heavy steps.

She picked a pair of black leather boots, bigger than she thought he would need, and several pairs of socks.

She didn't know exactly where she and Samuel would be going or even how they would get there, but in the meantime, she needed to make him easier to look at and accept.

Wallace Lancaster stood in front of a mirror as Mendelson measured. His eyes followed Emma in the glass. She could feel him looking at her, and she knew that as soon as Lancaster got home, he would tell his wife he saw Emma at Mendelson's, buying clothes for a boy who had been dead for nearly a year.

Let them think I'm crazy, she thought. *It doesn't matter.*

She took the clothes up to the register. Mendelson excused himself from measuring to attend to her, and Emma caught Lancaster's eyes in the mirror. They widened briefly, then he smiled and nodded. She smiled back, but even she could feel the falseness of it, the halfhearted way her mouth curved.

Mendelson came around the counter, measuring tape hung around his neck like an untied tie, his small, round glasses foggy with moisture.

"It's wonderful to see you again, Mrs. Pevensie," Mendelson said. The bald spot on top of his head shone. "These suits just came in from New York, wonderfully made. I should think all the boys in town will wear these soon enough."

"It seems warm," Emma said, because she was not sure what else to say. She still felt Lancaster staring at her, even though his back was turned. She opened her bag and took out some coins while Mendelson wrapped her purchases in paper.

"I hope Jeremiah is well," Mendelson said, without looking up.

"He is well and very busy," Emma said. She set the coins down on the counter. Lancaster had still not moved. He stood facing the mirror, and even though Emma could no longer see his face, she knew he was looking right at her. Sweat ran down her back. The room suddenly felt far too hot.

When Mendelson handed her the package, Emma saw a mixture of sadness and concern in his eyes. She pushed the coins closer, thanked him, and turned to leave. As she neared the door, she heard Mendelson's voice call out, "Mrs. Pevensie? Mrs. Pevensie?"

She reached for the handle to push it open, to get out into the fresh, cool air.

Mendelson's hand touched her elbow. Emma turned and forced herself to smile.

His other hand was open, holding two coins. "You gave me too much," he said.

Lancaster's eyes, there in the mirror, watched the whole thing.

"Keep it," she said. The small bell rang as she pushed the door open.

Mendelson's open hand came closer. "I couldn't possibly accept this," he said. "This is as much as the boots."

"Thank you for the suit," Emma said, and left the store.

Across the street, near the steps in front of the tavern, stood a tall man dressed in a strange black robe that hung to his ankles. Like a priest from another time, she thought. The man's face looked relatively young from a distance, but his hair was as white as a cloud on a clear day. The man's face moved, but his body did not. He followed her as she walked. More eyes, more staring. It had weight when people shamelessly stared, as though waiting for her to do something irrational. Their thoughts pressed down on her like stones and made her feel like she was suffocating.

She looked away from the man with the white hair and walked faster, her boots stomping along the boardwalk in the same staggered rhythm as her golden son.

51

THE WINDOW OF SAMUEL'S ROOM faced the forest, now mostly dark. The hills in the distance were a black outline against the burning sunset.

Jeremiah had put fresh wood on the fire before going downstairs to pay Abigail and send her home. Emma knelt in front of Samuel, who stood before her naked, the firelight making his golden skin shimmer and warp. The package of clothes lay unwrapped beside her.

The boy watched as she ran her hands over all the gouges and indentations in his body. Places where the flesh had rotted away, fallen in. Her fingers moved along his thigh, feeling the large divot where part of him no longer was. His penis was gone, replaced with smooth gold that grew over the space where it had been. His chest was pockmarked, but the holes did not look as deep as when she first saw him.

Samuel stood, arms at his sides, looking at his mother blankly. Emma had come to believe the boy was incapable of moving the muscles in his face. He really did look like a statue come to life. A study in decomposition made of solid gold.

Emma rapped her knuckles gently against the boy's chest. Her ring hit and rang hollow inside him. She put her ear against the cool metal and listened for a heartbeat. All she heard was air moving around—even though he did not seem to breathe—air that moved as it would over the mouth of a bottle or a jug.

Emma lifted one hand, four fingers touching her thumb, and moved it to her mouth.

"Do you get hungry?" she asked.

The boy's head tilted slightly.

"Do you need to eat?"

Samuel moved his head left to right, once.

Golden bones were still visible along the top of his feet, inside large patches where the skin had decayed. It reminded Emma of how snow melted on the grass in early spring.

She unfolded the trousers, gently lifted one of Samuel's feet, and slipped it inside. She did the same thing with the other foot and hoisted the trousers around his waist.

"I don't understand how you got here," Emma said, putting one sock on him and pulling it up to his knee. "But I need to ask you something, and I need you to answer me."

She pulled the other sock up, and now those stiff golden feet were hidden. Emma took the shirt and guided his rigid arm into the hole.

"Do you want to go back to where you came from? The place you were before you woke up here?"

She brought the shirt up over the boy's shoulders, one of which hung a little lower than the other, and began fastening the buttons.

"Do you understand the question?" she asked.

Samuel nodded once.

"Do you want to go back?" she said again.

Samuel's mouth opened and closed. It reminded her, horribly, of a fish. The dead-eyed movements of something not quite alive. Then his mouth closed, and a sound came out of him.

"Mmmmm."

"Yes," Emma said, tucking the shirt into the trousers. "I'm your mother."

His eye stayed on her. She still could not look at the right side of his face. That gaping hole where his other eye should be made her feel like there was a small bird trapped in her chest, fluttering its wings, trying to get out.

She was about to ask the question again when Samuel's mouth opened and stayed that way. A scraping sound came from the back of his throat.

"Ack."

Emma stopped tucking in the shirt and leaned back, putting one hand on the boy's arm.

"What did you say?"

His eye closed and he made the sound again.

"Ack."

"Try again," she instructed. "One more time."

She took his hand, moved his arm, which was like pulling a horse that did not want to be led, and put his fingers to her mouth.

"Feel the sound," she said, and pursed her lips together. "Buh. Buh. Now you try."

Samuel opened his eye and watched her lips. He closed his mouth, and Emma heard vibrations coming from his throat and felt them shiver down his arm. He made a gentle sound like a drop of water falling into a puddle.

"Good," Emma said, smiling. "Very good. Now, say 'ack'."

Emma felt air move as it sucked into the boy's mouth, and just before she sensed that he was going to make the sound, she said, "Buh."

"Ack."

Emma took his hand in both of hers and held it. She didn't even feel the tears that ran down her face.

"Back," she said. "You want to go back?"

Samuel nodded once.

Emma turned his hand over and rubbed her fingers along the palm. The skin was growing back slowly, and it looked like ice on the outside of a window—golden ice that spread over the palm and up the thumb. She touched his long fingers and once again imagined them stretched out on the keys of a piano—stiff, golden fingers pressing down, making music rise out of the instrument and echo through the house.

She lowered his hand and looked into the boy's eye.

"Is it beautiful there?" she asked him.

Face still expressionless, Samuel nodded once.

Emma put both her hands on either side of the boy's face.

"I want to be there too," she said. "I want to be where it's beautiful."

52

JEREMIAH SAT IN A CHAIR by the fireplace, pipe clenched between his teeth, as Emma walked backwards across the boy's room. Samuel staggered in front of her, both arms stretched out. Emma held his hands. The new leather boots creaked on his feet.

"Heel first, then toe," Emma said.

Samuel's right leg lifted and moved forward. The left leg dragged along the floor behind it until he brought it level with the right.

"Heel, toe," Emma said, demonstrating. "Move the right leg first, and don't move the left until your right foot is flat on the ground."

Again, the boy staggered awkwardly, and although his expression did not change, Emma sensed embarrassment or disappointment radiating from him, like a change in temperature that she felt on her skin.

"It's okay," she told him. "Try again."

In the back of her mind, in a deep place where she stored her memories of Samuel as he had been, she imagined each memory as being kept inside a glass bottle with a stopper, and the memories were different-colored liquid. Something shook loose, and a bottle came tumbling to the front of her thoughts, shattered, and spilled the memory.

It flooded her mind.

Samuel as a little boy, just a little older than a baby. He babbled incoherently and crawled around the house, touching, exploring, giving his own names to the objects he found. When he began grabbing hold of furniture to pull himself up to stand, Emma taught him how to walk. She remembered the huge smile on the boy's face when he took his first step, and his brain lit up with the realization that this was how to get places. She taught him then as she taught him now, only then he had been so much smaller, and Emma was on her knees, face to face with him, encouraging him to keep going.

Samuel's golden face became blurry, and Emma's eyes filled with tears. She smiled at the boy, blinked, and let out a little laugh.

"You're doing great," she said.

The boy wore his new suit jacket and vest, a white button-up shirt with a black tie. Jeremiah smoked his pipe and watched Samuel's movements gradually grew smoother with each journey across the room. He still wasn't walking like a normal kid his age, but he was getting better, and the sound of his steps was softer.

Emma, still holding Samuel's hands and walking before him, neared Jeremiah.

"We need to talk about Abigail," Emma said, keeping her eyes on Samuel.

"What about her?"

"I don't want to keep him locked up in this room all day," she said. "I want him to be able to explore the house and go where he wants."

Jeremiah already knew what she was thinking.

"She's going to see him eventually," Emma said. "Don't you think it would be better if we made it happen, rather than let it happen by accident?"

Jeremiah had asked himself the same thing the night he sat in the study while Emma spent time with Samuel, and the idea made him feel anxious. The more people who knew about Samuel, the more likely it was that word would reach the town, and he didn't know what would happen then. He saw it going two ways. The townspeople would dismiss the story of a golden boy as a fantasy, or they would be afraid and want to confirm whether or not Samuel was real. Whether he had been brought back from the dead.

"She plays piano," Emma said. "Do you remember, she played in church once while Gretchen Hussel sang."

Emma stretched out the boy's long fingers. "I want him to play. I want her to teach him."

"We don't even have a piano," Jeremiah said.

"I think it would help him," Emma said. "Connect him to the music we can't hear, the vibrations of the world we can't see."

Emma made a wide turn, and she and Samuel began walking back to the opposite end of the room.

Jeremiah took the pipe out of his mouth. "What if she gets frightened and wants to leave? What if she's too afraid to work for us anymore? What then?"

Samuel moved slowly, lifting one leg and putting it down, then doing the same with the other. The motions moved him forward, but they were clumsy and stiff. His new boots clacked on the floor. Jeremiah noticed that Emma no longer winced at the sound of his footsteps.

"Pay her," Emma said. "Give her so much money that she can't leave. You know her family, Jeremiah. She wants to move out and get as far away from them as possible. Pay her and ask her to come live with us."

That was something Jeremiah hadn't considered. Emma was right, of course. Abigail's father, Lloyd Fletcher, spent as much time away from his family as he could. He had no job to speak of, and instead insinuated himself into the circles of the wealthiest people, and what little money he made was by doing small favors for them, usually hiding something or covering it up. The money was then spent on girls and booze, and whatever was left went to buying the whiskey that kept his wife in a haze. Their house was in permanent ruin, just outside town in the shadow of the forest. A leaning structure covered in moss that looked like it wouldn't stand for much longer.

When Lloyd Fletcher was home, he usually joined his wife in her drunkenness, but the alcohol did not cause him to fall into melancholy like it did her. Instead, it unbottled his rage. And his wife and daughter often paid the penalty. There had been enough bruises and cuts for Emma to know that Abigail was lying about how she got them, but she and Jeremiah had agreed early on not to intervene in the personal matters of the town. Occasionally, though, Emma would slip a few extra coins into Abigail's jacket.

Jeremiah was trying to imagine the future, to see how everything would play out, when Samuel started moaning. Emma stopped walking and looked at the boy with concern.

"Are you trying to say something?" she asked him.

The moan was different from any sound Samuel had made before. A sound that reminded Jeremiah of fresh pain, the immediate moment after an injury.

The boy let go of his mother's hands. They jerked and shook as he lifted them. He could not quite grasp his head, but he held his hands near his temples, like he wanted to push on them and relieve a headache.

"Darling, what's the matter?" Emma said.

The boy turned around, his one eye falling on, then moving past Jeremiah. Samuel staggered away from Emma, all progress lost, and stumbled across the room. Each step slammed into the floor, and Jeremiah heard the solid gold in each footstep. They landed on the wood with a thick and heavy sound.

Emma went after him, trying to put a hand on the boy's shoulder, but he kept stumbling forward, his upper body pitched so far that Jeremiah was amazed the boy didn't fall over.

Jeremiah stood from the chair as Samuel came closer, his eye staring directly at the fireplace. Jeremiah wasn't worried yet. He was curious what the boy was doing, and if he was going for the fire, it would take a lot more heat than that to cause any damage. Still, Jeremiah stepped to the fireplace as Samuel came near.

"Samuel," Emma said, "stop. Please, darling, listen to my voice."

Samuel went straight for the iron poker and lifted it from the stand. Jeremiah put his arms out and moved in front of Emma, half-expecting the boy to turn around and swing the poker at his mother.

"Son," Jeremiah said, trying to make his voice sound stronger than it felt. "Put the poker down. That's dangerous. It could hurt you."

"Darling," Emma said from behind him, "listen to your father. Put it down."

Samuel moaned again, and Jeremiah felt it inside him. The sound of that voice hammered down on a string in his heart, and it rang out like a note on a piano. The note was pain. It sounded again and Jeremiah's eyes burned.

Then Samuel lifted the iron poker and swung it into his own head.

53

THE IRON STRUCK SAMUEL WITH a dull sound and crumpled in part of his forehead. A sickening metallic vibration came ringing from the boy's open mouth. His one eye, open as wide as it would go, stared straight ahead.

Whatever Samuel had been trying to silence, it still made noise.

The boy tried to hit himself again, but Jeremiah rushed over and jerked the poker from his son's grasp. Samuel let out a high-pitched, metal-scraping scream. Jeremiah and Emma put their hands over their ears to drown it out. The sound pierced through anyway and made Jeremiah nauseous. It was a screech, part voice, part machine. It went on so long that Jeremiah thought he would pass out, then it stopped suddenly, and Samuel collapsed to the floor, moaning.

Jeremiah and Emma carried their son, so much heavier now than he used to be, to the makeshift bed on the floor and laid him down. Emma lay next to him and stroked his forehead like she used to do when he was alive. She ran her fingers gently over his face, tracing his eye, his nose, his mouth. She ran her fingers over the missing part of his face and sang to him. At the sound of her voice, the boy stopped moaning. He lay perfectly still, arms at his sides, and listened to his mother's voice.

Eventually, Emma fell asleep with her hand resting on Samuel's chest. Jeremiah covered them both with a blanket and watched from the chair. He smoked his pipe and tried to sort through all the thoughts crowding together in his mind.

It was hard to tell if there was any change in the boy after the blow, but he seemed the same. Jeremiah thought the indentation would heal with time, just like the rest of Samuel's body.

The boy's eye was still open, and Jeremiah knew it would not close. He would lay through the night, but the boy would not sleep. He pretended to sleep, or his body remembered that nighttime was when you lay down until the sun came up.

He doesn't eat, and he doesn't sleep, Jeremiah thought.

When Emma first saw Samuel, she asked Jeremiah, "What have you done?"

At the time, he thought he knew. But now, he wasn't sure. All the books and texts said nothing about what came next.

A slow and steady click-clacking noise came from the hallway. It paused at the doorway of the room, and Jeremiah saw two red eyes staring at him from the darkness. The shape of the wolf came into the room, into the firelight. It padded over to Jeremiah and sat down in front of the fire.

Jeremiah looked at the creature. It appeared exactly like a wolf, yet he knew it was something else. Was it that thing right now, but Jeremiah could not see it? Did it take the form of a wolf, or was something using the animal as a host?

Its gray fur was dark with dew, as if it had just come from the field. Jeremiah had no idea how it came inside the house.

YOU'VE DONE IT.

Jeremiah leaned forward and put his elbows on his knees. "I don't know what I've done," he said.

YOU HAVE BROUGHT HIM BACK.

"Have I?"

The wolf's head turned, looking at the boy and his mother on the floor. IS THAT NOT YOUR SON, SAMUEL?

"I honestly don't know. Maybe. Part of him anyway, but not all of him. Did I do something wrong?"

The wolf looked back at Jeremiah. HAVE YOU FORGOTTEN WHAT ABERNATHY TOLD YOU?

Jeremiah swallowed. He had not forgotten exactly, but he believed the old man was wrong. Jeremiah read the same books, and they said nothing of what Abernathy had told him.

THEY DON'T WANT TO COME BACK. DEATH IS ONLY MEANT TO BE ONCE. DEATH CHANGES THE SOUL, AND WHAT COMES BACK CANNOT BE THE SAME.

"He's in pain," Jeremiah said.

TO BE ALIVE IS PAINFUL.

Jeremiah's eyes burned again. He stared into the bright flames, devouring the wood. "How can I fix this?" Jeremiah asked.

The flames flickered in the wolf's red eyes and cast a long, wolf-shaped shadow that stretched across the floor and fell over Emma and Samuel.

MORE PAIN, the wolf said.

54

ABIGAIL FLETCHER HAD NOT SEEN much of her employers over the last two weeks. They spent most of their time on the second floor of the main tower, either in their bedroom or the room that held all of Samuel's things. She knew better than to bother them and tried to busy herself with keeping the house free of dust and mice.

She cooked their meals but rarely had to take them upstairs, as Jeremiah usually came down and gathered the food. Later, he would bring the dishes back and leave them in the kitchen.

Abigail often heard thumping from one of the rooms up there, but the sounds were not the typical rhythmic knock of the bed she was familiar with. They were not the sounds of a headboard banging against the wall, and the whimpers she heard from time to time were closer to crying than anything like passion.

Sometimes, she heard voices. Jeremiah's carried more than Emma's, and his deeper voice was often raised in what sounded like frustration.

Once, Abigail climbed halfway up the stairs and listened. She heard something banging into the walls, a dull thud that she felt in her forehead, because that's exactly what it made her think of. Someone hitting their head against the wall.

"Stop," Jeremiah's muffled voice said. "Stop it right now. You can't keep doing this. You have to control yourself."

Then came a sound unlike anything Abigail had ever heard, and if there had been someone she talked to, someone she confided in, she would not have known how to describe it. "Metal," she would have said. Metal scraping against metal. A sound that should make sparks."

From within this rasping noise came another sound much more like a voice, although it still had that same metallic quality. It rose and fell and rose again. There was no doubt in Abigail's mind. Someone, or something, was moaning. But she did not think it was Jeremiah or Emma, because she heard both of them speaking softly over the noise.

Whatever it was, it drew an icy line up her back and into her neck.

Although she would never admit it to anyone, Abigail sometimes pretended that Jeremiah and Emma were her parents. When she put on an apron and cooked a roast, chopped vegetables, or swept the floor, she was not an employee, she was simply a daughter doing her chores. Thinking this way made the work seem less like work and more like the mundane tasks of a life lived with a family who loved her.

She pretended the massive stone house was also hers and imagined climbing the stairs of the west wing at night to fall asleep in one of the large empty rooms. She walked the halls with her broom and dustpan, humming. Songs she made up and then forgot.

Abigail was in the great room of the west wing, sweeping dust and ash from around the fireplace, when she heard the sound of a wagon approaching. She carried the broom to the window and saw a large, covered wagon pull up to Garrett's camp. The driver jumped down, took off one glove, and shook Garrett's hand.

Garrett's cigar bounced as he spoke and pointed at the house. He saw Abigail standing at the window and nodded. His other hand absently stroked the top of his mutt's head.

The driver replaced his glove, slapped the side of the wagon, and five men dressed in work clothes emerged from the back.

Abigail watched as the men struggled to unload a large object. Covered in cloth held together by rope, the six men worked in unison until the object was free of the wagon. It was large and flat, and four black legs stuck out of the cloth. With strained faces and gritted teeth, the men carried this heavy thing up the steps to the front porch and set it down.

Even without seeing it unwrapped, Abigail knew exactly what the object was. Back when she went to church, she often sat at the bench of something like this and played music that made tears well up in the eyes of the congregation, notes and chords so beautiful they seemed to be telegraphed to her from some other world.

Her fingers twitched a little as she imagined placing them on this grand piano's black and white keys.

55

ABIGAIL RAN UPSTAIRS AND PAUSED at the door of the bedroom where they kept all of their dead child's things. Abigail thought it was strange to spend so much time in there. She wondered if Emma was pregnant again, and they had not yet told her. Maybe the room would be occupied by someone living soon enough.

She put her ear to the door and listened. All she heard was Emma's muffled voice, speaking the way a mother does when instructing a child. Abigail heard the metallic sound again, and this time, it was a soft hum—almost like a voice.

She knocked on the door. There was a shuffling noise and some clomping, like a drunk man stumbling across the room. Then the door opened a little, and Emma's face appeared in the crack. Her eyes were narrowed and intense.

"I'm sorry to interrupt you, ma'am," Abigail said. "There are men outside with a piano. I don't know where you want them to put it."

Emma's face relaxed. She looked over her shoulder, nodded, opened the door further and stepped out. She closed the door behind her and said, "Come with me, please."

The two of them went back downstairs. Emma straightened out her dress and brushed some hair away from her eyes before opening the front door. The men had set the piano down on the porch. A light rain fell just beyond them, turning the ground of Garrett's camp into soft mud. She could see a group of workers in an open tent, playing poker around a small table.

The lead man tipped his hat and handed Emma a piece of paper.

"We had it tied down good," he said. "Hit some bumps along the way but made it in one piece without scratches. Though I think it will need a good tuning before it's fit for playing."

Emma smiled and handed the paper to Abigail. She pointed down the hall to the west wing. "I'd like it to go in the great room just down the hall."

The man tipped his hat again, and the workers grabbed hold of the piano and tilted it, easing two legs through the doorway before bringing in the rest. They carried it down the dark stone corridor until they came to the great room. Emma went and stood at the south end, near the windows, and pointed to the floor.

"Please set it down here," she said.

The men did as she asked, untied the rope, and removed the cloth. Abigail had never seen such a beautiful instrument. The wood was a reddish brown, polished so bright her reflection glided over its surface. The legs were ornately carved with flowers and vines, and the feet were lion's paws.

One of the men ran back out to the wagon to get the bench, and when he returned, the whole crew left. Abigail walked around the piano, gently running her fingertips along the smooth wood.

Emma smiled at her. "You can play it if you want."

Abigail came around to the front of the instrument and put her fingers on the keys in the position of middle C. She glanced at Emma, who only nodded and smiled. Then Abigail pressed down, and the chord rang out from the body. It was slightly out of tune, but the tone and timbre of the strings resonated throughout the room. A rich, warm sound that filled Emma's chest. Abigail played a few more chords, a piece of music Emma had never heard before, and she felt each chord vibrate in her ribs.

"You play beautifully," Emma said as she came closer. "I remember being so moved every time you played in church."

"I didn't know you played," Abigail said.

Emma's face took on a strange expression. She looked to Abigail as though she was watching for a reaction.

"Oh, I don't," Emma said. "I've never even touched a piano."

"It's like anything," Abigail said. "It's difficult and frustrating at first, but the more you do it, the easier it becomes."

"Do you think you could teach someone to play?" Emma asked.

Abigail took her hands off the keys and smiled. "You want me to teach you?"

"No, not me."

"Jeremiah?"

"Someone else," Emma said.

Abigail looked confused for a moment, then composed herself.

"Of course, I'd be happy to teach someone. But who is it?"

Emma smiled just a little, but Abigail thought her eyes were sad and nervous.

"I'd like you to meet him," Emma said, turning and walking toward the corridor. Abigail followed a few paces behind, a tightening feeling growing in her chest.

Emma was already halfway up the stairs when Abigail began climbing them. When she reached the second floor, Emma was at the door of the bedroom she had been in before, her hand resting on the handle.

"You will have questions," Emma said. Her voice sounded different, a monotone. "And we are prepared to answer all of them as best as we can. But first, here is your student."

Emma pushed open the door.

56

A FIGURE STOOD JUST INSIDE the room. As tall as a young child, it wore a grey suit and vest with a blue flower in one of the button holes. Black boots on its feet, high socks.

The tightness in Abigail's chest grew until it felt like her heart was being suffocated, like it had no room to beat. She covered her mouth with a hand and took a step backward.

The figure's neck and head were bright, solid, and metallic. A few strands of hair were frozen to the head, gleaming in the grey light that streamed in from the windows. Its face was damaged, half of it collapsed inward. There was only one eye, and it looked right at Abigail.

It's gold, Abigail thought. *They are grieving so much they had a statue made to look like their dead son.*

She smiled nervously and almost laughed. Both of them had gone mad, spending so much time in this room and thinking of the past that they made a statue and convinced themselves it was real.

Abigail suppressed the laugh, unsure what to do or say, when the statue's golden hand lifted until it was extended straight out. The feet moved, bringing the statue two or three steps closer to Abigail. Now her lungs felt restricted. She couldn't get enough air.

The one golden eye swirled, seemed to look past her own eyes and straight into her thoughts. The statue walked closer, hand held out. It stopped close enough for Abigail to study the smooth, reflective surface of the skin. She took a step backward and bumped into the closed door. She wanted to scream. Black pressed in at the edge of her vision.

The statue moves.

But she knew it wasn't a statue. Her mind brought up different possibilities, and none of them fit. She started breathing heavier and her head went light.

"Samuel," Emma said softly, "say 'nice to meet you.'"

Abigail's fingers reached behind her for the door handle. She couldn't find it. Her nails scratched at the wood. Her feet were stuck to the floor, and her legs went weak.

Then, a sound, a voice, came from the statue's mouth.

Abigail closed her eyes, hoping the golden boy would be gone when she opened them. But he was still there, staring at her with that one eye, and Abigail felt as if her heart was about to seize up and stop beating.

"Ayyyyyy meeee yoooooo," the statue said.

Abigail finally found her own voice and let out a scream.

57

ABIGAIL RAN. SHE THREW OPEN the door, hit the stairs, and felt her body moving down, but she didn't feel her feet on the steps. When she reached the bottom, Abigail ran straight for the front door. She grabbed the handle, out of breath, when a pair of strong arms wrapped around her.

She thrashed and kicked, screaming as loud as she could.

"Calm down," Jeremiah said in her ear.

Abigail stopped fighting. Each inhale burned in her chest. Jeremiah relaxed his grip, and Abigail turned to face him. Her hair stuck to her face with sweat. She looked down at Jeremiah's hands, and they were both empty. No weapon. Just a leather glove worn over the right hand.

"I need to leave," she said. "I can't stay in this house. Not with… not with that. Whatever it is."

Jeremiah touched her arm and led her to the study. Once inside, he motioned to one of the chairs in front of the fireplace. Abigail sat down. Her dress was damp between her shoulder blades.

Shadows flickered on the walls as Jeremiah poured two glasses of whiskey. He brought one over, handed it to her, then sat in the opposite chair.

"Take a moment," he said. "Breathe."

Abigail held her glass and watched as Jeremiah drank his. Jeremiah's glass was empty before she had even taken a single drink. He rose to fill it again and sat back down.

Jeremiah raised his eyebrows and nodded at her glass. She hated alcohol. The only time she ever drank was when her father brought another man to the house, and then Abigail only drank to numb herself from what was going to happen next. But she lifted the glass to her lips and took a drink. She made a face when it hit her tongue, closed her eyes as it moved down her throat. When she opened her eyes, the room shifted slightly.

"Is it witchcraft?" she asked.

Jeremiah shook his head and leaned forward, elbows on his knees. He turned the glass in circles. Firelight glowed through the amber liquid and threw ripples on the walls.

"Not as far as I know," he said.

"Did you sell your soul to the devil?"

The glass stopped turning. Jeremiah stared into it momentarily, then looked up and met her eyes.

"I hope not," he said.

Maybe it was just the dim light, but Jeremiah looked very tired to her, burdened. His wife looked more vibrant and alive than Abigail had seen during her time working for them. It used to be the other way around.

"You knew who it was?" Jeremiah asked her.

"I thought it was a statue at first." She took another drink of whiskey, coughed once, and then asked, "Is it a statue? One of those mechanical statues that can draw pictures?"

Her face was hopeful. She wanted to know if what she saw was anything other than what her heart told her.

"It's him," Jeremiah said. "It's the boy."

Abigail let out the breath she had been holding. "How?"

Jeremiah turned the glass again. He thought it would be easier to tell the truth, but he knew that after he told her, she would never see him the same way again, and he was reluctant to watch her face change and become afraid.

Abigail saw his hesitation. "Please don't lie to me. I hate being lied to."

"I found something," Jeremiah said, "on a mountain. It came with great sacrifice, but you saw what it can do."

Abigail looked around the room. "This house, everything you have, is that how you paid for it?"

Jeremiah nodded.

She was surprised to find that she believed him. Maybe she would have felt differently if she hadn't seen the golden boy—the golden corpse. But the sudden wealth, the black castle they lived in—all of it made sense only if what Jeremiah said was true—that he could turn things into gold.

"What did you sacrifice?" she asked.

Jeremiah's eyes narrowed and his lips tightened, as though her words were something sharp that had stabbed him.

He stared into his drink. "Every single version of the future in which I am happy," he said.

"Is he..." Abigail stopped, took another drink, and felt her head get lighter. "Is he alive?"

"Partly," Jeremiah said. He swallowed the last of his drink and stood. "Pieces of him have returned, but not all."

"Is this power from God?" she asked, hopeful again.

Jeremiah smiled a little as he poured more whiskey into his glass, which made Abigail nervous. He walked closer and stood near her chair. She wrapped her glass in both hands, ready to jump up and throw it or smash his head with it if she needed to.

"This is a lot to take in all at once," he said. His voice was soft, kind even. "I don't expect you to be okay with it, but I can't change what it is."

Jeremiah drank the whiskey in one swallow, then slipped the glove off his right hand. Abigail gasped when she saw his golden fingers and an uneven line at the knuckles, as if he had dipped them into melted gold and let them dry. He crossed one finger over the other, then pressed his fingertips to the side of the glass. There was the sound of air squeezing through a tight hole, a bright light that enveloped the glass. Abigail blinked once against the light, and the glass was gold when she opened her eyes. Brilliant and shining. A small cloud of sparkling dust slowly drifted to the floor. Jeremiah held it out, and Abigail lifted one hand to receive it. It was heavier now, solid all the way through.

"No one knows of this except Emma, and now you," Jeremiah said.

Abigail turned the golden glass over in her hands, taking deep breaths to keep her head from going light. She swallowed hard.

"I can't have you leaving this house to tell the town what you've seen," Jeremiah said. "Do you understand?"

Abigail nodded, gripped each glass tighter.

"What do we pay you now?" Jeremiah asked.

She swallowed again. "One dollar a day."

"I will pay you fifty dollars a day to come live here with us. You'll even be paid on the weekends, your days off."

Abigail nodded. She felt dizzy trying to do the math of how much money she would make each week.

"You can choose any room in the west wing, and I will purchase any furniture you need."

Abigail tried to compose herself but knew her face could not hide her shock.

"What do I have to do to earn this?" she asked. But she knew that her answer would be yes, no matter what he said. She had waited so long for the world to shift in direction, for some chance or opportunity to appear that would enable her to be free of her mother and father. A way out of their house. And this man somehow, impossibly, had the power to transform anything into solid gold.

How could she say anything but yes?

"I want you to do whatever Emma asks," Jeremiah said. "No matter how strange it may seem. Teach the boy to play piano, if that's what she wants. If she asks you to read to him every night, read to him. Do not ask questions, and do not comment on the boy's appearance. Simply do what you're asked, and the money is yours."

Abigail nodded. "Yes, sir."

"Your other responsibilities still stand," he said. "We cannot have anyone else coming into the house now. So, you will still need to cook and clean, as you always have."

"Of course," Abigail said.

Jeremiah extended his hand to her. "Do we have an agreement?"

She set down her glass of whiskey, reached out her hand, and stopped. His two golden fingers pointed right at her. If he wanted to, he could pull her close, wrap an arm around her neck, touch those two fingers to her skin, and within seconds, her body would harden and change, turning into a glowing statue like the boy upstairs.

She looked into his eyes and placed her hand in his. The skin of his hand was rough, callused, but those two fingers were smooth and warm.

"I'll write up a contract in the morning," Jeremiah said, letting go of her hand. "In the meantime, pick your room and I'll have your things brought over from your parents' house."

Jeremiah picked up the leather glove and slipped it back into his hand. He nodded once and walked past Abigail.

"Sir?" Abigail said, turning in her chair.

Jeremiah stopped, his back to her.

"You said pieces of Samuel have returned. Will he ever be whole again?"

Jeremiah's head hung. He didn't turn around, and his voice was quiet when he spoke. "I don't know that any of us are whole."

He walked away. She heard his footsteps echo down the hall leading to the west wing. She turned back around and held the golden glass up to the light, turning it in half-circles and watching the way it gleamed. Her heart beat faster as she thought of melting it down and selling it to the bank. There was more money in her hand than she had ever made in her entire life—or her parents' lives, for that matter.

All these years, her father taking his belt to her face, her mother screaming and vomiting into the night, her father whoring her out to travelers who came through town. Who knew that all this time, her escape from that life would be the grieving preacher? The preacher who turned his back on God built a black castle in the middle of a field, transformed a corpse into gold, and raised it from the dead.

She would not walk away from this. Not until she had tucked away every dollar and golden cup she could.

58

JEREMIAH STOOD AT THE WINDOW in the empty room outside his secret room. He'd been up most of the night reading over Abernathy's books, looking for something he might have missed. Some small piece of information, or detail, that might explain Samuel's behavior. He found nothing and now wondered if the flaw was not in the power, but in his expectations.

He expected to get his son back.

What he had done was give life to a statue.

The field outside was covered in smooth, unbroken snow that sparkled brightly in the morning sunlight. A single note on the piano echoed up the staircase, down the hall, and into his ears.

Middle C.

It rang out again and pulsed behind Jeremiah's right eye, a pressure he felt like a second heartbeat.

Again.

He had heard that single note every day around midmorning for the last two weeks. Abigail sat beside Samuel on the bench and helped guide his stiff fingers. He still couldn't spread them apart to make chords, so Abigail stretched out his first finger and helped him push down on the C. Emma sat in a chair nearby, head resting in her hand, a contented smile on her face.

Jeremiah hated the sound—the metal ring of the string vibrating endlessly. He wasn't sure if he actually heard his son playing or if he was just imagining it, because he heard it all the time.

Middle C.

Maybe it wouldn't be so bad if the note was hit in rhythm, but there was no telling the next time Samuel's finger would fall on the key. Sometimes it was only a breath or two, and sometimes Jeremiah could almost believe the lesson was done for the day. And then…

Middle C.

Emma required the boy to do an hour lesson every day, and there was no progress beyond that one note, the first note Abigail had shown him. An hour a day was torture enough on Jeremiah's head. Still, the boy often found his way to the west wing and sat at the piano by himself, striking the middle C with his heavy golden finger until Jeremiah wanted to take an ax and smash the piano to pieces.

He closed his eyes and let the sunshine fall on his face. It was bright and blinding, and he saw red instead of black—the light shining through the blood of his closed lids. When he opened them again, he blinked away the dark snowflakes in his vision and left the empty room.

He walked down the staircase, that middle C growing louder with each step, until he heard Abigail's soft voice encouraging the boy to lift his left hand and hit a different note. Jeremiah couldn't see if Samuel tried to do what she asked, but what he heard was the middle C. The muscles in his neck tightened.

At the second-floor landing, he paused and tried to suppress his frustration. He didn't want either of the women to see any emotion on his face. He was about to begin walking again when he heard another sound echo. A loud knocking at the front door. Three bangs in quick succession.

The middle C rang out.

The knocks sounded again. Three, pause, then three more. Jeremiah went down the stairs, louder than normal, to signal he was coming, and reached the west wing. Samuel looked up when his father came into the great room. His smooth, expressionless face was unreadable. The one eye fixed on Jeremiah as he walked, and his body jerked as the middle C was hit again, filling the room as nerve-rattling as an unexpected gunshot.

Jeremiah tried to smile as he walked by Emma. Her smile was genuine, but her eyes were distant and open too wide. Something about the smile made the skin on his arms tingle. Thick dark curtains had been hung over the windows to prevent anyone from seeing in, making the room feel as though it were on a cycle of day and night separate from the rest of the house.

Three knocks, louder this time.

Abigail's eyes followed him as he crossed the room. Her gaze was more curious, but she had not looked at him the same since she met Samuel and learned that Jeremiah was the one who made him that way. She looked fascinated, maybe even a little frightened.

Jeremiah nodded at her and Samuel and then went down the hall to the foyer.

He unlocked the deadbolt and opened the door. Sheriff Brennan stood there, hat in hand, wearing a brown duster, his black boots shining with melted snow.

"Morning, Jeremiah," he said.

"Good morning, Sheriff."

Brennan rubbed the back of his neck. "There's no easy way to say this, so I'll just come right out with it. Reason I'm here, Abigail's ma and pa are worried about her. Say she's being kept against her will."

He raised a hand before Jeremiah could say anything. "Now, I know that's not true. But I promised I'd come out and make sure she's okay."

Middle C rang out, twice in a row.

Brennan's eyebrows went up.

"Emma is learning to play," Jeremiah said.

"Abigail teaching her?" Brennan asked.

Jeremiah nodded. "She's just starting."

"Well, she couldn't ask for a better teacher. As I remember, that girl can play like no one else I ever heard before or since."

Brennan shifted from one foot to the other. The duster moved, and Jeremiah saw the man's pistol hanging from his belt. The shiny, round ends of bullets stuck in the slots around it.

"Do you want some coffee?" Jeremiah asked.

Brennan smiled. "Yes, I would. Thought you were going to keep me out here in the cold."

Jeremiah smiled in return, felt the falseness of it, and realized he had not seen himself in a mirror since yesterday. He had been up all night with those books and knew he probably looked as bad as he felt.

Jeremiah let Brennan inside as another middle C came echoing down the hall. Jeremiah cringed as he shut the door.

"She's going to have that one note down, isn't she?" Brennan said with a smile.

His boots left wet footprints on the floor as they walked to the study. Jeremiah added a few logs to the fire and then went to the kitchen for coffee. When he returned, Brennan was standing by the fireplace, one arm resting on the mantle.

"We both know what they want," Brennan said, without looking up from the fire.

Jeremiah handed him a cup.

"Her ma and pa, they want money," Brennan said. "Accuse you of stealing their daughter, holding her captive, or whatever nonsense is going through their heads. You give them some money to be quiet, and suddenly they don't miss her so much anymore."

Brennan took a sip of the coffee and hissed at its heat. "At least that's the way I see it."

Jeremiah sat down in one of the chairs and took a drink as well. "Truth is," he said, "she asked to come live with us."

Brennan nodded and made a little humming noise. "Can't say I blame her. I don't know how God let someone as good as Abigail end up with parents like those."

"God doesn't have anything to do with it," Jeremiah said. The words just tumbled out, and he wished he hadn't said them.

Brennan turned to him and ran his fingers over his grey mustache. "You don't look like a preacher anymore," he said, "and you've stopped sounding like one, too."

The middle C again.

Jeremiah's teeth clenched so tight he felt them grind together. He closed his eyes in a long blink, and Brennan was staring right at him when he opened them.

"I'm going to need to see her," Brennan said, his face serious.

For a moment, Jeremiah was confused. It must have shown on his face because Brennan added, "So I can tell her ma and pa that she's healthy and fine."

Jeremiah nodded. "Of course. I'll get her."

He walked halfway down the stone corridor to the west wing, then stopped. The C note rang out, and a muscle in his shoulder twitched.

"Abigail," he called. "Come here, please."

He heard the scrape of the piano bench, and a moment later, she entered the corridor. Jeremiah stepped closer and spoke quietly into her ear.

"Sheriff Brennan is here to check on you. Your mother and father think you are here against your will. I told him you asked to come live with us."

Abigail's shoulders fell.

Jeremiah lifted his right hand, hesitated, then touched her arm gently.

"Don't show anger," he said. "Show Brennan you're okay, and that's what he'll tell your parents."

She let out a breath, nodded, and followed him back to the study. Brennan set down his coffee and hugged the girl when he saw her. He stepped back, keeping one hand on her shoulder, and looked at her as though she were someone he had not seen in years. Brennan smiled, and Jeremiah saw something in the man's eyes. Concern, maybe.

"You look well," Brennan said to her.

The fingers of her right hand rubbed together nervously, but Abigail's face lit up with a smile so genuine that Jeremiah couldn't tell whether she was acting.

"I am," she said, almost laughing. "I've got my own room here now. I'm giving piano lessons and working on writing my own music."

"Your ma and pa…" Brennan began.

She nodded. "I'm here because I want to be."

Brennan smiled a little sadly. "And that's what I'll tell them." He put his hat back on and shook Jeremiah's hand. "Well, I won't take any more of your time. It was lovely to see you, Abigail. I hope to hear you play again soon, and I'm glad you're doing well."

Abigail opened her mouth to respond when a terrible sound came from the west wing. The sound of something slamming down onto the piano keys. A discordant noise rang out, then another smash, more violent this time.

Jeremiah knew exactly what it was because it was the same sound he heard whenever he had imagined taking an ax to the instrument.

59

BRENNAN'S EYEBROWS ROSE, AND HE looked at Jeremiah, who did his best to appear unconcerned.

"What is that?" he asked.

Jeremiah put his hand on the sheriff's elbow and led him to the door. He glanced at Abigail and moved his eyes to the hall. Abigail nodded and walked quickly back to the west wing.

Jeremiah lowered his voice. "It's Emma. She's started drinking."

Brennan's eyes saddened. "What is she doing in there?"

They reached the door, and Jeremiah opened it. He stepped outside with him into the bright, cold air, and then closed the door behind them.

"She practices day and night, but the truth is she's not getting any better. She drinks to deal with the pain, and then it makes her play even worse, which makes her angry."

Brennan buttoned up his coat and shivered. "You be careful," he said, and Jeremiah noticed the man's eyebrows and mustache were the color of dirty snow. "There's a box inside all of us where we lock things up. All the stuff we don't want to face. The drink is a key. You understand what I'm saying? Get in the habit of unlocking that box, and soon, everything you hid away in there is out in the open. And it's ugly, rotten stuff we put in there."

"I'm trying," Jeremiah said.

Brennan's face went serious, "Try harder. Don't let your wife slowly bury herself with your boy."

He gave a tight smile, patted Jeremiah's shoulder, and walked down the stairs. He paused at the bottom and turned around.

"One other thing I wanted to mention. A stranger came into town yesterday, tall guy with white hair, wears something like a priest robe. Anyway, he's been asking about the house, about you, and why you don't preach anymore. Sound like anyone you know?"

Jeremiah rubbed a fist in his burning eyes. He wanted to close them and sleep for a year. Priest robe? He searched his memory for another pastor he might have known who fit the description.

"No," he said. "Doesn't sound familiar."

"Seems a little odd to me. Al Jenkins was out south by Fang Rock, chasing after a cow, when he says he saw a caravan of wagons go into the woods. Maybe forty, fifty people, he reckons. Next day, this tall fellow shows up asking about you."

"He knew my name?"

Brennan nodded, squinting at the sun glinting off the snow-covered field.

"Any of them handy with a gun?" he asked, nodding at the tent city.

"A few."

Brennan shielded his eyes and watched the men of Garrett's crew going about their tasks.

"I'd pay some of them to keep an eye on things for a few days, or at least until this tall fellow makes it clear what he wants from you."

Jeremiah tried to act like he was not worried, but Brennan's words set off a small bell in his head.

"I'll do that," Jeremiah said.

Brennan turned and looked up at the fortress that towered above him. He gave a small smile.

"And don't lose yourself in there, okay?"

60

AFTER BRENNAN MADE HIS WAY through the tent city and was halfway across the field, Jeremiah went back inside. In the west wing he found Emma sitting on the floor, dress spread out like a flower, and Samuel sitting stiffly next to her. Her arms were wrapped around him, one hand stroking his head as she rocked gently, humming in his golden ear. Abigail stood a few feet away, chewing her nails and staring at mother and son with a look Jeremiah thought was something between fear and disgust. She didn't seem to notice Jeremiah come into the room.

As he came toward them Jeremiah stepped on something hard. He bent down and picked it up, held it to the light. A piano key. He looked over at the instrument. Several of the keys in the middle were cracked while others were broken off completely, pieces of them scattered about the floor.

He went past Abigail and knelt in front of his wife and son. He didn't like Emma's expression at all. It was distant, too similar to the way she used to stare out the window at Samuel's grave, as if looking at a world that did not exist.

Jeremiah put a hand on his son's leg, looked at the boy's face. Deep lines were carved into his forehead, each of them the size and shape of the edge of a piano key.

Samuel had done it once before, but only that one time and for the most part Jeremiah believed the music, if that's what it was, soothed the boy. Now he had done it again, and much worse this time. Bashed his head right into the instrument until he broke it.

He was ashamed to admit it to himself, but Jeremiah was almost glad for it. He wouldn't have to hear that middle C any longer. It was the white key he now held in his hand.

The selfish thought grew in his mind, became a solid thing that he took and placed inside the dark box Brennan had talked about. Then Jeremiah locked it up tight.

61

JEREMIAH TOOK SAMUEL'S HAND AND helped the boy to his feet. A metallic moan came out of his mouth. So much of the boy's body was wrecked, yet those self-inflicted marks on his face made Jeremiah tense and angry. That blank golden face, that grating sound from its throat.

Jeremiah pulled Samuel towards Abigail. "Take him upstairs, to his room."

Abigail stared at Emma, still sitting on the floor, legs splayed, one hand held against her chest, as if feeling her heartbeat. Emma's eyes followed her son, her face full of longing and fear.

"Abigail," Jeremiah said, raising his voice, "take Samuel to his room."

His voice shook Abigail out of her trance. She took the boy's hand and led him off down the hall.

Jeremiah crossed the room and pulled open the curtains, letting in dim, cloud-filtered light. He went back over to Emma and lowered himself on the floor in front of her.

Her eyes met his. "I don't understand," she said.

"He doesn't belong here," Jeremiah said. "He never did."

Emma lowered her hand, placed it flat on the wood. "But he *is* here, Jeremiah. And we make decisions based on that fact."

Jeremiah said, "It's clear the boy is in pain. I can see it, Abigail can see it. You can see it too, but you choose to believe that it will go away."

Emma put both hands to her face and spoke from between her fingers.

"Samuel is learning. He's still growing, still getting used to his new body. He didn't ask to be here, just like a baby doesn't ask to be born, and that's what he is. Don't you see that?" She lowered one hand, put it on Jeremiah's arm and squeezed gently. "You think he's in pain, and I think he's just newly born. He doesn't know yet how not to hurt himself, but he'll learn. I know he will."

Jeremiah took her hand in his. Her skin was cold and sticky. Her eyes wide and red. There was desperation in her voice, in the way her body moved in frantic, jerky motions. He wondered how long it had been since she slept a full night.

"Emma, I read all the books again, looking for something I might have missed." He closed his eyes and continued speaking. He didn't want to see her face. "They don't want to come back. I pulled him away from something." His hand tightened around hers. "The way Samuel is, is how he'll always be."

With his eyes still closed, Jeremiah heard her inhale and hold it.

He said, "He's suffering, and it's cruel to keep him here with us."

The slap across his face hurt worse because Jeremiah didn't see it coming. He heard the swish of Emma's dress, then her free hand struck him. The skin stung and heat bloomed in the shape of a hand and fingers on his left cheek. He opened his eyes and looked into Emma's hardened face. Her lips were tightened into a thin line and her nostrils flared with heavy breathing. She pulled her hand away from his.

The muscles around her mouth moved as she tried to keep her composure. Multiple expressions flickered across her face.

"He's learning," she said, spitting the words out. "You don't see it like I do. You don't spend as much time with him. He's saying things."

Jeremiah sighed. "But none of it stops him from hurting himself."

"You want to take him away from me again?" she asked.

"I want to send him back to where he belongs, where he won't be in pain anymore," Jeremiah said.

Emma pushed herself up and stood. She smoothed out her dress and brushed hair from her eyes. She hurried away, leaving Jeremiah sitting in the middle of an empty room.

He looked down at the floor and saw the sweat-shape of his wife's hand on the wood. The same shape that still burned on his face.

62

SAMUEL WAS ON THE FLOOR in front of the fireplace, sitting in that strange way of his. Back upright, legs stretched out straight, as though they could not bend. The curtains were closed in this room as well, though there was little chance anyone could see inside. The embers still glowed and pulsed on Samuel's golden face, deepening the shadows where parts of him were missing. His expressionless face stared into the fire, his hands flat on the floor beside him.

Abigail sat in the rocking chair, watching him. He was silent. There were no sounds of breathing in and out, and it made her own breaths seem loud. She hated the silence. Hated the way his face never changed. Hated that she didn't understand how such a thing could live without a beating heart or breath.

Maybe she wouldn't hate him so much if he didn't frighten her. She tried to think of him as a boy, a boy she had known no less, but she couldn't see him as anything other than a golden statue possessed by something she didn't quite trust.

It might be Samuel in there, but she didn't know if he was all alone.

"Samuel," she said, to break the silence. "Samuel, can you hear me?"

The boy kept staring into the fire.

Abigail stomped her foot. Not hard, but enough to vibrate the wood.

"Samuel," she said again.

The boy's face turned, slowly. Shadows moved over his smooth, bright skin. The hole where his right eye should have been became a dark pool of shadow. His good eye looked at her.

Abigail leaned forward. "Can you speak? Can you tell me what you're thinking?"

The iris of the good eye swirled a little. The embers crackled as she waited. Samuel stared until Abigail was about to slam her foot down again. Then the boy's mouth opened and a sound came out.

"Huuuurrrrrrrr," he said.

Abigail got down on her knees and came closer to him, watching the mouth closely.

"Say it again, faster."

His mouth opened. There was a faint echo as air moved in him, in his hollowness.

"Huurrrrrrt," he said.

She looked into the swirling liquid color at the center of Samuel's eye and saw something reflected back at her, only it was not a thing, it was a feeling. Something she felt in her own thoughts. A boy was in the body, inside the gold, spread throughout every inch of the metal.

She played Samuel's drawn out word with her own mouth, slowed it down, tightened it.

"Hurt," she said. "Do you feel hurt?"

Samuel nodded.

"Where do you hurt?"

There was another long pause, but Abigail was patient this time. She somehow knew he was thinking. Finally, the boy said, "Alllllll huurrt."

Abigail reached out and took his hand, held his cool fingers.

"All hurt," she said.

63

ALL HURT. ALL TIME. THIS HOME NO HOME. BACK. BACK TO LIGHT. NO HURT IN LIGHT. BACK. BACK. BACK. NEED GO BACK. HERE DARK. NO LIGHT. IN LIGHT. NO HURT. NO MORE. NO TIME.

64

JEREMIAH LAY ON THE FLOOR in the great room of the west wing. Outside, the sky lowered and snow fell. Thick flakes that looked like ash. Pieces of the broken piano were scattered across the floor. Bits of black and white keys.

He closed his eyes, laid as still as he could and imagined he was in a coffin, buried in damp black earth. The fingers of his right hand moved until the first and second fingers were straight. He felt a burning pain deep in the bones of his hand, like something building up inside him that would split the skin and come pouring out.

He thought of Samuel but the name no longer meant his son. It meant the golden statue that moved through the house with heavy steps and spoke in metallic tones. His son, his true son, was somewhere else and Jeremiah wondered what that place looked like. He hoped it was beautiful.

Would it be so bad to let the boy remain, let Emma have something to love, to teach? Jeremiah knew he could convince himself to not follow through, but every time he saw the boy he thought of the horse his father had shot when Jeremiah and Elijah were young. The animal had stepped into a shallow ditch and snapped its leg. It lay in the field, pushing yellow foam from its flapping lips and breathing like there was no air left. Their father had taken them out to the field and told them that when a creature is in misery, the only thing left to do is end its suffering.

That's what Jeremiah saw in Samuel.

Suffering.

If he sent the boy back, his suffering would be over, and Emma's would begin all over again. Jeremiah only hoped hers would fade in time. He knew, though, that if Samuel remained his suffering would only get worse.

Jeremiah tried to be strong as he thought these things, but his eyes burned and he felt tears trace down his face.

Why did every choice have to be so painful?

A thought flashed through his mind and before he realized what he was doing, Jeremiah crossed the two fingers of his right hand and held them against his temple. He clenched his teeth and pushed until he felt the hard bone of his skull. He waited for the golden light to glow, to feel heat spreading over his head and down his neck.

Just let it be over, he thought.

But there was no light, no heat.

He yelled out once and slammed his fingers down onto the floor. This time there was light. It grew brighter and the burning pain he had felt in his hand subsided. When he pulled his fingers away, there was a solid gold floorboard beside him.

PART III

CONSEQUENCES

65

WHEN PASTOR CARLSON REID CAME out of the mayor's office, he saw the tall man with white hair walking down the main street, stopping at each storefront and glancing inside. Dressed in a strange black robe that hung down to his ankles, this stranger walked with a minor limp, hands clasped together behind his back. His shadow stretched out on the dirt. His deep-set eyes moved over the buildings, the signs, the horses and carriages that rumbled by. To Reid, it looked like he was studying the town, memorizing each and every detail.

The stranger walked past the tavern, avoiding the eyes of the men that watched him. When he came to the end of the street, the stranger looked up and stopped. Ahead of him, across the field, Jeremiah's dark fortress rose into the sky. Even from this distance the sounds of hammers and shouting voices could be heard.

People passed the stranger on the street, staring openly, but the man didn't seem to notice. He kept looking at the massive structure, and Reid thought there was a slight smile on his face the entire time.

Two days passed before Reid saw the stranger again. This time it was from the pulpit of his church. He stood looking out at the familiar faces of his congregation as he preached. The man sat in the very back, hands folded on his lap. His eyes remained fixed on Reid as the preacher spoke.

"The Lord Jesus himself talked more about the dangers of being rich than he did about hell. What does this tell us? Our almighty Redeemer taught that abundant wealth pushes a man's soul closer to hellfire than anything else. Remember the rich young ruler?" Reid paused as heads nodded and voices murmured in agreement. "He wanted eternal life, but he refused to part with all his wealth. He refused Christ's call to help the poor and needy."

The stranger sat motionless, expressionless, and his eyes never left Carlson Reid. It made Reid nervous, but he had a job to do.

Reid raised his voice so that it filled the room. "I choose to believe that this young ruler, this young arrogant man of wealth, walked away from the Lord and lived out his days in misery. I believe his guilty conscience would not allow him to sleep, and he lay awake every night in a cold sweat, feeling the fires of hell licking at his ankles."

Reid's voice went deeper as his face turned red. "And I do believe with all my heart that one black night, when this rich ruler was no longer young, but a lonely old man with no friends and no family by his side, that he lay upon his death bed, and those flames he imagined, they became real and the fires of hell burned him. And from the thick smoke that choked him came the hideous face of the devil himself, saying…" a loud whisper now, and the congregation leaned forward to hear it, "'…all you had to do was part with your money and help the poor. But you didn't, and now your soul belongs to me!'" Reid shouted. The room filled with applause.

"Do not be like that man," Reid yelled out, waving his arm over them. Sweat rolled down his back, and he felt like his collar was choking him.

"Do not be like our neighbor who secrets himself away in his castle, hoarding wealth." He clenched his teeth together and held up a fist, pointed in the direction of the field. His eyes went wide as he spoke in a low growl. "Do not be like him!"

The whole congregation rose to their feet, cheering and clapping. Reid felt the energy coursing through the room, the electricity of a group with an identified enemy. Someone to blame. Someone to hate. Jeremiah, his predecessor, had never preached so powerfully. Had never given his congregation this sense of unity against a common threat.

The stranger with the white hair was the only person still sitting.

Carlson Reid stood just outside the church doors shaking hands as his congregation exited. One person after the next all told him how much they enjoyed his sermon, how necessary and important it was. It was a test, really. A test to see where they all stood, and now he knew without any doubt.

The white-haired stranger remained seated just inside and Reid could think of little else, even as he shook hands and ruffled children's hair. His wife, Laura, stood nearby on the lawn, also greeting families, and she caught his eye, smiled at him. There was something carnal in that smile. Something that made Reid's blood run hotter.

After the last person had gone, Laura took the children to their home behind the church, and Reid went back inside to confront the stranger. When he entered the empty building, the stranger was now sitting on the stage, his long legs bent, sharp knees jutting out. The stranger rose and began clapping. A lonely sound that echoed harshly.

The clapping stopped suddenly. "Well done, sir," the man said. "I have not seen such a passionate display of righteous fury in God knows how long." He smiled with teeth the same color as his hair. "It is good to know the reality of hell has not been forgotten in at least one church in this country."

His voice was smooth and clear, and a hint of an accent, vaguely British, colored his words.

"Allow me to introduce myself," he said, holding out a hand. "My name is Solomon Anders."

Reid took the man's hand and shook it. The skin was smooth, cold.

Solomon looked up at the ceiling. "You have a beautiful church, and such a vibrant congregation, no doubt thanks to your fiery preaching."

"This church wasn't always mine," Reid said.

"So I've heard," Solomon replied, sitting back down. Reid sat in the pew across from him. "The previous pastor," Solomon continued, "I was told he lost his faith."

"He lost his son and his faith followed," Reid said. "Death is many kinds of loss."

Solomon tapped a knuckle on Reid's knee. "But surely not for a man like you?" he said, smiling. "Death is to be celebrated, is it not? The soul no longer imprisoned, no longer in pain. Free to fly back to its true home. What a wonderful hope!"

Reid couldn't tell if the man was mocking his faith and remained silent.

Solomon spread his fingers and touched the tips to his temples. "Allow me to read your mind," he said, his smile fading. He closed his eyes and hummed for a moment. "You are wondering who I am, and why I'm here."

He leaned forward so their knees were almost touching. Reid could smell the man's breath, stale like a hole in the ground. As he looked into Solomon's face, he noticed something strange about his eyes. One was lightning blue, sparking as it stared at him. But the other eye was stone grey. It made Reid uneasy to look at them.

"I have traveled long and far to be here," Solomon said, all trace of his good humor gone.

Reid swallowed with a loud sound. "Have you come alone?" he asked, feeling nothing like the man of strength he pretended to be while preaching.

"I am with my family. We are camped just outside town."

"You should bring them," Reid said. "You all would be welcomed."

The corner of Solomon's mouth turned up a little. "In time, I will. But not yet."

Reid tried to smile also but wasn't sure what he was smiling about.

"What, in our humble town, could warrant such a long journey?" Reid asked.

Solomon's long fingers laced together. "I am a seeker. Would you believe me if I said there is a world inside the world? Something invisible that's above us, beneath us, all around us?"

"You speak of the spiritual world?"

"I speak of the world before the second flood."

Reid's face twisted in confusion. "The second flood?"

"The flood that Noah survived," Solomon said.

"But that was the only flood."

Solomon shook his head slowly and smiled. "When did Lucifer fall?" he asked.

Reid's brow creased. "The Bible doesn't say, so we cannot know for certain."

"Think about this, preacher," Solomon said, lifting a single finger. "The serpent was in the garden of Eden. He was already here. He had been here for a long time."

Reid closed his eyes tight for a moment, then opened them. Black stars scattered from his vision. "This is beginning to sound like heresy," he said. "Are you a God-fearing man, Mr. Anders?"

"Oh, I am," Solomon nodded. "I do fear, indeed." Then, rising to his full height, he said, "Listen to me, Carlson Reid. We were not the first, and we will not be the last. There was a world that existed before Adam and Eve were made, and its fragments remain here with us. All of the mysteries, the unexplained, the evil spirits and hauntings. Echoes of this past world."

Reid felt the man's voice vibrate in his chest, kicking his heart out of rhythm. He pressed his back against the hard pew, his fingers gripping the edge.

Solomon leaned in close, his stale breath filling Reid's nose. "Now, tell me about Jeremiah Pevensie."

After Solomon Anders left the church, Reid sat in the pew alone, his head spinning. He stayed there until the sounds of a strong wind blowing through the trees stirred him from his thoughts.

He went outside and walked the short path to the home he shared with his wife and children. His temples throbbed and he wanted nothing more than to lie down, let the day be over.

When he opened the door of the house, the voices of his two daughters fighting over a doll caused the pain in his head to grow even sharper. He had to hold back from screaming at them to be silent.

Laura greeted him with the same smile she had given him at the church, but he was too lost in thought to notice. Even the smell of the meat she was cooking made him feel ill. He brushed her aside and went to their bedroom where he lay down on the bed and closed his eyes. His pulse pounded at the base of his neck.

Reid could not get the stranger's words out of his mind.

Just before Solomon Anders had left, he had torn a blank page out of a hymnal and drawn a map on it. He handed the map to Reid and told him to wait until dark, then follow it to where Solomon and his family were camped.

Reid stared into the stranger's eyes, and cursing his lack of inner strength, could not find a way to say no.

66

CARLSON REID WAITED UNTIL THE children were asleep and his wife settled in by the fire to read a book. Then he gathered his hat, coat, and gloves, made for the door, and told Laura he was going for a walk. Her voice followed him out the door.

"Carlson, dear? It's so late. Why are you going for a walk at this hour? Carlson?"

When he was out of view of the house, Reid took the map from his pocket and looked at it in the moonlight. It was crudely drawn, but he recognized the landmarks. He walked south outside town, past mostly dark houses with the occasional lantern flicker in the windows. He continued until the buildings fell away and he was alone in the snow-covered field, under a sky full of dust. The cold stung his nose and cheeks, and his breath came out in clouds.

By the time he reached Fang Rock, Reid's feet were stiff and aching. If he had been thinking clearly, he would have brought a bag of water to soothe his parched throat.

Reid folded the map, took a deep breath, and walked into the forest.

Moonlight trickled through the treetops, making the snow a ghostly blue. The trees creaked with a high breeze. Branches clacked together. Reid stumbled over a stone and regained his balance, cursing out loud. As he righted himself, Reid thought he saw two red orbs hovering in the darkness. He blinked once and they were gone.

He heard voices coming from up ahead. He walked a bit further until he saw the orange glow of firelight pulsing on the trees. Reid wasn't sure whether to announce himself, so he started walking heavier, crunching the snow beneath his feet.

The trees thinned and then opened into a large circular clearing with a bonfire blazing at its center. A series of nine coaches and wagons stood in a semi-circle in front of the fire. A dozen or more tents were scattered around.

Reid stepped into the clearing. A group of men and women—all dressed in long robes, like Solomon's, only white—moved about the space, focused on particular tasks. A man to his right held a cleaver and was in the process of butchering a deer. He hacked away at the meat, and the dirt around the carcass was soaked a deep crimson. A few women sat huddled in blankets by the fire, all of them sewing. Another man was digging a hole, for what though, Reid could not tell.

Reid was about to clear his throat and draw attention to himself when something moved to his left. His fist clenched on instinct.

A man, about his same age, white robe stained with dirt, stood before him. His eyes were deep-set and shadowed. Each hand held a strange object made of twigs and string. The objects were very similar, a triangular shape with rounded corners. The strings criss-crossed in patterns over the open space, making something that looked very much like a face. Teardrop eyes and a thin mouth, surrounded by beads and feathers and the bones of small animals.

Reid glanced past the man and saw these faces hanging at intervals from low tree branches all around the camp. Similar totems were laid out on the ground behind him in a line.

The man stared at Reid, unsmiling. "You are the one the Guide is waiting for?" he said.

"Do you mean Solomon?" Reid asked.

The man set down his objects. "I will take you to him."

Reid followed him through the clearing, past more people, some of whom were making the twig and string faces this man had been hanging. All of them dressed in the same white robes, and Reid shivered to think how cold they must be.

Reid was led behind the wagons where there was a smaller fire and a large, round canvas tent. The man gestured to the tent, then turned and left Reid standing alone. Firelight glowed in the space between the tent flaps. Reid would have stood there longer, questioning his decision to come all the way out here, if a gust of frigid wind had not blown across his neck and made him want to seek warmth.

He went to the tent, and after clearing his throat, said, "This is Carlson Reid."

"Come in," Solomon's voice answered.

Reid pulled back one flap and stepped inside.

Two hours later, Reid stumbled out of Solomon's tent and into the snow. His stomach clenched violently, and then he doubled over and vomited. He retched so hard that he tasted blood.

The people in white robes watched Reid stagger past their tents. Some of them stopped what they were doing, as if frozen, and stared at him as he tried to walk normally, but his whole body was sending too many signals, feeling too many things all at once.

He was hot, he was cold. He was dizzy and ill, and his feet looked a long way down.

Reid's hands opened and closed rapidly as he passed by the fire. A young woman whose white robe stuck out with a pregnant belly stopped her sewing and followed Reid with her eyes.

Did they know? They had to. Solomon must have told them why they were here. Why else would they follow him?

Once he reached the forest, Reid took one look over his shoulder and started running, and he didn't stop until he made it back to Fang Rock. He leaned back against the cool stone, pointed his face to the sky, and tried to slow his breathing. Sweat ran down his back and chest. He felt drunk, worse than drunk. His legs were weak and heavy, like they were made of stone.

Reid took off his collar and let the cold air hit his throat. His scalp was hot and itchy. He breathed fast, and the air puffed out like clouds from a steam train.

The sour taste of bile was still on his tongue, so he scooped up a handful of snow, put it in his mouth, and let it melt. Then he swished it around and spat it out.

Up until tonight, Reid had thought he understood how the world worked. He studied and taught from the Bible, he tried to live righteously, and he knew death was not the end of the soul. But what Solomon had told him, showed him, made Reid realize he knew nothing. He felt as if the earth had just opened beneath his feet and swallowed him whole.

He knew nothing, except that he was more afraid than he had ever been in his life.

Reid shivered and buttoned his coat back up. He looked at the sky, at the dusty lights of the galaxy stretched out above him, and Reid felt so small and insignificant.

Even inside the gloves his fingers were stiff and cold. He rubbed them together for warmth and started walking back to Charwood. Reid knew he would not be able to sleep once he got home. He could not stop thinking about the task he had been entrusted with. A task given to him by Solomon.

67

ABIGAIL HAD NOT SEEN MUCH of Jeremiah since the incident with the piano. He almost never left the west wing, and although she had been instructed to never go to the fifth floor, one night she snuck out of her room on the third floor and climbed the stairs.

Halfway between the fourth and fifth floors the air became thick and electric. The hairs on her arm raised up and she felt a tickling in her nose when she breathed. It made her think of the little sparks she could shoot from her fingertips when she shuffled over a rug in her stockinged feet as a girl. Sparks that would shock another person when she touched their skin.

She climbed higher, trying to breathe through her mouth. Still, the air charged through her teeth and made them tingle.

There was a sound, too. A subtle vibration in the curve of her throat, and it made her feel like she was humming. It grew stronger the higher she climbed, until the hum had a tone, like a piano holding out a note. There was a metallic quality to it, a bell that had been rung somewhere far away and just kept ringing, faint but never diminishing.

When she reached the fifth floor, a golden glow lay on the floor just outside one of the rooms halfway down the dark hallway. The hum was stronger here, and the electric feeling grew until it was almost painful, like a sewing needle gently pricking her skin. The thin blond hairs on her arm were standing straight up.

She knew she should turn around and go back to bed. If she got caught, Jeremiah might make her leave the house. Or worse, she could lose her wages and end up right back where she started—living with her mother and father—and there was nothing in the world she feared more.

But the hum and the lightning in the air and the golden glow made her feet move forward.

The hum had a pulse to it now that reminded her of a beehive. Steady and droning, it rose and fell in intensity. Abigail finally reached the door where the light came from, and opened it slowly, just enough so she could see inside.

The room was empty. No furniture, no curtains, just like every other room on this floor. Nothing except a large painting hung on the far wall. Abigail pushed the door open further and put her head inside.

Behind the painting, a rectangle glowed on the wall. Thin lines of bright golden light in the shape of a door.

68

REID WENT STRAIGHT TO THE church, locked the doors behind him, and sat at his desk in the office behind the stage. He lit a lantern, took off his coat, and hung it on the chair. Against the far wall was a bookcase filled with volumes of commentary on the Bible, works written by spiritual luminaries who studied the words of the prophets.

How quaint they all seemed now. Books written by men who only saw the surface of a deep black ocean. Some part of Reid wanted to burn them, because he would never be able to read them again, not after what he'd been shown.

What had Solomon said? *A world inside the world.*

Too many thoughts were storming in his mind, and it made him dizzy. He tried to focus and pull one thought out of the hurricane, but he couldn't. Inexplicably, he wanted to cry. He put his head down on the desk and pulled at his hair.

He wished Solomon had never opened the box and had shown him what was inside. Even thinking of that box made the back of Reid's neck ache again.

Reid's eyes fluttered open. Gray morning light came through the windows. He sat up, feeling tired and sore. The lantern had burned out, and the office was so cold that Reid could see his breath. He heard voices coming from town, the rattle of wagons, the clang of the blacksmith's hammer.

Reid stood unsteadily, and his head seemed to float above his shoulders. He blinked away spots, and once he regained his balance, he put on his coat and gloves and left the church. As he passed the cemetery, he glanced over at his house. Smoke rose from the chimney, and he knew Laura was probably making breakfast for their daughters and wondering where her husband was. He wanted to go to them, to take them in his arms and hold something real, but he kept walking.

People he passed in the street waved to him and said good morning. Reid could only nod in reply. Each footstep hammered in his temples, and even though the sky was covered in clouds, the filtered light burned his eyes.

He walked until he came to the sheriff's office and went inside.

Brennan's deputy, Franklin Denney, was sitting at the desk and looked up when Reid entered.

"Morning, Reverend," Denney said.

"Where's Brennan?"

Denney jerked his head back toward the jail cells. "Picked up Fletcher again last night, probably saved his life. The fool was passed out in the snow."

Reid stamped his feet to knock the snow off his boots and removed his gloves. He blew into his hands, but they still felt frozen.

"I need to speak with him right away," Reid said.

Denney stood, pushed his hat back, and narrowed his eyes. "You okay, Carlson?"

Reid tried to speak, but his lips were numb. His teeth chattered together. He moved closer to the stove. "It's important," Reid finally managed to say.

Denney's face creased with concern. He got up and went into the back hall.

A moment later, Brennan came walking out, Denney following behind him. He wore no coat, and his shirt sleeves were rolled up.

Brennan took one look at Reid and said, "Frank, why don't you head on over to Fletcher's place and let his wife know where he is. He'll be around once he's sobered up."

"Okay, boss."

Denney grabbed his coat. When the door opened, a burst of cold air hit Reid, and he backed up so close to the stove that he thought his legs might get burned.

Brennan took off his hat and tossed it on the desk. He sat down and motioned to one of the other chairs. "You look like you got a head full of things that need saying."

Reid hated to leave the stove, but his legs were shaking so badly he didn't think he could stand any longer. He took a seat on the other side of the desk and tried to look Brennan in the eye. He wanted to tell Brennan everything, but Solomon had been very clear that he was not to say anything about what he had seen.

Brennan leaned forward and put his elbows on the desk. Wrinkles deepened around his clear blue eyes.

"You been drinking, son?"

Reid laughed, even though he didn't mean to, and his teeth knocked together when he did. He shook his head. "I've been asked to come and speak with you."

Brennan's expression did not change. "Well, here you are."

"There's a stranger in town, a man named Solomon Anders," Reid said.

"The fellow in the black robe. I've seen him."

"He wants to meet with you."

Brennan rapped his knuckles on the desk. "He knows where to find me."

Reid rubbed his hands together but stopped when he realized how nervous it must make him look. "He requested that you come to his camp," Reid said. "There's something he'd like to show you."

Brennan leaned back until the chair creaked. He unrolled one shirt sleeve and buttoned it at the wrist.

A moan and a curse came from the back hall. Fletcher was waking up, Reid guessed. He could not stop shivering, but sweat slid down his back, and the skin on his face tightened with heat. He could smell himself, smell the sweat and the fear.

"And he sent you to ask me," Brennan said, looking into the preacher's eyes and rolling down the other sleeve.

Reid spoke slowly so the words wouldn't shake. "He has information about Jeremiah Pevensie."

Brennan's hand stopped moving. "What about Jeremiah?"

"He wouldn't tell me, only that he is not what he appears to be. Solomon says he's dangerous."

Brennan huffed through his nose and resumed buttoning the sleeve. "And what about Solomon, Reid? Is he dangerous?"

Reid looked down at the floor, at the puddle of melted snow under his boots. "I don't know what Solomon is. I've never dealt with anyone like him."

Brennan's eyes narrowed as he watched Reid squirm in his seat. "No. I don't suppose you have."

There was another moan from the back hall, followed by yelling. Brennan stood with a groan and picked up his hat.

An unexpected shiver ran down Reid's back and shook his body. "You need to hear what he has to say."

Brennan watched the man silently. Observed the little twitches and jerks, the wide eyes that moved from the floor to the ceiling to the paper on the desk, and his fingers kept rubbing together with an abrasive sound. One word came to mind when Brennan thought of Reid, and that was composed. He may have been conniving and manipulative, but he was always in control of how he appeared to others. Something had gotten to him and scared him, bad.

Brennan let out a slow breath. "Okay, meet me here at sundown. If I'm going out there, you're coming with me."

Reid opened his mouth to object, but Brennan's stare reminded him of his father. He looked back at the floor and nodded.

Then Brennan turned and went into the hall. He yelled, much louder than he needed to, "Good morning, Fletcher. How's your head feeling?"

Reid stood on legs that did not feel like legs and went back outside into the cold.

69

REID AVOIDED GOING HOME AND spent the rest of the day in his church office. He opened the Bible several times to find some comfort, some wisdom, but the words just bled together into splotches of black and red ink.

He waited until the sun went down, then Reid put on a second coat and trudged through the snow into town. The sky was dark and the moon shone from behind silver clouds.

When he arrived at the sheriff's office Reid found Brennan inside drinking a steaming cup of coffee. Deputy Denney was nowhere to be seen.

Brennan stood when Reid came into the room and grabbed a thick coat that hung on the wall. He went over to the gun rack and took down a rifle, a repeater, and handed it to Reid.

"How good are you with one of these?" Brennan asked.

Reid took the weapon, not sure how to hold it. "I haven't shot anything in a long time," he said.

Brennan cinched his gun-belt tight around his waist. "You aim at what you want to hit and pull the trigger. All there is to it."

Brennan buttoned up his coat, put on his gloves and scarf, and opened the door. A flurry of snow came rushing into the office.

Brennan held out a hand. "Lead the way."

They walked in silence until Fang Rock came into view. Reid stayed a few paces ahead of Brennan, their boots crunching through fresh snow the only sound. He was again reminded of his father, of how he could remain so quiet for so long. Only his quiet was loud, in its own way. His disappointment showed on his face, in his eyes.

They stopped at the rock and Reid pointed toward the forest. "It's not much further."

Brennan took off his hat and rubbed a forearm over his grey hair. The shadows on his face made him look older, frail. He sighed and replaced the hat. "I need you to do something for me. If things go bad out there, get back to town, find Denney, and protect Jeremiah."

Reid laughed, but Brennan put a hand on the preacher's arm, and those shadow-enclosed eyes stared at him.

"I need you on this, son," Brennan said. "If things go bad, I need to know that you'll help make things right."

Although his father had been dead for several years, Reid still heard his voice sometimes, heard his sharp criticisms delivered with a tone so close to disgust it made Reid's face burn just to think of them.

What Brennan asked him to do was exactly the sort of thing Reid's father would have told him he could never do. Because he wasn't strong enough, he wasn't righteous enough. Because he was too full of sin. But when Brennan looked at him, Reid did not see any doubt in the man's face. Brennan not only knew he could do it, but he was also counting on it. And more than that, Brennan hadn't told him what to do, he had *asked* Reid for his help.

"When I was just a boy, my father used to gamble all our money away," Brennan said. "Every week he'd try and win it back, and he almost always ended up with less. One night, he won big, bigger than he ever had, but someone accused him of cheating and before my father could collect and take off, someone punched him in the face. My father swung back, someone else joined in, and soon the whole place was in chaos."

Brennan paused, smiled a little and shook his head. "My father was there with a couple friends. They all knew they weren't getting the winnings, so they gathered around my father and pushed through the crowd, all of them swinging the whole way to the door."

Brennan held up a gloved hand and made a fist.

"That's what you do when there's enemies all around. You fight your way out. And you don't ever let go of the thing that might save you. You understand? I need you to promise that you'll do what's right even if a storm comes."

Reid gave Brennan a grim smile and nodded. "I promise."

Brennan patted his shoulder. "Good man."

It was not until they had entered the woods that Reid realized he was holding the rifle tightly in both hands, like a trained soldier and not like a man afraid.

When they stepped into the clearing, there were even more people in white robes than Reid had seen before. The whole camp was unusually quiet, and those who were talking spoke in hushed voices, as though the silence were something fragile that could break.

Reid took a step and heard a crack. He looked down and saw one of the wooden charms under his boot, the strange face broken in half.

The pregnant young woman Reid had seen last night struggled to her feet when she saw the men. She came over to them and smiled.

"You're here to see the Guide?" she asked.

Up close, she looked much younger than Reid expected. Her blonde hair was done up in a braid wrapped around her head like a crown. There was a small dusting of freckles across her nose.

Brennan looked to Reid. "The guide?"

"Yes," Reid said. "We're here to see Solomon."

The girl pointed towards Solomon's tent. The sleeve of her robe slid up her arm and Reid saw her pale skin. He wore two coats and still couldn't fight off the cold, but this girl wore just a thin robe and there were no bumps on her skin. She didn't even shiver.

Brennan tipped his hat, and they walked toward the large, round tent. The men and women sitting around the fire watched silently.

The strange tent was even bigger than Reid remembered. A perfect circle, large enough to park a coach inside, built on top of a round wooden base. Smoke rose from a hole at the very top.

Reid's hands started shaking with more than just the cold, and he gripped the rifle tighter. Brennan put a hand on the preacher's shoulder and looked him in the eye. He did not say anything, but Reid understood all the same. It was a look that said, *remember what I told you.*

Brennan's arm lowered to his side, fingers barely touching the gun hanging from his belt.

"Mr. Anders," he called out. "This is Sheriff Charles Brennan and Reverend Carlson Reid."

A breeze blew through the trees and knocked loose some snow. It fell with a soft sound.

"Mr. Brennan," Solomon's voice said, "please come in. Mr. Reid, I'll thank you to wait outside. I'd like to speak with Mr. Brennan alone."

The two men looked at each other. Reid's eyes were big. He was not expecting to stand outside alone in the cold with Solomon's strange family watching his every move.

Brennan held up both hands and made fists. Reid understood. *Fight your way out.*

Reid held the rifle like his father had taught him, one hand on the barrel, the other on the trigger, and nodded.

Brennan nodded back, walked up to the tent and stepped inside.

70

A FIRE BURNED AT THE center of the room, the floor around it covered with the fur of various animals. Several makeshift bookshelves lined the walls, filled with leather-bound volumes. Solomon Anders sat behind a desk at the far end, hunched over what looked like a scroll. Yellowed parchment with faded red ink. A journal lay open next to it under the glow of a single candle.

"Please remove your boots," Solomon said, without looking up.

Brennan did as he was asked, then waited. His ears became attuned to the sounds within the tent—the gentle crackle of the burning wood, the scratch of Solomon's pen as he wrote in the journal, and something else, a sound like breathing coming from just behind him. Brennan turned around and nothing was there. Nothing except a shelf that contained crystals, strange wood carvings, and something that looked like a tomahawk. A small ax made of wood with a bright green piece of jade stuck through a hole in the handle and lashed to it with strips of leather. It looked old, ancient even.

Brennan ran his thumb against the edge of the green blade. It was rough, recently sharpened.

Next to the ax was a human skull. The empty eye sockets and grinning mouth unsettled him, and he couldn't help but wonder who this skull belonged to. Was there a headless skeleton lying in a grave somewhere?

Solomon's voice spoke, coming from right behind him. Brennan spun around to find the man looking directly into his eyes.

"He was a silver miner who stayed with our family for a short time," he said, as if peering into Brennan's thoughts.

Solomon's black robe blended into the shadows, made his face look like it was floating.

"He was ill when he came to us. Weak, coughing up blood. A lifetime of breathing in the dust of the mines had taken its toll. We did our best to keep him comfortable until the end came, but death is never comfortable."

He walked on bare feet over the furs and came next to Brennan. He stood a full head taller than the sheriff, and the candle behind him created a halo around his white hair. Hair as white as the snow on the ground outside.

Solomon picked up the skull, cradled it in one hand. "On the day he died, he was in so much pain. He screamed for hours and would not stop. I remember his bony fingers gripping the blood-stained sheets of his bed. He clenched his teeth so hard that one of them cracked. If you look closely, you can see it."

Brennan did see it, a fissure that ran from top to bottom on one of the front teeth.

"I offered to end his suffering," Solomon said, "but he refused. He said it was his journey, and his alone. When the end came, I asked him to tell me what he saw in those brief, final moments. He said, 'I see everything.' And then he was gone."

Solomon placed the skull back on the shelf, gently. "He had no family of his own, and he asked me to remember him. This is how I honor that request."

Brennan thought it a strange way to memorialize someone, but then again, nothing this group did was normal. A roaming caravan of robe-wearing zealots who protected their camp with occult charms. Brennan felt as though he had wandered into a dark ocean and his feet no longer touched the ground.

"I was told you have information about Jeremiah Pevensie," Brennan said.

Solomon nodded and smiled. "I do indeed."

That smile made Brennan think of a spoiled child about to tattle on a friend.

"Where do you think Jeremiah acquired all his wealth?" Solomon asked.

Brennan looked to the other side of the tent and saw more bookshelves full of strange trinkets and totems, books and scrolls. There were also two small metal chests, side by side, against the curved canvas wall.

"He told me he and his brother found a gold vein up in the mountains," Brennan said.

Solomon's eyes seemed to glow. His smile grew bigger and his teeth looked yellow in the firelight.

"His brother," Solomon said. "Fascinating. And is this brother as wealthy as Jeremiah? Did they split the gold fifty-fifty?"

Brennan turned back to the shelf behind him and saw the translucent scales of a shed snake skin winding through some of the artifacts.

"I don't know what their arrangement was," Brennan said.

"Where is the brother now?"

Solomon's eyes did not look away from Brennan's and it made Brennan uncomfortable, like he was being stared into rather than looked at. He forced himself to stare back, even though it made the skin on the back of his neck start to itch.

"I don't know," Brennan said.

Solomon held his hands in front of him, fingers laced together. A faint smile curled the corners of his lips. "Of course you don't. I doubt anyone but Jeremiah knows, except perhaps his lovely wife."

Solomon moved a hand to his mouth and tapped his chin with one finger. "They lost a child, did they not?"

Brennan's jaw tightened and his eyes narrowed, but he did not look away.

"Fortunate, don't you think, that Jeremiah should find such enormous wealth only months after his son dies?"

Brennan didn't like the look of pleasure on Solomon's face, or the feeling that he was being played with.

"Listen, Mr. Anders, it's late and I'm tired. So, unless there's something specific you wanted to tell me, I'll be on my way."

The smile disappeared from Solomon's face. He stared at Brennan as the fire crackled, then said, "I'd like to show you something."

Brennan followed him around the fire to the other side of the tent where the two metal chests were.

"When I was young, I went on a quest. A spiritual journey," Solomon said, pulling a necklace over his head. From it hung a key. "I wanted to know the true history of the world, and I was told there were ancient cities in South America that contained the answers to every question man has ever asked."

Solomon knelt, unlocked one of the chests and opened it. "I spent six years wandering the jungles, walking through the ruins of these cities, studying their culture, their rituals."

His hands went into the chest and came out holding something wrapped in black velvet. He laid this on the floor and began very carefully unfolding the fabric.

"There was a world before ours, Mr. Brennan, and it was ruled by the very gods who had been cast out of heaven after their rebellion against the Creator. Some of them taught man how to do things, things we presently believe are impossible."

Solomon folded back the final piece of velvet, and there, glowing brightly on the black cloth, was a golden statue. Brennan inhaled sharply. It couldn't be what it looked like. It was, as Solomon said, impossible. The man's eyes watched the sheriff, reading his every muscle twitch and expression.

Brennan shook his head. He closed his eyes.

"Look at it," Solomon hissed.

Brennan clenched his eyes tighter and prayed that when he opened them the golden object would be changed. But it wasn't, and it was even worse than he thought, because the thing, for that was all he could call it, appeared to be in pain.

"It isn't real," Brennan whispered to himself.

"It is more than real," Solomon whispered back.

The sheriff was breathing so quickly his head started to spin. The tent and fire began to fade away until all he could see was the golden object, so small and so detailed. The skin and wrinkles, so lifelike. The tiny hands balled into fists. The downy hair on its head.

His knees buckled and he went down to the floor. Solomon reached out and grabbed Brennan's wrist, pulled it toward the thing.

"Touch it," Solomon said, his mouth so close to Brennan's ear he felt the heat of the man's breath. "Know that it's real."

Brennan jerked away and tried to stand, but his legs were too weak. Solomon leaned over, and slipping both hands under the thing, lifted it as though it were something fragile, alive. It looked even smaller in his hands.

"If you do not," Solomon said, his voice soft and gentle, "you will live the rest of your days wondering. I know you go to church. You claim to be a God-fearing man. But how can you hope to understand Him if you don't know what He is capable of?"

The object came closer to Brennan, and without realizing what he was doing his own hands moved to receive the thing. The smooth gold touched his skin and a shiver traveled up his arms, into his neck. He couldn't stop gasping for air. Tears burned his eyes.

Charles Brennan's mind dragged up memories of holding his sons for the first time. Their small frail bodies so new to the world. He remembered the way their eyes clenched shut against the light, so used to the warm darkness of their mother's womb.

This golden infant Brennan held in his hands had been there once too. He could no longer pretend it was a statue or a carving. It was too...perfect. Every single detail of the child was intact, and frozen.

Solomon silently put one hand on top of the infant, and his other hand beneath Brennan's. Then, he very gently tilted their hands. First one way, then the other. Brennan felt something move inside the infant, something that felt and sounded like sand shifting around in the hollow space.

Solomon, his face only inches from Brennan's, looked him in the eye and said, "That is its soul."

Solomon moved his hand away so Brennan could see the infant once more. So much smaller than his sons ever were, but just as dead as they were now.

"This," Solomon said, "is what Jeremiah Pevensie can do."

71

SOLOMON REWRAPPED THE TINY GOLDEN statue in the black velvet and placed it back inside the chest. Brennan sat on the floor, and he couldn't stop the tears that coursed down his cheeks.

"Something still clings to it," Solomon said as he unlocked the other chest. "Pain glows the brightest, I think. Takes the longest to fade away. A painful death, a death that happens too soon, rips something apart in the tapestry we're all connected to."

He removed a tiny skull from the chest and set it down on the fur. The fire had burned down, making the tent colder.

"I don't understand," Brennan said, finally looking up.

"There is nothing to understand," Solomon replied, reaching into the chest once more. "It is only there for you to accept."

"Then I refuse to accept it," Brennan said as he wiped his eyes and sat up straighter. He hoped his voice sounded stronger than it felt. "I refuse to believe this is possible."

Solomon pulled out another skull, the size of a small apple. Two dark lines crossed over the white bone and met in the middle.

Solomon's face grew hard, and the wrinkles beneath his eyes deepened.

"It does not require your belief," he said, his voice low. "It is something that's been here since long before you were born and will be here long after you're dead."

Brennan's heart beat so hard that his breath became shallow. The truth was, Solomon's story made a certain amount of sense, and Brennan had long suspected there was more to Jeremiah's wealth than simply stumbling across a large vein of gold in the mountains. He found something there, but something dark had followed him back home. A darkness hovered over his fortress like a storm cloud.

He looked at the skulls. "What are those?"

"Keys to doors," Solomon said. He took another skull out of the chest, this one misshapen. The back of the head was flat, rising to a point. He reached into the chest again and again, each time removing another skull and putting it in a line on the fur. Brennan counted twenty-seven in all.

Brennan clenched his sweaty hands into fists. He wanted to stand up, to run outside and fill his lungs with the frigid air, but his legs were numb.

"I have been searching for so long," Solomon said. He picked up one of the skulls and stroked it gently. "These were my children. Born to me with one purpose."

He lifted the skull and stared into the empty eye sockets. Brennan saw the man's eyes fill with tears, his lips tighten.

"They were my sacrifice, my payment," he said. He put the skull back down and laced his fingers together in front of his mouth.

"Jeremiah found what is rightfully mine. As you can see, I have more than paid for it. My family, those who travel with me, have followed me on this journey, and we have come to take back from Jeremiah what he has stolen."

During his years as sheriff, Brennan had looked into the eyes of many murderers and madmen, and not once did he feel the heart-squeezing fear he got from Solomon. His mouth had gone dry, and his hands trembled.

"You mean to kill him?" Brennan asked.

Solomon looked almost apologetic. "Only one may hold it at a time, and it does not belong to him. Besides, he must pay for his sin."

"Sin?" Brennan said. "You think God will be on your side in all of this?"

Solomon smiled again. "God is not on anyone's side. He is neutral, indifferent. The only evil or goodness that exists in this world is that which we create."

The fur under Brennan's fingers was warm from the fire, and for a moment, he thought it was still attached to something living.

"What sin?" he asked.

"The first sin committed in the fallen world," Solomon said. "The sin of Cain."

"Elijah," Brennan said and closed his eyes. He felt like a fool for not seeing it before.

From the chest, Solomon removed a jar of cloudy liquid and a plate of twisted-looking wafers.

"This is my communion," Solomon said. "When I eat the bread and drink the cup, I am given visions." He lifted a wafer and held it up. To Brennan, it looked like a rotted piece of bread.

"There is a world inside the world," Solomon said, "and our shadows live there. Versions of ourselves without substance. Sometimes I can find things in this place, information, people. I can learn things my true self cannot know. I found Jeremiah there, and I saw his sin."

"Where is Jeremiah's brother?" Brennan heard his voice ask from somewhere far away.

"He is light now," Solomon said. "He is on the other side of the other side. The place we're all trying to get back to."

Brennan looked around the tent at all the shelves, the scrolls, and artifacts, and the desk with its open journal.

"Why am I here?"

Solomon smiled, set the wafer down, took Brennan's hand, and held it.

"We have traveled for far too long looking for this mountaintop, this holy of holies. It was always my plan to settle once we found it, and now your town will be our new home."

Brennan swallowed, and his throat burned. "I'm just the sheriff," he said. "I have no influence."

Solomon raised a finger, "Ah, that's where you're wrong. I've met some of your people, spoken with them. They don't respect the mayor or the ones who work for him. They fear Jeremiah, as they should, but they respect you, Mr. Brennan."

Solomon's grip tightened around Brennan's hand. The man's face came closer. Flames from the fire flickered in his eyes.

"Once Jeremiah is gone, I will remake this town from the ground up. There will be wealth and prosperity. We will be one family partaking in the riches we all deserve. I want you to be there with me, to help me."

Brennan's body ached, and he was aware of his age in a way he had not been for a long time. There was more of his life behind him than there was ahead of him, and he knew that, felt it every morning he woke up in the bed he once shared with his wife, walked through the house where his sons had learned to crawl, to speak. He had nothing now, and although he was as afraid of dying as the next man, it didn't sting to think of it as he did when he was young.

"I won't help you," Brennan said. "Not if it means murder and destruction."

Solomon's brow lowered, and his eyes went cold. The hand slowly tightened on Brennan's.

"When I came to this town," Solomon said, "its judgment came with me, riding on the dust of my horse. I arrived here to find that my birthright was stolen and used to create that stain on your valley. That disgusting castle towers over everyone and everything. It's a dark house because darkness lives within it."

The bones in Brennan's hands scraped together as Solomon squeezed even tighter. His lips formed a thin line as sweat ran down his face.

"You all watched it happen, just hoping that Jeremiah would leave some scraps for the rest of you. But no, a man like that hoards it all for himself and lets the rest of you starve. I will balance the scale, Sheriff, and by the time it's all said and done, no one will even remember who lived and died during the process."

Brennan kept his eyes on Solomon's and pulled his hand away.

"Ashes to ashes," Brennan said. "Give it enough time, and no one will remember any of us. I don't want any part of the world you want to make. And if that is to be the future, I'd just as soon stay in the past."

It could have been the firelight, but it looked to Brennan like something close to disappointment crossed Solomon's face. The lines around his eyes deepened. Did he really think that Brennan would give up his town and his responsibility so easily? Maybe it had happened before in other towns. Maybe there was a whole swath of burned-out, used-up places on the map just like Charwood. Places no one would notice if they just disappeared.

Solomon sat up straighter. "These gifts were left here for us to remake the world as it was meant to be," he said. "I'm sorry you won't be joining us in the glorious future that awaits."

Brennan stood, feeling the old ache in his knees as he did. He went over and put on his boots as quickly as he could. Through the tent flaps, he saw Reid standing just outside, rifle held in front of him, watching the crowd gathered at the bonfire. Brennan could taste the cold air.

Then he felt a vibration in the fur blankets under his feet. He heard something scraping on wood and more vibrations. He started to turn toward the sound when a bolt of white-hot pain bloomed between his shoulder blades, followed by a wet warmth that spread down his spine and into his legs, which lost feeling and folded. Brennan dropped to his knees. He cried out when his left kneecap cracked on the hardwood under the fur. He fell to all fours and twisted his head to see Solomon standing over him, holding the jade ax. Dark liquid dripped from the blade.

"If you are not for me, you are against me," Solomon whispered.

Brennan knew something important was severed. All the pain was secluded to the upper part of his body. Everything from the waist down had gone dead. He gripped handfuls of fur and pulled himself toward the tent flaps that fluttered with a cool breeze. He heard voices coming from outside, a song—Solomon's family had begun to sing something with a haunting melody.

The cold air felt so good against his skin. Salty sweat dripped from his brow and onto his hands. His face was nearly at the gap now. Reid turned, their eyes met, and Reid's mouth fell open. He took a step back.

"Fight your way out," he said, and the words came out as a whisper between clenched teeth.

Reid nodded once, then looked up, and his eyes went wide as a shadow fell over Brennan. Solomon swung the ax into Brennan's head, and the white snow at Reid's feet was splashed with red. Reid watched as Brennan's eyes dimmed and went colorless. Reid turned and, holding the rifle against his chest, took off running into the forest.

72

THE PIANO STILL SAT BROKEN in the great room of the west wing, but another sound now filled the house—a percussive banging, like a hammer on wood, that shuddered through the walls. It echoed in the kitchen while Abigail made breakfast. She made smaller meals these days, as the dishes were still mostly full of food when she collected them. She took Jeremiah's plate, which he placed at the top of the fifth-floor landing, and Emma's plate from the room she rarely left. The room where she stayed with Samuel. She slept in there now, and as for Jeremiah, Abigail wasn't sure where he slept or if he slept at all.

The banging came from above Abigail's head as she put eggs and potatoes on the two plates. Dust shook loose from the ceiling and drifted down, and she held her apron over the food to keep it from getting dirty. There was no rhythm to the pounding, much like the way Samuel played the C note on the piano.

Abigail sprinkled a pinch of salt from the bowl over Jeremiah's eggs. A loud thump rattled some of the cups in the cabinet, and

Abigail dropped all the salt. It fell on the eggs in a white pile. She stamped her foot so hard pain shot up into her shin. She cursed and tried to scrape off as much salt as she could with a fork. Then, she stirred the eggs to distribute the seasoning evenly. Not that it mattered. Jeremiah probably wouldn't eat more than a few bites anyway.

She picked up one tray, left the kitchen, went through the foyer, and down the stone corridor to the west wing. She paused near the piano and looked at the cracked wood and missing keys. She had tried to play chords on either side of the damage, but the structure was too warped, and the notes rang hopelessly out of tune.

The banging came again, fainter because of where she was, but it still made her heart push a little harder. It came again, louder. She blinked with each hit, waited until it stopped, then started climbing the stairs.

As soon as Abigail's feet touched the first step, she felt as though she had walked into an invisible spider web charged by a lightning storm. Stinging strands clung to her skin, and she heard the distant hum coming from Jeremiah's secret room.

Her feet felt heavier as she climbed to the third floor. The sound vibrated in the walls, making the muscles in her arms twitch and the fork bounce on the tray. She wet her dry lips, and her tongue tickled when it touched the air.

She reached the fifth floor and walked the hall to the empty room with the elk painting. The hum was so strong that she felt the vibrations in her skull and eyelids. She took a deep breath, and the hum seemed to move inside her, rattle around her throat, and slide into her chest. The sensation was oddly pleasant.

A golden band of light glowed in the wall, and she knew Jeremiah was in his secret room, changing broken, ugly things into objects of beauty. Abigail set the tray on the floor, closed her eyes, put her lips together, and began humming. She made her voice match the sound that filled the space and hummed in time like her body itself was an instrument.

Back in the kitchen, Abigail collected the second breakfast and made her way up the main staircase. She reached what she now thought of as "Samuel's room" and gently knocked on the door. Something knocked back. A quick and forceful blow against the wood.

Emma's faint voice called out, "Just a moment."

Slow footsteps approached, and then the door opened. Abigail hoped her expression didn't show her surprise when she saw her employer. Emma's face was thin, near gaunt, and ashen skin sagged beneath her eyes. Eyes that were wet and red.

"Come in," Emma said, stepping aside. Her voice was low and hoarse.

As soon as Abigail entered the room, there was another loud thud from her left. She spun and saw Samuel nearby with his face to the wall. He stood perfectly still, staring at the wall as though it were something of interest. Then, his head moved back and slammed into the wood.

Abigail's body jerked, but she kept her grip on the tray. Emma crossed the room and sat in the rocking chair near the fire. She put a hand to her face and held it there, fingers spread out, nails digging into her skin.

"He won't stop," Emma said, closing her eyes. "I don't know what to do for him."

Abigail set the tray down and knelt by Emma's side.

"You need sleep," Abigail said, putting one hand over Emma's. Her skin was cold, and she could feel the woman's small bones.

"How can I sleep when he doesn't?" Emma said.

Samuel continued to make his way around the room. He clomped a few feet further, stopped, and once again slammed his face into the wall.

Abigail tried to imagine what she would do if she were the mother of this...thing—this boy-shaped hunk of metal that moved of its own will but could not communicate whatever thoughts it might have.

"Ma'am," Abigail said softly. "Have you thought of tying his hands and feet at night? So you can sleep?"

Emma's hand dropped from her face. Her head turned, and her wet eyes glared at Abigail.

"Tie him up?" she whispered. "He is a boy, Abigail. How would you like to be tied up, unable to move?"

"Ma'am, I'm only saying—"

"I know what you're saying, and it's disgusting."

Another bang as Samuel put another dent in the wall.

Abigail's face burned with shame. Tears flooded her eyes, and she tried to blink them back.

Emma's cold hand moved on top of hers and patted gently. "I'm sorry, I shouldn't be angry with you. You were only trying to help. I'm just very tired."

"No need to apologize, ma'am," Abigail said.

"It's not your fault," Emma said. The skin between her eyes folded, and she started breathing heavier. "It's Jeremiah's fault."

"Ma'am?"

"I see him clearly now," Emma said, watching Samuel shuffle to the corner. Abigail closed her eyes, but the sound still made her shoulders jump, and a soft metallic ring hung in the air afterward.

Emma put both hands to her face, and the fingers threaded up into her hair, clawing at the scalp.

"I almost believed he wanted to fix everything," Emma said in a raspy whisper. "But he knew, deep down, that it couldn't be done. The world is so dark all the time, and I think he just wanted to make it shine."

Emma lowered her hands and let out a long sigh.

"He couldn't have known what would happen. Still, some part of me hates him for what he's done, and I don't know if that will ever go away. Look at him. How can something that shines so bright still be so dark?"

Abigail opened her eyes and watched Samuel, dressed in his grey suit. The golden head was damaged and bent. Those golden hands hanging stiffly at his side. She felt her heart would pump cold blood whenever she looked directly at the boy, and she knew what Emma meant. Something clung to him, making her eyes ache, and her heart skip beats. She didn't know what else to call it but "dark." She did not believe the boy was evil, but something in his structure, maybe even the gold itself, was corrupt.

Emma put her hand on Abigail's again and leaned closer.

"Jeremiah put us in this halfway world, but we can't stay here. We won't stay here."

The woman's mouth did not smile, but her eyes changed and grew brighter.

"What do you mean, ma'am?" Abigail asked.

Emma's eyes drifted from Samuel to Abigail. "We won't stay here," she said.

73

REID TORE THROUGH THE WOODS, branches ripping at his face, his breath a howling wind that filled his head. He held the rifle in one hand and pumped his legs to work them free of the thick snow. He looked over his shoulder to see if he was being followed, saw no one in the blue moonlit glow, and did not stop running until he broke into the field and made it to Fang Rock.

Every breath scorched his chest, and his lungs burned as if they had caught fire. His head throbbed with each heartbeat like it had moved from his chest and up into his skull.

Reid could barely feel his nose or the snot running around his mouth, but the rest of his body radiated heat. His long underwear stuck to his legs. He moved around the backside of the rock and kept one eye on the forest's edge while he took off his outer coat and let it fall to the ground. He unbuttoned the other coat and let the icy breeze cool him down.

Fear had carried him this far, but now that he had stopped running, something caught up to him, something he had glimpsed when Solomon's axe fell. Here it was, a looming shadow that fell over his mind and made him nearly choke on his tears.

He was the one who had taken Brennan to Solomon's camp. He led Brennan to his death. No, he didn't swing the jade axe, but for a moment, it felt like he had. Hot tears ran down his cold cheeks. He wiped his nose with the stiff leather of his glove.

Guilt.

It washed over him like dark water and flooded all his thoughts.

If what Solomon told him was true, then Jeremiah could turn anything he touched into gold, and he killed his only brother to obtain that power. No matter how much Reid hated Jeremiah, the former preacher was part of their town, and his power, if it did exist, was theirs as well. If Jeremiah was going to be punished for his crimes, it would be for the people of the town to decide, not this murderer who had appeared suddenly as if he had stepped straight out of the shadows.

Reid looked around the edge of the rock to the woods. He listened. All was quiet.

He started to feel cold again, so he buttoned his coat back up.

Almost all the men he saw in Solomon's camp were young and strong. They followed their guide this far, and there was no doubt they'd be marching behind Solomon when he came for Jeremiah.

Fight your way out.

Reid needed men to fight. If that gift belonged to anyone, it belonged to the town, and he'd be damned if he was going to let this heretic steal it away. But he would need an army, and as the burning in his lungs subsided, Reid realized Jeremiah already had an army camped outside his castle.

Reid picked the gun back up and started running again, leaving his outer coat lying in the snow. This time, he didn't look back.

74

REID CAME INTO CHARWOOD FROM the south end and made his way straight to the sheriff's office. Deputy Franklin Denney jumped out of his chair when the front door flew open. His hand went to his belt and came up holding a pistol before Reid could even speak a word.

Denney took one look at him and rushed over. He helped Reid to a chair and knelt before him, putting a hand on his shoulder.

"Where's the sheriff?" he asked.

Reid kept one arm to his side to hold back the cramp that twisted his stomach into a knot. He felt the cuts on his face crack open and leak fresh blood when he tried to speak. His mouth was dry and raw.

"Dead," he managed to say. "The tall man with the white hair, Solomon Anders…" Reid coughed, and it felt like thorns were in his throat. "Solomon Anders killed him."

Just saying the words out loud did something to Reid. He saw the fear in Brennan's eyes just before the axe fell, the pain that warped his face as he tried to crawl out of the tent.

Denney's fingers tightened around a handful of Reid's coat. "Dead," the deputy repeated. His eyelids fluttered as he stared at the floor. His body swayed a little. He stood and paced across the room, his hands opening and closing. "Why?"

Reid closed his stiff fingers into a fist, and the knuckles felt like sore, rusty hinges. "He wants Jeremiah, and he wants Charwood." Reid reached up and grabbed Denney's arm as he paced by. "Listen. You need to hear this."

Reid told the deputy everything he had heard as he stood in the cold outside the tent, but he decided to leave out the part about Jeremiah's power and invented a different story about how he acquired his wealth. He and Elijah had robbed a wealthy man and stolen everything from him, then killed him. The man was wealthy, but he was also evil.

The words just came out of Reid. He didn't think about the lie, and he didn't know exactly why he told it. He said Solomon had known the wealthy man, and a significant portion of that wealth was meant for Solomon himself.

And Reid did not say anything about the fact that he had been to see Solomon the night before, and he knew exactly what the strange visitor wanted. If Reid was honest with himself, he wanted it too. He wanted to live in a town run by a man with immeasurable wealth. A man who could transform the very trees and stones into gold. What a world a man like that could create if that man wasn't selfish and uncharitable like Jeremiah.

Reid had hoped Solomon would convince Brennan that the future he proposed was so much better than the present they lived in. But now that Reid saw just how far Solomon was willing to go, he knew the man could not be allowed to take Jeremiah's power. It belonged to the town, to all of them. And they would have to fight to defend it.

Deputy Denney listened. He wiped his eyes with one hand, the other occasionally touching the gun on his belt. His mouth was a tight line, so tight that Reid sometimes heard the man's teeth click together.

"When is he coming?" Denney asked.

Reid didn't know for certain, but with Brennan's blood still drying in that round tent, Solomon would not wait much longer to make his move.

Reid met Denney's eyes.

"Now," he said.

75

CARLSON REID AND DEPUTY FRANKLIN Denney stepped out into the cold. Snow fell and swirled over the main street, drifting in and out of the orange lantern light.

"Hurry," Denney said. "I'll meet you there as soon as I can."

Reid nodded, and the two men walked off into the dark in separate directions. Reid knew he should head straight to the castle and talk to Garrett, but he had no idea what the night would bring or whether he would still be alive when morning finally came.

He walked down the center of the main street, looking at the shops and houses, roofs covered with thick snow. This town was so beautiful. How had he not seen that before? The dark shape of the castle loomed across the field, blocking out part of the sky. The white tents of Garrett's crew cut a straight line in front of it.

Reid glanced over to his left and saw the church. Even with its peeling paint, it was still beautiful in its own way because it was his, and he felt alive inside that building—alive in a way he felt nowhere else.

Without thinking, his feet moved toward it, but instead of going inside, he walked past the cemetery, with its stone markers rising out of the snow.

All those people, he thought, were dead and buried. All those lives that have been forgotten. We're only given such a brief moment in the history of everything.

He went to his house, opened the door slowly, stepped inside, and closed the door behind him. He took off his boots and walked over to the chair where Laura had fallen asleep. Her chin rested against her chest, and a book lay open on her lap. The fire had burned down to embers, but the room was still warm.

Reid put his face near her hair and breathed in her scent. He was ashamed he couldn't remember the last time he told her he loved her. She stirred a little when he picked up the book so it wouldn't fall and wake her. Then he went down the hall to the girls' room.

The door creaked when he pushed it open, something he had meant to fix but never got around to. He leaned over each of his daughters and kissed their cheeks. He pulled the blankets up and watched them from the doorway, their soft breathing filling the room.

Reid closed the door gently and went into his own room. He felt something course through him when he opened the chest by his bed and took out the pistol. It had been years since he held it. Its cold weight is slick steel. Even the feel of the hammer on his thumb sent off a charge that electrified him.

It reminded him that a man who carried a gun was no longer just a man. He was, or could be at any moment, a killer. The power of death lay just beyond the twitch of a single finger.

He strapped the gun around his waist and filled the empty slots of the belt with bullets.

At the front door, he put his boots back on and went outside. He stood and listened to the whisper of the falling snow, then pulled on his gloves and began walking toward the fortress.

76

JEREMIAH DIDN'T HEAR THE HUM anymore but felt it on his skin. He stood hunched over the table in his secret room, wearing a pair of tinted lenses to protect his eyes from the bright glow beneath his hand.

Gold filament grew along the surface of the object in symmetrical patterns, and Jeremiah felt something flowing through him, from the center of his chest, down his arm, and into his fingertips—a warm sensation that made him a little dizzy.

He waited until the new layers had covered a small section of rough gold, then pulled his hand away. He removed the lenses and looked at one of the several books that lay open on the table.

He read the same words over and over again, but there were no instructions for what he attempted now. All he had were bits and pieces he pulled from the different texts and assembled into something new.

Doubt crept in the back of his mind like a spider with needle-sharp legs. He reread another passage, and his brain ached at thinking of what could go wrong. He didn't have any other options, though, not that he could see. Emma was right, taking Samuel away again would crush her. He would lose his son again, and he would lose his wife. He told himself everything he'd done was to bring them together again, to fix what had been broken. But now, he wasn't sure he believed his own motives.

The wolf's words came back to him.

MORE PAIN.

Jeremiah closed the book, put the lenses on, and went back to work.

77

FRANKLIN DENNEY HAD NOT YET arrived when Reid approached the white tents. Four men huddled around the fire, playing cards and laughing quietly. The fortress towered above them, black stone rising into a black sky. Orange light glowed from the windows in the west wing and from one of the bedrooms at the front of the house on the second floor. The rest of the house was dark.

Garrett sat on a log away from the poker game, smoking a pipe, one hand petting the mangy dog that lay at his feet. The snow around the fire had melted and turned the ground muddy, and the dog's white fur was spattered with it.

Garrett looked up as Reid came closer, motioned him over, and pointed to the log across from him. The men playing cards stopped and watched Reid with blank faces. Poker faces, Reid thought.

Reid sat down, and as soon as he stopped moving, he felt the cold again. He crossed his arms and rubbed each shoulder.

"Awful late for a preacher to be out," Garrett said, the pipe clenched between his teeth.

Reid nodded, trying to keep his chin from shivering. The card players had not resumed their game and kept a close eye on Reid as if they couldn't fully enjoy playing with the reverend present.

"You about some business, son?" Garrett asked. His pale eyes looked Reid up and down.

Reid took a deep breath and tried to keep it quiet, but his chest shook as he exhaled, and he knew his voice would shake if he spoke. He looked around the camp and noticed fewer tents than the day before.

"Where are the others?" he asked.

"Gone," Garrett said and spit in the dirt. "Back home. We had ourselves a little mutiny this morning. They think this place ain't ever going to stop being built. Can't say I disagree. Some were cold, some tired. Most just missed their families. Decided now was the time to move on."

Garrett leaned forward and rested his elbows on his bony knees. "Why don't you say what you came here to say?"

Reid met the man's eyes. "I have a favor to ask."

Garrett took the pipe from his mouth, and smoke came spilling out. "Night is the worst time of day to be asking favors," he said, "but I'll hear you out."

Reid wished Denney were here to explain things. Reid had no problem getting up in front of his congregation every Sunday and preaching, but he was something inside the church. Out here, in the real world, he was nothing, and he felt it in the way Garrett looked at him and the way the card players watched. Reid knew he was not just talking to Garrett, he was talking to the whole crew.

"Sheriff Brennan has been murdered," Reid said, "and the man who killed him is coming to kill Jeremiah also."

Garrett's eyes opened a little wider. He stopped petting the dog.

Reid looked down at his boots. "This man, he goes by the name Solomon Anders, and he's camped in the woods past Fang Rock. There's a whole group with him. They think he's some sort of spiritual guide."

The card players rose and came closer. One man sat on the log beside Reid, cards still in his hand.

Reid paused and tried to conjure up some tears. It wasn't hard. Just thinking about Brennan lying half in and half out of Solomon's tent, blood leaking from his mouth, was enough to make Reid's eyes burn.

"We can't let him get to Jeremiah, not after all he has done for this town."

Reid's legs were weak, and his feet numb, but he had to stand. The words came slow at first, but now he felt just like he did behind the pulpit.

"It is our duty to defend a neighbor. And more than that, Jeremiah will pay each of you three months' salary if you'll stay and fight."

Anger rose up in Reid as he spoke. It warmed his skin. The arrogance of Solomon was absolutely staggering, believing he could come to Charwood and kill at will, take whatever he wanted. Reid did not want to fight, and he certainly did not want to die, but neither did he want to live under the control of men more powerful than him. He became a preacher only because it was what his father had wanted. So he entered a profession he had no desire for and found himself with a family, a congregation, and no skills to do anything other than what he had never wanted to do.

This decision, to ensure Solomon did not take what he came for and that it stayed in Charwood, was the first thing Reid had ever done that seemed right.

"Solomon Anders is a murderer and madman," Reid said. "I know you don't call Charwood home, but Solomon plans to stay here and use this town up, take everything he can before moving on again. And maybe the next place he goes is your town. He must be stopped here tonight."

The man sitting next to Reid stood up and held out his hand. He was tall and broad with a thick beard. His large hand engulfed Reid's.

"I'll stay," he said in a deep voice. "I got no one out there waiting for me."

Another man stepped into the light, much younger than the others, barely out of his teens, if that. His face was smooth and free of wrinkles, but his jaw was tight, and his grip was strong.

"Jesse Hartfield," the young man said. "My papa was a lawman and he always told me justice outside the law is no justice at all. I'll stay and help if I'm able."

Reid shook his hand. "Thank you, Jesse."

A third man, standing off in the shadows, spoke softly. "Three months' pay? Is that guaranteed?"

Reid nodded.

"Count me in, then."

Garrett watched silently as the three men pledged to stay and help. But the fourth man stayed seated. He stared into the fire, one hand picking at the fingernails of the other hand.

"What about you, Russell?" Garrett said.

Russell's head snapped up. He looked first at Garrett, then at Reid.

"No," he shook his head. "I ain't staying. I'm sorry, and I wish you all success, but I don't know this, Jeremiah, and I sure as hell ain't gonna die for him."

Garrett nodded slowly. "I understand." He reached into his pocket, took out a few coins, and dropped them into Russell's hand. The man's shoulders fell, and he hung his head.

"Go on into town and get yourself a room at the inn," Garrett said. "There's no shame in walking away from a fight."

Russell stood without looking any of them in the eye. He went back to his tent and emerged a few minutes later carrying all his belongings. He stopped and looked like he wanted to say something, but he nodded instead, turned away, and walked toward Charwood.

Garrett put the pipe back in his mouth and smiled.

"All right, preacher. You got yourself four men. One too young to shave and one too old to be of much use. I sure hope you've got some other folks coming to help."

Reid stood up quickly and squinted into the dark. Something moved across the field, a series of shapes and dull yellow lights casting halos. Reid stepped away from the fire and watched, his heart thudding like a war drum. A group of men, too few to be Solomon's, marched through the snow. Reid recognized some of the faces in the light of the lanterns they carried.

He pointed. "Here they are now."

78

FRANKLIN DENNEY LED A GROUP of twelve across the field. They were all he could find and, more than that, the only ones he trusted. He'd spent the last hour going from house to house, rousing men from sleep, breathlessly explaining the situation as best as he could before moving on to the next house. After a few agreed to join him, he sent those men out to find more. Twelve was all they managed to come up with, and Denney hoped it would be enough.

Denney had hardly said a word after he gathered the men. He marched in silence with a burning in his chest as he thought about Sheriff Brennan, slaughtered. He didn't know what Jeremiah had done or not done, but he would be damned if he'd let a man like Solomon Anders kill again. Not without a fight.

Several of the men carried lanterns to light the way. All of them carried guns. One man, Henry Sayer, brought his grandfather's sword from the War of Independence. It had been well-cared for over the years and now hung from his belt in a scabbard. Abraham Carmody, the oldest man in the group, wearing a long heavy coat that concealed the large knife on his belt, looked down at the ground as he walked, the steam of his breath trailing behind him.

The sky was clear, and the stars shone brightly. The cold crept in through Denney's coat and chilled his skin. Ever since Reid told him about what Solomon did to the sheriff, the dark seed of thought had been slowly growing.

Is tonight the night I die?

He tried to push the thought down, suffocate it, but no matter how strong his anger was over Brennan's death, the thought slipped free and floated back up to the surface.

He wished he had said goodbye to his wife and three sons, the youngest of which would not even remember Denney's face if he was killed tonight. His eyes burned, and his hand squeezed the rifle until his knuckles went hot.

Thomas Shelton, a small, wiry man with a black beard and thick mustache, trudged through the snow with each hand on a pistol. He was as good a shot with the left as with the right. Denney suspected Thom had been drinking, but the flesh under his eyes was always a bruise-colored shade of purple, so it was difficult to know for certain.

Fewer white tents were camped in front of the fortress, and the large group Denney had expected to see was only four. That dark thought in his mind grew heavier.

As they approached the house, Denney looked up at the castle. Only a few windows were lit, hovering in the dark like orange eyes. He shivered and pulled the collar of his coat tighter around his neck.

When they reached the fire, Reid came over, and Denney was surprised to see that he wore a gun.

"The others left," Reid said, his face drawn and tired-looking.

Denney nodded to Garrett and the three other men and tried not to look disappointed.

The group gathered around the warmth of the fire, except Abe Carmody. A breeze blew over the top of the house, and he thought he heard a distant voice inside it—a woman's voice, screaming in agony.

Carmody walked closer to the black fortress and had to crane his neck to see the top. When he was a young man, he and some friends had come across a woman living in a shack in the woods. When he saw her, every good feeling Abe had ever felt evaporated in a cold burst of pain that left him clutching his head. He spent three days in bed with a fever after that, and the whole time, he was afraid he would never be happy again.

He felt the same way as he looked at the house—that something inside was pulling light into its center and giving back nothing but darkness.

Abe Carmody stood silent and listened. The house groaned and creaked as the cold air moved over it. He wore no hat, and his white hair blew wildly in the icy wind. He didn't hear the voice again, but he still felt it inside him—that fear, that pain. He shivered once and went back to the fire to get warm.

The wind drifted over the field and caused the forest's treeline to sway. Reid looked at the faces of the men with him, all of them somber and pale in the moonlight. Their eyes were alert, and their bodies tense. Franklin Denney was sweating despite the cold. Reid could smell it.

Over the next hour, the conversation grew quiet, then stopped altogether. The men stared across the field and watched the light on the snow-covered main street of Charwood.

They watched, they listened. They waited.

Abe Carmody stayed awake while the others closed their eyes and tried to sleep. He listened to the breeze but didn't hear any more voices.

He sat up straighter when he saw the light darken at the edge of town. A group of shadows moved into the open whiteness of the field. Abe shook Garrett and Reid awake and pointed. They roused the rest of the men, and each drew their weapons, spread out, and took positions behind the tents. Abe unsheathed his knife and gripped it tight. Sweat ran down his back, so he took off his coat and laid it on the log where he had been sitting.

He wondered if he would ever put the coat on again.

79

AFTER DENNEY'S GROUP ARRIVED, AND while the men intro-
duced themselves, Garrett stood slowly, stretched, and silently walked
toward the castle. His mutt stayed close behind. Garrett's stiff knees
crackled as he went up the steps. His thighs quivered.

The mutt sat down next to him as Garrett knocked on the door.
He waited, looking over his shoulder to see if any other men had
followed him. It didn't look like anyone noticed he had left.

Garrett rapped his knuckles against the door again and heard
the sound echo into the house. He petted the dog's head until the
door opened, and Abigail Fletcher stood there, arms folded across
her chest to hold a sweater in place.

Garrett nodded. "Evening ma'am."

Abigail's face was pale and tired. She looked past Garrett to
the group gathered at the tents.

"What's going on out there?"

"What I came to talk to you about," Garrett said. "Seems the
sheriff's been killed. Some stranger done it, and he's got a group with

him hell-bent on killing Jeremiah, too. So I'm told."

Abigail's mouth fell open. She took in all the men and their weapons.

"I'll get Mr. Pevensie," she said and turned to leave.

Garrett reached out and grabbed her arm as gently as he could.

"I don't think that's wise," he said. "Listen very carefully, you need to keep everyone inside the house. Do not let them come out for anything. No matter what you see, no matter what you hear, keep them inside." He lowered his voice and leaned in. "All of them."

Abigail took a quick breath and searched Garrett's face. "Should I tell them?"

Garrett took Abigail's hand in his own. Her soft skin, like his wife's used to be when she was young and alive, was warm. He placed her hand on the mutt's head, and the dog leaned into her touch.

"They'll know soon enough," Garrett said.

Abigail waited in the open doorway until Garrett rejoined the camp's men. She let the cold breeze blow on her face and looked out at the dark outline of Charwood across the field. Shapes moved down the main street, casting shadows on the lantern-lit snow.

Abigail squinted. The shapes did not appear to be human. Each breath she took felt small and insufficient. Reid, Garrett, and the other men must have also noticed the movement, because conversation came to a halt and each looked across the field.

Garrett glanced back at Abigail, his eyes dark and sad, and nodded once. Abigail nodded back and shut the door. She ran up the staircase to the boy's room and tried to open it, but it was locked.

She banged her fist against the wood. "Ma'am? I need to speak with you."

She put her ear to the door and listened. She heard footsteps on the other side, a woman's voice humming a lullaby.

"Ma'am, it's very important. I need to speak with you right away."

No response. Abigail leaned her forehead on the door and tried to calm her breathing so that her words would be clear.

"Emma, someone is coming. Someone who wants to take everything away from you. Please, open the door."

The footsteps stopped for a few heartbeats, then resumed. Abigail clenched her fingers into a fist and raised it to hit the door. Something was wrong. She wasn't sure how she knew it, but she felt it as strongly as she did the strange hum coming from Jeremiah's secret room.

She lowered her hand, then turned and ran down the stairs. She ran down the corridor to the west wing and up five floors until she came to the hall where the air crackled. Abigail entered the empty room and went straight to the elk painting. Its eyes seemed to move in the blue moonlight streamed through the windows. She gripped the edge of the frame and swung open the wall.

She banged on the hidden door until Jeremiah opened it. Brilliant yellow light spilled into the room from behind him. Abigail put a hand over her eyes. The hum was so much louder now, overwhelming. Her knees wanted to buckle, and she struggled to stand.

Jeremiah looked angry and frightened. Sweat glistened on his face like liquid gold in the light surrounding him. He opened his mouth to speak, but Abigail's words rushed out breathlessly before he could.

"He's here," she said. "He's here."

80

SOLOMON AND HIS FAMILY FOLLOWED the same trampled snow path through the moonlit field. Twenty-two men and one woman. Not a single one of them carried a gun. Solomon believed that since the ancient people did not need such weapons, neither did his family. If there was to be warfare, they would fight using the tools of their spiritual ancestors. The act of taking a man's life should be close and personal, close enough to feel his blood splash on your face. It was, after all, a spiritual act, killing a man. You were setting free his soul from a prison of dust and blood.

Solomon motioned for them all to remain quiet, though none of them were making any noise. He closed his eyes, let the breeze blow on his face, and inhaled slowly. It carried a scent—sweat and fear. He was sure of it—there were others near the white tents in front of Jeremiah's fortress. He sensed their silence, it had weight.

Solomon walked, the hem of his black robe dragging behind him like a second shadow. He stopped when he saw a lone figure standing before the dying fire. Solomon closed his eyes again and listened. He heard the breath of the other men, a sound like someone trying not to breathe. It carried on the breeze. He walked closer until he saw Reid's pale and stern face.

The family spread out in a line behind Solomon, and Reid tried not to let his face show the shock he felt. To Solomon's right was a shirtless man wearing a leather skirt. His head was covered with a pale mask of some kind, what looked like a cow's skull. Its upper teeth stretched across the man's forehead, and its lower jaw wrapped around his own. The horns, one of them jagged, were silhouetted against the sky. In one hand was a spear, in the other a blade.

To Solomon's left was a woman holding an elk antler in each hand—the points polished and sharpened. Her hair was braided and tied back, and streaks of white paint were on her face.

Solomon stepped forward and smiled, holding his arms out. "Mr. Reid," he said. "What a glorious night."

Reid did not smile back. His arm was outstretched, pointing a revolver at Solomon's chest.

"Don't take another step," Reid said.

Solomon stopped moving. He didn't like Reid's tone of voice. There wasn't enough fear in it, enough awe, and for a moment, Solomon himself was afraid the preacher had already found Jeremiah.

Solomon lowered his arms. His eyes narrowed. "It was a mistake coming here tonight. You are not needed."

Reid jerked the gun toward the fortress. "How is this possible?"

Solomon smiled again, but it was cold and lifeless. "Everything is possible," he said, "we have only forgotten how to do it."

Reid's face twisted up for just a second. "How…how do we take it from him?" he asked.

Ah, Solomon thought. *He is afraid.*

"You don't have the time to understand it all, Mr. Reid. That is why I am here. Remember what we discussed. There will be a place for you in what comes next, but first, I must finish what I've started."

Reid stepped forward, his gun now pointed at Solomon's head. "Tell me how. Tell me how I take it from him."

"Mr. Reid," Solomon said, "you would not be taking it from Mr. Pevensie. You would be taking it from me."

"It doesn't belong to you."

Solomon's eyes narrowed. "Like Jacob and Esau, Mr. Pevensie stole my birthright, and I have come to take it back."

Reid shook his head, eyes set and steady. "No, it belongs to the town. It is for all of us to do with it as we wish. You and your group are strangers here, you have no claim to anything."

Solomon tried but could not control his breathing. Clouds of vapor came out of him faster and faster.

"You know nothing," Solomon yelled across the distance. "You are like a child that thinks fireworks are magic. There is machinery in the universe, Carlson Reid. Wheels and gears turning in endless motion. Have you studied this machinery? Do you understand what it requires in order to turn so perfectly?"

Reid stood silent, still aiming his gun at Solomon's head. Snow began falling from the sky.

"Do you?" Solomon screamed, taking a single step forward. "I have bled and starved just to glimpse the inner workings." Jabbing a finger at his chest, he said, "I have given up more than you've ever had in pursuing the knowledge the Watchers gave God's early creation. And you, you act like it's some toy you can just steal and play with. You are a child, Mr. Reid. A spiritual infant."

Silence hung between the two men. The snow creaked as some of Solomon's warriors shifted their weight.

Finally, Reid said, "You are not leaving with it."

Solomon nodded and lifted his head toward the sky. He closed his eyes as snowflakes drifted down, touching his cheeks and mouth. His tongue licked at the flakes on his lips. He opened his eyes and smiled, looking now at the fortress.

Solomon nodded again. "This is the place people come to die," he said. "Why should we be any different?" He moved his left hand behind his back and held out three fingers.

Reid saw the movement and said nothing, but his hand gripped the pistol tighter. Sweat trickled down his face and neck, urging him to wipe it away, but he remained still and focused.

"You don't know the secret," Solomon said, lowering one finger. "You would end up killing him and getting nothing. I promise everyone in your town will be wealthy if I have it. Are you willing to risk losing it all just to keep the gift from me?"

Solomon lowered another finger and looked past Reid to the tents behind him. "You have seen what is possible. I'm sure you asked yourself, is this gift evil? Perhaps, perhaps, it is. But nothing in this world is all one thing. Think of the good such a gift could do. So, I ask you again, do you want to be rich, or do you wish for everything to remain as it is?"

Reid's vision became blurry as sweat rolled into his eyes. He blinked away the salty sting and kept the gun trained on Solomon.

Solomon nodded toward the tents.

"Do they know?" he said. "Do the men hiding there know what Jeremiah can do?"

Reid's eyes flicked to Garrett, crouched out of view a few feet away. Garrett looked at Reid, but his face did not change. His jaw was clenched, and he held his gun barrel up.

Solomon smiled. "You didn't tell them? Oh, for shame, Mr. Reid. For all your talk about sharing this gift, you apparently have very little intention of actually doing so."

Reid swallowed hard and looked back to Solomon. "You will not take it," he said.

"Very well," Solomon said. "It was written that the road shall be paved with blood, and blood shall follow wherever it goes."

He lowered his final finger, then flung open his robe with the other hand and grabbed hold of the small ax that hung from his belt. With one swift motion, Solomon pulled the ax out and threw it. It spun, end over end, trailing a green arc, and embedded itself in Reid's chest. Reid's gun discharged in a cloud of smoke, a shot that went straight up into the sky.

Solomon dropped to the ground on his back just as Garrett and the others began firing. The warriors behind him scattered, ducking low to the ground and moving forward.

Reid did not remember falling, but he looked up at the sky and felt it was lowering upon him like a blanket. He heard gunshots and screaming coming to him distantly through a rushing wind. With great effort, he lifted his head and looked at his chest. The jade ax he'd seen in Solomon's tent had pierced his lung, he could hear and feel the air wheezing out of the hole. Blood gushed up around the wound, pouring down his side, turning the snow red. The flow pulsed with each heartbeat. Pain flooded through his body. He felt each limb begin to shut off, one by one.

Someone fell to the ground next to him, groaning. Reid turned his head to see Henry Sayer lying face down in the snow, eyes wide, his throat cut open and spraying blood. His grandfather's sword was still clutched in his hand.

More voices screamed, some in pain, others in rage. Reid looked to his left and saw Abe Carmody fending off a man with a bear's claws strapped to his hands. The old man's face looked hardened as he swung his knife. But then another one of Solomon's warriors snuck up behind Abe and stabbed him in the side with an obsidian blade. At the moment Abe arched his back and cried out, the other man rushed forward and slashed at Abe's face with the claws. Lines appeared in his cheek, then split open so wide Reid could see teeth. The old man crumpled to the ground, fingers grasping for his knife even as his eyes rolled back.

The world grew dim. Colors turned grey. Sounds were filtered through the liquid. Reid closed his eyes, overcome with a sense of failure, of futility. His whole life had come down to this moment, and he didn't even have the chance to fight. Suddenly, time seemed clear, and he knew his existence would be forgotten once everyone who knew him was gone. So fleeting, he thought.

He lifted his head and saw Garrett fire a shot into the woman's shoulder just before she plunged a sharpened antler into his gut.

Garrett dropped his gun and coughed out a spray of blood. He doubled over, both hands gripping the antler and trying to pull it free. The woman staggered forward with her teeth bared and stabbed the other antler into Garrett's face.

Reid closed his eyes and tried to ignore the pain. Pain that settled inside his ribs and became a burning ball of light so intense he could not wait for it to be over. Hot tears ran down his face.

Something pressed down on his chest, and a new spark of pain lit up. He opened his eyes to see Solomon kneeling atop him, the man's hot and stale breath blowing on his face.

"You're so close," Solomon said, leaning down and speaking directly into Reid's ear.

Then Reid felt something tearing out of his center, pulling muscle and bone. A searing pain followed, and he screamed with what little breath he had left.

"Do you see it opening up?" Solomon asked, holding up the jade ax he'd pulled out of Reid and wiping it on the dying man's coat. "The doorway between this world and the next?"

Solomon sighed. "I envy you, Mr. Reid. You'll get to see the other side first. But I do wonder..." Solomon looked at the bodies strewn around him, "what if you've been wrong about everything? What if there is no one waiting to greet you, no streets of gold, no crowns? What if your pain is only just beginning?"

Tears ran from Reid's eyes as he looked into Solomon's black pupils.

I tried, Reid thought. *I tried to fight my way out.*

Then Solomon swung the jade ax and cleaved Carlson Reid's skull.

81

JEREMIAH RUSHED THROUGH THE WEST wing and into the foyer. Abigail was somewhere behind him, he could hear her heavy breathing. Gunshots echoed outside, along with shouts and screaming. He stopped and glanced out a window near the front door, and it looked like an army of monsters had invaded Garrett's camp. A skull-headed man stabbed a spear through one man's leg, while a creature with antlers for hands slashed wildly at anyone that came near. Bodies fell to the snow, blood spraying from their wounds.

A figure with white hair, wearing a flowing black robe, moved through the camp like a shadow up a wall, hacking at necks and arms with a green ax. His teeth were clenched together and bared like an animal's. More screaming, followed by moaning from those who had already fallen.

Jeremiah backed away from the window, one hand held over his heart as it thudded away like a stone in his chest. Abigail came up beside him and tried to look out the window, but Jeremiah took her by the shoulder and turned her away.

"You don't want to see this," he said, leading her to the stairs.

She saw tears on his cheeks as they climbed to the second floor.

When Jeremiah reached the door of Samuel's bedroom, he tried the handle, found it locked, and rapped his fist on the door.

"Emma, open the door."

Her boots echoed across the room, but she said nothing.

Jeremiah banged on the door again.

"Open it," he said. "I need to get you and Samuel out."

He heard the faint sound of glass tapping against metal, so he put his ear to the door and listened.

"Emma, say something."

Liquid was being poured out, running down a smooth surface, dripping. He thought of the bath, but there was no tub in that room. Then a smell came through the keyhole, seeping out from under the door—a pungent odor that made him dizzy.

Jeremiah struck the door harder this time and shouted her name. The door rattled against the frame.

"Emma, we are in danger. Do you hear me? We need to get to the west wing immediately."

The smell grew stronger. Jeremiah took a few steps back, then ran at the door and threw his shoulder against it. The wood that held the lock cracked a little. He did it again, putting all his strength into it, and the wood shattered. The door flew open and crashed against the wall.

Emma stood at the center of the room, Samuel next to her. The boy's skin glistened, and he stood at the center of a dark puddle. Liquid dripped from Samuel's chin, ran down his arm, and fell off his fingers.

An unlit lantern lay on its side nearby. Emma held another lantern above her head, and as soon as her eyes met Jeremiah's, she tipped it and let the oil drench her hair and gown. The room wavered with the fumes, like the horizon on a hot summer's day.

She took steps backward toward the fireplace.

"Either he stays, or we both go," Emma said, oil running around her mouth.

Jeremiah held out his hands. "You don't know what you're doing."

"You never knew what you were doing," she said. "And you can't even see what you've done."

Jeremiah took one step forward, and Emma took one step backward.

"Please," he said. "Don't do this."

Emma reached the fireplace and, keeping her eyes on Jeremiah, felt for the iron poker. She took it and glanced down quickly, jabbing it at a thin log until it shifted away from the flames.

Jeremiah took another step.

"I don't want to be here anymore," she said. "I'm sorry, Jeremiah. Truly, I am. But if you take him, there is nothing left in this world for me."

The boy stood perfectly still, the one eye moving between his mother and his father. Emma reached up, grabbed the sleeve of her gown, and tore it at the seam. She slipped her arm out, wrapped the cloth around her hand, and knelt. She grabbed the end of the log that was not burning and stood, holding it at arm's length.

She took a step toward Samuel. So did Jeremiah.

"Emma, there's another way. If you don't come with me right now, we will all be killed. I've been working on something, another way out of this."

"A way out of this?" Emma said, and her face held a dark smile. "Another map that leads us to a place even worse than where we started? You're lost, as lost as I am. Only you won't admit it."

Jeremiah pointed at the log with one finger. "Put that back in the fire. Right now."

Emma kept walking. "This," she said, moving her eyes around the room, then coming to Samuel, "this is all wrong. But I'm going to make it right. I don't want the hurt anymore. I don't want to wake up and face each day with this hole inside me. I want to be with him, and if you're sending him back, he's not going alone. It's your choice. You either keep us both or lose us both."

Jeremiah raised his voice and nearly shouted, "Do not take another step."

"Or what?" Emma said. "Are you going to kill me like you killed your brother?"

Jeremiah inhaled sharply, like he had been punched in the stomach. He swallowed and shook his head. He looked directly at his wife and said, "If I could have sacrificed you instead, I would have."

Emma gave him a faint, sad smile as tears slid from her eyes into the oil that covered her face. She nodded slowly. "There really is nothing left for me."

They were both equal distances from the boy, and Jeremiah ran as fast as he could to put himself between Emma and Samuel. As soon as she saw what he was doing, Emma ran also, leaving oil-soaked footprints on the wood. Jeremiah reached the boy and spread out his arms as Emma rushed at him. She thrust the torch toward Samuel, but Jeremiah knocked it back with his forearm. The burning end singed his eyebrows.

"Emma, stop! I found a way!"

She stood there, panting, drenched in oil, holding the torch. Her eyes looked around Jeremiah to the blank face of her son's golden corpse. Then she raised her eyes and met Jeremiah's.

She said, "No matter what we do, no matter how hard we try to fix it, the end of everything is the same."

Emma rushed at Jeremiah, pushing him back with one arm and reaching for the torch for Samuel. Jeremiah grabbed her arm with both hands and twisted. He felt and heard a snap. She let out a cry, and the arm went limp. When she looked at him, Jeremiah saw nothing but pain and anger reflected in the flames in her eyes. The torch fell from her grip. She tried to catch it, but the burning edge touched her skin.

Emma screamed. The flames tore up her arm and into her hair in a blue-white blaze. The dress ignited and looked as if it were made of flames.

She fell to her knees with a sickening crack. Her screams grew louder. The oil on the floor around her caught fire, and she jumped to the oil-stained footprints that led back to the fireplace.

Jeremiah grabbed Samuel under the arms and dragged him away from the inferno. The skin on Emma's face boiled and cracked. Her screaming cut through Jeremiah's heart. He left Samuel and rushed over to his wife. He made the symbol with his hand and reached out, touching his two fingers to the center of her chest. He closed his eyes as he felt the change happening.

Emma's screams became narrow, higher pitched, as though coming through a tunnel. Then, the sound of air being pulled inward and a muffled explosion. Jeremiah opened his eyes just as Emma's ghostly shape, made of gold dust, rose into the air. It hung there for a moment, suspended, then rained down on him.

Fire still burned on the floor around her. Jeremiah took off his coat and threw it on the flames, stomping on it to put them out. Black smoke filled the room.

Jeremiah knelt and put his hand on the golden statue of his wife. Her mouth was open in a permanent scream, hands held in front of her, twisted and contorted. The boils on her face, the open hole in her cheek, the feather-shaped flames that covered her body, all solid.

His breath came faster, and his heartbeat fell out of rhythm. He wanted to scream, but he had no air. He groaned and lowered himself until his chin touched his knees.

The room was silent except for his breathing and the gentle crackling of the fireplace. Then, a metallic hum came from behind him.

"Mmmmmmm…."

Jeremiah turned. Samuel stood perfectly still, staring at the statue of his mother. His expression had not changed, but Jeremiah somehow sensed pain. Or maybe it was his own pain he saw reflected at him.

Samuel's legs moved, not with the smooth gait Emma had taught him, but with the clunky steps he had when he was first made.

He came closer. He reached out and touched his golden fingers to the golden skin of Emma's face.

"Muuutthherrrr," he said.

82

GARRETT SWAM UP OUT OF a terrible blackness. He heard gunfire and screaming. He opened his eyes but only saw light out of the right one. A hot pain throbbed in his belly. He put a hand to the heat, and it came away sticky with blood. Air whistled out of a hole in his chest where the antler had punctured a lung. He blinked, and with it came an awful realization—there was something hard jutting out of his left eye socket. His fingers reached up and felt something wet and viscous running from the hole and down his cheek. He felt something else, too, something smooth and hard. His fingers wrapped around it, and he knew at once what it was. One point of the woman warrior's antler was still embedded in his eye, and another was twisted into his neck.

Garrett's breathing was shallow and scorched, which meant the point in his neck had missed the windpipe, but he still felt like he was drowning. He could feel liquid seeping into his lungs, diminishing the space he had for air.

He turned his head slowly. The snow of the camp was churned up into pink icy chunks and painted with blood.

A shirtless man wearing a skull mask and carrying a spear walked amongst the dead. He came to the groaning body of Franklin Denney, lying near a white tent splattered with red. One hand was pressed to his stomach, thick blood pouring between his fingers. Denney held up his other hand, his voice made a pleading sound, and the skull-masked man plunged the spear into Denney's open mouth.

Garrett looked through hazy red vision as the jade ax split Carlson Reid's head. Solomon, this tall man with hair as white as the snow had been before the battle, had a wild look in his eyes. A look of crazed passion and something else, something that froze the thoughts in Garrett's mind, pushed him away from his own body and made him feel like a stranger staring through his remaining eye.

Pleasure. This horrifying figure in the long black robe took pleasure in what he was doing.

Solomon closed his eyes, and a light smile played on his lips. Flecks of blood shone bright in his white hair. Wet red streaks and trails ran down his face. When Solomon opened his eyes, he was looking directly at Garrett.

Garrett searched for his heartbeat, but he couldn't feel or hear it. He breathed faster, and every inhale pushed him further underwater. He reached for the antler again and thought to pull it out of his body and use it as a weapon, but his fingers were weak, and his hand would not stop shaking. When he finally managed to pull on the bone, bolts of white lightning shot through his skull, and he let go.

Solomon came over and knelt next to him. His black robe spread out on the snow like dark oil. Screams echoed behind him as the warriors finished off the wounded.

"I saw you," Solomon said, pressing a blood-speckled hand to Garrett's forehead. "I saw your thread intersect with mine. I'm sorry it had to end like this."

Garrett tried to speak, but blood came up his throat and filled his mouth.

Solomon put a hand on Garrett's chest. "It's okay, you don't need to speak. Just hold up one finger for yes and two for no. Do you understand?"

Garrett lifted a single weak finger and winced at an icy pain. He looked down and saw the finger cut deep, white bone visible inside the open flesh.

"Good," Solomon said. "I know you built this house and have been camped outside it these many months. So, tell me, how many are inside right now?"

Garrett's throat gurgled, and Solomon touched the man's forehead and stroked it gently.

"Just use your fingers," Solomon said. "How many?"

Every part of Garrett's body was sparking with pain signals. He could no longer feel his legs, not like he should. They were going cold. Cold and pinpricked. His teeth ground together as he used all his strength to open his hand wide, all five fingers, close it into a loose fist, and open it again. He did this until Solomon said, "Stop."

Solomon's face lost all expression. His dark eyes peered into Garrett's, and the prone builder watched the man's nostrils flare.

"I asked you a simple question," Solomon said. "If you are unwilling to answer me, then I'm afraid this is where your thread and mine separate."

The last thing Garrett saw was a brilliant flash of white light, and the last thing he felt was a surge of freezing cold water as it flooded through his body.

Solomon stood and wiped the jade ax on his robe. The moaning had stopped, and his warriors stood, watching him. Solomon held up his hand for them to wait, then walked to the castle. He wanted to meet Jeremiah face to face, man to man. This former preacher was a thief, yes. But he was like a child carrying a gun, unaware of how dangerous it was. Maybe he would give it to Solomon willingly because surely Jeremiah had learned by now how heavy the gift was.

83

ABIGAIL BACKED DOWN THE HALL into the shadows, but she could still see the light falling on the floor from the open door of Samuel's bedroom. She heard voices, mostly Jeremiah's, as he shouted at Emma to stop whatever she was doing. Emma's voice was just a faint murmur. Jeremiah's shouting became more frantic, and there was fear in his voice, genuine terror.

Abigail took a few steps toward the door but stopped. There was nothing she could do.

Then Emma started screaming, her torn voice full of pain. Thick black smoke came pouring out of the room, rising to the ceiling. Emma's voice changed as if she were being choked, then cut off abruptly with the sound of distant, quiet thunder.

Abigail's skin felt electrified in the silence. Even Samuel's grating voice trying to say "mother" could not change it. She smelled the odor of burned flesh and fabric.

She was about to make her way to the room when something moved deeper into the darkness of the hall—a darker shape that seemed to be formed of black space. Two red eyes glowed as the shape came closer. It looked and moved like a dog, but not a dog, something wilder—a wolf, maybe. It had pointed ears and a long snout. It was larger than any of the dogs in town, and it walked softly on padded paws as though it were stalking prey.

Abigail held her breath, afraid to move. How had it gotten into the house? She thought that one of Garrett's workers must have left a door open or a window.

The darkness seemed to move with the wolf as though it were a black cape the animal pulled behind it.

A smooth voice spoke her name, and she heard the word inside her head.

ABIGAIL.

The wolf approached, and cold air came with it. Abigail shivered and felt the skin rise up on her arms and shoulders. Her breath came out in shallow clouds.

I'VE WATCHED YOU FOR SOME TIME.

Abigail backed away until her heel hit the wall. The sound of Jeremiah weeping came drifting down the hall.

YOUR WHOLE LIFE HAS BEEN A TRAGEDY. BUT HERE YOU ARE, STRONG AND CAPABLE. YOU HAVE LEARNED TO SURVIVE, TO USE TERRIBLE CIRCUMSTANCES TO YOUR ADVANTAGE.

She saw an animal, but the thing before her was not an animal and Abigail could not find the words to explain to herself how she knew this. A form, she thought. A representation of something.

She struggled to breathe normally to keep her teeth from chattering.

"I can hear you?" she said.

IS IT ME YOU HEAR, OR ONLY YOUR OWN THOUGHTS? the wolf said.

Abigail's chest went tight with her rapid heartbeat. "Is this real?"

AS REAL AS ANYTHING.

She thought she saw a faint smile on the wolf's mouth. The animal was close enough to touch. It looked real enough to run her fingers through the soft grey and white fur. Real enough to attack her.

"Why were you watching me?" she asked.

IT'S WHAT I WAS MADE TO DO. I'VE SEEN WHAT YOU WANT.

"I don't know what I want," Abigail said quietly.

WHEN THE TIME COMES, TAKE WHAT YOU CAN AND RUN FAR AWAY FROM THIS PLACE.

More sobbing came from the open doorway. Abigail looked toward the room.

YOU KNOW WHAT YOU'LL FIND IN THERE.

Abigail opened her mouth to answer, then looked into the wolf's eyes and felt them pull on her. The floor turned to liquid beneath her feet. Her vision shifted, moving back and forth like someone was shaking her head. She closed her eyes.

THIS IS NOT YET FINISHED. DO NOT LEAVE UNTIL YOU HAVE WHAT YOU DESERVE. The wolf turned around and disappeared back down the hall. The dark swirled and followed.

84

ABIGAIL CREPT TOWARD THE OPEN doorway, her eyes burning as they adjusted to the light that spilled into the hall. Jeremiah's crying had grown quieter, but she could still hear him taking deep gasps of air.

She came into the room and stopped when she saw Emma's body. The gold shimmered differently than it did on Samuel. It seemed to move, waver, as though it were something melted and not yet dried.

Emma knelt in a burned black patch of wood. Smaller black marks led back to the fireplace. Both hands were twisted, palsied, in front of her neck, as though she were reaching up to grab hold of a noose that was strangling her. The eyes were closed so tight, deep lines spread from their corners, but the mouth was open so wide that Abigail could see the back teeth.

Jeremiah was kneeling in front of Emma's corpse, hands flat on the ground, muttering things Abigail could not quite hear. Samuel stood by himself, still and expressionless, his one eye moving between his father and mother.

Abigail took a step and let her boot make a noise to alert Jeremiah. He sat up quickly and looked at her, fear and shame twisting his features.

When Jeremiah looked into her eyes, all the muscles in his face fell.

He said her name once, then lowered his head and began to sob.

Abigail crossed the room and knelt next to him. Jeremiah's hands clutched her arms and neck and finally gripped the back of her blouse to support himself. He pressed his face to her chest and wept, his whole body shaking.

Abigail put her hands on Jeremiah's head and held him. She looked up at the statue of Emma and hated how it made her feel, as though her throat was closing.

Jeremiah groaned, and his fingers gripped her blouse even tighter. She felt each wracking sob as it shuddered through him.

Abigail realized the strange shimmer on the statue was flames frozen in place on Emma's dress. They were frozen as they danced up the fabric and devoured it, shimmering shades of gold.

Jeremiah's muffled voice spoke into her chest. "I had no choice."

He pulled his head back and looked up at Abigail, his eyes red and swollen. "She was going to kill Samuel and herself."

Abigail put her hands on either side of Jeremiah's face, feeling the slick tears and sticky heat of his skin.

"You did nothing wrong," she said.

Jeremiah closed his eyes. His mouth contorted as he tried to keep his sobs from making sounds.

Abigail's fingers caressed the skin around Jeremiah's eyes, softly tracing the lines.

"She got lost," Abigail said. "You tried to help her find a way out."

Jeremiah's eyes opened, and Abigail tilted his head until he looked at her.

"You did nothing wrong," she said again.

She moved Jeremiah's head back to her chest and held him there, gently stroking his hair. She stared at the golden statue of Emma, finding it hard to believe it had once been a woman. It looked like something from a storybook—something precious, priceless, and impossible. Jeremiah's hand rested in her lap, the fingers curled into a fist. She reached down and touched his hand, uncurling the two golden fingers. The hand was warm to the touch, the color of a sunburn.

Jeremiah's head jerked, and he pulled away from her. He stood up and looked toward the door.

"The gunshots have stopped," he said. His eyes grew fearful. "I don't have enough time."

Abigail started to ask what he meant, but Jeremiah had gone behind Emma's statue. He grabbed a few strands of golden hair and bent them until they snapped.

"Take Samuel and leave through the courtyard," he said. "Head for the trees and make your way to Brennan's house. Stay there until I come for you."

Abigail nodded, and Jeremiah left the room. She heard his footsteps slamming down the stairs and echoing as he ran across the house to the west wing.

The statue mesmerized her, the gold was so brilliant and shining. She crawled closer and touched the metal. It was cool on her fingers. She knew it was once a woman, but all Abigail could think of was how much money was there. Money shaped like a person.

Samuel started walking across the room, leaving a puddle of oil where he stood. He came closer, picked up a piece of firewood from the floor, and staggered past Abigail, but she hardly noticed him. She stood and went behind Emma, took a few strands of hair in her hand, and bent them like Jeremiah had until they broke off.

Abigail saw her distorted reflection in the golden fire on Emma's dress. Some of those flames looked like they could be broken as well. Emma grabbed hold of one, but it was thicker than the hair, and she struggled to bend it.

A scraping sound came from the other side of the room. She glanced over and saw Samuel bent over, pulling a log from the fire.

She yelled his name. He turned around and looked at her, his face eerily calm and expressionless. Oil dripped from his hand.

"Mmmmm," his metallic voice said.

Abigail walked toward him. "Samuel, you need to put that down very carefully."

The boy hummed again and pointed the burning end of the log down at his mother's oil-soaked footprints.

The first one caught fire and jumped to the second. Samuel let go of the log and stepped backward, away from the flames. The fire moved across the floor and roared to life in the puddle surrounding Emma's statue.

Abigail yelled for Samuel to get against the wall as she ran to grab blankets from Samuel's makeshift bed on the floor. She came back to the fire and tried to smother it with the blankets, but they, too, caught fire and burned. The flames grew beyond the oil puddles and spread across the floor. The edge of one curtain caught, and the flames tore up to the ceiling.

Abigail turned to grab Samuel and get him out of the room. But the boy was already gone.

85

PALE BLUE MOONLIGHT FELL THROUGH the windows and illuminated the stone corridor where Samuel paced. He walked to the west wing, then turned around and staggered back to the foyer. His gray suit was still wet, and small black spots glistened on the floor where oil dripped from his fingertips and pants.

He paced, back and forth, back and forth.

When he came to the foyer for the sixth time, Samuel paused and looked up at the window near the front door. A man-shaped silhouette was peering inside. Samuel stared at the shape until it moved away from the glass, and then there was a light knock on the door.

Samuel shuffled over to the door, put his hand on the handle, and wrapped his fingers around it, but the oil was slick, and they slid off.

Three more knocks.

He gripped tighter and pulled the door open.

A very tall man stood before him. His hair was as white as the moon hanging over his shoulder in the sky. He wore a black robe that went to his feet. His long fingers were laced together at his waist.

The man was smiling with teeth as white as his hair. There were dark red dots and streaks all over his face.

Silence passed between them. Samuel's mouth opened and closed. A faint metallic sound came from the boy's throat, and the tall man leaned forward, still smiling, and his eyes grew wider as though he was very interested in what Samuel had to say.

Finally, the golden boy, dressed in a suit still soaked with oil, spoke as clearly as he could. The words came from some old memory of what he was supposed to say when a guest arrived. "Ayyy hellllllllp yoouu?"

The tall man's smile grew wider. He reached out one hand and gently touched the boy's face.

86

ABIGAIL WATCHED AT THE TOP of the stairs as the tall man in the black robe stroked Samuel's head. She didn't realize she had put a hand over her mouth until her eyes stung from the stench of oil, and she tasted it.

A group of shadows gathered behind the man, waiting outside the doorway. His steps echoed as he walked closer to the stairs and stopped where a pale band of moonlight divided the room. He looked up and saw Abigail. A smile spread across his face, and he waved a hand.

"Come join us, my dear," he said. "You will not be harmed. You have my word."

Abigail hesitated, looked behind her, and saw the glowing orange light of the fire pulsing in the hall just outside Samuel's room. She felt heat growing at her back. Thick smoke poured out of the doorway and rose to the ceiling.

"It looks like we don't have much time," Solomon said. "Join us, please."

Abigail inhaled and choked on the smoke. She came down the stairs coughing, eyes burning.

Solomon watched her, one hand on Samuel's shoulder, the other holding an ax.

"What is your name?" he asked.

Abigail wasn't sure what to do with her hands. Her fingers twisted the fabric of her blouse.

"Abigail," she said. "Abigail Fletcher."

"What a strong name for such a strong young woman," he smiled. "You must have seen everything that happened in this house."

He leaned in and smiled again, like a conspirator. "Of course you did! Look at those eyes, they don't miss a thing. You knew what he was, and you still remained. That, my dear, is strength of the rarest kind. Standing beside a man while he does terrible things requires a certain kind of honesty, does it not?"

The ax hung at Solomon's side, blood dripping down the green blade. The man's voice was surprisingly warm and inviting.

"I could use a woman like you, Abigail Fletcher," he said. "Right now, your future is nothing. Do you understand that? If I so decide, you will be nothing in a matter of minutes. A body on the floor with all your blood leaking out of you. All your memories will just fly away and scatter. But I am offering you a place within our tribe, our family." He waved a hand to the shadow shapes behind him. Inhuman shapes make human sounds, still breathing heavily from the battle. Reeking of blood.

The tall man leaned in. "You will have a home, you will have wealth, and you will have a position of power by my side. More than that, you will have a future. You see, Miss Fletcher, I am remaking the world, and what a glorious thing that it starts here in your humble town."

Solomon waved his free hand as if stopping a protest that had not yet happened. "I know, I know. You see savagery, but that is not who we are. Savagery was called for tonight, but it is merely one part of us, one small part. Without a battle to fight, that savagery is used only to protect our family. It is a large and loving family, and many call me Father."

Solomon stepped into the moonlight. The streaks of blood had hardened on his cheeks, and Abigail thought she had never seen anything more dangerous in her life.

She turned her head at the sound of wood cracking as the fire moved into the upstairs hall. Smoke rolled along the ceiling above their heads like black thunderclouds.

Solomon held out his hand. "Come, do not let this be the end. Do not let death be your future."

"Death is the future for all of us," Abigail said.

Solomon smiled, one hand stroking Samuel's head. "Surely, we cannot say that anything is impossible."

Samuel looked from Abigail to Solomon and back again. There was no fear in his face, no confusion. Just blankness. Tendrils of smoke came rolling down the staircase.

Solomon took one more step forward, his eyes black and wild. The pale light made deep shadows in the creases of his face. He looked not just old but ancient, and Abigail thought, ill. He looked ill. A man approaching death, maybe even already feeling its icy grasp, and he was desperately trying to find a way to keep on living.

"Let me put it to you a different way," Solomon said, all the warmth gone from his voice. He held the jade ax up so the blade was only inches from Abigail's face. "If you don't take me to Jeremiah, I will kill you right here, then I will seek out your family and kill them. Next, I will steal into every home and slaughter every single person I find. Then, I will burn the entire town right off the map. Like it never existed."

Looking into Solomon's demented eyes, Abigail knew his words were not threats. He was speaking a version of the future, a version that would surely come to pass if she did not do what he asked. The roar of the fire grew louder, and the smoke was now so thick she could not even see the upstairs hall. There was just a wall of black smoke with a throbbing orange light inside it. Twisted fingers of flame curled up the walls and ignited the framed paintings.

Abigail pointed down the stone hallway that led to the west wing.

"You are wise, Abigail Fletcher," Solomon said. "Soon, you will be wealthy enough to build your own world. Now, take me to him."

Abigail turned and walked toward the west wing. Solomon waved his hand, and the inhuman shadows that waited entered the house.

87

ABIGAIL LED THE WAY, AND Solomon walked beside her, one hand on Samuel's shoulder to guide the boy. The warriors followed close behind.

Samuel's clunky steps echoed off the stone corridor, and Solomon occasionally moved his hand to the boy's golden neck and stroked the smooth metal.

Abigail looked back to the entryway, and the whole room was glowing with red light. Smoke poured into the corridor as if it were chasing them.

When they reached the west wing, the warriors gathered in a half-circle around Abigail, smelling of sweat and blood. Air rushed in and out of the man with the skull mask as he breathed heavily— one animal wearing the skull of another. The woman with them was short but powerfully built. Dark liquid leaked from a deep wound in her thigh and pooled on the floor.

Although Solomon was not smiling, Abigail saw a knowing, haughty look that made her feel dirty and used. An expression similar to the ones she'd seen in the men her father used to bring to the house—a perverse desire that burned so hot inside them that it twisted their features into horrible, ugly masks.

Solomon pointed his jade ax toward the dark stairway. "The future is waiting."

Abigail turned silently, took Samuel's hand, and walked toward the staircase.

"Stay and keep watch," Solomon said to the warriors. "More may come." Then, he followed Abigail.

The staircase twisted into darkness. Samuel's knees bent stiffly, and Abigail had to help pull him up each step. They reached the third floor and continued climbing.

"You feel it, don't you?" Solomon asked. "The air is different here." He held up a hand and rubbed two fingers together. "Something is happening."

They reached the fourth floor, and every muscle in Abigail's neck started to cramp as they climbed higher.

Solomon paused and closed his eyes, slowly turning his face like something invisible was brushing against his skin.

"I saw this moment," he said quietly. "This house, these stairs. Even you, my dear. I saw you. This moment has been an outline with countless threads leading to it. I know how this ends."

He opened his eyes, smiled at her, and started up the stairs again. Abigail felt like she was falling, and her heart dropped in her chest. The smoke-filled air made her dizzy and turned her stomach sour. All she heard were their footsteps and their breathing, out of rhythm, out of time. Finally, they reached the fifth-floor landing and stopped.

The jade ax made small twisting motions in Solomon's hand. His nostrils flared beneath his wide eyes, eyes that peered at Abigail with a mad eagerness.

"He's close?" Solomon asked.

Abigail closed her eyes and nodded.

"Show me."

Abigail walked down the long hallway, her sweaty hand slick on the cold metal of Samuel's hand. The dim light reflected off the snow in the courtyard and came in through the windows to their right.

Abigail sensed Solomon lean in closer every time they passed a closed door. The man's movements were tighter now, his head jerking in quick motions like a bird's. Abigail stopped at the second to last door.

"This is it?" Solomon asked, pressing in close.

Abigail lowered her head and did not speak.

Solomon's hand tightened and released around the leather grip of his ax. Tightened and released. It made a small squeaking sound each time.

"Open it," Solomon whispered.

Abigail pushed open the door, and they stepped into the large empty space, filled with a metallic hum so loud that the windows shivered with the vibrations. A rectangle of moonlight lay on the floor, dividing the room.

Abigail pointed to the painting of the elk. "If you open that, there is a door that leads to another room."

The hum was so loud Abigail felt she was shouting.

Solomon smiled, his white teeth shining. "You have done well, Abigail Fletcher." He put both hands on the young woman's shoulders, the blade of the ax touching her spine. "Look at the force of this world," Solomon said. "It kills, burns, floods, destroys. It makes chaos from order. It is indifferent to our morality. It does what it is meant to do and never questions it. Morality is an invention, Abigail."

His fingers tightened painfully. "We all have a role. I have always known mine, and tonight, you find yours. Your place is with us now. Soon, you will have everything you deserve. Everything you've ever wanted."

He loosened his grip on Abigail's shoulders and took Samuel by the arm. Solomon's face tightened, and the shadows made it look as though his features were carved out of stone.

Abigail stood aside and let Solomon and Samuel walk past. Halfway across the room, Solomon paused and smiled again, moving one hand through the air as though it were made of water.

Solomon tapped a finger to his ear. "Do you hear that? That is the sound the universe made when it was created."

He turned in a circle, his black robe flowing around his legs. One hand held Samuel's arm, and the other rubbed against the leather handle of the ax. He exhaled quickly as he neared the wall, grabbed the frame of the painting, and swung it open to reveal the door to the secret room.

The metallic hum grew in volume, pulsing through Abigail's jaw and rattling her teeth. Solomon held up the ax and looked at it curiously. The hum was vibrating the green blade, causing it to make a faint hum of its own.

With his eyes on the second door, Solomon took deliberate steps toward the hum, looking like a man caught in a trance. He reached out and held his hand to the surface of the door, feeling the vibrations through the wood. Solomon smiled as the energy coursed through his fingers.

His hand moved to the brass handle and opened the door. The room that lay beyond was bathed in rippling orange light. Solomon smoothed out a wrinkle on his robe and tightened the belt. Then, after taking a deep breath, he gripped the jade ax tighter and walked into the secret room, Samuel by his side.

As soon as the door closed, Abigail slumped to the floor, that metallic hum vibrating every drop of sweat on her skin.

88

IT TOOK SOLOMON'S EYES A moment to adjust to the pulsating orange light. Ribbons of white danced along the walls like reflections of water. He tried to stop his hands from shaking, but he couldn't. His eyes filled with tears as the hum passed through him, warming his bones. The years of searching were finally over.

Keeping one hand on Samuel's shoulder, Solomon walked deeper into the light, the hum, and felt like a swarm of insects fluttered around in his chest. Tiny beating wings moved up his heart and lungs, pushing into his throat. Solomon opened his mouth, and his breath came out in a vapor like it would in the cold, only this breath sparkled as it hit the air—sparkled and floated like gold dust.

The orange light revealed vague shapes that slowly became more defined. Solomon expected to encounter Jeremiah alone, but other people were still and unmoving in this room. He took a step back and held up the ax.

"Jeremiah Pevensie?" he said. "Are you here?"

A voice came out of all the light. "I was wondering when you would find me," it said.

"Did you see me like I saw you?" Solomon asked.

Silence.

Solomon tried to calm his breathing, but the hum was energizing. It was more than just a sound, he realized. It was a musical note, lifting him from the inside out. Evaporating every fear and every doubt. It sang through his blood, took his thoughts and shaped them, clarified them.

Solomon remembered stories from the Hebrew Bible, stories of their tabernacle and the Holy of Holies, where God dwelled and only priests could enter. Those who went into that place without a pure heart were killed by God's glory. He thought that same power was residing in this room, doing work on a level beyond the physical. Something was happening. He felt it. Something was being created.

The fluttering wings moved through Solomon's throat and into his skull. He was immediately overcome with dizziness, and he felt as though his body was miles below his head. Afraid that he would fall over, Solomon reached out an arm to support himself. His hand touched a smooth, warm surface, and all at once the light dimmed, and the hum receded until it was nothing but background noise.

Solomon blinked at the sudden shift, and everything in the room was clear. Shelves against walls were filled with ancient books and scrolls. His senses were so alive he could smell their age, the dust of the places they had come from. The fireplace glowed with faint light, casting shadows on the ceiling. The shapes he had seen inside the orange light were statues and various golden animals on the ground.

A thought appeared in Solomon's head. *You have been given this gift and this is what you do with it? Thousands have been slaughtered in search of it. Kings have spent their entire existence trying to find it. And you use it to kill animals and hide yourself away? You are not worthy.*

This thought had its own hum, its own rhythm, and Solomon realized it was his vocal chords vibrating. He had spoken the thought as soon as it came to him.

Three human shapes stood near the fireplace. One of them turned slowly.

"I may not be worthy," the voice said, "but it belongs to me, and you cannot take it."

The shape turned until Solomon found himself looking into the eyes of Jeremiah Pevensie.

He was thinner and more fragile than Solomon expected. The wrinkled suit he wore hung on his frame, and the work shirt underneath was stained with sweat and dirt. The skin on his face was sallow, the cheeks sunken in, lips cracked. His eyes were set deep within dark circles, but those eyes burned with a feverish intensity.

Jeremiah moved around the table and stood before it, holding out his arms as though trying to block Solomon's view of what was on it. The other human shape standing near the fireplace was as tall as a man but wider. A round, hairless head, and sloping shoulders. Solomon squinted into the light.

"Do you know of Titus, the Roman emperor?" Solomon whispered. He pressed his thumb into the still-wet blood on the ax and made a red line on Samuel's smooth forehead.

"His last words were, 'I have made but one mistake.'"

Solomon made another line on the boy's skin, a bloody cross. "Scholars believe he was referring to his brother, Domitian, who poisoned Titus. His mistake was not killing his brother when he had the chance." Solomon smiled. "But that's not a mistake you made, is it?"

"Turn back," Jeremiah said, his voice weak. "There is nothing for you here."

Solomon saw another golden shape on the other side of the fireplace, this one much smaller. Nearly the size of the boy in front of him. Solomon tightened his grip on Samuel's jacket and took one slow step forward. "If you knew how long I've been searching, you would not say such things."

To Solomon, it looked like Jeremiah had not slept in days. The man seemed to have no weapon, at least none Solomon could see, and judging by his weak appearance, Solomon guessed he could easily overpower him.

"It doesn't matter how long you've been searching," Jeremiah said, spreading his arms out. "It belongs to me."

Solomon looked to his left and saw another golden shape near the bookshelves. This one, though, he recognized. Only half a body was less human than the others, though still transformed and beautiful in its own way. The flesh on the face and hands was partially eaten away. A good portion of the skull had been caved in. Golden clumps of earth still clung to its skin and clothes. The eye sockets were empty grooves, and the nose was gone, leaving only two narrow holes. The bottom half of the body was melted into a hardened gold puddle as if the man were sinking right into the floor. A puddle attached to him, part of the gold he was made of.

"Did you try to bring him back?" Solomon asked.

Jeremiah moved and used his body to block whatever lay on the table. He lowered his eyes for a moment.

"You knew him?"

"I sent him," Solomon said, "to find what you now have. So, you see, it was never yours to begin with. It's always been mine."

"I buried him when I found his body," Jeremiah said. "But I wanted to know what he'd learned during his time with the gift. What came back was not human, it spoke in another voice. So, I changed him. Changed him into something that would last forever."

Solomon caught a glimpse of something at the far end of the table, something that caused his blood to run cold. A chill ran from his neck and down his spine. A crudely shaped golden foot connected to a golden leg full of bumps, like clay when it is being fashioned.

"What else are you changing?" Solomon asked, moving closer.

Jeremiah's eyes glanced down at the jade ax in Solomon's hand. "Give me my son back," he said.

"I can feel it," Solomon said softly. "It's in the air, the creation. But what you're doing is very difficult, isn't it? Maybe even impossible."

Jeremiah shifted his weight, and the thing on the table was momentarily visible. It was even more horrifying than Solomon had thought.

"If you take one more step, I will make you like him," Jeremiah said, nodding his head toward the statue of the man from the woods.

"Someone once told me they still dream," Solomon said, "after they are changed. Some parts of them still remain, and if you listen closely at night, you can hear them whisper. When a person is changed, gold becomes much more delicate. The soul requires a fragile home. It's inside every inch of the gold, part of it." He held the edge of the jade ax to Samuel's head and pressed it against the metal until it made a mark. "The gold is corrupted by the soul, which is why it melts much faster. Have you found this to be true?"

He took another step. "Do you hear voices, Jeremiah?"

Jeremiah jerked his head to look at a dark corner behind him.

"I hear only one voice," he said. "Always one voice."

"And what does it say?"

"It tells me God has abandoned me, and life is suffering, but I can make a world inside the world."

"Then the voice lies," Solomon said. "There is not just one God, there are many. Thousands of them. They have been here since the earth was formed and will be here long after we are gone. And the world is not made, Jeremiah. Anything we build is only created for the universe to tear down. I've studied the texts and spoken with the priests and shamans. The universe is a clock made to tick backwards, it counts down to the end of all things. Nothing we do can stop that. The mortal will always die."

Solomon took another step, close enough now to smell Jeremiah's sweat. He looked into Jeremiah's eyes, then slowly moved his gaze to the foot at the end of the table. "Nothing will ever bring her back," Solomon said. He touched the back of Samuel's head. "Just like him."

Jeremiah's mouth tightened into a thin line. His eyes stared into Solomon's with pain, fear, and anger. Two fingers of his right hand stretched out while the other three folded inward. His nostrils flared wide.

"You see these books?" he screamed. "You see these scrolls? I have read every single word written in them. I know it's possible, you liar. You filthy goddamned liar! I know it can be done. It has been done."

Solomon nodded slowly. "I did not say it was impossible, only that they could not be returned to you. Not the way they were. That part of them is gone. You would only be resurrecting the surface layer of the soul, which has no memory, no language, and no love. It's a shell, Jeremiah, nothing more."

Jeremiah doubled over suddenly, like he had been stabbed in the stomach, and roared with a cry so fierce it struck some deep chord in Solomon, in some deep place he never visited.

"I need more time," Jeremiah yelled.

Solomon's voice spoke softly. "We all wander this earth with an invisible hourglass inside us. No one knows how much time it has, only when it has run out. And your time is up, Mr. Pevensie. The upper half of your hourglass is empty."

Jeremiah looked up at him, tears filling his eyes. "You don't decide when my time has come."

"I have been studying and searching for most of my life," Solomon said. "I've always known what it would cost, what must be sacrificed. I have had many children, and I have fathered them all with a single purpose, that their blood might one day provide the required payment for the gift you now possess."

Solomon's eyes glazed over and lost color. He stared at Jeremiah but was looking elsewhere, somewhere beyond.

He said, "I have held the knife and pierced the heart. I have paid again and again, receiving nothing in return. Do not moan to me about the reality of what you face. Life is temporary, Jeremiah, it always has been. And this lack of understanding is why you are unworthy of this immense gift. Your hands are too weak to hold it."

Solomon reached into his robe, and his hand came out, holding something Jeremiah could not see.

"Samuel," Jeremiah said, and the boy's one good eye floated until it came to rest on his father. "Come here, son."

Samuel did not move, but his mouth opened. "Mmmm…."

Solomon's hand opened and revealed a box of matches. He took one out and struck it against the box. The small flame reflected off Samuel's golden skin and illuminated the boy's oil-soaked suit.

Solomon held up the match. "If you will not willingly give me what is mine, I will take it from you and everything you love in the process."

He set the match against Samuel's suit, and before Jeremiah could take a breath, the entire boy was engulfed in flames. He stood perfectly still as the fabric of his suit was consumed. Pieces of it fell off him, and the oil on his golden skin continued to burn.

Jeremiah screamed and ran over to his son, afraid to touch him. The boy's expression remained unchanged, but his mouth opened wide as though he wanted to say something, and Jeremiah saw all the way back to the glowing metal of his throat. As the flames covered Samuel's body, the gold began to loosen and change shape. The boy's lower jaw elongated and hung down to his chest. The good eye turned to liquid and ran from its socket. Droplets of gold fell to the floor.

Jeremiah tore off his jacket and tried to wrap it around his son, but the jacket caught fire and stuck to the melting gold. A sound came out of Samuel's mouth, like a hushed scream.

Solomon rushed forward, brandishing the jade ax, and swung. Jeremiah straightened up just in time to deflect the man's arm, but the force of the blow knocked him back against the table.

Solomon's eyes burned with anger, and spit dribbled from his gritted teeth. He swung again. Jeremiah moved aside as the green blade slammed into the table and stuck, but Solomon immediately let go of the ax and struck Jeremiah in the side of the head with his fist. He fell to the ground, holding a hand to his ear and groaning.

With Jeremiah out of the way, Solomon could now see the full body stretched out on the table. A crudely shaped woman with a dark gaping mouth and eyes. Solomon had seen the texts and knew the figure on the table was hollow. He knew that Jeremiah would try and melt down his dead wife and fill all that empty space with her gold.

"Just a shell," Solomon said.

The other two figures near the fireplace—the man-sized one and the boy-sized one—served the same purpose. Solomon understood: Jeremiah planned to be done with his human body and join his family inside these hollow, golden shells.

Jeremiah struggled up to his knees and screamed. Samuel's body warped and collapsed, slowly melting into a puddle of gold that spread across the floor.

Solomon gripped the ax again, pulling the handle up and down to work it free from the wood. He looked at the preacher, kneeling like a man confessing sin, and felt disgusted that such power should be granted to someone so undeserving. He swallowed hard, readying himself to swing the blade, to split the wretched man's head in half, and then Solomon saw a fleeting movement from the table. Something so small he might have missed it if he was turned just a little more. But he did see it, and he couldn't look away.

One empty eye of the woman-shaped shell filled with gold and fluttered slowly, like a butterfly emerging from a cocoon, and opened. Solomon backed away, feeling curiosity and horror in equal measure. Inside the socket was a golden orb, smaller than a normal human eye, perfectly round and unblemished. There was only a slight discoloration in the gold where the pupil would be, just enough to know it was there.

The orb rolled until it came to rest on Solomon, and he felt as though the coldest winter had come rushing into the room, freezing his skin and his blood. The orb stared lifelessly, but Solomon sensed some knowing energy radiating from it. Some force or intelligence on the other side was waiting for the transformation to complete.

A shadow appeared in the doorway and entered the room, stealthy and low to the ground. Solomon narrowed his eyes and thought he recognized the shape, but it joined the other shadows before he could get another look.

In that moment of distraction, Jeremiah rose to his feet, lowered his shoulder, and hurled himself into Solomon's ribs. The two men fell to the floor, grappling, clawing at each other's faces. Jeremiah managed to stay on top, hammering his fists on Solomon's chest as hard as he could. Jeremiah screamed as his fingers grasped a handful of Solomon's white hair. He slammed the man's head into the floor again and again, and he did not let go until Solomon's legs stopped kicking and a trickle of blood ran from his ear.

Jeremiah fell back, gasping. Each breath sent a bolt of pain through his ribcage, and he was certain that one, if not more of them, was broken.

Solomon lay motionless, thick blood leaking from his ear, staining his white hair. His black robe pooled on the floor around his body like dark water. Jeremiah knew now was his chance. His fingers moved into position as he stretched out his right hand and touched Solomon's leg.

The glow was so bright Jeremiah had to close his eyes. Heat grew under his hand as Solomon's leg hardened and turned into shining metal. Like paper burning, a bright edge of light spread slowly, turning his legs and robe solid as it rose toward his knees. Solomon stirred, opened his eyes, and began screaming. He tried to kick at Jeremiah, but his legs wouldn't move. His arms thrashed wildly, and froth came from between his gritted teeth as he grasped at the floor, trying to drag himself away.

Jeremiah turned his head away, waiting for the process to end. Dark thoughts clouded his mind as the power flowed out of him. Every bitter and hateful emotion he ever felt, every curse and blasphemy he had ever uttered seemed to gather and form a hole at the center of his chest. He could feel it pulling on his insides, on his soul.

With his head turned Jeremiah didn't see Solomon's hand reach for the jade ax that had fallen to the floor. He didn't see the man push himself up on one elbow and swing with all his strength. Jeremiah felt something like a snake bite, quick and sharp, then an icy sensation on his wrist. He looked back and saw his hand on Solomon's leg, but something was wrong. He lifted his arm to see empty space where the hand should have been, angry red flesh surrounding white bone. Hundreds of small liquid pearls floated through the air, splashing onto the floor, onto Solomon's robe. Streams of liquid shot out of the stump. They burst out in time with his heartbeat, each pump sending out a fresh spray.

Solomon's mouth twisted, his black pupils large and glistening with pain. His face was covered in droplets of blood.

Jeremiah clamped his other hand over the stump to staunch the flow. He wanted to cry out, to scream, but the room spun in circles around him, blurring into a kaleidoscope of orange and red. Black moved in at the edges of his vision, and then the room tilted sideways, and his head crashed to the floor.

Solomon lay back, breathing heavily, sweating. The lower half of his body was solid gold, the robe hardened around his legs, splattered with red. The two men were close enough to touch, and they stared at one another across a growing pool of blood. Jeremiah's eyes ached to close, remain closed, and slip into an endless sleep and awake in whatever world came next.

"I have made but one mistake," Solomon said in a hoarse voice, as he lifted the ax once more.

Jeremiah let his eyes close, waiting to hear the blade whistle as it cut through the air, but he heard the click of claws on the floor, coming closer, faster. He opened his eyes and saw the wolf leaning its open jaws over Solomon's face. Solomon sucked in a breath to scream, but the sound never came. The wolf's teeth clamped over the man's mouth and tore. The flesh ripped away, leaving a gaping bloody wound and two rows of red-stained teeth clenched together in a nightmarish smile. Punctures in Solomon's cheeks leaked thick blood. A gargling sound came from the dark, wet hole in his face. The wolf opened its mouth again over Solomon's throat, and Jeremiah closed his eyes as the jaws snapped shut, and a flood of warm liquid inched across the floor, puddling under his head.

Jeremiah looked up to see the wolf standing over him, blood dripping from its muzzle.

"Is this the end?" Jeremiah asked.

The wolf blinked once.

"I'm not sorry to leave this world," Jeremiah said.

His vision broke down, and everything in the room fell apart and lost shape. He reached out his hand for his son, now just a shapeless mass of gold with no face or features. He closed his eyes, knowing he would never open them again. He held his breath for as long as he could, and when he finally exhaled, his body went still.

The wolf stood near him for a moment, staring at a face that was finally peaceful, no longer creased with heartache and fear. Then the wolf walked around the body and went to the door, leaving a trail of bloody paw prints.

89

ABIGAIL SAT IN A BAND of moonlight, her back against the wall, clenching her fingers into fists and releasing them. She heard noise from the room, screaming. She closed her eyes and tried to picture someplace faraway, someplace beautiful, like she used to when she lived with her mother and father, but her heartbeat was so heavy she had trouble taking in full breaths. Her chin shook, rattling her teeth together. Sweat slid down her neck and back.

Too much time had passed. Or maybe not enough. She had no idea what was supposed to happen next, or what she was supposed to do.

Smoke crawled past the open door that led to the hall. Silver fingers that crept further into the house, some of them trailing along the floor and into the room. Abigail covered her mouth with an arm and coughed. Her eyes burned from the smoke and her throat was sore every time she swallowed. She couldn't stay in the house much longer.

She was watching the way the smoke changed color in the moonlight when the door of the second room creaked open. She sat up straight, waiting to see who would come out. Which man had killed the other. But no one was there. The room beyond the door was all orange and crimson. A warm coppery smell drifted out. The wolf emerged from the shadows and came toward Abigail. Its muzzle was slick and wet, the fur clumped together, stained red.

IT IS FINISHED. TAKE WHAT YOU CAN AND LEAVE.

Abigail looked into the wolf's red eyes, seeing things she could not explain there. It left the room and went into the smoke-filled hallway.

Abigail got up and went to the entrance to the secret room. The hum was gone now, replaced with an eerie silence. She stepped around a shapeless mass of melted gold in the center of the floor, small flames still flickering on its surface. As she moved past, she heard a sound coming from inside it. A single letter hummed like an out-of-tune song.

"Mmmmm...."

Abigail covered her mouth and backed away. She could see it now: Samuel's collapsed and disfigured shape in the mass. The voice was weak but unmistakably his.

Abigail came closer and whispered, "I'm so sorry, Samuel. I'm sorry I couldn't do more."

The voice fell silent as the center of the mass folded inward, and a cloud of gold dust burst out. Abigail watched the dust settle into patches of drying blood and sparkle, and she wondered if each particle represented a memory, a lived-in moment that had been recorded in the soul.

Every thought, every emotion, every memory. Nothing but dust.

"Be at peace," Abigail said.

She approached the two bodies lying on the floor and knelt next to Jeremiah, seeing the stump and the surge of blood that had sprayed across the room. Even Samuel's mutilated golden body was stained with twisted trails of red.

Abigail touched Jeremiah's remaining hand and said a prayer for his soul.

Solomon's face was no longer a face. The skin had been shredded, the flesh still raw ànd bloody. The eyelids and lips were torn away, leaving bright white eyes and teeth gleaming inside a mutilated mass of tissue. There was red everywhere. Red splashed over every surface and wall. Dripping down the books and scrolls, falling from the ceiling. Solomon's white hair was now pinkish, wet and stuck to the floor in clumps.

Abigail stood and rummaged around until she found a canvas sack folded up near one of the bookshelves. She quickly started picking up some of the smaller golden animals on the floor and putting them in the pockets of her coat. She wanted to study each one, but she had to hurry.

On a bottom shelf, she found a small stack of gold ingots. Perfectly smooth and weighing only about ten pounds each, they were all stamped with the letter JP in the center. Abigail put several of these in the bag and lifted it to see if the canvas would hold. It did.

Leaving the bag on the ground, Abigail went around the room and pulled down as many scrolls and books as she could. She carried them over to the bag, but there was no way she could take everything. She would have to choose either the gold or the texts. Even then, she could not take all the books. There were far too many.

Sweat dripped into her eyes, and she wiped it away with the back of her hand. That's when she noticed the large gold object lying on the table before the fireplace. She walked around it slowly. It looked like a human-shaped suit meant to contain a body. The chest cavity was open, exposing its hollow center, but not until she saw the golden pieces of Emma's hair lying inside where the heart and lungs would be, did Abigail understand.

She looked up and saw the other two shapes, the other shells standing near the fire. A man and a boy. Her breath caught and her eyes burned with tears. She understood, not completely, but enough to see what Jeremiah was trying to do. He was going to save his wife and son in these new forms, and then join them. But he didn't have enough time.

All the gold, the money, everything was just to keep them together. She looked back down at Jeremiah's lifeless body.

"Dust," she said out loud.

At the end of the table, a journal was on top of several pieces of parchment paper. Whatever these were, they were what Jeremiah had been referencing for this final change. Abigail grabbed them all, went back to the bag, and put them inside. She was able to add a few scrolls and books before the canvas was almost too heavy for her to lift.

She twisted the top of the bag, hoisted it over her shoulder, and went back out into the empty room, so full of smoke now that she coughed until she thought she might vomit.

Dark smoke rolled down the hallway, and there was a red-orange glow where the staircase went down. The air was thick and suffocating. Abigail's eyes watered, and it burned when she breathed.

She turned to go further down the hall to the back of the house when she heard screams echoing up from the stairs—voices crying out from the west wing, some in anger, some in pain. Abigail pulled her blouse up over her mouth and nose and took slow steps toward the landing. The screams grew louder and more frantic. The furious snarling and growling of an animal cut through the cries and then stopped.

Abigail backed away as heat moved invisibly through the hall, warping the air. It pushed through her clothes, touched her skin. Sweat broke out everywhere on her body, dripped off her face. The damp blouse clung to her back.

The red light grew down the stairs, and Abigail turned and ran as a wall of flames burst out of the stairwell and came tearing down the hall. She glanced over her shoulder, momentarily struck by how the fire moved as though controlled by some fearful intelligence. Bright orange tongues licked at the air, searching for things to burn. Smoke spread along the floor, curling up the walls and rolling along the ceiling like dark storm clouds.

She ran.

Wood snapped as the fire spread its ragged fingers up the walls. Fibers on the rug popped and sparked. Abigail felt the floor shifting under her feet as parts of the house were consumed by the fire below.

She made it to the staircase at the far end of the hall and went down into the unfinished north wing. She moved as fast as she could through the skeletal structure until she reached a large open space and ran between pillars supporting the floor above her. There was a door up ahead. She charged through it and outside into the snow, taking deep breaths of the cold air. She was at the back side of the house, facing the field behind it. Beyond the dark tree line of the forest was a black, jagged line.

Abigail walked some distance into the snow until she could see the sunset-colored glow rising off the house. She went further along the back wall until she came to the edge. She leaned out and saw a group of townspeople, many dressed in nightgowns and overcoats, gathered in the field to watch the castle burn. A dark ring, where the snow had melted from the heat, surrounded the house like a black halo.

The hand holding the canvas bag shook as she thought of walking out to meet the crowd, the only survivor of a massacre. She saw flames twitching beyond the windows, tearing through the rooms, leaving black streaks on the glass. Ash snowed down from the sky, silver flakes still glowing at the edges.

Abigail gripped the bag with both hands and started walking toward the trees when a loud crack resounded in the air above her. She looked up just in time to see a chunk of roof break free and tumble into the courtyard, out of sight.

More townspeople crossed the field, coming to watch the end of something none of them fully understood.

The air changed suddenly, became superheated and charged. Abigail felt something press on her chest, like an invisible hand, and as it pushed the breath out of her, the air went cold for just a second, and then there was an explosion. A sound louder and deeper than dynamite. The force blew out all the windows, sending a shower of glass raining down on the crowd. A hole opened in the roof of the west wing, and a burst of fire and debris came rushing out, scattering wood and stone all over the ground. The gathered crowd backed away, covering their heads with their hands.

The roar of the fire grew in volume until it was all Abigail could hear. A massive column of smoke billowed into the sky. Somewhere deep in the house, beams cracked and shattered.

That's when the screaming started.

The figures crossing the field ran now—a group of ten, maybe twenty, men, women, and children. They ran awkwardly, stumbling through the snow, white nightgowns fluttering behind them like they were being chased by ghosts. Their cries and moans echoed as they came across the broken bodies strewn about the blood-stained snow. Then Abigail understood: These were the families of the dead men. The families who knew their husbands and sons had gone off into the night to defend the man who built the castle.

Minutes passed. The fire moved throughout the house until every hallway and every room was filled with bright flames. An orange glow surrounded the entire structure, as if a hole had opened in the ground and was pulling the house into it, piece by piece.

The roof at the center of the house began to sag, right above the room where Emma's statue was, still covered in frozen flames. Then, in a burst of sparks and ash, the roof collapsed. Glowing red embers shot up into the sky. The crowd gasped and cried even louder.

Abigail knew that now was her chance, and she took off running across the field, bathed in flickering firelight. Her shadow stretched out on the snow and ran beside her all the way to the barn. She went inside and stood in the dark, watching fire overtake the fortress.

She watched the east wing fall into itself. She watched the west wing crumble, the roof of the north wing crash into the courtyard, and then the center of the house buckled and fell forward onto Garrett's camp, burying all the bodies lying in the bloody snow. The mortar between the stones melted, and they fell to the ground with a sound like cannon fire. Even from the barn, Abigail felt the heat of the inferno that blazed relentlessly, tearing everything down.

Some of the families had fallen to their knees in the quickly melting snow, muddying their white gowns. One woman had her arms stretched out to the flames, crying in a loud voice as though her husband might hear her and walk miraculously out of the wreckage. A small child had his arms wrapped tightly around the woman, wailing.

Abigail watched it all from the shadows of the barn, unseen by the townspeople. As much as she knew or understood anything, she knew that Charwood was no longer her home. She couldn't stay, not after everything that had happened. So much death and darkness. There would be endless questions she could never answer. The accusing eyes, the suspicious glances, the outward displays of bitterness and resentment—she could foresee it all. What kind of life could she ever have in this town with that dark history following her?

But she also knew if she was dead, all would be forgiven.

The tower at the center of the courtyard shuddered and leaned. There was a series of loud snaps, and the top half of the tower separated from the base and fell straight down like the point of a knife.

90

ABIGAIL SADDLED UP ONE OF the horses, loaded the heavy canvas sack, and led the animal out of the barn. The castle was still ablaze, illuminating the forest and the crowd watching it burn.

When she reached the tree line, Abigail got in the saddle and rode into the forest. She looked back once and saw the orange glow of the burning house fading to the size of a lantern light behind her.

She didn't know where she was going. All she knew was that she'd ride until she couldn't ride anymore. The rest, she'd figure out once she got there.

Every once in a while, she would catch a glimpse of something moving between the trees. A flash of gray fur and red eyes would be watching her and speaking to her, and Abigail knew the path would reveal itself in time. For now, she rode away from the old life as fast as she could.

SAN FRANCISCO, CALIFORNIA, 1877

FOG DRIFTED IN FROM THE bay. Abigail watched from the balcony of her house on top of the hill as the silver mist touched the shore and spread inland. The poorly built shacks and homes at the bottom soon disappeared as the fog rolled over them. It looked like a cloud had fallen from the sky and covered the streets and the buildings. She couldn't even see the water anymore.

Nowhere near as large as Jeremiah's castle, the mansion where Abigail lived was much bigger than she needed. And unlike that fortress built of dark stone, Abigail's was painted bright white with red roofing tile. On summer days, the house gleamed so bright that it almost hurt to look at it.

Abigail avoided her neighbors as much as possible. In fact, she knew only one by name, and that was by accident. They probably all thought of her as arrogant and eccentric, but she didn't care. She had more money in her safe than they would see in two lifetimes.

She had invested in real estate and silver as much as the bankers and investors, but she did so to appear as though she belonged in the city, on the hill, and not out of any true desire.

Abigail went back inside and heard the voices of her husband and children coming from downstairs, the clink of silverware on porcelain. The governess would arrive soon to teach their daughter, Lily, grammar and mathematics. After that, the piano teacher would come, the home would be filled with beautiful music, and Lily's small fingers danced over the keys. Such a musical soul. She was only ten years old and already bursting out of her skin with ideas and dreams. And so lovely, with her mother's curly brown hair and large eyes.

Their son, Jesse, could not be more different. At fifteen, he was no longer a boy and longed for something more than wandering their home and its gardens. In recent years, he'd grown sullen and moody. Abigail often found him with his nose buried in a book of adventure, tales of outlaws and bandits.

It was her own fault, and Abigail knew it. Out of love, she created a family. Out of fear, she imprisoned them within the mansion's walls. The children never went into the city unless accompanied by their parents. They had few friends, and those they did have were not allowed to come and play. They were educated and raised under a roof and behind walls. Their knowledge of the world was limited to what they read.

It was only a matter of time before Jesse rebelled, so it was no surprise when he climbed out his window one night to be with others his age. He stumbled home the following morning, reeking of whiskey and perfume.

Benjamin lectured the boy and forbade him from sneaking out again, but Jesse only stared at his father and smiled with such a smug, haughty expression it made Abigail sick to her stomach. Jesse had reached the age where he no longer wished to live by anyone's rules but his own, and he didn't realize that rules were what kept their family safe. There was a reason Abigail had a ten-foot-high wall built around their property with only one large iron gate. The world was constantly trying to claw its way inside, rip away whatever it could sink its teeth into. And Abigail would be damned if she let that beast get to her children.

Yes, they were wealthy, but not like the other wealthy families who lived on the hill.

Whenever Abigail went into the city for business, what she saw terrified her. The extremes of the human condition seemed to converge in a single point at the center of all the madness of commerce and construction. The city kept growing, attracting silver miners, businessmen, and foreign workers. In just under a decade, the city that Abigail had begun to think of as home completely transformed, and she didn't recognize it anymore.

Abigail went down the staircase slowly, the rings on her hand clinking as she gripped the banister, the fabric of her expensive dress swishing with each step. Something about the stairs reminded her of Jeremiah's fortress, the home that wouldn't stop growing.

Those days returned to her more and more, and she found herself longing for something, but she couldn't put a name on it. Youth, maybe. But it felt like something deeper than that. Meaning, perhaps, came closer. Purpose.

When Abigail entered the dining room, her family was already seated at the table waiting for her, and a large breakfast was spread out before them. Her husband, Benjamin, smiled and reached his hands to either side, grasping Lily's hand and Jesse's.

Benjamin closed his eyes and led them all in a prayer of thanksgiving. At one point during the prayer, Abigail cracked her eyes open to look at Jesse. The boy sat, eyes wide open, staring at his father with hatred. Part of Abigail wanted to slap his face, but she restrained herself, and Benjamin finished the blessing.

As they ate, Abigail couldn't stop looking at her son. Her heart was half filled with a love so fierce it would destroy anything that tried to harm her child, but the other half was filled with anger, a rage so severe that she wanted to bend the boy's will until it broke.

After breakfast, the governess and Jesse's tutor arrived. The children were sent to separate rooms, where they each studied with their teachers.

It was the first day of the month, the day the teachers were paid, so Abigail went into her study to write up the checks. Benjamin followed her and closed the large, heavy door behind him. He sat in one of the chairs while she added wood to the fireplace.

"You're quiet today," he said, his fingers tracing patterns in the chair.

Abigail struck a match and set fire to the wood. She went and sat in the chair next to him.

"It's—" she began.

"Don't tell me it's nothing," Benjamin interrupted. "Don't treat me like a fool."

Abigail nodded once and reached for her tobacco pouch.

"I wish you wouldn't," Benjamin said with a sigh. "You know how that bothers my eyes."

Abigail nodded again, clenched her lip between her teeth, and bit down. Her husband was a kind man, which is why she agreed to marry him when he asked. When they met, she had been living like an impoverished woman. She did not want to announce her wealth to the world, and she had no idea how to live like a rich woman. So, she rented a cheap room with mold-covered walls and spent her time wandering the city streets.

"We're in this together," Benjamin said, reaching for her hand that grasped the arm of the chair. When his skin touched hers, she realized that her fingernails were digging into the upholstery.

"I need you to tell me what's on your mind," he said. "Don't keep me in the dark."

They had met by accident. He was engaged at the time to a woman he didn't love, but his parents approved of the union and pressured him until he proposed. Tired of eating overripe fruit and stale bread, Abigail wandered into a fine restaurant for a decent meal and glass of whiskey. She had sat at an empty table and waited for someone to take her order.

Someone approached and sat down across from her. When she looked up, she was staring into Benjamin Harrison's dark blue eyes. She had sat at a reserved table without realizing it. Once they had begun talking, Abigail found her nervousness slowly vanishing. She had never met a man so kind, someone who seemed to want nothing from her. Someone interested in her, not for what she could give him, but because he found her truly interesting.

He was kind but not strong, neither in character nor in body, and Abigail often wondered if these were the real reasons she married him. He was a threat to no one. She knew he would treat her well and would not try to stop her from building the life she wanted. Some of the men she did business with were surprised that she, not her husband, handled their financial affairs and investments. But they learned she had a sharp mind and trustworthy instincts over time. Meanwhile, Benjamin stayed in the house, read books, and painted the occasional landscape.

Abigail loved him, but she was stronger than he was, and they both knew it.

"Is it Jesse?" Benjamin asked. He held her hand gently, and those dark blue eyes were focused on her, reading every muscle twitch in her face. "I saw the way you were looking at him."

"He's becoming someone I don't recognize," Abigail said.

"It's a hard age."

A concerto played on the piano drifted into the room.

Abigail still held the tobacco pouch and turned it over in her hands. "She plays so well."

Benjamin nodded in agreement, but his eyes never left Abigail's face. "Tell me," he said.

The thought had been floating at the back of her mind for days, a foggy, half-formed thing that she only occasionally glimpsed. Whenever she did, she shoved it back into the dark where it belonged. It didn't even make sense, but it frightened her all the same. The thought had grown since it first appeared, and now it took up all the space inside her head. She couldn't go for more than an hour without it pushing aside every other rational thought. Soon, it was all she could think. Even then, it was only dust, and it wasn't until Abigail spoke that it became solid.

"How much time do we have left with him?" she asked. "How much time before he's on his own in the world? And how much of the world gets into him once he's there? Have we prepared him enough?"

She pinched the bridge of her nose and squeezed until it hurt. "The world is so dark, and he has no idea what it's like. I'm afraid he'll get lost, and we'll never get him back."

Benjamin tightened his lips together and squeezed her hand. The heat of their skin touching made her palms start to sweat.

"You talk about the world like it's a monster," he said.

Abigail opened the tobacco pouch, took out some leaf and sprinkled it on the cigarette paper. She carefully held up one side, licked the edge, rolled it, and lit it with a match. She inhaled, filled her lungs with smoke, and it made her think of the burning castle in Charwood.

She looked over at her husband. "What else do you call it?"

Later that night, after her family had gone to bed, Abigail stayed up and paced in her study. The flames became smaller and smaller until they were just orange pulsing embers. That one heavy thought rattled around in her head like a billiard ball, crashing into and obliterating every other thought. What most worried her was that the thought might not be her own, which is why she avoided it for so long. But there was no denying it now, it was too big to ignore.

She locked the door of the study, then went to the corner of the room, where she knelt down and pried up a loose section of floorboard. Underneath was the door of a safe she had not opened in years. She spun the knob until the tumblers fell into place, and she opened the door, reached inside, and pulled out two items tied together with string.

Abigail carried these things to the chair and sat down. The feel of them in her hands dragged up memories. If her mind was a clear river, these memories were the jagged rocks at the bottom. And now they were all she could see.

She untied the string that held the leather journal and the piece of parchment paper together. The paper crackled as she unfolded it. The memory of the first time she saw it grew inside her until those old images blended into what she now saw and held in her hands. A map that led to a mountain. At the top of the mountain was a dark hole in the ground. A man knelt near the hole, arms raised, mouth screaming in pain. Above him floated a hand, two fingers extended toward the sky, rays of light shooting from around it.

Blood pushed through the veins in her neck like it had grown thicker. The skin on her scalp tightened, pulling at her face. The hairs on her arms rose up, and that thought, the one taking up all the space inside her head, suddenly came into focus—it was the map, the images drawn on it. She'd kept it hidden for years, telling herself she'd never seek out what Jeremiah had found.

Whatever it was, it ended in death and pain.

Abigail crawled back over to the still-open safe and reached in. She took out a small, golden mouse that Jeremiah had created in what felt like another lifetime. The animal was frozen with its two front claws stretched out, reaching like it was trying to scurry away when it died. Abigail had still never seen anything as pure as the gold she held. The smooth metal reflected the light of the fire, an array of colors rippling along the ceiling.

Something moved outside, and the bushes along the wall stirred. A branch snapped, and dry leaves cracked. Abigail got up and looked through the glass into the darkness. Nothing but the silhouettes of the trees and flowers that Benjamin had planted created a garden oasis.

A sound somewhere in the house. A door opening and closing. Footsteps on the floor, slight vibrations moving down the stairs.

Jesse. It had to be.

Anger swelled up in Abigail. Her palms went sweaty. She opened the door of the study and heard voices coming from the foyer. She inched her way down the hall, listening. Three men stood in the dark, whispering to each other. Men she didn't recognize. She turned and went back to the study, opened the cabinet where she kept her guns, and grabbed a revolver.

Deep down, she'd been waiting for the day desperate men would break into her home to try and steal what they could. Fortunes came and went in this city daily, and sometimes, men would resort to crime to get back what they'd lost.

She opened the cylinder, saw the round metal eyes of six chambers staring at her, and slammed it back into place. Down the hall, the whispers grew louder and more aggressive. She moved with stealth from shadow to shadow, the gun gripped in two hands. One of the men was louder than the others, gesturing and telling the others they needed to leave.

The movement came from the staircase, and another person walked down the steps. It stopped halfway, and then Benjamin's voice said, "What are you doing in my house?"

The three men turned at the sound, and Abigail recognized Jesse's silhouette in the moonlight. She could see the fear in his eyes. She'd never seen the other two men before.

"Leave here immediately," Benjamin said, pointing at the front door.

One of the men lifted his arm and pointed a gun at Benjamin just as another shape came down the stairs. Smaller, long hair, wearing a dressing gown, rubbing the sleep from her eyes. Benjamin didn't see her.

Time slowed down, opened up. Abigail ran down the hall, screaming Lily's name, but her voice was drowned out by the deafening blast as fire spit out the barrel of the man's gun. Two more blasts followed in quick succession. Benjamin's head snapped back, and his feet left the steps. He slammed down hard, and his limp body slid down the remaining stairs until it came to rest on the floor, face down, arms splayed out, a dark pool growing beneath him. Then, a scream of pain came from the stairs as Lily slumped down against the wall, leaving a smear of blood.

Jesse fell to his knees at his father's body as Abigail came running out of the hall. The man with the gun saw the motion and turned the weapon in her direction. Abigail planted her feet, aimed, and pulled the trigger twice. The top half of the man's skull was blown off. He remained standing for just a moment, an upright corpse, before crumpling to the ground. The other man ran for the front door, and Abigail fired again, striking him in the back. Blood splattered all over the glass of the door. He kept moving, and she fired again, and again, and again. Her finger kept pulling the trigger even after the cylinder was empty--each pull making a quiet clink.

Her ears rang like a distant, prolonged train whistle. Jesse knelt by his father's body, weeping, touching his shoulder as though trying to wake him up.

"I told them to meet me outside," Jesse said, looking up, his eyes filled with tears. "Mother, I didn't know what they'd do. I thought they were friends. Please believe me." His voice fell apart, and he started crying again.

Abigail barely heard her son's voice. The space around her warped and tilted, and her head felt disconnected from her body as she stumbled toward her husband.

He was gone.

A moan came from the stairs, Lily's weak voice saying, "Mommy. Help me, please."

Abigail ran up the steps to where her daughter lay, blood leaking from a hole in her stomach. Her face had gone pale, and her skin was covered in beads of sweat.

"It hurts, Mommy. It hurts so bad."

Abigail reached behind Lily, fingers searching her back until she felt the torn flesh where the bullet had exited, which meant the metal was no longer inside her, but there was no way to know how many vital organs it had torn through on the way out. Abigail's hand came away covered in blood.

"Darling, listen to me. I need you to be strong and hold on, okay? You'll feel the dark want to pull you in, but I need you to stay with me. It'll hurt, but I can help you. Just be strong."

She stood. Jesse looked at her with a broken expression. Guilt, fear, pain, all of it creased into his features. Abigail wanted to hit him with all her strength and comfort him in equal measure.

"Jesse, hitch the horses to the carriage and meet me out front. Hurry."

He tried to stop the sobs that came out of him. He nodded, tears running down his face.

"Mother, I'm sorry. I'm so sorry."

She hurt for him. She hurt because of him. She fought her own tears and nodded.

"We'll fix this," she said. "We'll make it right. Now hurry."

As soon as Jesse went outside, Abigail ran upstairs and pulled the sheets off Lily's bed. She ripped them and used the pieces to pack Lily's wound, then she wrapped the longer strips around her stomach, tightened them until the girl groaned, and tied them in place. She squeezed Lily's hand, told her to be strong again, and ran downstairs into the study. She went to the safe, pulled out a large bag of coins, gathered the map and journal, and shoved everything inside a pack.

When she got back to Lily, the girl's eyes were rolling back in her head.

"There's a wolf in the house," she muttered. "It talked to me."

Abigail's stomach dropped. She shook Lily gently. "Come on, darling, stay awake."

Her eyes fluttered. "I can't feel my legs," Lily said. "Are they gone?"

Abigail slipped one arm under her daughter's back and the other behind her knees. She lifted the girl up, trying to ignore the blood that ran down her arms.

"Your legs are still there, but you don't need to use them now. Focus on me, my voice. Stay out of the dark, okay?"

She carried Lily outside, where Jesse was waiting with the carriage. Two horses stood harnessed to it, their breath like smoke.

"Go get some pillows and blankets," Abigail told him.

Once he returned, Abigail made up a bed on the floor of the carriage. It would be a long journey through the night, and she would not slow down or stop for anything. They would ride until the horses gave out, and then she'd carry Lily until her heart gave out. But she would not stop until they reached the mountaintop on Jeremiah's map. Whatever he found there gave him the power to bring his son back to life, and that power could somehow stop Lily from slipping over the other side. Whatever it was, Abigail had to try.

She gently laid Lily down on the carriage floor and then climbed up to the bench next to Jesse. She snapped the reins, and the horses took off into the night.

Abigail heard Lily moaning as the wheels bounced off ruts in the ground. She glanced over to see Jesse biting his lip, eyes closed, chin shivering.

She whipped the reins again, pushing the horses to go faster. Time felt like a weight pressing down on her, suffocating her.

"Stay out of the dark, Lily," she said to herself. "Stay out of the dark."

She would find whatever Jeremiah had found, but she'd be wiser and stronger than he was. Jeremiah was weak and wounded, he couldn't hold onto both the gift and his pain. One took over and destroyed the other.

She didn't know what she'd find on the mountaintop, but she was ready to give everything to save her daughter. And when she did, she would protect herself and her family. She would build something, a structure, a fortress, that would keep the world from getting in and ruining them. A barrier between them and all the decay, the suffering, the deception, and evil. Something that not even death itself could break through.

She would build a world inside the world.

ACKNOWLEDGEMENTS

PAUL MILLER, thank you for giving this book its first life, and to **STEVE BERMAN** for giving it its second. **JOSH MALERMAN**, for such a thoughtful and generous introduction. Pool at McMenamins? **JOSHUA MOHR**, for helping me see what this story wanted and needed to be, and for encouraging me the whole way. **BEN BALDWIN**, for the beautiful cover art. **LIAM**, the world is so much more golden with you in it. **QUINN**, you shine bright and light up the dark. **MOM AND DAD WRIGHT**, for always traveling the hard roads with us. **MOM AND DAD JONES**, for unwavering support. **ELIZABETH COPPS**, for championing this book with such enthusiasm and perseverance. **PHIL HAAGENSEN**, for your friendship and being the best beta reader a writer could ask for. **BRENNAN LAFARO**, for the continuing conversation on art and life, for the editorial insight and endless encouragement. **NEIL MCROBERT,** for allowing me to discuss the story on Talking Scared. **MARIANNE LEONE COOPER**, for sharing Jesse's story with us at a time when we needed it most. **GOLIATH**, it all started with you. **RAE LYN**, I am constantly amazed by your strength, your wisdom, and your selflessness. Amazed, but not surprised. I am so grateful to share this life with you. "I don't believe that anybody feels the way I do about you now."

ABOUT THE AUTHOR

TYLER JONES is the author of *Criterium*, *The Dark Side of the Room*, *Almost Ruth*, the story collection *Burn the Plans* (one of *Esquire*'s Best Horror Books of 2022), *Heavy Oceans*, *Midas*, *Night of the Long Knives*, and *Longsight M40*. His work has appeared in numerous publications including *Burnt Tongues* (edited by Chuck Palahniuk), *Cemetery Dance*, *LitReactor*, *PseudoPod*, *Tales to Terrify*, and *The NoSleep Podcast*.

He lives in Portland, Oregon.